"*Crafted with great cunning and flair which makes for a wild and electrifying read.*"
—Ann Coombs, futurist and best-selling author

"*A terrific tale, fast paced and gripping to the end.*"
—Mike Harcourt, author and former Premier of British Columbia

"*A band of 12th Century characters fan out across southern England, Europe and the Holy Land unraveling a mystery about lost birthright, power and magic. Full of twists, turns and incidents and vivid descriptions of the violence and lawlessness of medieval life and of the medieval landscape; a thought provoking read.*"
—Island Tides, newspaper

"*… A good story well told. Moves along with speed and clarity, and with such vivid imagery and dramatic action that the reader becomes excited and possessed, as are the book's characters themselves.*"
—Robin Skelton, poet, author of *Fires of the Kindred*

THE ANCIENT BLOODLINES TRILOGY

BOOK ONE
THE POWER IN THE DARK

BOOK TWO
SHADOW OF THE SWORDS

BOOK THREE
THE KEEPER OF THE GRAIL

THE ANCIENT BLOODLINES TRILOGY
BOOK ONE

The
Power
in the
Dark

BARRY MATHIAS

Agio
PUBLISHING HOUSE

PUBLISHING HOUSE

151 Howe Street, Victoria BC Canada V8V 4K5

For information and bulk orders, please contact
info@agiopublishing.com *or go to*
www.agiopublishing.com
Visit this book's website at www.barrymathias.com *and*
ancientbloodlinestrilogy.com

ISBN   978-1-897435-11-3 (trade paperback)
         987-1-897435-12-0 (electronic edition)

10   9   8   7   6   5   4   3   2   1

Printed on acid-free paper made without fibre from
old growth forests.

DEDICATION

This is dedicated to Clare,
my soul mate and best friend,
who helped me, in so many ways,
to complete this book, and the other two of the trilogy.

ACKNOWLEDGEMENTS

I am grateful to my family for their encouragement and help through the long gestation of this story. My particular thanks to Natasha whose illustration has added immeasurably to this book.

I thank Bruce and Marsha Batchelor of Agio Publishing House who have enabled me to reach a wider readership, and whose expertise has been invaluable.

THE POWER IN THE DARK

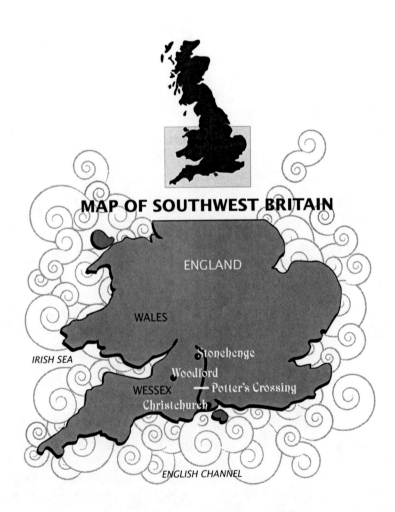

MAP OF SOUTHWEST BRITAIN

ENGLAND

WALES

IRISH SEA

Stonehenge

Woodford

Potter's Crossing

WESSEX

Christchurch

ENGLISH CHANNEL

PROLOGUE

A S DUSK APPROACHED, THE besieging armies made their long-awaited breakthrough. Hundreds of armour-clad men poured through the breach in the great walls of Jerusalem and massacred all who stood in their way. It was 1099, the culmination of four years of travelling and almost constant warfare, and the Crusaders burst like a wave into the city, searching out the infidels and securing the Holy City for Christianity.

Among the first to reach the Great Temple was Gilles de Beauchamps, who, with others of an elite brotherhood called The Order, had sworn to preserve and defend the holy manuscripts lodged in secret vaults under the huge building. However, his most important role, known to only a select few of the brotherhood, was to identify and rescue the surviving members of an extraordinary bloodline, and defend them with his life.

Gilles de Beauchamps rested wearily on the hilt of his great sword, and leaned his back against one of the massive marble pillars. He had sustained numerous small wounds and some severe bruising on his arms and shoulders. It had been a remarkable day, and now he was exhausted and feeling his forty-nine years. He roused himself as Charles De Ville approached, the red cross vivid on his white tunic.

The younger man looked grave, and did not speak until he was standing directly in front of Gilles.

"My Lord, the news is not good."

"Give it to me, quickly."

"The families have been betrayed. All are dead except for a young boy and a girl child."

Gilles de Beauchamps bent his head, and let out a deep groan as waves of disappointment wracked his tired body. Outside the temple, the night air was rent with terrible screams and demented laughter as the victorious soldiers took their revenge on the luckless inhabitants of the city. In a secret room in the Temple, two small children wept piteously; their secure world was gone forever.

CHAPTER 1

ONE DAY, WHEN HE was almost sixteen years old, he awoke as if from a long dream. It was a bright, sun-blessed morning. The cock was crowing, a gentle breeze was fanning his face from the open door of the cottage, and he realized he was different. It was as though he had been swimming up from a great depth in murky water and had suddenly burst through the surface; the drowned had been reborn. Yet, although he knew where he was, he had no memory of his arrival. His previous life was a mass of faint impressions that remained on the edge of his recall, and he was unable, or subconsciously unwilling, to bring them into the light.

"My name is John." He repeated the words over and over in a soft whisper, like an incantation. He knew the bed on which he had been sleeping; he recognized the sounds of the strident rooster in the yard outside and the old red cow complaining in its small barn. He knew the old woman with whom he shared the modest cottage, his friend Peter with the limp, and the path to the village. Yet, he could not recall his parents, nor could he remember how he had come to live in this lonely place.

He lay back on his straw palliasse and stared up at the thatch ceiling, focusing his mind on recent events. Last night something had happened. He knew it was important, and yet it was not something on which his mind wished to focus. It was as if some part of him was trying to rub out the picture while another part was repainting it.

"It's power," he muttered aloud. "It's to do with power." Then he remembered.

· · ·

HE HAD BEEN DOZING after a late supper in the warm and smoky room. All day he had been gathering the dry, golden hay Old Mary used as winter-feed for the cow. His arms ached, but he felt content with his day's work.

"What did you say about power?" John asked, suddenly alert.

"I said you will have power some day," Old Mary answered.

"What sort of power?"

"You are special, like me. You will come to know all things when the hour is right."

She had said it before. Always the same response: "When you are older," and "When the hour is right." Most of the time he did not understand what the old woman was talking about, but she was kind to him, and her Wessex home had been his refuge for many weeks. He looked closely at her as she slowly crushed herbs in a smooth wooden bowl. She was very old, yet still a large woman, with big hands, a prominent nose and deep, black eyes. Her hair was silvery white and was worn in a plait that hung on one side of her head and reached down to her waist.

She was so old that the boy wondered how many more years she might live, for without her he would be homeless again. Perhaps, if she lived another few years, he would be able to look after himself. She might even leave the cottage to him. Immediately, he was ashamed of his thoughts and hoped she would live forever. As he looked at her, she turned to him and smiled.

"I shall not live forever," she said. "Not in this form. But you will carry on the power, as will your children."

The boy felt his face burning with embarrassment. Could she read his mind? Did she really have power? It did not make sense.

"If I am to have this power, why am I no different to other boys?"

"You are different, but just as small plants look much the same, so you seem like other young men. When you are older the difference will be clear, even to you."

Her smile deepened. He was just as she had known he would be: strong and healthy, with a keen eye for detail and a questioning mind. Although he was only about fifteen years old, he was already taller than other boys of his age and could stand up for himself. He had wavy, black hair and dark eyes and his high cheekbones and well-proportioned mouth gave him an aristocratic appearance that marked him out from the other boys in the area. It did not appear to worry him that his new friends in the village said that the woman he lived with was a witch.

He found himself gazing into her bright, twinkling eyes and had a brief vision of himself: he was standing in a field of flowers holding a long sword in both hands. The sword gleamed in the hot sun with a strange light, and there was something large and black on the ground. As his attention was drawn to this thing, the picture blurred as when wind blows the surface of a pool.

"What did you see?" she asked.

"Nothing." He shrugged. "I saw nothing. I was just thinking of something." The experience had unnerved him. "You once said this power was all around." He now spoke aggressively to cover his confusion. "You said a person only had to look and he could possess it. Why can't others possess it too?"

"Only some are chosen." She moved towards the open door and contemplated the early evening sky. The west was ablaze in fiery light. The sun's last rays coloured the high clouds in reds, yellows and blues, which merged with the deeper mauve of night. It was warm and the air was still, and the isolation of the thatched cottage was increased by a total absence of sound.

"Imagine," she said, in a quiet, thoughtful voice, "that you are up a high tree. It is dark and you have a sword in your hand. Somewhere below is the scabbard; it is stuck into the ground with the open end upwards and you have to make the sword fit into the scabbard. What chance would you have?"

"That's silly," he said. "There's nobody could do that even if they could see where to throw the sword."

"That is how it is with the power. It is there, but few are able to understand it, and those who do, are either very lucky, or unfortunate, to unlock the secret."

"Then how do you come by this power?"

"Most people stay up the tree, not even guessing that the power is within their grasp. A small number see through the darkness of superstition and recognise the scabbard of power. But it is a rare person who can think to climb down from the security of the tree and walk to the scabbard and fit in the sword." Her voice had risen in volume and he sensed a strange excitement in it.

"What does one do then?"

"With the sword and the scabbard you have the power. From that point you become the guardian and the defender of the ancient ways." Her eyes stared out into the night sky.

"Have you fitted the sword into the scabbard?" he whispered. He was suddenly afraid of her. She seemed different.

"I have the power," she said thoughtfully.

She had often spoken in a strange way, but he had thought that it was because she was old and, like him, had moved into the area from far away. But now she was changed. In the reddish light from the doorway she looked younger, larger and immensely strong.

"But why have power if you don't use it?" he murmured. His voice trailed away....

"I do use it. You have seen the ones who were ill and are now cured."

He remembered. The people with ugly swellings and red, painful sores, the injured soldiers who had returned from the Crusade, and people who could hardly walk; she had cured them all. Some had received herbal potions and some she had merely held with her strong hands. When she released her grip, they had seemed cured, and claimed they could walk, when before they had been lame. He had seen all these things, but being young he had supposed she was just another wise woman, a natural healer. Most large villages had one. But now he felt there was something more. She was quite unlike any person he had ever met.

"But there must be more to it than that?"

"There is, much more."

"Then why don't you use it to become rich?" he asked.

"What would I want with money?"

John was confused. Everyone wanted money. He knew she was poor. Her cottage had been an open secret to him from the time he had arrived; he had investigated all parts of it. There was the one large room in which they spent the day and two small, curtained sleeping areas. She had all the necessary things, but there was nothing of value, and she only earned enough from selling her herbs to pay for food. Surely she must want money.

"You could buy new clothes and boots," he muttered.

"I have everything I need. What would I want with extra clothes?"

"You could have gold and jewels."

"What for?"

John was amazed at the question. What for? What did she mean? Everyone wanted gold and jewels. "Well," he stuttered, "everyone wants them. You can buy things...."

She fixed him with a fierce stare. "I have real power: the sort that gold and jewels can never buy. When you are older you will understand. Real power concerns life and death, and the eternal battle between good and evil. Riches are drawn from the earth and will go back to the earth. My power is eternal and its value is greater than anything you can imagine." Her eyes were like the sunset; they blazed in a wild, passionate way. Her voice resembled a mighty queen addressing her massed subjects. She was all-powerful; she was terrifying, and John hid his face in his hands.

"What is the matter?" The voice was, once again, soft and homely.

He raised his head slowly, expecting... he knew not what. Fearfully, he looked into the kind, handsome face of the old woman with whom he had lived for the past weeks.

"I... I... You look different. A moment ago you were," he paused, "someone else."

"One day you will be someone else. Someone you have been before, and will be again."

He did not understand. The time was not yet come. The hour was still a long way off, but the evening would stay in his memory as a constant reminder of the old woman's power.

CHAPTER 2

I T WAS SEVEN MONTHS later at the end of a cruel winter. The snow was slowly fading on the high hills, and the frozen puddles in the cart ruts were melting to form muddy pools. Everywhere, the signs of spring reassured the travellers that the biting cold and the fierce blizzards were over for another year.

"Are you going to market today?" John asked.

"I am," the old woman replied. She busied herself with the preparations for her journey. She was well wrapped in thick woollen clothes: a brown tunic, blue skirt and fawn, knitted stockings enclosed in tough walking boots. Around her shoulders she spread a large brown cloak, and adjusted the hood under her firm chin. Then she selected a strong hawthorn stick, picked up the cloth bag in which she carried her dried herbs, and moved towards the door.

"Take me with you." It had been a long winter and John was keen to meet his friend in the nearby village of Woodford. It had been nearly three weeks since he had seen anyone other than the old woman. The last snows of winter had blocked all the roads, and he had felt as if the two of them were alone in a frozen, deserted world.

"You must stay here. You will be needed."

"Why will I be needed? There are only the cats, and the other animals will come to no harm for one day. Please let me come with you. I want to see Peter and my other friends in the village. I won't be any trouble," he pleaded.

The old woman turned quickly to face him and looked gravely into his dark brown eyes. "What is your name?"

He was puzzled. "My name is John, but you never call me John; you say it is not my real name."

"What do I call you?" She was staring hard at him, willing him to understand.

"You call me...," his voice faltered. "You call me Giles."

"Why do I call you that name?"

"Because I am the Keeper of the Grail." He had learned it by heart. It was part of the ritual she had made him learn through the long winter evenings. He had wanted to please her, and in a strange way he had found it exciting, but now the winter was over, and he wanted to be free to see his friends and in particular Peter, the boy with the limp.

"You are Giles Plantard, you are the Keeper of the Grail, and you must stay, for the moment of truth is near."

He was suddenly afraid. "What do you mean?"

"You must stay. Much will be revealed." She picked up her purse and prepared to leave. Her dark eyes were thoughtful but her mouth was set in a tight line. When she reached the door she turned to face him. "Be strong and be guided by your own true self, Giles. Remember all that I have told you this last winter, and remember above all that nothing of value is gained without great effort and hardship. I shall be with you in your greatest need."

Then she was gone. The boy stared at the closed door. What was he to make of her strange statements? He felt he should laugh, but could not. It was as though he was a poor animal in a trap, waiting for the hunter.

"You don't frighten me!" he cried aloud to the empty room. "It's all woman's talk. I don't have to stay here. I can go if I want to. You don't own me. I'm not your son, and I'm not Giles Plantard, whoever he might be!"

He rushed to the door and flung it open. The sky was clear and the bright light from the early sun shafted over the distant hills. He shielded his eyes with his hand, searching the track that led in the direction of the village. The old woman was nowhere to be seen.

After a few moments, he felt the cold breeze of the April morning, and retreated inside. As he closed the door, his resentment exploded into rage. He would not be put upon like this, he silently ranted while pacing the stone floor. He was almost grown up. She could not frighten him with her strange tales and weird prophecies. He would go to the market and if she saw him, so much the better. He knew she liked having him about the place. He was quite sure she would not throw him out onto the road, and she had never raised her stick to him or even threatened him and he had been with her for almost a year.

He picked up his cloak. It was dark blue with a deep hood, unlike the other village youths'; they wore brown capes, or none at all. She had made his cloak soon after he had arrived, sick and penniless, at her door. As he felt the texture of the garment, he experienced a pang of guilt. She had been good to him and had not asked much in return, only that he learn the lists of words and strange signs she said were the keys to the power. He had found them easy to learn and had seen it as a game and partly as an interesting exercise during the long days of winter.

"It's stupid!" he grumbled. "There's no reason to keep me here." He remembered, with a smirk, she had often said a man must be guided by his own judgement. Well then, that was what he would do.

He strode over to the heavy door and tried to lift the latch, but suddenly he felt as though his strength was ebbing away. Struggling with the handle, he slowly forced up the catch. John prised open the door a few inches and then, using both hands, pulled it back. It seemed to take a long time and he was aware of an odd creaking in the hinges he had not noticed before. He gave a final shove and, without warning, as though on a spring, the door swung violently away from him and crashed against the inside wall. The metal hinges burst out of the wood and the door toppled over with a loud crash onto the stone floor.

John was appalled. How could he have done such a thing? He had caused enormous damage to the old woman's home. The door was larger than most and the hinges were huge, yet, he had apparently pulled it from its mountings. It was unbelievable. He rushed forward and tried to lift the door. It was impossible. He could hardly raise it a few inches. He felt close to tears as guilt and frustration battled within him. How could he explain such a happening? He would have to repair the door before she returned, and that would mean getting help from the village. But now he would have to be careful to avoid the old woman.

As he crossed the threshold, he saw the cat. It was one of a number the old woman kept around the house and outbuildings. He had never had much time for cats and the creatures had exhibited the same feelings towards him. They had never been unfriendly, just aloof and distant, and had never sought his company. But this cat seemed strange and threatening. It was black and heavy and stared at him with green, unblinking eyes, as if it were blaming him for the damage he had done. As he moved to pass, the cat began to hiss and snarl and braced itself as if to spring.

John stopped, uncertain what do, and involuntarily stepped backwards. The cat relaxed its body and resumed its baleful stare. He took a step forward and the animal immediately arched its back and spat at him. He noted its sharp white teeth and the vicious claws and something else: this was no ordinary cat, for its eyes were much larger and it seemed to be hypnotizing him.

"Be off!" he yelled, trying desperately to sound courageous.

The cat resumed its unblinking stare. Both cat and boy remained like wax figures, warily watching each other. Time stood still. Finally, John retreated into the house and grabbed one of the old woman's walking sticks.

"Get out of my way!" he roared as he charged back through the doorway. Halfway over the front step he stopped in mid-stride and the colour drained from his face. In front of him was not one cat, but more than a dozen ferocious, hissing creatures, all staring at him with enormous green eyes, all angrily intent on preventing him from leaving.

John retreated back into the house, wondering if the cats would follow, but they remained guarding the entrance. Slowly, he sat down on a stool near the fire; his mind was in turmoil. How was it these cats had suddenly become his gaolers? Did the old woman have power over cats as well as sick people? Was she more than just a wise woman? John remembered what Peter had said when they last met: "My farder says your old woman be a witch. She arrived from nowhere and suddenly her be livin' in that cottage all by 'erself. An' what 'appened to the family what used to live there?"

"She bought the cottage from them. They moved to live by the sea. She told me," John had replied, angry that his friend should have spoken that way of the old woman.

"Oh ah! Then why'd they just go like that wiv' no leave-takin'? They was called Turner. He be quite well known in the village. Nobody's 'eard from 'em since."

"Perhaps they had to go because of illness or something."

"My farder thinks her killed 'em," Peter had said in a voice hushed and fearful. "My farder says 'e be afraid of 'er and that I'm not to mix with 'ee any more."

"What? You mean you won't see me again?" John had been distressed; Peter was his only real friend.

Peter had laughed. "O' course I will! What sort of a friend d' ye think I be? Anyway I 'ate that farder of mine, 'e beats me wicked 'e do." Peter had limped up to him, "I'll be your friend even tho' ye be a witch's apprentice."

They had wrestled playfully in the road until the curfew bell had reminded them of the time. Snow, light as goose feathers, began to fall from the grey sky.

"I'll see 'ee tomorrow," Peter had called as he dragged his withered leg along the muddy lane. John watched as Peter hobbled away, his thin body and his ragged clothes made him appear sadly comical.

That had been over three weeks ago. John suddenly realized this was the first time he had remembered Peter's accusation. The words swirled around his mind: "She killed them… he is afraid of her… not to mix with you." The words were like alarm bells sounding in his head. Before it had seemed superstitious nonsense. But now? He could not believe it. She had always been good to him. She was kind and gentle and… suddenly he remembered that evening many months ago, when in the vivid sunset she had talked about her power. She had not been gentle then. She had been like a goddess; like a mighty warrior. At that moment she could have destroyed anyone. She had been a different person: no longer old, but ageless.

Now she had made him a prisoner, guarded by her fierce cats. But why? What was it all about?

He gnawed nervously on his lower lip. He wished his father were alive. John had a vague memory of a tall, silent man racked with illness. Had that been his father? He did not remember his mother, but vaguely recalled being told that she had died when he was very young. Images, like flashes of lightning, illuminated his consciousness. There had been a storm at sea, and many men were in armour; he was with his father on a huge horse; then there was a long journey that had ended in a rain-swept barn one cold, winter's night. His next memory was of a man with a tired face telling him his father was dead and he must be brave. John had stayed with a number of families whose faces he could not clearly recall. His earlier life seemed a dull dream from which he had awakened when he had arrived, as if by chance, at the door of the old woman.

He remembered. She had not been surprised to see him, but welcomed him with a warm drink and food and a straw bed already made up. When he woke a long time later, it had been an amazing experience. Suddenly his senses had come alive: he was aware of colours and sounds and could recall in precise detail everything that he saw; yet he was unable to remember any clear details about his earlier life. Since then, the old woman had looked after him. Her house had become his home.

He looked up from his contemplation of the fire, and regarded the fallen door. It lay like a brown tongue across the stone floor, and behind it the open doorway gaped like a huge mouth.

"What a strange thought," he murmured, "to think of the door and the opening as if they were a tongue and a mouth."

Instantly, he was on his feet. "A mouth and a tongue!"

What was it the old woman had said one night? *When the mouth is open and the tongue hangs out, you will see a stranger with a twisted jaw.* At the time, he had smiled; she was always making these strange prophecies. But he recalled her making him repeat her words, and saying one day he would be glad of the warning. When he asked about the stranger with the twisted jaw, she had stared hard at him, as if she was peering into the very essence of his soul. Then, she had given him a small silver amulet with some curious runes on it.

"You will be safe only if you get him to accept this. Until then, keep it close by you and never be without it."

He felt inside his woollen shirt. Around his neck was a small leather purse attached to a leather thong. He slipped his fingers inside the purse and removed the silver amulet. The strange runes seemed to glow and become more distinct, and in the light of the fire the silver appeared red. He sensed the room had become dark. A weird wave of excitement swept over him and he felt stronger and more alert, like plunging into a cold river. A new confidence and cheerfulness pervaded him and he experienced a sense of vigour in his mind and in the muscles of his body.

He was about to replace the amulet into his purse, when he heard the geese hissing and calling as they did when a stranger approached. Gripping the silver piece in his hand, he moved cautiously towards the open doorway to see who was there.

"I wish you a good day, young John!" a voice boomed out. John jumped. It was not the strength of the man's voice that surprised him, or the fact this stranger knew his name, although that was mystifying in itself; it was the man's face. He had a twisted jaw!

John was determined not to show any fear. The amulet, gripped tightly in his hand, gave him added confidence. John watched the man shamble towards the door. He was a big fellow with matted, black hair and huge, scaly hands. He might have been mistaken for a young man, but for the many lines on his face. There was something sinister about him, and it was not just his yellow, broken teeth, his odd lower jaw, or his large cavernous nostrils. It was not even his musty odour wafting over John at a distance of five feet. It was the man's eyes: they were black as pitch and seemed to have an unnatural depth. John was aware of being drawn into a dark place where no man had ever before set foot. Far, far away. A place of empty, endless days… then a cat brushed against his legs, and it was as though he awoke from a deep sleep.

Immediately alert to the danger, John jumped back and retreated into the room as the man reached out for him. A look of disappointment passed over the twisted face to be replaced instantly by a surprised smile. He lowered his hand.

"Did I scare you, young John? You seemed to be a bit sleepy." He smiled an ugly smile revealing again the mass of broken, yellow teeth. He advanced to the entrance of the cottage and stopped before the open doorway. "I see you've had a little accident," he said, pointing to the fallen door. He laughed again, an odd mirthless sound that resembled the braying of a donkey.

"What do you want?" John's voice was louder than he had meant it to be. "How do you know my name?"

"Well now, young John, that is quite a tale. Are you going to ask me in?" His voice was sugary and coaxing.

"It's not my cottage, I can't ask you in," John spluttered, faintly puzzled. The man seemed to have come as close as possible while not actually crossing the threshold. It was as though an invisible barrier prevented him from moving any nearer.

"Old Mary won't like it if you don't ask me in," the stranger persisted. "I'm an old friend of hers. How do you think I would know your name unless she'd told me? She always speaks of *her John*, who is so good to her."

"That's—" he stopped himself from yelling it was a lie. Old Mary never called him *John*, let alone *her John*. Instead he coughed on the words and said, "That's strange, she never mentioned you."

"How odd," the man's ugly features twisted into a semblance of a smile. "Well, are you going to invite me in? Or do I have to stay on the door step until Old Mary returns?"

"No, I suppose you had better come in," John murmured. As he spoke, he was gripped by a sudden terror, and felt defenceless. In that second, he remembered two things that the old woman had said and which he cursed himself for forgetting. The man had said *Old Mary*. Nobody ever called her that; usually it was *Ma'am*, or occasionally *the Herb Woman*. John called her *Ma'am*. She had warned him: *When Old Mary is called, the devil's abroad.* He had not understood, until this moment, what she meant.

The man was lumbering through the door, a look of triumph twisting his ugly face. His enormous hands were held stiffly in front of him and his foul breath came in loud gasps.

The other saying John recalled, with horror, was one evening when a night insect battered its wings against the window. She had taken his hand and declared, with an intensity that frightened him, *Never ask the devil into this home. He can't get in unless you give him leave.*

The man's arm was reaching out to grasp him. John stared helplessly at the approaching hand like a mouse, mesmerized by a viper. He sensed that once in that huge grip he was doomed. This was the evil the old woman had warned him of during those long winter nights, when he had taken so little notice. In one brief second John experienced horror, despair and a sense of bitter failure. His eyes were drawn to those of the large cat, which had previously prevented him from leaving the cottage. It jumped onto the stool by the doorway, and was behind, and just to the right of the advancing figure. John felt the cat's green eyes boring into his. Instantly, a vision flashed into his mind of the ancient runes on the silver amulet. As in a dream, when actions are slowed down, he felt his clenched fist enclosing the amulet move up to meet the oncoming hand. John's fist smashed into the huge palm, and the long fingers of the stranger closed like a vice, but not before John's hand opened and squeezed the amulet against the man's flesh.

All movement ceased. The fearful hand seemed to be frozen in mid-air. The stranger's dark eyes suddenly glazed and his twisted jaw trembled. An ear-piercing shriek shattered the silence. John smelt a dreadful aroma of burning, like charred flesh, and a blue mist formed in the air. As the echo of the terrible cry faded, it was replaced by a roaring wind, which hurtled through the door, tossing the boy, like a rag doll, against the back wall. In seconds the gale was gone, and with it all trace of the man, the mist, and the amulet. John lay on the stone floor, his ears ringing and eyes watering. He felt sick, light-headed and oddly numb.

He knew he had been in mortal danger. What came quickly to the front of his confused thoughts was how much of the encounter had been foretold by the old woman. John opened his eyes and tried to focus on the room. The cat was watching him intently; its green eyes seemed to be smiling. John groaned, annoyed with himself; he had behaved badly, and forgotten almost everything the old woman had told him. He had not taken her forewarnings seriously, and without the cat, the evil thing, masquerading as a man, would have destroyed him.

Yet, the same cat had prevented him from leaving, keeping him there like a mouse in a trap. The old woman and her strange cats had forced him to face the monstrous creature that had nearly destroyed him. She had wanted him to suffer! The more he thought about it, the more his anger, hot as sparks, flamed within him at the injustice of the old woman's actions.

He struggled slowly to his feet. His shoulder hurt from his fall against the wall, and his hand that had held the amulet felt very sore. He examined his palm and his eyes grew round in amazement. A round burn seared the middle of his hand, with the imprint of the runes branded into the flesh. The pain was so great he cried out and fell to his knees, weeping loudly. In the midst of his wailing the old woman returned.

• • •

JOHN SLEPT FOR MANY hours, and awoke feeling refreshed and optimistic. He remembered the old woman had given him a sleeping draught and had comforted his pain and fears with her seemingly endless warmth and good humour.

From his pallet, he reached out and moved aside the rough hemp curtain. Through the open doorway he could see blue sky. Small puffs of clouds moved slowly across the bright, azure canopy. He lay back and listened contentedly to the comforting sounds of the place. Outside, the geese squawked and hooted, the hens kept up their unending clucking, and the old, red cow complained in its enclosure. Enveloping all was the gentle whisper of a warm breeze, full of promises.

"Giles! Are you awake?" The old woman's strong voice called from the other side of the room.

"Yes, Ma'am, I'm getting up." He wondered how she had known he was awake, but another part of him was already accepting that the old woman knew more, much more, than he ever imagined, and she possessed powers at which he could only guess. The events of the previous day served to awaken a much greater respect for this woman. Despite her age, she was never tired, never unhappy, and seemed to care for him in a comforting way, strangely frightening in its intensity.

When he had accused her of leaving on purpose and forcing him to face alone the horror of the stranger with the twisted jaw, she had smiled and asked him if he was still alive.

"That's a silly question," he had grumbled. "Of course I'm still alive, but I could have died if...."

"If you had not remembered what I taught you. If you had not worn my talisman to protect you, then you would have been in danger, which is why I told you to stay in the house."

Slowly, it dawned on him it was he who had been in the wrong. If he had followed the old woman's advice, the door would not have come off its hinges; the stranger could not have entered the house, and he would not have had to use the talisman.

The talisman! He opened his right hand resting on the blanket, and raised his head to look. In the centre of his palm was a clear imprint of the runes, as though painted on by a remarkable artist. But now the red, sore burn was gone and it looked as though he had always worn such a mark. He stared at it for a long time, and then forced himself to get up.

He put on his clothes, and prepared himself for a hard day. There was no doubt he would have to mend the door and clean up the room. He remembered the chaos caused by the violent wind sweeping through the cottage. Almost certainly he would have to go into the village to get help to raise the door. He pulled back the curtain separating his bed from the rest of the room and stared, open-mouthed. The cottage was its normal state of clean, ordered tranquillity. The fire burned cheerfully in the grate; the stone floor was spotless and the rows of herbs hung from the wooden beams, as usual. But the most astonishing sight was the door. It was fixed, as if it had never come off its hinges.

John went up to the heavy door, which was ajar, and slowly opened it. It swung easily on its strong iron hinges without a sound. He examined the hinges and could find no mark on them or on the wooden doorframe. It was as though the events of yesterday had never happened.

"Oh, you're up then!" The old woman came through the door with an armful of washing. She smiled at his questioning face. "I had it fixed while you were asleep."

His mind tumbled with unanswered questions, but she was already past him and was hanging the clothes on a wooden rail by the fire. There was something forbidding in the determined way that she moved, as though avoiding his questions.

"Have you seen my hand?" he asked at last.

Her busy fingers paused in their task; she slowly replaced a damp apron on to the pile of washing. When she turned to face him, her dark eyes were smouldering with frightening intensity.

"The time has come and you are now ready for what will be," she said, taking his hand in hers. "The mark on your palm will open many doors to powerful people. Some will become your friends and others will wish to use you for their own ends, and you will learn whom to choose. But just as the mark will identify you to your friends, it will also draw your enemies."

"What enemies? I have no enemies."

"You carry the mark of greatness; you will always have enemies from now on. But you will also have wonderful friends, and there is nothing in the world as wonderful as the love of one person for another." Her eyes grew big, as they had on that earlier occasion. Her hair was still white; her face still wrinkled, yet, once again, she radiated a youthfulness that made her almost beautiful.

CHAPTER 3

T HE NEXT TEST CAME after three months. John, meanwhile, had learned
many things. Old Mary taught him how to use herbs and powders to
cure illnesses, and how to gain power through intense, mental concentration,
so he could approach problems in a logical and imaginative way. She insisted
he exercise, in order to strengthen his rapidly growing frame, and with his
physical development had come a greater mental maturity. She urged him
to relearn the mystical signs and chants he had first encountered in the
winter; this time he found them easier and more meaningful. However,
in some things, he was not changed: he still insisted his name was John,
while she continued to call him *Giles Plantard*; he also believed he was no
different to other boys, while she maintained he was special, and pointed
to his hand as proof.

John was taking the calf to market. It was a fine young bull, the latest in a
succession of sturdy animals produced by the red cow; the only large animal
the old woman would keep. When he asked why she did not keep the calves
and build up a herd, the old woman said that one cow was all she needed.
He tried to point out there would be more profit in building up their own
herd and she reminded him sternly of the life he would have to accept.

"How many times do I have to remind you," she said, her voice unusually
sharp, "we only need enough to live by. There is no point in earning more
money than we need. Most people spend their lives trying to earn sums of
money to spend on things they don't really want. They kill animals and eat
more than is good for them. They cut down trees to make houses that are
too big, and then they have to make weapons to protect those things they
never really needed in the first place."

"But we need more money," John had argued.

"You think you need more money, because you think you need a new
tunic."

John blushed. Once again she knew his thoughts.

"Which is the reason," she continued, "that I am going to sell the calf and not give it away."

"Give it away!" John was flabbergasted.

"You will learn it is better to give than to receive. It is not an easy thing to learn, and some never learn it, and are unhappy and discontented all their lives. But you will come to understand, because you are different. You will have no choice."

The last statement mystified John, but he felt humbled enough by the conversation not to ask any more questions. A new tunic was something to look forward to.

The local market was held every two weeks in the village of Woodford, almost four miles away. The day was very hot and the ground was dry and dusty. The July drought was in its third week, and life seemed an unending succession of blue skies and blistering, windless days.

The path he walked along was narrow and little used. At times, the track passed through small copses of tall trees with thick clumps of bushes. Then it wound through wide fields, where the grass was waist high and filled with multitudes of insects. He had walked this path a few times and marvelled how the turning of the year brought such changes to everything. The calf was content to follow him, and although a strong rope secured the animal, John found little need to pull the docile creature, which followed like a pet dog.

Having never met another person on this route, it came as a surprise to see a girl about sixty paces ahead of him, picking flowers at the side of the path. John was passing a large oak tree, and his first reaction was to jump back and hide behind it. The girl was unaware of his presence, and it pleased him to watch her as she carefully selected each colourful bloom. Red poppies, purple vetch, blue cornflowers and yellow daisies; he knew them all by name since being with the old woman.

Now his attention was fixed on the girl. She was about his age, perhaps slightly older. Her hair was long and black and reached down past her shoulders in a loose wave. Her skin was deep brown on neck, arms and legs, and she wore a simple woven gown of blue, coarse material. She had her back to him, and he noticed she wore sandals and had a thick silver bracelet on her left wrist. He knew most of the village girls by sight, but could not remember seeing anyone with such beautiful hair, or such long, graceful limbs.

On an impulse, he decided to move closer to see her face. Leading the calf, he moved to his right and took cover behind a clump of small beech saplings and then moved in a semi-circle through the shade of larger trees until he could creep up behind a thick hazel bush, less than ten paces from where the girl was kneeling.

He was about to introduce himself, when he heard the distant rumble of hooves galloping along the track from the direction of the village. The girl jumped up, and seemed uncertain what to do. She glanced towards the bush where John was crouched, and at that moment, a horse and rider appeared from around a bend in the path and galloped towards the bush, forcing the girl to run into the field.

The rider was a very large man dressed in dark clothes, with a wide-brimmed hat shading his eyes. He pulled the horse to a stop so violently that the huge beast reared up into the air and whinnied loudly. The girl ran like a hare across the field; only the upper part of her body visible in the long grass. She seemed desperate as she lunged through the dense vegetation.

"Come here, girl!" the man yelled. His voice was harsh and the words were spoken with a heavy accent.

John had no experience of accents; to him the speaker was a stranger from far away. In his first, brief glimpse of the man, John noticed many things: the horse was the largest animal he had ever seen. It was more than sixteen hands high, jet black with enormous staring eyes and a foaming mouth. It was in a constant state of motion, pulling at the reins as if in terror of the vicious spurs that the man wore on his boots. With every moment that John stared, the rider became more sinister. His hat obscured the top of his face, and a thick, ugly scar was visible across his left cheek, stretching from his large hooked nose to a place below the ear and hidden by thick red hair that poured out from beneath the hat. On his left hip, he wore a long curved dagger attached to a black belt studded in gold. A long sword and a small round shield were fixed to his saddle. He seemed immensely strong and frightening.

"Stop or you will be punished!" he called. His voice boomed like thunder.

The girl continued her headlong flight towards the trees at the far side of the meadow. The man dug his spurs into the flank of the horse and, with a cruel laugh, galloped off in pursuit. It was an unequal race. The girl was only half way across the field when the horse and rider were upon her.

John watched, outraged, as the stranger deliberately rode into the girl, knocking her sideways, and she disappeared into the tall grass. Again, the rider pulled the horse to a violent halt. As the horse turned, the girl leapt to her feet and began to run diagonally towards the trees, frantically lashing out with her arms to part the thick grass. John could now hear her voice screaming, "No! No!" and the man's laugh echoing across the field, loud and brutal.

Anger welled up inside John, but he felt helpless against such a powerful enemy. His mind raced. He had no weapon, and even if he had, what use would it be against an armed man on such a horse? He knew he had to do something and tried to concentrate as the old woman had taught him. He searched quickly around for a rock or a stout stick or anything he could use as a weapon. Nothing came immediately to hand.

He looked up in time to see the horseman knock the girl to the ground a second time. As he turned his horse, the girl staggered to her feet, and tried to limp away in a different direction. Her head was bent over and she seemed to be holding her side. She took a few, faltering steps and then stopped, swaying from side to side. Before she finally collapsed, the rider trotted over and leaning down, dragged her across his saddle. She lay limp and apparently lifeless. Her legs hung loosely on one side of the horse's neck, and her arms and her head, with its long black hair, drooped down on the other. The man gave another bellowing laugh and began to walk his horse back towards the path.

If he was going to do anything to help, John realised it would have to be when the man reached the path, and before he urged his horse to greater speed. It was at that moment that John's eyes seemed drawn to some objects lying in a large clump of ferns by the side of the track. He stared hard, and slowly understood what was compelling his attention. Nestled in the undergrowth and partly covered, were two long poles; the sort woodsmen often cut as struts for fences. The ends nearest John were both pointed in readiness for fixing into the ground and they must have lain there for weeks, unobserved by passing travellers.

The rider was about eighty paces away; a dark shape in the bright field, and moving slowly towards the deep shadows of the track, near where the poles were hidden. This made it impossible for John to reach for them and still avoid being discovered before the rider passed by. To wait too long would make any action futile. While he was labouring with this problem, he felt a gentle pull on the rope. The calf! He had forgotten all about it. The docile animal had followed him behind the bush, without complaint, but was now becoming restless.

In a flash John knew what to do. Still crouching behind the high bush, he untied the rope from the animal's neck and gave a vigorous wallop to its flank. The unsuspecting creature was so surprised by this sudden violence that it careered off into the field, kicking its back legs in the air, bellowing loudly and prancing about as if on springs.

The rider was about thirty paces from the track, when the calf burst into the field, causing the horse to shy away. Then, seeing the horse and rider, the beast stopped and regarded them with mute suspicion. After his initial surprise, the rider seemed vaguely amused and urged the horse forward, whereupon the calf turned about and with much prancing, raced off in the direction of its former home. As the man continued to watch the antics of the calf, John stretched his arm through the branches until his hand closed on the first of the two poles. He remained perfectly still as the horse and rider approached with the motionless body of the girl. John held his breath as they passed close to his hiding place. He sprang to his feet pulling the pole from its grassy bed.

With a wild cry, he ran forward and rammed the pole into the back of the rider, hitting him on the right side of his body below the arm. Luckily for the man, it was the unsharpened end that hit him, and, although it knocked him to one side, he was not seriously injured. The unexpected noise and action caused the horse to rear up. The man was pushed to the left as the girl dropped to the right, headfirst on the ground. She lay only an arm's length from the rearing horse, her black hair spread over her face, and her limbs twisted at odd angles. She did not move.

John tried to get between the huge beast and the fragile body, using the pole as protection. The man fought to regain control of the frightened animal and retain his balance, but the blow had winded him and his right arm failed him. Nevertheless, he possessed great strength, and in a moment, it seemed to John, the stranger was turning his horse while drawing his sword from its scabbard.

John knew instinctively once the sword was drawn and the horse controlled, he would have no chance against his powerful adversary. The

21

horse was side-on and the man's sword was on the other side. It was then or never, and with all his failing strength he swung the heavy pole.

At that moment, the horse reacted to the violence of its rider's spurs and kicked out its back legs, and moved suddenly to the right and away from John. The pole arced through the air, missed the horse and rider and continued its circular path with great velocity. John, unbalanced, whirled round until he lost his footing and fell in a heap in the grass; the pole fell from his grip.

As he fell to the ground, he knew if he did not get up the moment he landed, he would die. Somewhere within his mind, a hidden power calmed his panic. Everything seemed to happen in slow motion. One part of his mind recalled the same feeling when he had confronted the awful stranger with the twisted jaw, while the other part watched as the horse and rider charged down on him.

He hit the ground, turned, rolled over and slid across the path towards the hedge behind which he had been hiding only moments before. John came to rest with his hand instinctively reaching for what his mind calmly reassured him was there: the second pole.

Still, as in a dream, he rose up, gripped the end of the pole and turned and swung it as though in slow motion. He had a vision of huge black eyes, a white frothing mouth and the flash of a sword in the sun. His ears reverberated with the thunder of hooves and there was a sudden jarring in his arms. He was falling over again; his arms were strangely loose and he was diving into a sea of green.

Seconds later, he tried to sit up. He was tangled in the branches of the bush, his shoulders felt as if they had been pulled from their sockets and there was the salty taste of blood in his mouth. Focusing his eyes, he saw the horse lying on its side a few paces away. It was not moving and the position of its head looked unnatural.

He climbed awkwardly and painfully out of the branches of the bush and staggered towards the huge mound of flesh, already surrounded by buzzing flies. Then he saw the man. The stranger was lying spread-eagled on his back beyond the horse. His dark clothes contrasted with the bright green of the grass and the blood red of the poppies. John stopped at a safe distance from the still figure. Was he dead? It was impossible to tell if he was breathing. Only moments before, this man had tried to kill him. Even in death he was frightening.

The devil doesn't die, he only lies down. John repeated the line over and over in his mind. It was yet another of Old Mary's sayings, which he had learned by heart.

He edged nearer. The man's eyes were closed and he wore an expression of grim disdain. The lordly effect was lessened by a small trickle of blood that slowly oozed from his nose. His left leg was twisted under him and in his right hand, he held his sword, which gleamed in the sun, its blade edge sharp and dangerous. On the middle finger of his hand was a large gold ring with a strange design that looked familiar, even from a distance.

John approached the fallen warrior. As a precaution, he placed his foot firmly on the sword. The powerful hand did not slacken its grip. John's eyes were riveted on the ring. Now he knew what it was. The design on the ring was a replica of the one ingrained in his hand. He stared at his palm and back again to the ring; there was no doubt it was the same.

What did it mean? Had he killed a friend or an enemy? Up until then, he had not doubted the man was his foe. After all, this stranger had mistreated the girl and had then tried to kill him. But supposing the girl was evil? The man might have been capturing a known wrongdoer. The stranger had every right to draw his sword, for John had hit the man first. Imagine if it had all been a terrible mistake?

He stared at the huge body. The blood had stopped oozing from the stranger's nose, and he was not breathing. Using both hands, John forced open the long fingers and levered the sword from the immense hand. As the weapon fell free, he examined the man's palm, but there was no sign on it. He lifted up the sword and found, to his amazement, the same strange runes were engraved on the gold hilt, in which were set many precious stones. As he held the hilt next to his open hand, there was a noisy outrush of air. John glanced up to see two large green eyes staring at him with great intensity. Any doubt he had about the nature of the man, vanished instantly. The stranger possessed the most evil eyes John had ever seen, with a depth and an unnatural brightness that caused him to tremble. In those eyes were measureless cruelty and hatred.

John jumped back as the left hand swung over to grab him. Luckily, the man was still suffering from the effects of the fall, and his movements lacked co-ordination.

"You will die," the man hissed. His eyes blazed with hate as he struggled to get to his feet.

John groaned and backed back. The old woman's words *The devil doesn't die, he only lies down,* came clearly to his thoughts. When would he ever learn? If only he had not ventured so near.

The red-haired stranger finally staggered to his feet. Without his horse, he was even bigger than John had imagined. The black hat had fallen off and, from the crown of his head to the bottom of his high boots, he must have measured nearly seven feet.

He stood swaying slightly, as John, with the sword in his hand, retreated behind the dead horse. The weapon was so heavy, John found he could barely lift it with one hand; even using two hands, it would be difficult to defend himself with it.

"I'll kill you!" the giant yelled.

Terrified, John turned and ran for the cover of the trees, carrying the sword on his shoulder. When he reached the first tree, he stopped and looked back. The man was standing by the dead horse and in his hand he held a dagger. He was limping badly and seemed in great pain.

He looked towards the boy and roared, "I'll kill you. You'll not get away!"

John turned, and looked for the girl. She was nowhere to be seen. His eyes searched the track and the open field. Nothing. She had literally vanished into the air.

He ran into the wood, searching the bushes and trees to see if she was hiding there. When he failed to find any trace of her, he returned toward the track. From the shade of a tall oak, he watched the stranger. The man had drawn a large circle in the dust enclosing the body of the horse and himself, and was scratching a series of intricate signs in the earth. After each sign, he chanted a stream of violent words in a strange language.

"He's a magician," John muttered. He felt cold and his legs trembled. With the girl no longer in visible danger, there seemed no need for him to stay. Whatever the stranger was trying to achieve, it was certain to be unpleasant. John turned into the woods and began to walk in the direction of Old Mary's house.

He had only taken a few paces, when he felt the sword begin to move in his hand. Was it his imagination? He stared at the hilt as it slowly began to twist like an eel. John gripped it as hard as he could but to no avail. The sword seemed to have a will of its own. He dropped the weapon on the ground and stood back, watching mesmerised as it began to twist its way through the grass and scrub towards the direction of the stranger. It moved like a snake, avoiding the trees, its sharp blade cutting a path towards the field where the evil being was chanting his spells in a loud, wailing voice.

Again, John had the sensation of a bad dream. Had he really rescued the girl? Was the terrible stranger hurt because he, a mere boy with a pole, had toppled him from his horse? Was this magic he was witnessing, or just a trick of the eye?

He moved back to the edge of the forest and watched as the heavy sword crossed the path and snaked its way to the edge of the circle, where it stopped and lay still. Without even checking to see if he was being observed, the magician drew a line with his dagger in the edge of the circle and the sword entered and lay motionless at his feet. The man lifted it high above his head and cried out in his alien language. Almost immediately, a cloud appeared in front of the sun, in a sky that, moments before, had been cloudless. Darkness thickened and a wind sprang up, causing the trees to moan as their branches stirred.

The change had happened so swiftly, John could only believe this evil man was responsible. Quickly, he turned to go, but the trees and the undergrowth that, until then, had been a friendly protection in which to hide, barred his progress. In moments, or so it seemed, the wind reached storm force. The bushes writhed and clutched at his legs. Leaves and twigs battered his face and from above, heavy branches thundered to the ground.

John was dismayed. He sensed he was in great danger, yet found it impossible to move on. The violent wind forced him backwards. He tried to hide behind a large elm but a violent crack above his head made him jump aside, in time to avoid being crushed by a heavy bough that exploded in an avalanche of wood and leaves on impact with the earth.

He was being dragged back towards the field by a power greater than anything he could imagine, and the thought terrified him. Desperately, he fought to prevent it. He clutched at small trees that broke in his grasp; he tried to hold on to the ground and tore his hands on roots and sharp blades of grass. There was a deafening increase in the roaring sound. The wind lifted him off the ground and catapulted him on to the track, with branches and debris whirling around him. He struggled to regain his balance but was thrown forward and rolled head over heels until he fell heavily against a solid, smooth object still hot and wet with sweat. He knew it was the horse.

Everything went quiet. He opened his eyes and saw the awful face of the stranger glaring down at him. The man's eyes were pure hate and exultation. In his hand he held the sword.

John experienced a mixture of emotions: fear of dying, disappointment at the injustice of it all, and a great anger at his own weakness. He raised his hand in a feeble attempt to ward off the blow, and found himself yelling his other name.

"Giles Plantard! Giles Plantard!"

He felt the imprint of the runes vibrating; it was as if he was holding an impregnable shield over his body, yet one that was pushing out a force of its own. It was not just defending, it was opposing.

The sword stopped in its downward movement, the clouds moved away from the sun, and the evil creature staggered back with a look of horror on his face. As John sat up, the man fell backwards out of the circle and instantly the sword sprang out of his hand and hung suspended in the air like a hawk. As the giant crashed to the ground, the sword spiralled over and descended like an arrow and sliced into his chest.

Once again, a weird silence settled over the field. The sun blazed down and the wind was gone. Nothing moved. The change was so eerie that John sat staring at the motionless body for many minutes, unable to take in the enormity of the events that had happened. Then he looked up at the sky, his thoughts in a tumult.

"Who am I?" he whispered, "Who am I?"

Had he really killed a man? What was it about the name the old woman had given him that possessed that sort of power? What did the runes on his hand mean? He lay back in the springy grass, closed his eyes and drifted into a deep sleep, as exhaustion overcame him.

· · ·

THE GIRL RAN AWKWARDLY through the trees, gripping the right side of her belly. She felt dizzy and sick, but her wish to live overcame her pain. Blood trickled down from her forehead and her face was grey. Her breath came in quick gasps.

"Don't let him catch me, God. Please don't let him catch me," she moaned as she staggered through the clawing bushes and sharp brambles that blocked her way. In her panic, she had fled into the dense forest and had lost the path. She glanced over her shoulder to check she was not being followed, tripped and fell headlong into a small patch of dry grass.

She lay quite still where she had fallen. Every nerve of her body tensed and she listened for any sound of pursuit. Nothing. Except the repetitive sawing sound of a wood pigeon in the high branches of a nearby tree. There was not a breath of wind, and a soft silence enveloped the wood. She remained there for several minutes, as the blood dried on her face and the heat of her body cooled. She felt safe. He would never find her in this forest.

The girl must have dozed for a short while, for she was aware of less pain in her side, but it was something else that had awoken her. She clambered to her feet and looked about. A curious noise seemed all around her. It was as though the forest was beginning to move and the trees were whispering to each other. She stared frantically in all directions, her eyes wide with fear. Then she realized it was the wind.

Even as she became aware of what the rustling was, the wind became a gale. Quickly, she crouched behind a large sycamore, as the world went mad. Branches lashed from side to side; the wind howled and roared; leaves and twigs whipped through the air like arrows and the sky went black. She lay flat on the ground gripping on to the roots of the great tree.

Huge and powerful forces pulled at her; the noise was all around. She felt weak and helpless as her body was wrenched out of the protective area of the sycamore's roots. Her hands clutched the gnarled wood in a frenzy of despair. The evil stranger was drawing her back to him.

She felt her body lift from the earth, yet still she held on to the tree, her nails and fingers ached with the effort and her whole being concentrated on the one action of gripping the safety of the bark. Her black hair streamed back, her legs were stretched out behind as though she was swimming; she could not breathe as her entire body vibrated in the violent wind.

The end came suddenly. One moment she was holding fast, the next she was prised away, like a limpet from a rock. She had a brief sensation of flying and then her mind passed into oblivion.

When she awoke it was getting dark. Her left arm was aching and there was more blood on her face. She tried to move, and winced as she felt the pain in her side. Slowly, and in agony, she sat up and looked about her.

She was lying beneath a large oak. About ten paces away was the sycamore she had tried to hold on to. The memory of the great storm slowly returned, and Gwen realized she must have been thrown against the tree beneath which she lay. She slowly massaged her tender shoulder, feeling an aching in every limb.

The strange wind had completely vanished and it was a warm, still evening. Birds sang their sunset melodies, and the world seemed at peace. It was hard to believe the horrors of the day had ever happened. As she staggered uncertainly to her feet, her body confirmed the terrible beating she had received, and she cried out with the pain.

CHAPTER 4

I T WAS LATE SATURDAY afternoon in the village of Woodford, a small sleepy
habitation nestled in a clearing surrounded by thick forest, and close by
a fast-flowing stream. Thomas Roper, the village blacksmith, was working
at his forge. Tom, as everyone called him, was a large man with powerful
shoulders and strong arms. He had inherited the forge from his father, and
was much respected in the village. Tom was a silent man, not given to long
sentences or any great show of emotion, and he was never so content as
when he was beating and shaping the hot metal to make shoes for horses,
implements for farming and weapons for war. His forge and small cottage
were at the southern end of the village and most people would call a greeting
as they passed.

"Tom! Be you there?"

Tom recognized the shrill voice of his wife, calling as she always did when
she came out of the house. He wondered where else he was likely to be, and
began to hammer out the blade of an axe.

"Oh, Tom, there you be," she said, as she always did. It was an unconscious
ritual, which was her introduction whenever he was working. Elizabeth was
a slim woman of medium height with light brown hair, going grey at the
edges. Twenty years ago she had been thought by some to be pretty, but in
her middle age she wore a worried frown and always appeared to be in a
hurry.

"Tom, have you seen that girl?"

Why did she always have to call her *that girl?* Tom wondered. He stopped
his hammering and glanced round at his wife.

"Gwen's gone to pick flowers for the church," he said.

"Well, she should 'ave been back hours ago. She hasn't done a stroke of
work all day." She suddenly sneezed. "I'm not 'ere to wait on 'er like she be
some princess." She sneezed again and blew her nose loudly.

The reference to the princess was not lost on Tom. Ever since Gwen had been able to walk, Tom had called her his little princess, although she was not so little now. He scratched, absent-mindedly, at his thick, black beard.

His wife sneezed again. "I can't stay out here," she complained. "The pollen makes me ill." She turned for the house, and Tom watched her hurry to the door with a rag held to her pale face. He tried to remember when he had last seen Elizabeth smile.

"Send her in 'ere as soon as she...." The last words were lost in an enormous sneeze.

Tom resumed his work. His thoughts returned to Gwen. A lovely girl, who was gentle, caring, but with a strong will and a great sense of right and wrong, which was why none of the village boys ever called: she made them feel uncomfortable. They admired her, but from a distance. Gwen was taller than Elizabeth and in the last few months had reached, what his dead mother would have called the *bloom of youth*.

"How be', Tom!" The voice belonged to an old, broad-shouldered man, who continued on past the open forge towards the main part of the village. He carried a sturdy axe on his back.

"You be early today, Will!" Tom called after him.

"Same as usual," the old man answered, as he moved slowly down the road.

"You seen my Gwen?" Tom called after him.

"No," the old woodcutter paused and turned round, "but I saw a stranger on a big horse who asked after 'er today."

"Who be this man?" Tom asked, his voice betrayed his anxiety.

"Never seen 'im before. Big feller. Bigger 'an 'ee. A fightin' man. Dressed in black, wiv' a scar 'cross 'is face. Didn't like 'im. Spoke foreign." He turned and resumed his slow walk up the road.

Tom wanted to question him further, but knew old Will was not a man to alter his routine for anyone, especially at the end of a day when his food was on the table. It occurred to Tom that if he had not asked about Gwen, Will would not have bothered to mention the stranger, although the arrival of such a man was a rare event in the village.

"Silly ol' fool," Tom muttered. He looked up at the setting sun, which hung like a copper disc above the forest, and realized it was later than he had thought. He had been busy all day and unaware of the time. But Gwen had left before mid-morning to pick flowers for the church. More than seven hours had passed!

Tom walked slowly towards the brazier in which he heated the metal strips. His eyes stared unseeing at the hot charcoal. She was a big girl now, almost old enough to be thought of as a woman. He wondered if she had stopped off at the cottage of a friend, but he knew she would never have tarried so long. Then there was the stranger who had asked about her. He did not like the feel of it. Something was amiss. "This could be what I've feared for so long," he whispered.

He moved swiftly to the back of the forge. On a high shelf was a long object wrapped tightly in sackcloth. He reached up and removed the dusty sacking to reveal a heavy sword. Its blade was bright and the pommel, of yellow metal, was engraved with strange signs. It was a weapon fit for some great lord and seemed out of place in a small country forge.

Tom balanced the heavy sword in his right hand. His eyes took on a far-away look as he raised the weapon high above his head. The moment passed and he shuddered as if he had been woken from a dream. He placed the sword gently on the hard ground and selected a number of stout poles, which he tied in a bundle, with the sword in the middle. Finally he made a long loop and swung the load over his broad shoulders. To the casual eye, he was only collecting wood.

Without a word to Elizabeth, he slipped silently out of his old forge, and moved quickly down the dusty lane leading to the church, and beyond stretched the meadows where Gwen always went to pick flowers. She had a love for wild flowers, but was never allowed to bring them into the house as Elizabeth claimed all plants made her sneeze. However, the old priest welcomed such gifts, and Gwen always found time from her work to decorate the church before Sunday service. It was part of the duties she performed for the old man in return for the education he had given her over many years. Tom often joked that she spoke more like a titled lady than the daughter of a poor blacksmith. However, he was proud of her ability to read the Bible and understand Latin, even though Elizabeth complained that Gwen did not spend enough time helping with the chores. "You remember now, she be different to us," he would remind his wife. "We must never forget she be special."

Tom went straight to the church, but it was empty and there were no flowers. His anxiety increased as he made his way to the fields. He reached the Flower Meadows a short while later; it was his own name for them, and went back to the time when Gwen had been a small child. He remembered when he had first brought her to these wide tree-lined fields. She had been about three years old at the time; a small, beautiful but very unhappy child, and the sight of the masses of yellows, reds and blues had caused her to smile in spite of her misery. Since that moment it was her favourite place.

He was half-trotting, half-walking and his large face was flushed with sweat running in rivulets down his cheeks. The bundle on his back had grown heavy and he was conscious of his thirty-nine years. Tom paused at the edge of the forest. In front of him was the first of the long meadows, and to his left and behind him was the dark line of the forest. The track stretched ahead, shadowy in the evening sun.

"Gwenny!" he called. There was no answer. He called again, much louder, and a flock of crows erupted noisily from the trees above him, their black bodies swirling into the air, their rasping cries drowning all other sounds.

Tom stared at them. "Unlucky birds, always the bringers of bad fortune," he muttered. He immediately dismissed the thought. "Nothing will 'ave 'appened to Gwen. I won't let it," he growled, and hurried down the narrow track.

His mind returned to the springtime more than twelve years before, when Gwen had arrived at their house, a small infant wrapped in a soft cloak. It was evening when the riders had thundered to a stop outside the forge. Looking out from his window, Tom thought it was a robber band intent on murder, for he saw their weapons in the moonlight. He remembered placing a sharp knife in Elizabeth's trembling hand and pushing her into their sleeping area. Then, grabbing a heavy axe, he opened the solid door of his house and waited for the horsemen to make the first move.

"We are looking for Tom Roper!" a voice announced from the darkness. There were eight of them. Their horses stamped and fretted as though eager to be off.

"Who wants 'im?" Tom answered.

"Sir Maurice de Ridefort!" came the reply. "Don't you recognize me, Tom Roper?"

"M' Lord," Tom stuttered. "Be it really thee?"

The leader dismounted and approached the door. He was dressed in a suit of chain-mail over which was worn a white tunic with a large red cross emblazoned on it. Most of this was concealed beneath a dark cloak, discoloured with dust. With a tired movement Sir Maurice removed the chain-mail hood.

Tom stared. It was unbelievable. This was the man whom he had last seen in the Holy Land at the head of one of the most powerful armies in the world, and here was the same general at the door of Tom's poor home, deep in the forests of Wessex.

"Will ye come in, m'Lord?" Tom said, standing aside.

The old man entered. He glanced quickly around the small room, then looked earnestly into Tom's face.

"Do you remember when we last met?" Sir Maurice asked, his voice confirmed the tiredness showing in every feature of his lined and sun-tanned face.

"Yes, m'Lord," Tom answered. "By the walls of Acre in the Holy Land. Ye had me wounds tended by your doctor. Ye saved me life."

"It was no more than you deserved, Tom. If all my soldiers had fought as hard as you did, we would have finally defeated the infidel." He paused and seemed lost in his thoughts.

Tom waited, knowing the old general had not called merely to exchange remembrances. Outside the horses stamped their hooves and snorted, and there was a clink of metal.

When at last Sir Maurice spoke, there was a different tone in his voice. It was as though he was saying something important and pretending that it was not so. "This is your house then?"

"Yes, m'Lord."

"You have a wife?" he said, looking at some of Elizabeth's knitting by the fire.

"Yes, m'Lord. Her name be Elizabeth," Tom added, wondering why this important man was bothering with such details.

"You have children?"

"No, m'Lord. God 'as not blessed us."

"You are a good man, Tom Roper. God has other plans for you. Bring forth your wife."

"Elizabeth!" Tom called. "Come out. All is safe."

She parted the curtain slowly. Her eyes stared and she carried the knife in both hands as if carrying a candle.

"Have no fear, woman," the knight said and indicated a stool by the fire.

Elizabeth sat down and seemed embarrassed by the knife, which she tried

33

to hide under the stool. She passed her hand over her hair, and patted her skirt.

"Your Tom was a brave man in the Holy Wars," Sir Maurice said, looking carefully at Elizabeth. He seemed to be making up his mind about something. "I remembered what you said, Tom, when you spoke of your father's forge. You said it was the quietest place in the world, just forests and birds and God-fearing people."

"An' so it be still, m'Lord. 'Cept my father be dead a year or so now."

"Do you like children?" the old knight was addressing Elizabeth, but he appeared to be speaking to both of them.

"Yes," Elizabeth murmured. The blood rose to her cheeks. "But God 'as not...."

"Would you look after a child for me?" he interrupted. "She needs a good home where she will come to no harm, and where people ask no questions."

"Ye wants us to look after a child?" Elizabeth could hardly believe what she heard.

"Bring her in!" Sir Maurice called, and almost immediately a tall knight appeared with a small girl wrapped in a thick cloak. She was sleeping soundly.

"The child is drugged to help her survive the journey," Sir Maurice said. He looked at the sleeping child with a great tenderness, and when he came to take her from the arms of the man who held her, the knight lifted the child with such care that it seemed as though he felt she might fall apart in his hands.

"This is no ordinary child, Tom, she is from a very old and important blood-line. She has enemies who wish to kill her because of her family, and I am sworn to protect her." Sir Maurice stopped and, raising his gaze from the peaceful face of the child, he stared into Elizabeth's. His eyes blazed with fanatical fire and she felt a sudden fear of this old man.

"I would die for this child," he said. His voice was soft, but the intensity of the words was breathtaking.

Tom was aware of the silence in the room. He was conscious of the thumping of his heart and of a lump in his throat. "My wife and me, we would...." He hesitated, uncertain of what to say.

"I want you to look after this child until such time as it is safe for her to take her rightful position. They will not think of looking for her in such a place as this. In my company she is always in danger, and her enemies will stop at nothing to kill her. Will you take her, woman, and treat her as your own daughter?" Sir Maurice had not removed his eyes from Elizabeth's, and she stood like one in a trance.

Tom cleared his throat. "We be 'onoured, m'Lord, but I'm only a poor—"

"You will be well paid for your service," the tall knight interrupted.

"That was not my meanin'," Tom replied, his face burned with embarrassment.

Sir Maurice turned to the knight, "You do not know this man; he is not concerned with money but with the lifestyle that he can provide for the child." He turned to Tom. "She cannot have riches and a royal education, for that would bring attention to her. I want her to become a country girl; I want her to blend into this village so that no passing stranger will ever notice the difference. Treat her as your own daughter; do not tell her more than is necessary. Children soon become used to changes. All I require of you is that you will guard this child as you would your own flesh and blood. With you, there is a chance of life, with me there is certain death for her. Will you do this for me, Tom Roper?" The old man was almost pleading.

"We'll do anything ye ask, m'Lord," Tom murmured. It seemed hardly possible that this great general, in whom thousands of soldiers had placed their trust and whose reputation was well known in the courts and palaces of Europe, should be asking, even begging, a favour of a mere country blacksmith.

"Take the child," Sir Maurice said to Elizabeth. "It will be some hours before the drug wears off. When she awakes tell her you are her new parents. In time she will become used to it. She has no choice in the matter," he added, and his face was creased with anxiety. He turned to the tall knight and gave some hurried instructions. The man handed Tom a plain canvass bag, and then moved quickly out into the darkness, where he could be heard organizing the other men.

"We must leave immediately if we are to keep ahead of our pursuers. There is a long journey ahead of us and we must lead the enemy far from this place if the child is to survive." He turned to Elizabeth. "Give her all the love you can and may God smile on you for your good deed…." He took a final look at the sleeping infant and, when he faced Tom, there were tears in his eyes.

"Take this," Sir Maurice said as he unbuckled his sword. "Use it only in defence of the child. It is more than just a sword, as you will discover when you have need of it. But remember, use it only to protect her, for no other reason. There is money in the bag. Use it wisely. Do not bring attention to yourself. Keep the sword hidden at all times, and when we leave put out your candles, bar the door and admit nobody. After tonight you should be safe."

"'Ow long does we keep the child?" Elizabeth asked, her voice taught with worry.

"Until I send word, or until a person comes bearing these signs." He pointed to the hilt of the sword on which were engraved a series of designs and symbols unlike any that Tom had ever seen.

At that moment a rider approached at a gallop and there was a shout of warning from outside.

"It is one of my scouts. The enemy must be close at hand." Sir Maurice grasped Tom's shoulders, "You are a good man, Tom Roper, may God be with you." He turned to go. Outside Tom could hear the movements of the horses and the voices of the men as they prepared to leave.

"What do we call 'er?" Tom asked as the old knight reached the door.

"Call her what you will, she must not know her true name. Neither must you. What you don't know can't harm you." He raised his hand in a final farewell. "Guard her with your life!" he cried, and disappeared through the door.

Almost immediately, there was the clatter of the horses as they broke into a gallop, their hooves drumming on the hard earth. Tom and Elizabeth stood listening to the sound as it slowly faded away.

Without a word they secured the door, damped down the fire and extinguished the candles. Elizabeth took the child to bed with her while Tom hid the sword and the canvass bag, then both prepared for bed. Neither slept as they lay, with the child between them, going over in their minds the events of the night. Both realized that their lives would never be the same again.

It was in the early hours of the morning when they heard the thunder of horses galloping along the road. They held their breath until silence returned, punctuated only by the hoot of an owl in a nearby tree.

"Well, that's that then," Tom said and turned over on his side and closed his eyes.

Elizabeth lay staring into the darkness. "What do it all mean?" she whispered. But Tom was asleep.

CHAPTER 5

JOHN WOKE WITH A start, fearful and wide-eyed. It was early evening and the sun was starting to set in a pastel-coloured sky. Birds were singing and the hum of the insects was loud in his ears. The smell of horse sweat was all around him, and he felt an emptiness in his stomach.

He scrambled to his feet, aware of the ache in his arms. The dead horse was covered with buzzing flies and was still warm to the touch. Beyond, only ten paces away, lay the body of the stranger, the sword deep in his chest like a gravestone. His eyes were open, staring unseeing into the darkening sky. The cruel lips were parted, revealing stained teeth that were clenched together, giving the face an expression of agonized terror.

It was some minutes before John could drag his eyes from the awful corpse. Slowly, a feeling of fear and guilt began to overcome him, as he remembered the questions that had tormented him before he had collapsed, utterly exhausted. On his hand, the imprint on the palm was still as clear as before, but the power he had felt surging from his hand was now only a memory.

John moved cautiously to the edge of the circle, watching the sword, fearing its deadly force. Nothing happened as he placed first one foot, then the other over the circular mark on the ground. He released his breath loudly. The circle, like the sign on his hand, had lost its power and was just a dusty mark in the field. Whatever magic had been conjured up had vanished, and he was left with a dead man and a putrefying horse.

He stared at the sword. Should he take it and bury the body? If he removed the saddle and the rest of the horse's equipment, the animal would appear as if it had broken its neck in a gallop and had been left by its rider for the crows and wild creatures to pick clean. Perhaps he should just leave the body and return home? Old Mary would know what to do. But then there was the girl. Supposing she was still close by and was lying badly injured, unable to reach her home or call for help? If he pretended that nothing had happened, she might die. Then again, if she had somehow reached home, what story would she tell her family? When they found the body, they would know that he had been responsible for the man's death. It would be useless to try to explain what had really happened. Nobody would believe such a story when he could hardly believe it himself. He would be branded a murderer. However, the man had been trying to catch the girl and did attack her. But who was the girl? She could well be a thief or even a murderer herself. Yet even as he thought this he knew, in his heart, that it could not be so.

The thoughts pushed and pulled at him. He stood staring down at the sword and at the evil, twisted face of the dead man, and was unable to decide what to do. He remembered the runes on the sword and once more compared them with the image on his palm. They were the same. He came to a decision: he would remove the sword and take it back to the old woman. Darkness was falling, and with luck nobody would see the horse or the body until morning, by which time he would have been able to share the problem with her. She would know what to do.

He moved hesitantly towards the huge body and stared steadily at it. There was no doubt the man was dead, and had been so since the sword had transfixed him to the earth. John grasped the hilt of the sword with both hands and, closing his eyes tightly together, he pulled hard. It came away remarkably easily, but he dared not open his eyes until he had turned his back on the awful corpse. He felt he might be sick, and stood very still, breathing deeply.

Then he walked quickly away towards the path, and wiped the sword on a tuft of grass. The blood was thick and sticky and left a dark stain on the green blades, that were already a deeper colour in the thickening dusk.

As he turned for home, he heard the sound of crows flying up from the trees further down the track. Their raucous cries echoed a warning to the whole area. Someone was coming.

John flung himself behind some bushes and lay flat on the ground. Panic overcame him once again. To be found with the sword in his hand would take some explaining, and if they found the mark on his hand and the same mark on the sword, what conclusions would they draw?

Some moments later John saw a large figure coming quickly down the track. He was moving at a fast, awkward trot, his breath sounding in loud gasps, and he carried a bundle of wooden poles on his back. As he came closer, John recognized the man as the village blacksmith. His black beard and his broad shoulders were unmistakable.

As the blacksmith approached, he paused in his stride to yell "Gwenny!" His powerful voice disturbed more birds as the sound spread through the forest. John had only seen the man from a distance as he worked in his forge, but Peter had said that he was the strongest man in the village, and probably in the whole area.

"Gwenny! Can ye hear me?" he bellowed.

There was no doubt in John's mind, the blacksmith was looking for the same girl whom the dead warrior had attacked. Should he reveal himself and try to answer the questions that were sure to follow? Suppose the blacksmith did not believe him, and accused him of murdering the girl? After all, a man was dead. When John thought about it, he realized he was no longer the same person who had left for market that morning. He had killed another human being. He closed his eyes to shut out the horrible thoughts and felt tears run down his burning cheeks.

"Gwenny!" The blacksmith gave a final cry and continued his lumbering run. When he was a short distance from John's hiding place, the blacksmith stopped and let out a cry of alarm.

John raised his head and rubbed his eyes as he watched the man dart quickly towards the dead body of the stranger. The blacksmith examined the corpse, walked over to the dead horse, and slowly surveyed the field. Then he noticed the flattened vegetation and followed the channel through the high grass where the girl had been chased and knocked down. The blacksmith looked about, returned to the body once more, and pondered the scene. He stared hard at the deep forest and seemed to be looking for something. After a pause, he trotted over to the path and began to search along the grass verge. It was not long before he came to the spot where John had cleaned the sword. The blacksmith bent down to take a closer look and touched the bloodstained grass with his forefinger.

"So?" he said in a long-drawn out sound. "So?"

John lay very still and tried not to breathe. He felt the sweat form on his brow, as he watched the blacksmith in the fading light.

The man was staring closely at the grass and at the bushes. Then he stood up and said in a loud voice, "Nothing more to be done here for now." He turned to the south and began to walk with great strides along the path, away from the village, and soon disappeared from view.

It was some time before John moved. He held the heavy sword in his right hand and felt a certain security from it. The copper sun had finally set behind the western hills, the shadows had increased, and everything looked different. It was a clear sky with a bright half moon, which produced a silvery light in the field, intensifying the darkness under the trees.

John could hear the flutter of birds as they settled down for the night, and somewhere close by, small creatures writhed in the undergrowth. There was no wind and a heavy brooding silence enveloped the forest.

"I must get back to the old woman," John said to himself. He moved cautiously onto the track that looked like a silver river in the moonlight. In contrast, the edge of the woods was dark and menacing. Nothing moved, and after a moment John decided it was safe to continue. It would take about an hour to get to the cottage and he began to walk quickly, holding the sword in his right hand and resting the blade on his shoulder. Every few paces he paused, listened, and checked the path behind.

He jumped violently when a white owl glided silently across the field, and again when a rabbit broke cover almost under his feet. The trees on his left appeared to get bigger, and at times he was almost certain they moved. He thought of Old Mary's saying: *Fear is the enemy. He who does not fear, has no enemies.* If only he could stop being afraid.

Ahead was the end of the open fields, where the track disappeared into the woods and weaved its way through oak, elm and ash before it climbed gently up into open ground again. John approached the dark mouth of the wood with staring eyes and a pounding heart. By day this had been a pleasant, cool refuge from the burning sun. Now it was a place of terror. He was tired and hungry, and his one thought was to reach the security of the cottage and sink into the softness of the straw palliasse on which he slept. Although he felt the blood pounding in his neck, he knew he had the key to unlock his fear, if only he could force himself to use it.

The sword was becoming increasingly heavy and he was aware of the bruising he had received both during the fight, and as a result of the battering from the strange wind. Tomorrow, he said to himself, he would learn Old Mary's ways in earnest. Tomorrow he would start afresh and practise what she told him. She had been right so many times that day.

"Don't move or I'll kill ye!" A huge, dark figure sprang out from the shadows. John froze, unable to speak.

"Lay down that sword!" the voice roared. "Now!"

John saw the flash of metal in the moonlight and cringed as he waited for the blow to come.

"Lay it down slowly," the voice commanded.

John realized he was fully visible in the moonlight, while his adversary was half in shadow, and had the advantage.

Slowly John removed the sword from his shoulder and laid it on the ground. If the man was going to kill him he would have done so without giving a warning.

"Who are you?" John asked in a faint voice.

"Never ye mind who I be. Just what 'ave ye been up to?" the man spoke with a strong local accent. His voice was cold and threatening.

"It was an accident, sir."

"Accident! Did ye kill the man back there?"

John recognized the blacksmith as he moved out of the shadows.

"Yes," John spoke quickly. "He was attacking a girl, I tried to defend her and he came off his horse. Later he tried to drag me back by magic."

"Magic!" the blacksmith echoed in an incredulous voice.

"Yes. Then the girl disappeared and I was drawn back by a mighty wind towards him, and at the last moment I raised my hand." John faltered, knowing how unbelievable his tale must sound.

"Your 'and?"

"Yes, I have a..." he paused, "a sign on my hand. It is too long a story to tell you why. But I raised my hand and yelled my other name, and suddenly the sword turned and killed the man. I didn't mean to kill him. It was the sword. This sword," he added lamely.

The blacksmith said nothing. Then he came forward and took hold of John's hand and held it up against the moonlight. Although he could not see clearly, he could see enough. The sign resembled the one on the sword he carried.

"I'm Tom Roper, the blacksmith. Now ye must tell me all ye knows. What was the girl like?" His voice revealed his concern.

"She was... my height with black hair. Long. And she wore a blue robe."

"What 'appened to 'er?"

"She was knocked down by the man on the horse. He dragged her over his

41

saddle. I knocked him off with a pole," John spoke rapidly, as he relived the experience. "Later, I realize she had vanished."

"Ye 'aven't seen 'er since then?"

"No."

"When was this? What time o' the day?" The blacksmith was very agitated.

"It must have been..." John thought, "early afternoon."

"Ah. Early afternoon," Tom repeated. "That be the last time ye saw 'er?"

"Yes, I... so many things have happened. I... I passed out at one time. I don't remember much," he apologised.

"An' this sword ye be carryin'?"

"It was his sword. It's got the same marks on it I have on my hand. It flew through the air and killed him."

Tom regarded John in silence. He felt the boy was telling the truth, but what sort of truth involved magic? Yet the boy appeared to have killed a fully armed fighting man who, by the look of him, had been both strong and fearsome. Also the boy had the marks on his hand. Tom had only ever seen those marks on the sword that had remained hidden in the forge since the night when Gwen arrived. Now there was another sword with the same marks. What did it mean? Who was the enemy?

"We'll go back down the track to the body and ye'll show me where ye last saw 'er. I 'ope for your sake 'er ain't come to no 'arm."

John was dismayed. "I tried to help her. I didn't harm her!"

"I only 'ave your word for that. It seems mighty strange t' me that a mere boy like 'ee could kill a fightin' man like 'im." Tom had encountered strange things in the Holy Land, but this was Norman Britain where such things did not happen. "Right then, ye keep up mind."

John knew he had no choice. He feared the strength of the blacksmith and although escape by running away was a possibility, John was equally certain Tom would follow for as long as it took to recapture him.

The blacksmith set a brisk pace down the silvery path. Once again, the woods on the right seemed full of terrors. Although Tom feared the blacksmith, yet in a strange way he wanted to stay near him, for at least he was a fear that John could understand, while the wood represented the hidden, evil horrors of his worst dreams. So, reluctantly, yet unwilling to be parted from him, John followed close behind.

It was not long before they came to the scene of the fight. Tom, who was still leading and carrying both swords on his shoulder, let out a loud cry and ran into the field. As John caught up, he could see, in the silvery light, that the bodies of both the man and the horse had disappeared, and something heavy had been dragged into the woods.

. . .

GWEN HAD BEEN DOZING fitfully. It was dark and she lay propped against a broad tree, too weary and sore to do more than slowly alter her position. Every joint in her body ached and her head throbbed. She knew her father would be looking for her, and if she stayed where she was, he would be sure to find her as soon as it got light. Also, when the sun had risen she would be able to decide the approximate direction of the village, and make her own way out of the forest.

She guessed it was past midnight. The moon was up and although darkness surrounded the trees like a thick cloak, there were areas where its light shone through, illuminating the paths and small clearings. There were the usual night sounds, but slowly other noises began to invade her semi-conscious mind: the crackling and crunching of dry twigs and leaves as many people moved along a nearby path.

Without a second thought, she staggered to her feet and held on to the tree for support. Her body's injuries made her groan with pain and she took a deep breath and called out as loudly as she could, "I'm here, father! I'm here!"

There was an immediate silence, as though the seekers were listening. Gwen called again: "I'm over here! I'm over here!" Even as she cried out, a fleeting suspicion crossed her mind. If it was her father and the men of the village they would surely have called her name and given a cheer when they heard her call. But still there was no friendly reply. Gwen heard, instead, muffled speech as of men debating in whispers. Then a loud crashing as many bodies ran towards her. A voice called out, "Show yourself!" It was a harsh voice with a foreign accent, unlike any she had ever heard in the village. She began to fear for her safety, but her injuries prevented her from hiding and there was little to be gained by keeping silent. As a precaution, she slipped off her silver bracelet and placed it in a deep pocket of her gown.

"I'm here!" Gwen called; her voice rang out in the still air. Almost immediately, a number of figures appeared in the moonlight spaces, and behind them came the sounds of horses. As she stared at them her worst suspicions were confirmed: these were not local men, and her father was nowhere to be seen.

Rough hands grabbed her and she cried out in pain. She had a glimpse of strange helmets, grim faces and staring eyes. She was half-dragged, half-carried towards the main group who could be heard advancing through the trees.

The pain was intense, and it was in vain that she cried out to them that they were hurting her. Then she was in a tight circle of faces. Gwen was so afraid that she could not tell if she was standing or being held off the ground. There was a large man in front of her; his eyes glowed red in the light of a burning torch that was held near her face. He gave an order in a language unknown to Gwen, and many of the other faces disappeared. She could hear them as they searched the area.

"Who are you?" the man asked in a slow but intense manner, as though he was unfamiliar with the English words. As she looked at him she was forcibly reminded of the man who had attacked her that afternoon, and fear gripped her like a cold plunge in an icy stream; it took her breath away. The man in front of her was dressed like the other stranger, and had the same evil eyes and cruel mouth.

His rough hand smacked against her soft cheeks, first one way then the other. Her head was knocked from side to side, shocking her out of her thoughts.

"Speak!" he roared. "Who are you?"

"Gwen Roper, sir," she gasped, choking on her tears. "I'm hurt, please don't hit me."

Since her earliest days her father had warned her never to speak to strangers, especially those with foreign accents. He had never given her a clear reason, but had said that they were often up to no good. As she stood captive in front of this man, she understood why her father had given this warning. Her cheeks were on fire and tears coursed down her face. No man had ever hit her or even threatened her in her whole life, and now in the space of one day two men had assaulted her.

"Are you alone?" the man demanded, unmoved by her distress.

"Yes, sir," she stammered as sobs racked her body.

"Why are you here?"

"I was injured… I hurt my head, your honour. I did not know where I was.

I thought you were my father with the men from our villager. Please take me home, sir," she pleaded.

The man exchanged some words with the others. She sensed that there was disagreement and that she was the reason.

"Where do you come from?" the leader demanded.

"From…" she paused, her mind racing. The other stranger had been looking for her and had tracked her down. If these men were his companions they might be seeking her too, though she could not imagine what reason they might have. "From Little Woodley," she gasped, her breath still coming in spasms. She averted her eyes, ashamed of her lie.

"Where is that?"

"A few miles from here, sir."

"Why are you in these woods?" The man raised his hand.

"I hurt myself and got lost in the dark," she began to sob again, fearful of further violence, and convinced he would know she was lying.

"You live near here and yet you get lost?" he mocked. There was more to this and he was going to get the truth.

"I was looking for herbs, sir," she sobbed. "I'm not used to these woods in the dark. I'm hurt bad, sir."

A man on her left spoke rapidly and pointed to the sky. She guessed he was referring to the passing of the hours of darkness.

"You will come with us!" He turned away and mounted a huge horse. Towering over her, he bellowed further instructions in his strange language.

"Where are you taking me? Please don't—" A tight gag of foul-tasting material prevented further speech. Her hands were bound behind her back, and she was thrown like a sack of flour across the neck of a horse for the second time that day. The pain and the shock were so great she fainted and her mind released its hold on her pain-filled body.

CHAPTER 6

Peter Halfcart limped home feeling hot and bad tempered. He had been at the market all day in the hope of seeing John, who had not appeared, in spite of his promise.

"See if I care, John Witch!" he yelled at nobody in particular.

Some travellers on the road exchanged glances and pulled a face as they passed him, but Peter did not notice, his mind was consumed with the injustice of it all. John had promised to meet him and was going to sell a calf. It had all seemed so easy. Peter had told his father about the calf, and his father had told an important friend from another village.

"The ol' witch be not interested in money. Give the boy enough for a tunic, and ye could make a goodly profit!" his father had boasted, pleased to be able to impress his friend.

"I'll make it worth ye while, Dick," the man had answered. The two men had gone to the alehouse in high spirits.

Peter had been told to wait for John and prevent him from reaching the market. The plan was for Peter to say his father had a buyer for the calf, and all should have gone smoothly. Peter had felt some unease when he had first heard of his father's scheme, but his father was a hard man and often, when he was in a bad mood, he would beat his son, blaming the boy for his own lameness. Also, Peter knew the old woman did not care about money, so where was the fault?

Now, at the end of a wasted day, his father would be waiting with his leather belt in his hand. The thought made the boy's eyes water.

"It's not my fault," he murmured, practising his excuse. "John did not come to market today. He must be ill. He's bound to bring it next market day." Peter began to shake with fear. He knew his father would not accept such excuses. Dick Halfcart spent a lot of time in the alehouse, and to lose face in front of the man from the other village was something he would not accept. Even now he would be standing with his back to the hearth, the heavy belt in his rough, hairy hands. He would probably be drunk, as he was after every market day.

Peter could imagine his father's voice, slurred and menacing: "Come 'ere, ye limping devil. I'll teach ye to make a fool o' me. Ye young waster, I'll skin ye this time. Come 'ere!" The coarse voice filled his mind with terror, and he found himself warding off imaginary blows, and whimpering as he did so.

He turned off the main road, up a narrow track leading to a small group of tumbledown hovels, clustered round the other side of a large, evil-smelling pond. There was nobody on the weed-covered track, but on the other side of the pond there was noisy activity. A woman was running from one of the shacks, screaming and waving her arms, and a large man was staggering after her, hitting at her with a leather strap. He was obviously drunk, and his actions were violent and inaccurate, but he was still able to catch her a vicious blow across her shoulders. She gave an agonised yell, and disappeared behind the shed. The man stopped, his body heaving for breath. His face was red and his eyes stared wildly around.

Peter froze, mesmerized with fear, like a rabbit that sees a stoat. It was his father, who, having warmed himself up on the luckless female who was Peter's mother, was now intent on finding the reason for his day's disaster.

It was too late for Peter to hide, he was a mere forty paces away, on an open track, with only the deep pond between himself and his drunken, angry father.

"I see 'ee! Ye crawling dog! Ye limping mother's boy! Come 'ere!" His voice boomed across the water. "I'll make 'ee sorry ye was ever born!"

"I hate ye!" Peter yelled back. He was amazed at what he had said. It was true, he did hate this man who bullied his mother, wasted all their money on ale, and was always violent and cruel. Peter had lacked the courage to say it before, but now he had done so, he knew there was no going back.

"I hate ye!" he yelled again. "Ye be a no-good drunken bully. I hope ye rots in hell!" He made a rude gesture as a last farewell, and limped off quickly down the track.

• • •

IT WAS ALMOST DARK as Peter made his way past the small stone church, and with the fading of the light his spirits reached a low ebb. At first it had seemed a wonderful thing to be free. He had told his father what he thought of him, and not before time; he had escaped a beating, and now he had the chance to travel the country and be his own man. He spent the first hour imagining all the things he would do, and how sorry his father would be having forced his own son to leave home.

But after a glorious hour of freedom, the chains of the world slowly encircled him. He had eaten very little during the day, and was tired and thirsty. Gradually, he became aware of the need for a place to sleep for the night. What of the next day, and all the following days? He knew his father would not miss him, and his mother would have one less mouth to feed. They would be glad to get rid of him! The thought was a bitter blow, and he sat down on a small mound and sighed deeply, his eyes moist with emotion.

After a while, he became more aware of his surroundings. He was in the burial ground, and the grassy knoll he was sitting on was someone's grave. He jumped up, afraid of what he might have done. He remembered the stories the boys of the village would tell each other, of dismembered bodies rising out of their temporary graves and searching for human blood. His eyes darted round the quiet, tree-lined patch of ground that served as the village graveyard. Nothing stirred in the windless air; no unusual sounds. Nothing. Yet, deep shadows had formed around the brooding trees as the twilight thickened.

Holding his breath, he stepped carefully out of the graveyard and back onto the twisting path that led south. If only John was with him, it would have been all right. John always knew what to do.

"That be it!" he exclaimed. "I'll go to John's cottage. He'll get the old witch t' give me some food and a place to sleep." Peter was not too sure about the old woman, in fact he was afraid of her. His father said she had murdered the Turners, who had lived there before. Others spoke of her power as a witch, and hinted at strange practices which happened at full moon. He hesitated, but then he reasoned that John lived with her, and he was not afraid, so she could not be too bad. Anyway, he decided, his lack of a home was John's fault. He was supposed to be a friend, and Peter recalled what his father had always said: *Make use of friends, it's what they be for.*

With this happy thought, he set off along the path leading in the direction of the old woman's cottage. He had never been there, but he had seen it from a distance, and he knew it was just a matter of following the path for about four miles. Having solved his immediate problem, he felt better, and much of his tiredness faded away. It was only a short time before it would be night, and as a form of defence, and as a way of moving faster, he selected a sturdy hazel sapling for use as a stick. He always carried a small rusty knife he had found one day near a haystack, and hacked at the sapling until it was a suitable length. Then, resting on it, he continued his journey along the path.

It was night before he covered the first mile. The meadows were bright in the moonlight and the path was easy to follow. Above his head the stars were a million tiny fires, and it was possible to believe, on such a night, a person could see almost as well as by day. Peter, however, had no such thoughts. The dark wood on his right was a constant worry to him as he moved silently down the path. He had inherited his parents' superstitions, and coupled with a colourful imagination, he was in terror of those things of the dark hours that the worst horror stories brought forth. In the past, with a crowd of other boys, he had ventured into the black forests, pretending to a kind of shared bravery. But by himself, he was terrified.

Peter stopped to massage his leg, and as he bent down to rest the stick on the ground, he heard voices. He panicked, and flattened himself on the earth and remained very still.

After some moments he heard the voices again. There were a number of them speaking in hoarse whispers, and in a language he did not understand. Slowly, as his courage returned, he raised his head and was able to identify the direction of the speakers. They were about thirty paces in front of him, standing in a dark group in the meadow grass. Peter realized he was lying by the side of the path, and would easily be seen if they decided to return his way. Cautiously, he moved himself into the tall grass, trying desperately to avoid scraping the loose stones littering the ground. As soon as he was hidden, he stood up, slowly, taking the strain on his stick. His dark hair and unwashed face provided excellent camouflage as he peered over the tops of the uneven grass.

There were four figures outlined in the moonlight, with their backs towards him. They appeared to be very excited about something, and every now and then one would speak in a louder voice, his speech fast and emphatic. Other voices murmured in reply, and even though the language was quite indecipherable, Peter was able to judge they were having a disagreement. It appeared the main speaker wanted to leave two of the men and depart with the other. He was waving his arms and pointing at something on the ground. The other two men were shaking their heads and appeared to be unwilling to stay. After some minutes of argument, the leader came to a decision and, having given a short command, they all crossed the path and disappeared into the forest with a speed and quietness of movement that was both impressive and unnerving. Not a twig cracked, not a bird was disturbed as the four strangers faded like shadows into the trees.

It was a long time before Peter felt it was safe to move back to the path. Whoever the men were, he was certain they were up to no good. People never ventured out after dark unless they were hunting, and these men were not hunters. Besides, they were foreigners and the only ones that he had ever heard or seen in his whole life. He had listened to the ex-soldiers at the market talk about the Turks, who were the soldiers of Satan, and how they sacrificed Christians in their devil-worship. His father had once met a Spanish merchant, and a man in a nearby village was supposed to be married to an Irish woman. That was the extent of his knowledge of foreigners. It was possible these were not human beings at all. They had all disappeared without a sound and they had looked unnaturally dark in the white glare of the moon. Perhaps the forest was full of spirits and he had witnessed some strange ceremony. As his imagination began to blossom, he moved, almost in spite of himself, down the edge of the path. As his anxious eyes left the shadows of the forest and flicked across the meadow, he saw the dead horse.

He remained frozen for some seconds, as his mind tried to sort out the meaning of the black shape. When the panic subsided, he moved hesitantly towards the silent outline, and breathed with relief when he realized what it was. "It be an ol' dead 'orse!" he exclaimed. "Just an ol' dead 'orse."

It was then he saw the body of the dead rider. Peter let out a cry of alarm, as he expected it to jump up and attack him. He even turned, in a half-hearted attempt to run away, but when the figure remained totally still, Peter eventually summoned up enough courage to approach the silent shape.

In the moonlight the awful corpse was hideous. The staring, lifeless eyes glared out from a yellowy-white face and the teeth were revealed in a demonic grin. There was a deep gash in his chest.

The horror of the sight was too much for Peter. His legs buckled under him and his empty stomach heaved in a series of uncontrolled convulsions. After a while he was able to stagger to his feet and limp painfully away towards the path. He was emotionally exhausted and, having had no food or drink for many hours, he collapsed into the nearest clump of bushes, intending to stay the night there, rather than risk any more horrific encounters.

He had just dozed off in a sitting position among the thick greenery, his knees drawn up to his chin, his stick clasped firmly in both hands, when he was awoken by the sound of horses moving out of the forest. With trembling hands, he parted the bushes to see a large group of armed men, some on horses, approach the corpse. The figures were dark but their sharp weapons gleamed in the moonlight. A huge man on an enormous horse was giving instructions in a low, authoritative voice, while the rest moved like ants, in a flurry of activity. As Peter watched, the dead man was strapped over a spare horse, which was led away, while a large group tied the carcass of the horse onto a litter made from branches. Four horses were attached to the litter and it was dragged into the forest, with the men fanning out on both sides. Two remained behind to quickly replace vegetation to cover their entry into the forest, and then, they too were gone. The whole operation had been completed in a matter of minutes, and Peter found it hard to believe he had not imagined it.

He sat for some time, unwilling to leave the safety of his hiding place. His father had always said one should never do anything unless one was going to get something out of it. *Ain't nobody can fill 'is belly with a thank-'ee-kindly. If there be no profit in it, let it be.* The advice had usually been given with a hefty blow. Peter could never remember when his father had been kind to him. Always, there had been the constant reminder that his lameness meant he was useless. Once, when his mother had drowned her sorrows in a flagon of cider, she revealed it was Peter's father who had caused his son's lameness.

Peter was only a year old when his father threw him from his cradle because he was crying. He received a broken leg from this assault, but his father was too drunk to care, and his mother was too frightened to seek proper advice, which was why Peter grew up with a twisted leg. Some weeks after this revelation, Peter blurted out his knowledge to his father while trying to avoid a thrashing for being slow. The result was a systematic attack on every member of the family, which only ceased when Dick Halfcart exhausted himself. Nobody ever mentioned it again.

"Ain't none of my business," Peter reassured himself, and settled back into the cover of the bushes to await the dawn.

. . .

"THERE BE MORE T' this than meets the eye," Tom whispered. He was a simple man, and given to making obvious statements. But because of his deep voice and powerful body, he always sounded impressive.

"What do we do now?" John asked. He was tired, frightened, hungry and quite unable to understand why anyone would want to drag away a dead horse in the middle of the night.

Tom's eyes searched the forest for signs of movement. "We must follow 'em, whoever they be. They may 'ave Gwenny. If we waits 'til daybreak, them could be miles away. Come on!" He looked at John and noticed his weariness, "Ye'd better do the best ye can."

"Why don't you follow, and I'll go to the village for help," John said.

"Oh no ye don't, m'lad. Ye don't get off that easy. Ye got a lot of questions t' answer. For all I knows ye could 'ave somethin' t' do with all this." He paused, "If ye 'ave been tellin' the truth, then I reckons ye be wise t' stay with me 'til we knows what's what." Tom turned into the forest.

John took a deep breath and followed him. Perhaps the blacksmith was right. The thought of having to make his way home in the dark, and without a weapon of any kind, was a daunting prospect. At least he had some security with this powerful man, who seemed to have only one concern, and that was for the lovely girl he called Gwenny.

They soon picked up the broken path along which the dead horse had been dragged. Even in the blackness of the forest, it was not difficult to follow the trail. The fresh tracks of the horses and the ruts of some heavy conveyance were easy to feel under foot, in contrast to the more level spongy feel of the forest floor. At times they could see the tracks when they came to small clearings illuminated by moonlight.

"Is Gwenny your daughter?" John asked.

It was a while before Tom answered with an abrupt "Yes." Then he added, "We'd best be quiet."

They crept forward silently, listening for any sound which might give them an indication of the whereabouts of the group ahead. Tom had reasoned that there must be at least two men, and perhaps many more, to have been able to remove the horse and the body so quickly. John found his legs were moving mechanically, and his mind was half-asleep as he strove, in vain, to keep up with the determined blacksmith.

John was rudely jolted awake by a large, hard-skinned hand across his mouth. At the same time he was pinned against a leather jerkin. He fought vigorously to release himself.

"Keep still an' listen," Tom hissed in his ear.

They stood as though rooted to the earth. John was aware of the thumping of his heart and the heat of the blacksmith's hand, which remained clamped over his mouth and cheeks. As John slowly removed the pressure of the hand, he heard the sound Tom had heard. It was the rustle of something, or someone, moving through the forest on the right of the path.

Tom released his grip of the boy and removed the two swords from his shoulder. "Hold this," he growled, and handed a sword back to John. He knew it was the one he had taken from the dead stranger. He did not know how he knew, but it felt right as he held it, and his palm tingled.

As he clasped the sword, a faint voice could be heard in the quiet night. It was a long way off, like an echo on a foggy night, but there was no doubt that it was a girl's voice, and it came from along the path they were following. There was no longer any sound from the trees on their right. Whoever or whatever it was remained, like them, motionless. Again, the girl's voice could be heard calling out in the still air. It was a frightened call for help in a dangerous world.

"Come on!" Tom urged. "That be Gwenny callin'." He began to run, and moved surprisingly quickly for a big man. John tried to keep up, but it was a losing battle; he was tired and the sword weighed him down. As he turned a bend in the path, he tripped over a thick tree root and sprawled headlong on the ground with a jarring thud. Tom vanished into the night.

John lay where he had fallen, fighting for breath. He felt exhausted after his headlong gallop. He raised himself to his knees, and was in the act of forcing himself to his feet, using the sword as a prop, when a demonic figure lurched up beside him.

The shock was so great that John flung himself to the side, lost his balance and rolled over, pulling the sword round to protect himself as he did so. The outline of the person could be seen silhouetted against a patch of clear sky, holding a knife in his hand.

"Who are you?" John gasped. He gripped the sword, holding it in front of him as he lay partly supported by a tree.

"Be it, John?" a timid voice enquired.

"Peter! What are you doing here?" John's voice was faint with amazement.

"I thought it be thee," Peter said. "There be many strange things goin' on an' I be real frighted."

John used the sword to lever himself to his feet. "I'm glad to see you, Peter, even though you nearly scared me to death." He laughed nervously.

The two youths stared about them. Enormous trees were etched out in the dark by patches of moonlight, and everywhere there was a strange brooding silence. The forest seemed full of menace.

"The blacksmith's gone on ahead," John whispered, unaware that he had lowered his voice. "I suppose we'd better follow him."

Peter grabbed his arm. "Don't do that, John," he pleaded. "There be a horde of 'em soldiers, an' they got swords an' things. It'd be better if we went back to the cottage, then we—"

His words were interrupted by the sound of a man's deep voice bellowing something from far down the track, followed by a wild eruption of screaming and shouting, and the dull clank of steel hitting steel.

"Come on!" John shouted, and he began to run towards the noise of the fighting.

"No, John!" Peter screamed, hobbling behind him. "Let's go back!"

"We've got to help!" John yelled back. "He's trying to save his daughter."

"It be no use!" Peter gasped. "We can't fight soldiers. We'll be killed. Don't leave me, John!"

But John was already disappearing into the darkness, and Peter, still hissing out his protests, limped frantically behind, desperate to avoid being left by himself. As John ran towards the conflict, he rested the sword on his shoulder, his eyes staring into the darkness ahead. He knew if he stopped to think he would not continue, but something inside was urging him on and he felt a strange exhilaration, as though he were diving into a deep pool.

The path bent sharply to the right, past some dark trees, and opened up into a large clearing. The air resounded with screams of pain, the whinnying of frightened horses, and voices yelling in a strange, harsh language. There was confusion and panic and the loud crashing of metal. By the glow of some flickering torches, he could see the blacksmith holding his long sword with both hands and lashing out at a tight semi-circle of soldiers who were attempting to get close to him. Some of the attackers held swords, while others carried torches. Tom Roper was an awesome figure in the red glow;

his broad shoulders provided enormous strength to his blows, and with his back to a massive oak tree he seemed to be more than a match for his opponents.

Two bodies lay sprawled on the ground, twitching convulsively and moaning. John watched, as another man fell to the ground with an agonizing cry and then lay still. Meanwhile, more soldiers on horses galloped back along the track on the left hand side of the tree, where the blacksmith fought for his life. John approached on the right hand side and was behind most of the yelling, heaving bodies. His first thought had been to attack some of them from the back and try to create a diversion. But the arrival of the horsemen confused him and he waited in the shadows uncertain what to do.

The first rider, a large bearded figure with a short dark cape, reined in his horse and drew a short spear from the side of his saddle and edged the animal towards the swaying mass of men. Slowly, he drew back his arm and waited for a clear throw at the blacksmith, who continued to scythe the air with incredible speed and power.

Without a conscious decision, John ran towards the horseman, impelled by a force greater than himself. For a brief time, he was outside his own body, watching with a feeling of detachment as he saw himself swing the sword wildly at the back of the horseman at the very moment that the short spear was being thrown. The sword's blade cut deep into the flesh, just above the hip and the spear, deflected from its path, plunged into the neck of one of the torch-bearers. The rider jerked in a violent upward movement, before collapsing backwards over the flank of the horse.

John's sense of reality returned and he was aware of the ache in his shoulders and wrists, and watched, horrified, as dark red blood dripped from the blade of his sword. The noise of the fighting, the frantic shadows and the rearing of the riderless horse overwhelmed him. He turned to face an oncoming horseman, and ducked as something flew past his head. The leading rider, having failed with his spear, attempted to ride his frothing horse into the bewildered boy. John leapt to the side, and with his sword poked at the passing animal, wounding it in the side of its neck and causing it to swerve violently into the foot soldiers, adding to the confusion.

The other horsemen were galloped towards him, and in the confusion he fell backwards into a small thicket of saplings as a sword embedded itself, with a thud, into the trunk of a young elm just above his head. The horseman lost his grip on the weapon, and with a jarred arm, careered past, desperately reining back his horse with the other hand.

More horsemen galloped up, searching for the elusive enemy, and were attracted to the furious battle being fought around the oak tree. After losing another man, the foreigners were content to keep out of range of the merciless blade, and Tom Roper, unwilling to leave the security of his tree, stood boldly facing them. The horsemen, spears in hand, moved closer in a wide circle surrounding him.

"Throw down your sword or you will die now!" a rider called out. His voice boomed over the heads of the soldiers. To emphasize his words he threw his spear that plunged into the oak, a hand's width from Tom's head.

"I want me daughter back!" Tom bellowed. "I don't want to fight with 'ee. Give 'er back an I'll…"

"Throw down your sword!" the leader interrupted. "Now!"

The blacksmith stared at the ring of swords and the line of horsemen with their spears raised. He twisted his head as he searched for an escape, but there was none.

The leader spoke again. "You have fought well. Lay down your sword and I shall spare your life. If you do not, then the girl dies with you."

Tears of frustration welled up in Tom's eyes, and with a loud sigh he threw his weapon on the ground. The soldiers edged forward. They were uncertain of the power of their dangerous adversary. One grabbed the sword, while the others flattened Tom against the tree, the weapon against his throat.

The man who had picked up the sword let out a cry of alarm and shouted loudly in his harsh language. The leader urged his horse forward and grabbed Tom's sword and examined it carefully in the light of the flickering torches. He too let out an exclamation and began to speak quickly, then held up the sword for all to see. The soldiers pushed and shoved one another in their rush to look at the weapon and there was much excitement. Those holding the blacksmith laughed violently, their white teeth gleaming in the torchlight.

The horsemen appeared to have forgotten about John for the moment, and he turned and crept through the bushes and hid behind a gnarled tree. Once he was hidden from view he edged his way further up the track keeping well into the shadows, but still able to see what was going on. Some more horsemen passed him, as they moved back to join the others. By the light of their flickering torches, John could see that four of the horses were pulling a litter with the dead horse on it. The last rider was carrying the girl, who was tied hand and foot and draped over the front of the saddle like a large doll. The men talked excitedly and waved their swords as they spoke.

As soon as the riders had moved past his hiding place, John darted across the track and began to edge back on the other side, towards the flickering lights. Soon he was near enough to see clearly what was happening. The leader, a huge man dressed in black with a full red beard, was speaking to the assembled soldiers. He raised the blacksmith's sword above his head and a cheer went up from the group. He spoke again and the blacksmith was dragged forward; his arms had been bound tightly, and there was a rope around his neck.

"Where did you get this sword?" the leader demanded in a heavy accent.

"I was given it," Tom answered. He stared defiantly up at his captor.

"How long have you had it?" the man asked. His voice seemed unnaturally gentle as though he was coaxing a naughty child.

Tom hesitated and seemed to realize the importance of the question. "I can't remember," he replied slowly. "I got it from a man in the Crusade. I saved 'is life."

The leader stared at Tom without moving. "Who is the girl?" his eyes narrowed.

"She be my daughter."

"How old is she?"

"About sixteen."

"How long have you had the sword?" This time the question was sharp and aggressive.

"I told 'ee, I don't remember," Tom growled, straining at his ropes. Then, staggering a pace forward he yelled, "The sword ain't important t' me! Ye 'ave it for all I care! Ye can 'ave me an' all, just let my Gwenny go."

"Which came first, the girl or the sword?"

The blacksmith seemed to be struggling with the answer when there was a cry from the direction in which John had injured the spear-thrower. This started a general commotion as horsemen and soldiers rushed into the trees behind them. Almost immediately, there was a triumphant yell and two of the soldiers emerged, dragging between them a small figure, which sobbed and cried out alternately as the men prodded with their swords. The limping walk confirmed that it was Peter.

The two men spoke quickly to the leader and pointed to the trees as they did so. One of them waved a short sword. Peter was speechless with terror. His eyes rolled in his head, he uttered high-pitched whimpering noises and, when the men let go of him, he collapsed in a heap on the ground. The soldiers immediately jerked him upright, where he remained, twitching in all his limbs.

"Who are you?" the leader asked. His voice was slow and menacing.

"I be only Peter 'Alfcart, your 'onour. I ain't be doing no 'arm."

"Ha!" the leader exploded. "No harm! You nearly kill one of my men and wound another, and you talk of doing no harm!" He paused, "You don't look much of a fighter." He translated this to his men and a great laugh went up.

"I'm not," Peter protested. "I didn't kill no one. That sword, 'tain't mine. I found it in a tree, o'er there," he added, pointing to the thicket into which John had fallen only a few minutes before.

"Enough!" The huge man glanced at the sky. The first glimmers of light were appearing and a bird began to sing in a nearby tree.

John watched as the leader spoke to the two soldiers who were holding Peter. Then he beckoned to the horseman who was guarding Gwen. The soldier dismounted and walked his horse towards Peter.

"Who is this girl?" the leader demanded. He reached down from his horse and grabbed the hair of the unconscious girl, forcing her head back.

Peter gave a gasp. "That be Gwenny Roper. 'Is daughter." He pointed at the blacksmith.

The man released the girl's head so that it fell hard against the side of the horse.

"Leave her be, ye accursed infidel!" Tom roared. He tried to move forward, but the man holding the rope pulled hard and the noose bit tight into the blacksmith's thick neck. The other soldier kicked violently at the back of Tom's legs and he fell backwards in an ungainly heap, gasping for breath. A roar of approval went up from the soldiers.

"I could kill you all now," the leader said. He gave an order and a horse was brought forward with an enormous body strapped across it. John recognized it as the warrior who had died in the flower meadows. The rope around Tom's neck was loosened and he was dragged to his feet.

"Did you kill my brother?" The leader spoke slowly, his voice taut with emotion. His right hand slowly drew his sword from its scabbard.

"I've never seen 'im alive," Tom growled.

"You speak in riddles. Have you seen him before... alive or dead?"

Tom hesitated. The sky was growing lighter and John was aware of a great volume of bird song filling the glade.

The leader backed his horse towards the limp figure of the girl, still lying like a corpse across the saddle. He reached down and, with his left hand, once again lifted her head by the long black hair. The blacksmith watched, his eyes blazing, unable to do anything. One of the soldiers thrust a dagger to Tom's throat forcing his head up. Slowly the leader allowed the long strands to pass through his hand. He gripped the end of the hair so that the girl's head was suspended. He suddenly brought the sword down in a fierce slicing movement.

John let out a gasp of horror. He wanted to rush out and attack this vile man who had so mercilessly butchered the girl. But once again it seemed his body was not his own, and although his mind cried out for action, his limbs remained motionless.

The blacksmith struggled hopelessly. There was blood running down the side of his neck, and he made horrible gargling sounds.

The leader was sitting quite still on his horse, watching the blacksmith carefully. John relaxed when he saw the warrior was not holding the severed head of the girl, but merely a hank of her long black hair. The girl hung motionless over the side of the horse.

With a toss of his hand he threw the hair into the blacksmith's face. Then, he grabbed the remainder of the girl's hair and, once again, forced her head into an upward tilt. He raised his sword. "Speak or she dies!" he roared.

John was in no doubt the huge man intended to kill Gwen if he did not get an answer to his question. But, as in a bad dream, John found he was unable to move or cry out. He felt paralysed, yet his eyes and ears continued to function.

"All right," Tom gasped, "I'll tell 'ee what I knows. It be the truth, even if it ain't what ye wants to hear."

"Did you kill my brother?" the leader hissed.

"No, I never did. I saw 'im lying dead on the ground, 'an 'is horse with 'im. He 'ad a great wound in 'is chest. When I found 'im he'd been dead a while."

"Where is his sword?"

"He 'ad no sword when I found 'im. I swear to God I be telling the truth."

The leader raised the girl's head a bit higher, and her mouth fell open. He made small movements with his sword, raising and lowering the weapon. He kept his eyes fixed on the blacksmith.

"Why did you attack my men?"

"Ye 'ad my daughter! I didn't kill that man. I swear to ye!" The blacksmith was yelling his answers in an agony of desperation.

There was a long pause when nobody moved. Then very slowly the leader lowered Gwen's head and replaced his sword in its scabbard.

"There is a lot I need to know," he murmured. His cruel mouth formed into a mirthless smile. "I think the girl is important and I need to know a lot more about this friend, who gave you the sword."

The leader turned his horse and gave a series of abrupt orders. Then he approached Peter who had remained sniffing and trembling throughout. "What shall I do with you? he asked meditatively. "I think you are of little value."

While he spoke, the soldiers were moving quickly and efficiently around the glade, collecting the scattered weapons and laying the bodies of the dead soldiers in a line. The injured were bandaged and were helped onto horses, while a few with various wounds were tied on to the litter that had been used to carry the dead horse. The dead animal was stripped of its harness and saddle, and was dragged into the bushes.

Peter was staring fearfully at the man's red beard and thin, cruel mouth. "Don't kill me, sir!" he quickly blurted out. "I could be useful, sir. I knows the girl and 'im," he pointed to the subdued blacksmith.

There was a silence. "I knows all about this area; I knows all the people. I could be useful, sir," Peter pleaded.

The man sat unmoving, he regarded the boy with dark, unblinking eyes. Then he gave a short command and turned away. The two soldiers, who had been holding Peter, tied him with a rope and began to drag him towards the line of dead bodies. Peter screamed in terror.

John reacted to Peter's scream, and it was as though his body had suddenly been released from a vice. Even while the sound echoed in his head, he was aware of a group of soldiers moving towards his hiding place. They were carrying one of their dead comrades. As the group of men approached, John flattened himself against the earth and hoped that his brown tunic would not be noticed in the gloom of the dawn light. The soldiers quickly stripped the body of all clothing and removed rings from the fingers, then they wrapped the corpse in a piece of material and bound it tight with strong ropes.

The men were within a few paces of where he was hiding and had stopped beneath a large beech tree. The first man attempted to climb the tree, but was unable to get a purchase on the lowest branch, which was just beyond his reach. The rest of the group lowered their burden and formed a platform on which the first man could stand. During this diversion, John was able to move further back into the forest, for he realized that the climber would have a clear view of his hiding place. As he edged back, he could see another group carrying a similar roped bundle into the forest.

He clambered slowly around until he was in a position where he could observe what the soldiers were doing, without the climber being able to see him. The first man clambered high into the tree and sat astride a broad limb. He held in his hand a rope that he dropped over the branch. The men at the bottom began to pull on this rope, and John saw that the other end was attached to the corpse that began an uncertain ascent up into the great tree. The man at the top directed the body and used the rest of the rope to secure it firmly to the branch. This took some time, and the soldiers at the bottom became increasingly agitated. Eventually, the first man climbed down and was helped to the ground, and all of them hurried back to the glade without a backward glance.

John wondered what would happen in a few months when the ropes became slack and the body was dislodged by the wind and the carrion birds. Some traveller was in for an unpleasant shock.

When all evidence of the fighting had been hidden, the group reformed and the leader uttered a weird chant during which every soldier prostrated himself on the ground and repeated certain words. The ritual ended with the leader holding up the golden sword towards each of the trees in which a dead soldier was hidden. Then he gave some brief commands and the party extinguished all torches and moved off in a southerly direction.

The soldiers conducted themselves like a well-disciplined army. Two horsemen cantered ahead, while pairs of foot soldiers fanned out into the trees on both sides. John was able to count sixteen horsemen, at least two of whom were wounded, with a further three figures strapped to the litter, which was pulled by two horses. The blacksmith had certainly made his mark! John had not been able to count the foot soldiers, but there were at least thirty and maybe more. In the grey light of the early morning, he could distinguish the burly shape of the blacksmith. A rope around his neck was connected to the saddle of one of the riders. There was one horse carrying the dead brother of the leader, but there was no sign of Gwen. John was straining his eyes to see where she was, when he noticed a slim figure staggering along in the midst of a party of foot soldiers. Gwen had obviously recovered enough to be able to walk. There was no sign of Peter.

John sat down against a tree and rubbed his face. What was he to do? Peter was dead, and the blacksmith and his daughter were captured, and here he was in the middle of a forest. He had seriously wounded one man and had been responsible for injuring at least two others; and his sword had killed one man by itself. Even if he found help, who would believe such a fantastic tale? An army of foreigners, magic spells, swords that moved by themselves, and dead people in trees: he would be called a liar.

He thought of Peter and his eyes welled up. Peter had not been without his faults, but he had been the only real friend that John remembered having. Before he arrived at the old woman's cottage, John's life had been a succession of brief encounters with people who, though kind in their fashion, failed to make any impression on him. He had a dim memory of a large, cold building occupied only by women dressed in brown robes and hoods. Then he had lived with a tall man in a rambling mansion. There was a long hall, and on one wall a white banner with a vivid red cross… something had happened, but he could not remember what. At times he felt he could recognize places. Much of what the old woman taught him seemed familiar, but at other times it was as though his life had begun from the time he arrived at the solid, oak door of her lonely cottage.

As he sat thinking, he was conscious of his misery fading in intensity and he began slowly to experience a sense of wellbeing and confidence. The old woman taught him that positive thought was the only way to cope with difficulties: *Speak your mind*, she said, *for words make bright the gloomy path of life*. Once again, John regretted the casual way he had treated the old woman's teachings.

"There are two things I can do," he said aloud. "I can go to sleep and in the morning return to the old woman, or try to help the blacksmith and his daughter and also get revenge for Peter's death." He paused, and in his mind's eye he could picture himself, sword in hand, defending… not his dead friend, nor the blacksmith, but the girl with the black hair. "Gwenny," he murmured and found himself smiling. There was no longer any doubt as to what he should do. He picked up the sword and, forgetting his tiredness and his hunger, began to trot in the direction that the enemy had taken.

CHAPTER 7

G WEN REMAINED IN A state of semi-consciousness for some while as her mind began to clear, and the realities of the situation started to demand her attention. She was first aware of the hot sun on her eye lids, then of the continuous jerking and rocking of her body, coupled with a strange sense of security, as though she was unable to fall no matter what vibrations she received. Finally, Gwen was aware of people groaning on both sides of her. Perhaps she was in hell, or maybe on her way to heaven and these were the sounds of the lost souls journeying in the opposite direction?

As she toyed with these first threads of consciousness, she knew she would have to open her eyes. Time passed and reluctantly, she glimpsed the real world under her trembling eyelashes. Some moments before, the pains in her head, stomach and limbs had begun to compete for her attention. All around new sounds burst into focus: she recognized the snorting of horses, bird song, people talking, and still the unnerving sound of groaning in her ear. When her left arm began to feel warm and wet, she knew it was time to open her eyes.

Very carefully, she raised her lids and immediately closed them. Then she knew. She was strapped onto a litter with two wounded soldiers, one on each side of her, and the one on her left was bleeding badly. There was no point in revealing she was awake, for her captors were unlikely to attend to her needs when they were prepared to allow one of their own men to bleed to death. So, very slowly, she peered out at the world under her lashes, and closed her eyes again and tried to remember what she had seen. She counted the horsemen, the soldiers walking alongside the litter and anything else that might be of use to her. Most of the time she drifted off into unconsciousness and woke believing she had remained awake all along. The sun beat down on her and she felt very thirsty.

It was many hours before they stopped, and Gwen was shaken awake by rough hands releasing her from the ropes securing her to the litter. She felt herself lifted clear and two men carried her to the shade of a tree. One made a comment and both laughed in a cruel, mocking way. After some time, she heard the deep, reassuring voice of her father, and she raised her eye-lids enough to see the soldiers securing his hands in front instead of behind, so he could eat and drink and attend to her.

Tom knelt by her side and whispered her name, "Gwenny, can ye hear me?"

"Yes, father," she croaked. "I've been awake a goodly while."

"Drink this," he said, and carefully arranged her head before he poured water into her mouth from a leather bottle. The water was warm and tasted unpleasant, but she gulped it down greedily. After a short while, her head cleared and she was able to eat some dry bread.

Tom kept his face close to hers, and whispered encouragement in her ear. "That's the way, princess. You'll soon be fine, Gwenny. Now get your strength up, but pretend to be 'alf asleep. They's all havin' a rest 'cept for some guards. Later on I'll move away 'cos it's me they be watchin'. Keep ye eyes closed an' then try an' crawl off when they ain't paying attention."

She nodded, but her tongue felt sore and rough, and her head throbbed. She wanted the water, although it was warm, and also the stale, hard bread that was difficult to swallow. Both would help to get her strength back and she persevered, even though she was racked with nausea. Tom did the best he could to feed her, but it was not easy with his hands securely tied. The soldiers took little notice of them, being more concerned with their own refreshments and the chance to relax after the long march. In a short while most of the men were asleep, except for the guards who were placed at regular intervals around the camp. One guard stood watching the blacksmith from the shade of an old chestnut tree, but he too began to doze as Tom feigned sleep. The leader was nowhere to be seen.

There was a slight breeze, but even in the shade the heat was oppressive. Gwen could feel the sunburn on her face, and her arms were red and painful. She had a raw cut on each elbow, where the ropes had chaffed the skin, and her whole body ached. She doubted if she had the strength to crawl away, let alone avoid the soldiers when they came to search for her.

She watched Tom through half-closed eyes as he staggered to his feet and moved to another tree. He indicated to the guard that it provided better shade, and after an initial suspicion, the guard relaxed. Almost immediately

Tom appeared to fall into a deep sleep. Gwen glanced around her, and could see only one other guard. He was standing near the horses and was looking in a different direction. The guard opposite them kept nodding his head, and had propped himself against a low branch. As she watched, his head dropped forward and he remained quite still, his arms clasped around his spear.

Gwen knew there would be other guards. She could not see them, and the chance of her escaping was slight. She felt her silver bracelet in her pocket and wondered why the soldiers had not stolen it. It seemed they had not searched her, and apart from the crude laughter as the two guards had carried her from the litter, she had suffered no obvious indignities. But if they found her bracelet, they would have a way of proving where she came from. The old priest in Woodford had given her the bracelet, and he had made her promise to wear it as a token of her Christianity. She realised that it was both a security and a danger; she tried to decide whether she should retain or discard it. As she pondered what to do, an acorn landed on her leg. She glanced up and then continued to watch the guard under her long lashes. Another acorn landed near her leg. This time she took more notice. Acorns did not fall in July, and never from an elm tree, under which she was lying.

Very slowly she rolled onto her stomach; her body felt bruised and tender, but at least she could see what was happening behind her. Far over to her left she noticed the helmet of a guard, and in front was a small thicket. She gasped as the branches parted to reveal the face of a young man. Although she had seen him for only a brief moment, as she had escaped the warrior in the flower meadows, she was certain this was the same person who had rescued her. She had feared the terrible stranger might have killed him, yet he seemed very much alive and was beckoning to her to join him.

With great care she turned to check on the guard. His chin rested on his chest, and he breathed in a regular heavy movement. There was no doubt he was in a deep sleep. She glanced towards her father who also appeared to be dozing. She desperately wanted to attract his attention, but he had told her what she must do, and now there seemed a chance of help.

She turned back onto her stomach and began to crawl slowly towards the thicket. Her limbs ached and her back felt stiff and painful. Every moment she expected to hear a cry and feel rough hands grabbing her. However, everything remained quiet. Dry sticks and leaves crunched under her and sounded loud in the heavy silence. As she reached the thicket, a strong hand guided her through; on the palm of the hand was a strange design that sent an incomprehensible thrill through her body, although she had no memory of ever seeing it before.

"Over there is the bed of a dry stream," he whispered urgently, pointing behind him. "Follow it until you reach a large fallen tree. Wait there until I come. A guard is just beyond, on the right of that oak. I shall try to attract his attention if he moves towards you. Go now." The young man had an air of authority in the way he whispered his instructions, and he carried a magnificent sword. It bore the same device that she had glimpsed on his hand.

"Who are you?" she asked quietly.

"My name is John. Go quickly before you are missed."

"What about my father?"

"I shall try and get help. Go now."

Gwen crawled in the direction he had pointed. Everything was bone dry in the forest and even the patches of brown grass felt brittle. Soon she came to the arid bed of the stream. It was a shallow gully about five paces across and waist deep. The passage was strewn with large rocks, stones, branches, and clumps of desiccated reed grass. She lowered herself hesitantly into the channel, and once again her body protested. She lay perfectly still on the warm sandy bed and listened for any sounds of alarm. There was nothing to be heard except for the monotonous cooing of a wood pigeon and the gentle swish of small branches moving in the breeze.

Gwen was in agony as she crawled on her hands and knees along the shallow passage. The large stones and branches made her progress slow and awkward as she tried to pass them without making a noise. Somewhere in front was the guard. She wondered if she would recognize the fallen tree, as there were many large boughs both in the channel and over-hanging it. Supposing she had gone past the meeting place and the guard was just above her? Her mind wrestled with these fears and her body complained with each movement she took. It was nearly ten minutes before she rounded a bend in the channel and saw the tree her rescuer had obviously meant. Its massive trunk lay across the depression like a fallen monument. Its violent fall had smashed down the sides of the gully, and there was barely enough room for Gwen to crawl under the gnarled trunk. It was a perfect hiding place, as she would be visible only to someone approaching down the way she had come.

Thankfully, she stretched out under the wooden shelter, and waited for the youth called John. She lay on her side staring back down the track, and ignoring the wood lice and beetles that crawled around her. After some minutes she began to be alarmed. Supposing John had been caught? What if they blamed her father for her escape? How long should she remain where she was? The thoughts weighed down on her. Gently she massaged her arms, and replaced the comforting silver bracelet on her left wrist, and then levered herself up on one elbow. Gwen began to examine the damage her body had suffered in the past day. Her nails were broken; there were numerous cuts and grazes on her arms, and her sunburn was beginning to throb. Her blue gown was torn, and she blushed when she thought of how she must have looked strapped to the litter, and of the way the guards had laughed as they had carried her to the tree. She tried to straighten her hair, and realized it had been cut. With a gasp of dismay she began to feel with both hands, trying to visualize what it must look like. She discovered that the sides were mostly still long, but a large area of the hair in the middle of her head had been hacked off, and was barely a thumb's thickness in length.

Gwen was not a vain girl, and had never coveted fine clothes, but she had always been proud of her thick, long hair with its deep, glossy blackness. It had marked her out as being different to the other girls. Now it was ruined. This final revelation sapped what little energy she had left, and she lay with her head on one arm staring vacantly down the gully, with tears streaming down her cheeks.

She did not hear the approach of the men until they began to speak. From the sound of their voices she knew they were only a few paces away from where she was hiding. Gwen recognized the alien language of her recent captors, and she prepared for the worst. However, the men did not appear to be searching for her, and their talk was frequently punctuated by savage laughter. Then there was a pause, and twigs crunched almost over her head. When they spoke again the sound was directly above her. They were sitting on the trunk of the huge tree and at any moment they might decide to jump down into the gully. There was nowhere else to hide.

·   ·   ·

JOHN KNEW WHAT HE must do. He felt confident and purposeful. Earlier in the day he had refreshed himself with water from a small spring, but it was more than a day since he had eaten anything other than berries, yet his mind was centred on the action of the moment and hunger was forgotten.

He waited impatiently until the girl crawled out of sight. Then he glided away in the other direction, his sword held in both hands. It took him longer than he had expected to make his way to the other side of the camp: twice he was forced to creep past sentries. One had been sharpening a piece of wood, and the other had been dozing. John experienced no fear; he did not hesitate, even when he passed within an arm's length of the sentries. Everything was very still except for the whisper of the warm breeze blowing from the south.

Eventually, he could see the horses. There were more than two dozen of them; large, black creatures with coats like velvet. They were standing in a line, their reins secured to a taut rope fixed between two trees. They stood patiently in the shade, occasionally shaking their long tails and manes to remove the buzzing flies that tormented them. John understood the importance of horses to the foreigners. Without transport the men would become tired and would travel much slower. He had noticed while he was shadowing them during the morning, that there was a regular system of rotation between riding and marching. They had all appeared to be excellent horsemen.

Near the animals, a solitary guard leaned heavily on an upturned spear. He was dressed, as all of them were, in a black tunic, with a black leather belt and a helmet that looked like a pointed skull cap with a thick flap to protect the back of the neck. On his feet were heavy, laced sandals. A little way off, the rest of the armed camp slept in the deep shade. John could see the blacksmith propped against a tree with his thick, hairy legs sprawled out in front of him. He appeared to be asleep.

John backed slowly into the forest until the horses were out of sight, and walked on until he came to a small clearing with dry grasses and a small holly bush. He checked that the breeze was behind him, and from a pouch in his belt he produced a small tinderbox that Old Mary had given him. *Fire is a cruel friend*, she had warned. *Never take your eyes off him once you have set him free.*

Quickly, he gathered a pile of dead leaves and twigs around the holly bush and placed some dry grass on top. After a number of attempts he produced a spark that ignited the grass. It flared up immediately. He heaped on more twigs and dry wood. The forest floor was covered in dead bracken and fallen branches: all were tinder dry. The flames spread rapidly, enveloping the desiccated holly bush, leaping up at an ever-increasing height, until within moments, the branches overhead were smouldering. There was a sudden flare-up as the breeze intensified the combustion, and yellow flames raced outward, fanned by the moving air.

As yet there was little smoke, but John was amazed at the fierce roaring of the monster he had released. He grabbed a flaming branch and dragged it over to the right. After about twenty paces, he stopped and started another fire.

Smoke was beginning to rise and the breeze blew it in thin bluish billows into the trees and towards the camp. It would not be long before the horses raised the alarm. The first fire escaped its original confines and became a wave of flame that moved rapidly over the hundred paces to the encampment. The flames leapt from bushes to the surrounding trees, which became engulfed in an explosion of heat and burning embers. The noise increased in volume, and the blaze became a roaring, spitting, crackling demon, raging on in ever-increasing strength.

John was almost overcome by the heat as he reached for another flaming bough, and as he moved back, his hair began to singe. He staggered to the left in the direction from which he had come, with the burning branch trailing behind him. He stopped every few paces to ignite another patch of vegetation, while to the right and behind him the world became a thundering wall of destruction.

He could hear screaming and a furious yelling from the direction of the camp, as men and horses became alerted to the danger. He dropped the flaming bough and ran, holding the sword in both hands, oblivious to the scratches from thorns and brambles. He had only one thought in his mind, and that was to find the girl. The blacksmith could take care of himself.

Without warning, a man appeared from behind a tree. John stopped abruptly and held the sword in front of him. He stared at the black clothing and the lined, olive-coloured skin. Surprise showed in the man's eyes and he was slow to react. He carried a spear in his right hand, and his first movement had been to protect himself by grasping the weapon with both hands and holding it out before him. The point of the spear was at waist height.

The man stared at John and the bright sword. Three long paces separated them. Neither moved as they stared into each other's eyes. John could hear the menacing roar of the fire as it surged up behind him. In front, the woodland seemed so peaceful with sunlight filtering through leaves. The dark figure made a sudden movement and attempted to raise the spear for a throw. John knew instinctively that this was what he had been waiting for. In that moment of raising the spear, the soldier was defenceless, but if he completed the action, he would be in a position of superiority.

John lunged forward, a terrible cry echoed in his ears. The man seemed to fold up as though he was bowing, and the spear fell to the side as John charged past, staggering clumsily through the trees. His sword dripped blood and an inhuman voice continued to scream as he blundered on. It was some distance before John stopped running, and realized the voice was his own. His lungs sucked in air in great gasps, and his arms ached. He was racked by a fit of coughing as smoke enveloped him. The fire was gaining ground.

· · ·

A SOLDIER JUMPED DOWN into the gully, his sandalled feet were so close to Gwen's face that she could have reached out and touched them. Her heart was thumping and her body tensed for a terrified scream. She watched in horror as he bent down, but his back was towards her, and he only picked up a handful of dry sand to throw at his friend. His laughter was followed by a silence. The legs near Gwen straightened and a word was shouted and repeated with increasing emphasis. Then there was a frenzy of movement as the legs vanished and she heard both men crashing through the forest. Their excited voices and the noise of their departure faded, to be replaced by a new sound: a low rumble like an advancing storm.

Gwen glanced out from under the fallen tree. The sky was clear blue and the late afternoon sun was still hot on her skin. From the south a small breeze stirred the leaves. As she stared up at the trees a grey haze filtered through the branches. She crawled out carefully from her hiding place. Something was wrong; she could feel it. Her nose caught the smell of smoke and she understood.

The low rumble had become louder. It was a thunderous roll, still some way off, yet rapidly getting nearer. As she peered into the deep gloom of the forest, she could see, down a long corridor of trees, a faint glow that flickered and increased in size even as she watched it.

Where was John? The question assumed enormous importance as the sound of the fire grew louder. Blue, grey smoke was billowing above her head and the air was becoming acrid. Should she wait as he had directed? Or should she continue along the path of the vanished stream in the hope that he would catch up with her?

Gwen climbed out of the channel and onto the bank. Red flames were clearly visible now and the smoke was increasing, fanned by the breeze. She stared down the gully, but there was no sign of movement. A thick cloud of smoke and sparks obliterated her vision and she climbed onto the tree trunk to get a better view. But overhead the smoke increased in density and hot sparks began to rain down.

She had no experience of forest fires, and was amazed by the ferocity and violence of the inferno. The noise was overwhelming and already she was aware of waves of heat surging out on the breeze. A dense cloud of smoke enveloped her, and she was overcome with a fit of coughing. As the air cleared momentarily, she turned and climbed painfully down from the trunk back into the gully. She had no choice now, it was too dangerous to stay.

As she began to move down the channel her mind was numbed by the terror of the fiery holocaust. The thundering and crashing was like the fearful roar of a demented monster, and the acrid smoke burnt at her lungs. The air was alive with falling hot embers, and smoke was surging out from the trees in thick billows, hot and choking. She ceased to worry about the soldiers, about her father, or about the young man. Her mind concentrated on the single problem of survival.

· · ·

ON HIS WAY TO the dried-up watercourse, John caught a brief glimpse of the soldiers' encampment. It raised his spirits to see the panic he had caused. The scene was one of chaos: furious soldiers struggled with the terrified horses, as burning embers showered down, injured soldiers were flung across the backs of horses, and clung precariously, slipping on the bare flanks of the frantic beasts, and orders were yelled and ignored, and the organization, previously so impressive, vanished in the smoke.

He saw the leader with the red beard, trying without success to draw a circle on the earth with his sword, but panicking horses and soldiers ran through it and dissipated whatever power he was attempting to create. Everyone appeared to be oblivious to his furious orders.

The smoke was increasing and spreading under the branches of the trees like a ghostly mist. There were no guards to be seen, and John staggered, breathlessly along the channel as it twisted between the trees. He was head and shoulders above ground level, and in his desperation to move quickly, and yet still keep alert for any hostile soldiers, he frequently failed to avoid the obstacles littering the bed of the waterway. Once, he fell heavily and lay gasping on the sandy soil, his body crying out for rest. He tottered to his feet and moved on, desperate to reach the girl named Gwen.

At last he rounded a bend and saw the fallen trunk. The smoke was billowing overhead, but had not yet reached the lower level of this part of the forest. In a gap in the trees he could see a lurid glow in the sky. There was no doubt that the fire was out of control, and if he and the girl were unable to move quickly, they would be in danger of being cut off.

His ankle was bleeding from a sharp stone and he limped the last few yards, his eyes searching the shadows under the fallen tree. There was no movement, and a cold feeling came over him as he knelt down and peered into the recess. She was not there.

•   •   •

THE BLACKSMITH LAY UNMOVING in the deep shade of a huge oak, his muscular legs sprawled in front of him and his strong arms, fastened by the wrists, rested on his belly. His head, propped against the gnarled wood, was tilted slightly back; his mouth gaped open. To even the most attentive guard, Tom appeared to be asleep. An unnatural brooding stillness hung over the camp. Occasionally, one of the injured men, lying in the shade of the litter, would groan loudly. The guard opposite would jerk up his head, stare angrily about for a moment and then resume his dozing. A small breeze massaged the leaves of the lower branches and insects throbbed in the hot air.

Tom was aware of every slight noise. A flicker of his eyelids allowed him to note the state of the drowsy guard on the opposite side of the glade. Tom allowed his head to fall forwards and glanced to his left and slightly behind. It was enough to confirm his ears had not betrayed him. Gwen had crawled off into the forest. He saw a movement in the bushes behind the place where Gwen had been resting. A face emerged briefly, and Tom recognized the youth he had met the previous night. The dark hair withdrew into the bushes and did not reappear. Tom smiled grimly, at least Gwenny would not be by herself and her chances of escape were considerably improved. For the first time in nearly a day he allowed himself to relax.

He took a deep breath and settled down to wait for the guards to discover Gwenny was gone. He held no illusions about the treatment he would receive when they realized she had escaped. It was something he was prepared for. He had always known a time might come when he would have to risk his own life for his adopted daughter. He was prepared for the worst. "I'll wait an' see what 'em devils will do," he murmured to himself.

After a while, his keen ears caught the distant sound of crackling, and almost immediately an imperceptible rumble. Tom stared with half-closed eyes at the forest in front of him, for it was from that direction that the noise was increasing, and he was surprised to see a grey haze creeping through the trees. The faint rumble became a drumming sound, and he smelt smoke.

His first reaction was to yell "Fire!", but he held his breath when he realized the implications. If the fire was a big one, and the signs were that it was, then there would be pandemonium when the soldiers awoke, and in the disorder Gwenny's absence might not be noticed. He gave no thought to his own safety, but watched with growing excitement as the smoke increased over the treetops.

The horses gave the first alarm, quickly followed by their guard. In moments, yelling men were jumping up and running to release the animals. Smoke wisps began seeping into the clearing blown by the breeze, quickly becoming dense clouds that billowed out, obscuring patches of the clearing and adding to the turmoil. Orders, counter-orders and curses filled the air, coupled with the loud whinnying of the terrified horses and the screams of the wounded men as they were roughly hoisted onto horses, or thrown onto the makeshift litter.

The confusion was sudden and complete. Sparks rained down, smoke blotted out the trees, and the thunder of the inferno drowned the bellowed orders. The first concern of the soldiers was for the horses, and their wounded companions came a poor second. At that moment, nobody was concerned with the prisoners.

Carefully, Tom rose to his feet, his back braced against the tree and darted quickly behind the broad trunk. As he did so, a guard appeared, running towards the camp from the direction that Gwen had taken. The man's sword was drawn, and he raised it above his head and aimed a slicing blow at Tom. The blacksmith ducked to the side and, as the man ran by carried by his own frantic momentum, Tom swung with both his arms like a club, and caught the man a mighty blow on the back of the neck. The soldier collapsed to the ground and lay very still. His head hung loosely at an unnatural angle.

"Serves 'ee right," Tom growled, and coughed as a dense cloud of smoke enveloped him. Without a backward glance he charged into the forest, his powerful arms held out in front of him like a battering ram, and forced his way through bushes and briars. He was coughing and spluttering as he ran, with eyes stinging and tears flowing down his hot cheeks. Behind him the fire thundered in his ears.

He did not see the gully, and experienced a brief moment of alarm as his feet failed to contact the ground. There was a jarring impact as his body slammed into the hard earth and stones. Tom lay prostrate, gasping for breath, but his mind quickly took stock of the situation. He was in a shallow, dried-out riverbed, and for the moment the air was clearer; while above him the smoke flowed over like a thick fog. He began to crawl along the channel, but his tied wrists made the going difficult, so he staggered to his feet and ran, bent double, his head searching for the clear air, his eyes barely focused.

After a few minutes he was out of the worst of the smoke, which was rolling out before the breeze in thick grey waves and shrouding the channel behind him. In front, the air was relatively clear, but he understood the fire would be spreading to the sides as well as moving forward, and soon his position would be threatened. He stumbled on, until he rounded a small bend in the channel and was faced with an obstacle: a huge tree lay across the depression, its trunk almost touching the floor of the riverbed. Tom did not want to climb over it because of the danger of being seen, and the upper air was thick with smoke. It would also have been difficult with his tied wrists.

He knelt down like a supplicant in front of the narrow opening under the trunk. He could see light at the other end of the narrow tunnel, and began to wriggle his way through the gap. It was then that he felt the wetness on his hands. There was blood on the stones and a dark red patch on the sandy soil. He squeezed his eyes together in the pain of the moment, and clenched his hands until his knuckles went white. It had to be Gwenny's blood; it was the only logical answer.

The lack of food and sleep and all the exertions of the past day seemed to overwhelm him. If his Gwenny were dead then nothing mattered. He closed his eyes and lay with his face on the broken stones. Overhead the smoke billowed and the noise of the inferno grew louder. Sparks and hot embers fell like a fiery rain, forcing him, reluctantly, to move into the hollow under the fallen tree.

Smoke filtered down the trench and he was racked with another bout of coughing. But the exertion roused him from his stupor and he edged through the narrow passageway and out the other side. As he dragged himself forward, his face to the ground, he felt more blood. It was sweet and sticky. Tom immediately felt more hopeful, for it indicated that Gwen had passed through the same tunnel. Perhaps she was still alive and had not been recaptured. He crawled on rapidly down the channel, and found no more bloodstains but could not decide if this was a good sign.

Behind and to his right, the fire raged unchecked. In front, the dry riverbed snaked on out of sight, but the fire was advancing and might cut him off. He had not found Gwenny's body, and if she were alive she would surely have moved into the forest on the left. Tom made his decision, and plunged into the trees and away from the advancing holocaust, driven by his unswerving devotion to the young woman who had brought so much happiness into his loveless marriage.

• • •

GWEN HURRIED ALONG THE gully. Beads of sweat flowed like tears down her face, her breath was laboured and she ached in every limb. She reasoned that it was better to follow the twisting channel than to turn off into the forest on her left. For although this path kept her close to the fire, there was more chance of the young man finding her if she kept straight on, than if she attempted to escape through the dense and unknown woodland.

She travelled almost a mile before the noise of the inferno finally faded, and the air was free of smoke. On both sides there were tall trees and behind them the thick, dark forest. It spread out with only the occasional break in the dense canopy, through which the light shafted, partially illuminating the dry mossy floor. The channel became narrower and deeper, and Gwen began to feel an increasing sense of unease. Shadows moved as the breeze caused the bushes to sway, and there was a brooding presence that was almost tangible.

At one point a herd of roe deer burst out of the forest and jumped the channel almost over her head. The crashing of their feet and the speed of their passage was so unexpected that she had remained motionless and wide-eyed for minutes after they had vanished.

Now the forest was silent. No birds sang and even the occasional creaking of the upper branches ceased. Gwen stopped and listened. Nothing. No sound at all. She strained to hear the noise of the fire, but in vain. It was unlike anything she had ever experienced: a totally soundless world, and one that had become strangely dark.

"What's happening?" she screamed, using her voice to rend the silence.

As if her cry had broken a spell, there was a faint thud of pattering feet, which grew steadily louder. Gwen was scared beyond speech. Her eyes desperately searched the shadows above her. She turned quickly, waving her hands frantically, as she tried to locate the direction of the sounds. It seemed that waves of frightening creatures were advancing from all sides.

"Please, God, don't let them take me," she whispered. Her tongue felt large in her dry mouth. The running feet became a deafening thunder that overwhelmed her. She closed her eyes and raised her hands to protect herself, and felt a cool wetness pouring through the green canopy. It was rain! A violent, torrential downpour splashed over her, she sank down on the stony ground and lay back, letting the heavy drops splatter on her face and flow down her flushed cheeks. She was utterly exhausted.

• • •

John crawled through the narrow passage under the fallen tree; his ankle was bleeding profusely. He checked the ground and the nearby trees for any sign of Gwen. There was none. Uttering a low moan, he took a handkerchief from his pocket and began to bind the damaged ankle. The blood dripped onto the yellow stones forming red flowers in the dust. As he wrestled with the makeshift bandage, he realized how tired he was.

He finished tying the knot and closed his eyes. What would the old woman be doing now? Would she be worried about him? Was this another of the strange tests? He doubted that. No one could have predicted the past day: the strange foreigners in black; the awful magic of the men with the red beards, and the amazing power of the sword. Now, it was his sword, and the pattern on its hilt was the same as that on the palm of his hand. What did it all mean? His friend Peter was dead, and Gwenny, was she dead too? He chewed on his lower lip.

Something hot touched his hand, and he opened his eyes to see thick smoke swirling out of the forest, and hot sparks raining down on him. He realized he must move and rose to his feet, using the sword as a crutch, gripping hard on the hilt. It felt strange and tingled in his grip. He stared down the gully. Which way to go?

He decided the forest would be safer. As he turned to the left and gripped the side of the ditch, an acrid cloud enveloped him. He screwed up his eyes, and tried not to breathe in too deeply. With the sword in his right hand he swung his left arm over the bank with the intention of pulling himself up. At that moment he felt the sword tug him backward like a wrestler, and he fell heavily on the dry bed of the channel in a sprawled heap. Dazed, he regained his feet and gingerly raised the sword, then moved a few paces down the gully. Everything was quite normal; the sword felt firm and balanced. Perhaps he had imagined it? The smoke was getting thicker and coming in dense, gusting clouds. He took two quick strides to the left and reaching up with his free arm, he grasped an overhanging root and yanked himself up. But as he raised his right hand with the sword, intending once again to swing it over the edge, he was halted in mid-air. The sword lunged away as if from a catapult, causing him to do a backward somersault down onto the rocky floor. He lay there winded and amazed. There was no doubt this time; the sword was preventing him from entering the forest.

Warily, he stood up and tentatively moved along the gully. The sword lay dormant in his hand. Another wave of smoke swirled around him, and he broke into a staggering trot; the sword felt cool and comforting in his grasp. After a few hundred paces, when he had escaped the forward movement of the smoke, John slowed down to a fast walk, and carried the sword with the blade resting on his shoulder. The tingling sensation in his hand had passed away as if it had never happened, and he felt strangely refreshed.

Without any warning, rain began to fall. The sky darkened and large, cool drops splashed on his upturned face, and thudded into the dry ground like arrows. In the trees there was the sound of clapping as the parched leaves caught the first impact. John stopped walking and stood in awe, as the rain quickly became torrential. He had never experienced such a storm. Lightning flashed, illuminating the sky behind him, and he heard the thunder for the first time, louder than the distant drum roll of the fire, but still some way off. The rain was like a waterfall, and almost as impenetrable. It hammered on his face and head, and his clothes were soon saturated. In the bed of the gully, which only a short time before had been cracked and dusty, puddles formed and merged and began to flow past him in thin streams. He was aware that he had been moving gradually into higher ground.

It became impossible to see more than a few paces ahead, and he decided that he would attempt, once again, to climb out of the gully. As the fire was no longer an immediate danger, and the violent deluge was sure to prevent it spreading, he chose the right hand side. He was able to pull himself easily over the slippery edge, and with great caution he crawled towards the cover of the trees, while the sword remained inert in his hand.

· · ·

GWEN LAY ON THE ground for several minutes while the rain beat down. She was unwilling to move; it was too much effort. It was easier to lie there and let everything drift away. She thought of the boy who came to her rescue. Would he have been killed by the fire or captured by the soldiers? She thought of her father; what had happened to him? She felt no sorrow; she was too exhausted for tears. Gwen allowed her thoughts to float away, far off into a painless cloud of softness, a world of beautiful flowers and soft music. Her eyes were half-opened when a vivid flash of lightning seared the heavens, jolting her out of her lethargy. When the thunder followed, she knew there was no escape. She had to face reality again.

Groaning with the effort, she crawled up the left bank of the gully and sought cover in the dense forest. She remained huddled against a broad tree, while the storm spent its fury. Her eyes were closed, but her mind remained alert. When the rain stopped she found a small track that wound its way through the forest, and decided she would follow it, in the hope it would lead to some safe habitation where she could shelter for the night.

The forest floor was waterlogged, and Gwen found the going difficult. She had lost her sandals sometime during her capture, and her bare feet were cut and bruised. The moss underfoot was cold and slimy, like seaweed, and she staggered like a drunken person as she hurried along the track. There were many noises in the forest: water dripped from every branch and stem, and wild creatures fled before her approach, crashing away into the undergrowth. When a rabbit scampered past her, she was alerted to the danger from behind.

She slithered behind a tree, only moments before two riders, dressed in black, came into view. As they approached she moved round the trunk, her back pressed against the wet bark. She heard the horses' hooves splashing and slipping on the wet track, but the riders were silent as they passed by. She remained behind the tree long after all sounds of the horses had faded. Fear and her damp cold clothes caused her to shake violently, and she felt miserable and alone. Very slowly she peered around the tree and stared into the gathering gloom. The track was empty.

Gwen decided to continue in her original direction, even though it meant following the horsemen, for she reasoned that it was unlikely that others would be patrolling the same area of the forest. She forced herself to hurry, trying to overcome the chill that was seeping into her joints.

Eventually, she came to a point where the track divided. The hoof prints showed the horsemen had gone to the right, and so she chose the other, smaller path, that snaked away into the grey light. Dense bushes added to the deepening shadows. She knew there was no choice but to press on, and ignoring the fear clawing at her imagination, she hurried forward.

It was dusk when she saw the light twinkling amid the dark trees. The light shone through the open window of a large wooden hut that was surrounded by bushes and nestled in a grove of tall oaks. By daylight she might have missed it; in darkness she would certainly have passed it by, had it not been for the lamp shining brightly, like a beckoning finger.

She approached cautiously, but her need for food and shelter overcame her fears. The door was half-open, and from a little way off she glimpsed a fire burning low in an open hearth with an iron pot heating over it. As she crept closer she could smell the inviting aroma of a stew seasoned with herbs, and her body cried out for nourishment.

Gwen paused at the partially open entrance and cautiously pushed the door open until she could see into the room. Much of the interior was in shadow, and it was a few moments before she was aware of the two eyes that were staring at her from a dark corner. She gave a startled cry.

"Don't be afraid, my dear. You're quite safe. Come in and close the door now."

"Who are you?" Gwen asked.

"Bless you, my dear, I'm just an old woman who's glad of some company. Come in now and rest yourself, you look tired."

"Thank you. You're very kind," Gwen said. However, she still remained by the door. There was something about the way the old woman beckoned to her that reminded Gwen of a spider enticing a fly into its web.

"You don't have to be afraid of me, my dear. Not of Old Jude, you don't. I have some food you can have, and a warm place to sleep. You'll be quite safe here." The old woman moved slowly towards the cooking pot and indicated a stool for Gwen to sit on.

Reluctantly, Gwen edged towards the stool. Her eyes searched the room for any lurking danger, but she saw nothing. The bowl of stew was passed to her and its aroma was irresistible. After a first cautious taste she abandoned her suspicions and tucked into the meal in earnest. The old woman sat opposite on another low stool, and stared at Gwen with dark, unblinking eyes, gleaming red in the firelight. She had a broad, fleshy nose and large hands and her grey hair showed flecks of copper. She was a powerful woman and one who, in spite of her apparent friendship, possessed a sinister quality. Gwen had met few people outside of her own village, and never one like Old Jude, as she called herself.

"Drink this, my dear, it'll warm you. Then you must get out of those wet clothes."

Gwen took the metal goblet, and smelt the sweet fragrances of honey and crushed fruits. She drank deeply and felt revived. It was so pleasant she immediately drank some more. It was getting darker in the room, and she had a great desire to sleep.

"That's right, my dear, drink it all. There's a good girl."

Gwen was warned by the gloating quality in the old woman's voice. It was the voice of someone who knows they have power. Gwen tried to push back the waves of sleep threatening to engulf her. She placed the half-empty goblet on the earth floor and tried to get up, but her limbs would not respond. She saw the old woman rise and her face seemed to get very large as in a nightmare. The room was spinning and Gwen felt she could not breathe. With a final effort she half rose from the stool, staggered drunkenly about, and collapsed in a heap on the hard floor.

The old woman stood watching her for a few moments. Eventually, she bent down and grabbed Gwen's hair and gave it a vicious tug. The girl remained deep in her drugged sleep.

"Blue dress and cropped hair. Yes, you be the one the soldiers were after, my dear. I reckon you'll be worth some silver." Old Jude gave a bitter laugh, and carefully removed Gwen's silver bracelet and placed it in a wooden bowl on the table. She found a piece of rough twine, tied Gwen's hands together behind her back and pulled her unconscious body to the large, heavy table, and secured her to one of the legs. She closed the wooden shutters and put some small logs on the fire. Finally, she flung an old, stained wrap around her shoulders, picked up the lamp and hobbled out of the door, which she locked with a large key. It was pitch black as she took a narrow path that led to the high ground, and her small light was deceptively innocent.

. . .

WHEN THE BLACKSMITH RUSHED headlong into the forest, his main aim was to find Gwen, not just to avoid death. He chose self-preservation, not because he valued his life, but because he had decided to use it to save his adopted daughter. Without any clear plan, he ran wildly through the trees yelling her name, hoping that somehow they would be reunited. His wrists were still tied together in front of him, as even his great strength could not break the bonds, and he plunged through the undergrowth like a human battering ram, with the noise of the inferno drowning his cries.

The rain brought him to his senses. The cool, heavy droplets surprised him, and the sudden fury of the storm overwhelmed him. Almost instantly the rain became a pounding force, drumming on the hard earth. He gave himself up to the elements, his huge chest heaving with the exertion of his demented run, and he knelt down with his forehead resting on the ground and his bound arms stretched out in front.

After a few minutes his body began to cool, and the mad panic faded away. He became aware of his position and of the waterlogged ground around him. With a sense of weariness he stood up and sought shelter under a spreading birch tree, and regardless of the danger from lightning, sat down with his back to the smooth trunk, and stared listlessly ahead.

It was some while before he noticed the deluge had given way to a lighter, gentler rain. The sun reappeared and a rainbow arched across the sky. The storm was over.

Tom felt detached from reality. The rain had washed away his anger and his strength, leaving him drained of energy and without any desire to continue his fruitless search. The sun warmed him, and his eyes grew heavy as he gave himself up to the sleep that his tired body craved. With a groan he slumped forward across his knees, his tied hands hung limp between his legs.

"Who're you?" a voice asked. Tom was suddenly awake. "Who're you?" the voice repeated. "Is you a giant?"

A young child was standing in front of him. She was very small with long, dark hair and she had her thumb in her mouth. She seemed embarrassed, and had crossed one leg in front of the other while she twisted her free arm self-consciously behind her back.

Tom tried to smile, but the child jumped back in alarm. He realized his appearance must be frightening and tried another approach. He laughed in a soft, encouraging way, and spoke in a quiet, gentle voice. "I'm not a giant, m'dear. I'm Tom Roper, the blacksmith."

This explanation did not seem to mean much to the girl, who remained staring at him with her thumb in her mouth. He tried again. "D'ye live near here?"

The child nodded her head.

"I've got my hands tied together, see. I need to get ye father t' untie me. If ye takes me to ye father, I'll give ye a present."

"What 'tis it?" she asked, suddenly interested.

"Well it be a secret," Tom spoke softly as he carefully rose to his feet. The child backed away. "If ye takes me to y' father ye shall 'ave this special present."

The girl stared at him for a moment then began to skip off along a path that wound its way through the trees ahead. Tom followed at a distance making encouraging comments and trying to reassure the child in case she ran off. After only a few hundred paces, he came to an open space sloping down to a small stream that had burst its banks. On a grassy knoll on the higher ground was an ancient covered cart. A large horse was tethered nearby and various pieces of clothing material hung on branches or were draped over bushes.

"Mama, I've found a giant!" the child called.

"Joan, 'ow many times must I tell 'ee not—" the mother's voice stopped abruptly as she emerged from the wagon to see Tom standing beside her daughter. The difference in size added emphasis to Tom's huge shape.

"May God protect us! Come 'ere, girl. Stand by me."

"Don't ye fear me, ma'm. I be Tom Roper, the blacksmith from Woodford."

"Never 'eard of it," the woman replied, but her voice had lost its original panic. "What is it ye be wanting?"

"As ye can see," Tom said, holding up his bound wrists, "I've need of 'elp."

"Are ye an escaped prisoner?" her eyes were fearful.

"I escaped from foreigners," Tom protested. "They was soldiers in black, and they got me daughter Gwen as well."

The woman's attitude softened. "We've had reports of 'em. They been killin' lots of people." She released her hold on her daughter and moved closer to Tom. "Ye looks and speaks like a good man, Tom Roper." She stared intently into his face. Then after a moment's hesitation, she produced a knife from the folds of her dress and began to cut through the thick cords. He noticed she had blue hands.

Later, when his wrists were free and the circulation had returned to his fingers, Tom joined Joan and her mother, Martha, in a simple meal of freshly caught trout and newly baked bread. He explained briefly about the soldiers and his daughter, but did not refer to the sword. When Tom mentioned the fire she understood, for she had seen the smoke in the distance.

"Be ye by yourself?" Tom asked.

"Bless ye no!" Martha exclaimed, "Me husband is off sellin' our cloth. Ye see, he be a weaver and I be a dyer." She indicated her blue hands and the lengths of coloured material that hung from the trees.

"An' be he comin' back 'ere today?" Tom asked.

The woman looked awkward, and her face flushed.

"I didn't mean nothin' by me question," Tom tried to reassure her. "It was just that 'ee might of got some news about where them soldiers be."

"No, it ain't that I don't trust 'ee, Tom," Martha smiled. "It's just that we 'ave a problem. Ye see we two was supposed to travel south to meet my Sam at the village of Nether Burstock tomorrow, an' that be some miles away. The reason we be still 'ere is that we've lost a wheel." She laughed, "I told Joan to go an' find a giant to help mend the wheel, an' she found one an' all!"

Tom smiled with relief. "I could help 'ee with it," he said and followed Martha to the other side of the cart, where the broken wheel hung awkwardly on its axle. Martha had wedged a lump of wood underneath to support the vehicle.

"I tried me best to keep it from fallin' over," Martha explained.

"An' ye did a good job," said Tom as he made the log secure. "Do ye have anythin' of weight in the wagon?"

"We do an' all," Martha replied. "We got our spinning wheel, and our old hand loom, an' it be a real heavy one an' all."

"Of course, I'd forgot ye husband's trade. Well, we need to move it out an' everythin' else we can shift." Tom turned to the small girl and winked, then he reached into a small pocket and held out his hand. "An' I've a present for ye, me pretty girl." He raised his finger to his lips and winked again.

Joan reached out her hand and Tom placed a coin in her palm. The child looked at it carefully and skipped off laughing as she went.

"What d' ye give 'er that made her so happy?" Martha asked.

"Oh, just a small reward for bringin' me 'ere," Tom said. It was much later when Martha discovered that it was a solid gold coin. The only one the family ever owned.

. . .

IT WAS A SLOW business unloading the wagon, but the loom was easier than Tom could have hoped, because Martha knew how to take it apart, and the heavy wooden frame was eventually in manageable pieces. Once the wagon was empty, and with the help of the horse and a series of rope pulleys, Tom was able to raise the wagon and remove the wheel. His skill as a blacksmith enabled him to make a serviceable repair.

"It won't go on for ever, but it'll take ye a good few miles," Tom said.

It was near dusk as they finally repacked the wagon. The sky was clear and bats, like ghostly shadows, swooped around the flickering firelight.

"Seein' as how ye knows this area, I reckon that as soon as we've had a bit to eat, we could travel through the night and meet up with your husband tomorrow," Tom said.

"I was 'oping ye'd say that, Tom Roper," Martha said and placed a hand on his arm. "Ye be a good man, an' I be mighty grateful to 'ee."

Tom glowed with pleasure and turned away to hide his flushed face. His own wife never praised him in that way.

CHAPTER 8

J OHN DID NOT KNOW in which direction to go, but there was nothing to be gained by waiting in the torrential rain. He was soaked to the skin and his body heat was cooling. He shivered, and began to walk quickly through the dense forest, following narrow tracks that were fast becoming quagmires as the water poured off the upper branches and flowed down the thick trunks of the trees. Overhead, he glimpsed the frequent flashes of light as the heavens exploded and the world around him drowned.

Much later, as the darkness increased, he reached a man-made track. The rain had eased as rapidly as it had started, and then stopped. Everything dripped loudly, and underfoot the puddles and small streams were ankle deep. He plodded on with the sword heavy on his shoulder and his feet sore and mud-clad. The scenery held no interest for him, and one tree blended with the next as the shadows thickened.

He was approaching the final point of exhaustion, when he limped into a wide clearing. On the opposite side was a thatched hut with a covered area in the front. A small figure sat at the open doorway, stirring a pot that hung over a hot fire.

As John approached, he saw it was an old man who appeared not to notice him, even though he splashed loudly over the sodden ground. The little figure continued to stir the pot, and threw in some herbs.

"So, you're here at last then!" he said enthusiastically, and there was a trace of merriment in his voice.

John stopped a few paces from the fire and his mouth sagged. "You were expecting me?" he gasped.

"A while ago. But you must be tired. Sit down and eat." The man indicated a small stool.

Obediently, John lowered the sword from his shoulder and gently eased himself onto the stool; his back rested against a wooden post supporting the makeshift porch. Who the man was, why he seemed to expect John's arrival, and whether there was any danger, was unimportant. John was too tired to care, and gratefully accepted a bowl of hot stew and a hunk of bread, and made no pretence to cover his ravening hunger.

The man said nothing as John rapidly consumed the food, but he studied the boy in a fixed and meditative manner from under his bushy eyebrows. He was a thin man of small stature with grey hair and a large hooked nose. He sipped from a steaming pewter mug and occasionally nodded his head as though agreeing with an internal conversation of his own.

"Drink this, it will do you good." The man handed John a second tankard. It was a hot, sweet drink that tasted of honey. John drank deeply and felt his body relax. The ache in his muscles disappeared and he experienced a great sense of contentment.

"My real name is unimportant, but you may call me Owl." Once again there was a hint of amusement in his voice.

"Owl? What an odd name," John murmured. He had difficulty keeping his eyes open.

"A good name. You see the owl hunts at night and is rarely seen during the day. He has a great advantage over other birds." Owl laughed. It was a warm, throaty sound.

"How did you know I was coming?'

"I was told to expect you, John, or should I say *Giles*?"

John sat up with a start. "You know my name... my other name... nobody knows that except..."

"Except Old Mary? No, don't be afraid, I am not like the man with the twisted jaw. I know her as a friend." He smiled.

"But how?"

"It would take too long to explain. Just believe that you're in safe hands tonight. You will sleep soundly and tomorrow we shall talk." He stood up and, putting a firm arm on John's shoulders, led him into the hut where a candle revealed a small pallet bed with a thick woollen blanket.

"Take off your wet clothes. I will dry them for you before the morning." Owl went out of the door and put some more logs on the fire.

Almost in a dream, John removed his wet clothing, wrapped himself in the blanket, and lay on the bed. Immediately, he fell into a deep sleep. After a while Owl entered, collected John's clothes and placed them on twigs around the fire. Later, he re-entered with the sword and placed it by the side of the bed. As he straightened up, he noticed the palm of John's open hand lying on top of the blanket. With the light of a candle, he carefully examined the markings. As he left the room, there was an excited gleam in his eyes. For the rest of the night he sat at the open door, a still, silent figure. Occasionally, he restocked the fire, but otherwise he was unmoving, and only his bright eyes showed he was awake.

John woke with the first twittering of the pre-dawn chorus. He felt remarkably well, and sat up on his pallet holding the woollen blanket around him to fend off the early morning chill. By the light of the small lamp he could see his sword lying close by and his clothes arranged in a neat order on a bed of rushes. There was no confusion in his mind; he knew exactly where he was and what had occurred. The clothes were dry and still warm, and he dressed quickly. As he bent down to pick up the sword, Owl appeared in the doorway.

"Leave the sword, Giles. It will be safe there. Come and eat, you have much to do."

John followed him out to the open porch. The fire was burning brightly in the pale early light, and the two stools were placed as they had been on the previous evening. Instantly, John recalled his unanswered question. "You call me Giles, and you know Old Mary…" he began.

"Later. Now is the time to eat. You need strength and time to think." Owl handed him a steaming bowl of porridge, mixed with honey, berries and nuts. "Eat. It will do you more good than a bowl full of words." He laughed, and John felt pleased to be in his company.

"What do you think about the sword?" Owl asked as John was eating.

"I feel it is my sword… it feels as if it should belong with me." John spoke the words even before he had thought about them. But it was true; the adventures of the past two days had convinced him that the sword was a part of him. It was his sword.

"Tell me everything that has happened," Owl said, as he carefully arranged wood on the fire. The bird song increased around the clearing, but the light was still grey and the sun was yet to appear over the hills behind the small hut.

For some while, in between mouthfuls of bread and gulps of the hot honey drink he had enjoyed the previous night, John described the events that had occurred since leaving Old Mary's cottage. He had decided to call her Old Mary, as everyone else appeared to know her by that name. Throughout the story, Owl sat quietly, chewing slowly on a crust and gently inclining his head. At times, he asked a question in order to clarify a point, but all the time it was as if this strange man knew what was going to be said, and the questions were to help John understand what had happened, rather than Owl.

When the story was finished, Owl asked, "What will you do now?"

"I must try to find Gwen."

"What about the sword?"

"Do you think it's important?" John asked. It seemed right to ask such a question.

"Only you can decide what is important. Others may direct your thoughts, but the final decision is yours."

"That's not true!" John exclaimed. "Yesterday, I tried to go one way but the sword made me go another. I did not make the decision."

"But you did, Giles. In life we are all given a second chance to reconsider; it was up to you whether you went forward or not." Owl nodded to himself.

"I had to go forward, I would have been burnt otherwise."

"No, the rain would have saved you."

"But I did not know it was going to rain," John protested.

"Of course not. That is the wonder of living."

John was confused. He broke off some bread and chewed thoughtfully. "I think the other sword is important," he said at last. "Tom, the blacksmith, had it, and the foreigners were very pleased when they captured it."

"Do you think it has any connection with Gwen?"

"I hadn't thought about that. Yes, it might."

"So you both have a sword?"

"Yes, I suppose so."

"And they are both exactly the same?"

"Yes."

"And you have a device on your hand and it is the same as the one on the two swords?" Owl paused. "What is the link?"

"I don't know," John answered. "Do you know?"

Owl ignored the question, and put another log on the fire.

"Do you think you are someone special, Giles?"

"Of course not!" John replied sharply. "And my name is John. I don't want to be called Giles."

"Are you afraid?"

"No! Not in that way. It's just," he paused, "I want to be myself, not someone else. I want to lead my own life. I want to be free to choose. You said I should choose."

"You must decide on what you will do and what you will not do. But, like the rain there are some events that you can't avoid." Owl spoke softly, but with conviction.

John bit his lip nervously. There was something Owl and the old woman knew that directly affected him. He needed to know what it was, and yet he did not want to know. It was like waking from a dream, yet wanting to be back in it.

"Why do you call me Giles?"

Owl did not reply. It seemed as though he was listening to something that only he could hear. "Some riders are coming. If they ask any questions, act as though you are my son." He spoke urgently but did not raise his voice.

After a moment, two riders appeared at the other end of the clearing, from the direction that John had arrived. In the early light it was possible to see that they were dressed in black and carried spears and round shields. As they walked their horses slowly across the waterlogged ground, their dark faces and black helmets confirmed that they were part of the group that had captured Gwen and Tom, and killed Peter.

"Keep still and don't show any recognition," Owl muttered under his breath.

The two soldiers approached and stared hard at the old man and the boy. They had grim, cruel faces and dark, merciless eyes. "You are a woodcutter?" one asked in a heavy accent.

"Good day to ye, sir." Owl got to his feet and bowed.

"You live here?"

"For the moment, sir. Just for the summer."

"Have you seen any strangers since yesterday?"

"No, sir. Us don't see many strangers. Ye be the first."

The rider turned to go, but the second rider said something in his own language, nodded towards John and Owl, and put his hand on his sword. The first soldier shook his head and they turned their horses to depart.

"If we sees any strangers, sir, where shall we come to report 'em?" Owl called in a heavy local accent. He smiled like an idiot as he spoke.

"Over there," the first man replied, indicating a distant range of hills to the southeast; it looked blue grey in the early morning light.

"Right ye be, sir. We'll keep watchin'." He nodded furiously and waved his hands in a foolish way.

The two soldiers laughed and turned their horses. They continued to share the joke as they disappeared out of the clearing into the deep shadow of the forest.

"Owl, those were two of the foreign soldiers," John said. "They killed Peter. They could have killed us." He swallowed hard.

"One of them thought to do so," Owl replied. "But it was not to be."

"Do you think they were searching for Gwen? Perhaps she is still free after all?"

"Perhaps."

"Or maybe they were looking for the blacksmith?"

"Maybe." Owl appeared to be lost in his own thoughts. After a while he turned to John and smiled. "You look well."

"Yes," John answered. It was true, he did feel well and refreshed. The exhaustion of yesterday was gone and with it the doubt and uncertainty; even his injured ankle seemed to have healed. "I must leave now, Owl. If I travel quickly, I may discover their camp before they move on. Perhaps I can find out if they have Gwen." He stood up and stretched himself.

Owl watched him thoughtfully. "What will you do if they don't have Gwen?"

John paused. "I shall follow them until I have an opportunity to revenge Peter's death. They must be heading for the sea. They don't belong here. Eventually, they must pass near a town, and I shall get help." The idea was exciting and he was keen to be away.

"Remember what Old Mary taught you, and always consider your actions before you make them." He gripped John's hands and stared fiercely into the boy's eyes. "You will come to understand everything when the time is right. Now fetch your sword and guard it with your life!" He breathed out noisily and released his grip. He face suddenly broke into a smile and he turned away to stir the fire.

John smiled back, a little uncertain of this strange man, and walked quickly into the hut. He had a plan now and was keen to be away. He picked up the sword and weighed it in his hand, finding he could swing it easily with one arm. Yesterday, it had seemed heavier.

He glanced around the hut. The light was increasing, and he could see that apart from the straw bed, which looked very bare, and the pile of reeds, there was nothing else in the room. No tools, no clothes – nothing. Even the blanket was gone.

"Owl!" he called as he walked outside, "How do you manage to live here? Owl?" He stared about him. There was no trace of Owl. The fire had burnt out and was just white ash; no smoke or hot embers. There was a cold, empty feeling about the place as though no one had lived there for years. John walked up to the fire and tentatively touched the ash with one finger. It was cold and crumbled at his touch. The cooking pot was rusty with age and contained nothing more than rainwater and leaves. The pile of logs was covered with moss and mildew and the two stools were just round slabs of oak. On the ground lay a broken pottery bowl and, partly covered by leaves, was an broken pewter mug. Bewildered, John walked slowly round the outside of the hut, but there was no sign of Owl, or of any recent habitation.

John gripped the sword and stared about uneasily. The sun had risen behind him, and the opposite side of the clearing was bright and green, but the front of the hut was still in shadow, which increased the eerie quality of the place.

Where had Owl gone and what had happened? Had it been a dream? John moved out of the shadow of the hut and into the bright sunlight, and there on the soft mossy ground were the clear imprints of the horses' hooves. At least I did not imagine them, he thought, as he searched the edge of the forest for some clue to Owl's disappearance.

John recalled his own exhausted entry into the clearing, the bright fire and the hot food and drink. He remembered his dreamless sleep and the feeling of strength and vigour he had experienced after his early breakfast, and which he still felt. Most of all he reflected on the way Owl had enabled him to make his own plans by asking those quiet questions. But now, although he knew he was restored both in mind and body, there was no tangible proof that Owl had ever existed.

John looked up at the high ground where the soldiers had pointed and knew it was time to leave. There was nothing to wait for. He glanced back at the hut and noticed something strange on one of the round oak slices that he had mistaken for stools. He approached it slowly and felt a tremor of excitement pass through him when he realized what it was. On the wooden surface, in the place where Owl had sat, was a small compact bundle of bones and fur. It was a fresh owl pellet.

• • •

TOM AND MARTHA TRAVELLED through the night towards Nether Burstock; neither spoke very much, but each felt comfortable in the presence of the other. The child slept soundly, while the old horse plodded along and the wagon bumped from side to side. Overhead, the moon shone down from a cloudless sky and the stars were very bright. Sometimes, a shooting star would flash across the heavens, intensifying the magical quality of the journey.

"It's almost like day," Martha said as they followed the tree-lined path. There were deep shadows around the trunks, but the path was bathed in a silver light.

"It is an' all," Tom replied absent-mindedly. His thoughts had been on Gwen and where she might be. When he found the blood stains under the fallen tree, he was convinced she was dead. When he failed to find her body, he allowed himself to hope she was still alive. Now, in the early hours of the next day, his mind was full of doubt.

"You worrying about your daughter?" Martha asked.

"I don't know what to think. Maybe she got away with the boy who helped her escape. He was a strange boy, and yet not really a boy neither, more like a young lord," he paused. "There was something about him that made him different. When I surprised him in the meadow, he seemed scared. I would have been an' all. But then he got himself involved with the fight with the soldiers and must have escaped again, 'cos I saw him help Gwenny get away. I think he was the one who started the fire." Tom remained silent for a few minutes. It was one of the longest speeches he had made, and Martha waited for him to continue.

"What I don't understand is the business about the sword," Tom murmured.

"Tell me about it," Martha said. This was something he had not mentioned in their earlier discussions.

"Well, I don't know," Tom said. "Ye see I don't rightly understand much myself." He stared out along the moonlit path. "I'll tell ye the story of Gwenny an' how I came by the sword."

It was almost daybreak when Tom finished his story. Martha had listened carefully, occasionally asking a question, but mostly staring ahead, silently, as Tom's rich voice filled her ears. It was a story that she would enjoy telling her husband.

"So ye see, I don't know if the sword has magic powers like the boy said, or whether it just be something people want for its value. Ye see, it had gold on its handle," Tom said. He gave a big yawn.

"Have you ever seen that knight again? The one who gave you your Gwenny?"

"No. There's never been another word. But Sir Maurice was a good man, an' I believed what he told me. I did sometimes think that the old priest, the one who taught Gwenny, 'ad something to do with it, but I never discussed it with 'im." He sighed deeply. "I had stopped thinking about the sword and the gold, until I 'eard a foreign soldier was looking for Gwenny. It all seemed to come to life again." Tom paused. "The sword was just a sword with me, yet the boy claimed his sword, which was just like mine, 'ad magic powers."

"Magic powers," Martha repeated. "I don't know nothin' about anything like that."

"No, me neither," Tom replied. "I'm not what ye would call a regular church goer. But I am God fearin', if ye knows what I mean."

Martha nodded. "If this boy is special, then maybe he is keeping Gwenny safe." She looked at Tom in the grey light of the early dawn. "What will ye do now?"

"I bin thinking. Once I get ye to this village and find your husband, then maybe I'll buy a horse and try to find 'er. You'd already 'eard about them soldiers, so it follows that others will have 'eard about them an' all."

"So you think the soldiers might have got her then?"

"I don't know. But if I gets to them before they leave the country, I can make certain they don't 'ave her." He yawned again.

"You close your eyes awhile. I'll wake you when we arrive," Martha said.

"I will an' all," Tom mumbled. He was asleep in moments. His head lolled against the back of the rocking wagon.

Martha studied him for a while and then smiled to herself. "Ye be a good man, Tom Roper," she whispered.

• • •

IT WAS DARK, AND there was a painful feeling Gwen began to associate with her arms. She was lying on something hard and cold and her wrists hurt. Slowly the waves of drowsiness gave way to the more insistent thrust of conscious pain. Her head throbbed and her stomach felt weak. It was some time before she was able to recall her meeting with Old Jude, and comprehend her situation. Her wrists were tied together behind her back in a tight knot and, after a while, she understood: she was secured to the table. The cords had been tied tightly, and her hands did not seem to exist, but felt like iron weights on the end of her arms.

The pain helped to clear her head and she lay pondering on her predicament. She tried calling out, but there was no response, and it was clear that the hut had no other occupant. Gwen had no illusions as to where Old Jude was gone, and felt certain she would return with the soldiers.

As she lay in the darkness, with just a dull red glow to indicate the position of the fire, she reviewed the happenings of the past hours and wondered why her quiet world had been turned upside down. Who were these soldiers, and what did they want with her? The silence was oppressive and seemed to emphasise her loneliness. Her ears strained for the first sound that would announce the return of her captors, and her stomach contracted with fear.

An owl hooted outside. Gwen listened hopefully to the sound; it seemed to be the only recognizable element in a confused and lonely world. The owl called out again in a loud series of cries; it seemed very close. Gwen heard the faint answering calls of other owls that gradually increased in volume. Soon the shrieks and hoots of countless owls filled the night air, and Gwen suspected that her tattered mind was playing tricks on her. Owls did not behave in this way. The noise increased until it was deafening.

Suddenly, she heard another sound. Someone was yelling and roaring at the top of his voice. There was a scrabbling at the locked door. The owls seemed to be swooping down on the hut, their fierce cries tearing the darkness, and a pitiful voice screamed outside the door in an agony of terror. Huge wings beat the air and the solitary human voice reached an insane level of screaming. At that moment, the shutters of the high window near the door burst open, the wooden lock shattered in pieces and a dark figure exploded into the room, landing heavily on the floor.

It was like the silence after a landslide: one moment all thunder and commotion, then nothing. Outside, the owls departed as strangely as they had arrived, and inside the room there was an unnatural stillness as Gwen and the stranger each held their breath. The stranger breathed out loudly, and sat up, rubbing his limbs and trying to get his bearings in the room. The broken shutters allowed in some moonlight, and Gwen watched as the dark figure moved cautiously, in a limping fashion, towards the window.

"Tha' weren't funny," the stranger muttered as he reached the window and looked out at the silent forest. "Tha' weren't funny at all."

It was a young voice, and Gwen could see he was not very tall. He seemed to have hurt his leg, for he limped badly as he shuffled towards the fire. He blew on the embers, and added some kindling that he found near the grate. The flames leapt up and the room was lit with a rosy glow. The figure turned and was immediately aware of Gwen, who was only a few paces from him.

"Ahh! Who're ye?" he screamed. "I didn't mean no 'arm." He seemed about to run out of the hut.

"Please don't go, sir. I've been tied to this table, and I need your help." Gwen felt hot tears running down her face.

The figure paused and then crept closer, examining Gwen by the light of the fire.

"Ye be Gwen Roper!" he exclaimed. "I'm John's friend, I'm Peter 'Alfcart!"

Once the brief introductions were over, Peter quickly found a candle and, using his old knife, cut through Gwen's bindings. As she sat upright, slowly exercising her painful hands, Peter lit more candles and searched the hut for what he could find to eat.

"We must go," Gwen gasped. She suffered silently as the blood recirculated in her fingers. It felt as if they were being dipped in boiling oil, and the pain was excruciating. Her head throbbed from the sleeping potion and she had a foul taste in her mouth. "The woman who drugged me has gone for the soldiers. I know she has."

Peter had found some salted meat and was gnawing at it furiously. His need to satisfy his hunger was all-consuming. He came to the table and placed on it a half-eaten loaf and a jug of cider. His jaws moved convulsively as he forced more meat into his mouth.

Gwen stood up unsteadily. She took a long drink of the cider and, still rubbing her hands, she staggered towards the door. "We must go!" she repeated.

"No," Peter spluttered, his mouth full of meat, "I must eat first or I'll starve t' death."

"Oh, come on!" Gwen wailed. "The soldiers are coming. We must go!"

As if to confirm her fears, a distant owl shrieked a warning. Peter froze and his eyes widened. He was petrified. "I'm not goin' out there again. Them owls is waitin' for me." He sought refuge in his eating and broke off a hunk of bread and crammed it into his mouth. He chewed frantically and took a swig of the cider to wash it down. The liquid ran down both sides of his mouth.

"We must go!" Gwen moaned. She tried, in vain, to open the door, then lurched towards the high window. The sill was the height of her shoulders, and she was too weak to pull herself over the sill. "Help me!" she cried, but Peter appeared to be totally absorbed in the joint of salted meat.

She grabbed a stool and placed it in front of the window opening, and climbed through. So great was her anxiety that she catapulted herself over the sill and fell, face down, onto the damp ground outside. She lay for a moment shaking with exhaustion, while waves of nausea threatened to overwhelm her. The owl shrieked again, this time much closer. She fought back the desire to be sick, and holding on to the window frame she called a last warning to Peter.

"The soldiers are coming, I know it. They'll kill you if they find you here."

"I can't," Peter wailed. "Them owls will get me for sure."

"The owls are our friends! Believe me. If you don't come, I'll leave you," she threatened.

"No!" Peter cried. "I'll come. Don't leave me."

Almost immediately his thin face was framed in the window. He tossed out the joint of meat and the remains of the loaf, and clambered past the broken shutters. As he lowered himself down, the owl swooped out from the trees in front of the hut, hooted once and flew back the way it had come. Peter gave a terrified cry and scuttled towards the far side of the clearing.

Gwen picked up the food and followed him. They reached the trees and were immediately enveloped in the impenetrable darkness of the midnight forest. Glancing behind, they could see the clearing bathed in moonlight, while in front everything was black. The owl shrieked insistently as if trumpeting a warning, and they saw a line of dark shapes glide over the clearing towards the front of the hut.

With arms outstretched in front of him, Peter limped quickly away from the clearing, while Gwen followed behind, cradling the food in one arm and resting her other hand on Peter's shoulder. After a few minutes, far behind them, they heard an angry voice cry out.

"Poor woman," Gwen whispered.

"Serves 'er right," Peter answered. "Anyways, that be a man's voice, not a woman's."

They travelled for some miles before they were sure that they were not being followed. Finally, they came to an area where the forest canopy was less dense and shafts of moonlight illuminated their way. They stopped in a clearing by a gurgling stream and found a damp mound on which to sit and eat the remains of the food. After a silent meal, they drank from the fast flowing stream, which was cold and tasted brackish, but neither of them cared. Then they sat together and waited for the dawn.

"Thank you for coming to get me," Gwen said.

"I 'ad no choice," Peter answered, meditatively picking his teeth. "Them owls drove me to that hut. I 'ad no choice." He did not appear to find the event strange, just frightening and inconvenient.

"What were you doing in the forest?"

"I came to find John. 'E was supposed to sell me 'is calf."

"John? Is he tall with long black hair, dark eyes, and good-looking?"

Peter looked dubiously at Gwen. "That sounds like 'im."

"He was the one who rescued me in the flower meadows, and he rescued me again, just before the fire." Gwen could hardly keep the excitement from her voice. "Is he a friend of yours?"

"Ah, he be a friend of mine," Peter agreed, taking some pride in the obvious interest of the girl. "He lives with a witch," he added, hoping to add to the story.

"Oh," Gwen replied. She was not sure what to make of this, but so many strange things had happened that this piece of news was just one extra.

Peter was disappointed in her reaction, and continued with his story. "I saw them soldiers, and when I met John we heard ye screamin' an' he ran off. Then I be caught by the soldiers. But they didn't kill me," he paused to extract some meat from his teeth. "The leader of them soldiers, 'e was going to kill me, but I told 'im I could be useful an' he didn't kill me." He smiled at his own cleverness. "When that fire started, I 'scaped an' got lost. And that's when them darn owls found me."

"The owls are our friends," Gwen said, for the second time that night, although she could not decide how she was so sure.

"Well, I don't care for 'em," Peter said.

"What do we do when it gets light?" Gwen asked.

"I don't know. Find a place to sleep, 'an get some more food, I suppose."

"No, I don't mean that," Gwen said. She looked at Peter, searching his face, trying to understand what sort of a person he was. "I mean what are we going to do about the soldiers?"

"I ain't 'aving nothing to do with 'em," Peter said firmly.

"My father was a prisoner when the fire started. I think the soldiers could still have him." Gwen was staring hard at Peter; the whites of her eyes were accentuated in the moonlight.

"Ain't nothing to do wiv me," he said truculently.

"Then I'll go by myself."

"Where are ye going to go?"

"I don't know, but I'll find them," Gwen tried to sound confident.

"That's stupid! Ye've just 'scaped from them an' now ye wants to find them again. That's stupid."

"He's my father!" Gwen exclaimed.

"So what! I wouldn't do nothin' for mine. He 'ates me."

"My father's not like that. He risked his life trying to save me!" She began to sob loudly.

Peter was embarrassed. He was used to his mother crying, but this was different. He had never before met a girl like Gwen. There were things of which he had very little experience, and true affection was one of them. He sat picking his teeth and staring ahead. Gwen gave herself to her sorrow and in doing so allowed the memories of her recent sufferings to be washed away. By the time she had finished sobbing, Peter was fast asleep.

It was the damp cold of the early morning that caused Peter to wake up. Gwen was curled up in a tight ball; her hair covered her face. Peter stared at the cropped area in the centre of her head and vaguely wondered why it had been cut. Then he remembered. Gently he touched her shoulder.

· · ·

DAWN WAS BREAKING, WHEN Old Jude reached the foot of the higher ground. She had covered some miles in the dark, and her breathing was laboured, but she pressed on with a fanatical haste bred of greed. As the ground began to rise, the darkness faded and the first traces of iron light appeared on the horizon to her left. Birds began to stir and small creatures scampered across the path.

"Gold," she wheezed, "I'll get gold for 'er." Her eyes blazed with an unnatural brightness, and her face was grey and damp.

The path rose steeply for a few yards before opening out into a broad band of scrubland with more forest beyond. In the gathering light, she could see a blue haze of smoke curling up above the trees, indicating a number of campfires. She turned off her lamp, and clambered up the steep incline; her chest heaved painfully and her mouth was dry. As she staggered across the band of scrub, she saw two horsemen ride out of the forest about a hundred paces away. They were dressed in black.

She had found them. She would get the reward. Gold. She tried to hurry, but her legs felt like lead, and her lungs were bursting. She raised a hand to wave, and felt a hot pain shoot through the left side of her chest. She stopped moving, and her eyes bulged. She tried to speak, but no words came. With a look of astonishment on her mean face, she crashed to the ground and lay very still. Her lamp lay broken beside her.

The two horsemen cantered down the path and stopped next to the body. They regarded her unemotionally, and one of them dismounted. As she was lying face down, he turned her body over with his foot. Her eyes were staring and her mouth gaped. The soldier glanced up at his companion, shrugged his shoulders, and spat into the heather. Then, he knelt down and ripped a thin golden chain from her neck and placed it in his pouch. Uttering a humourless laugh, he grabbed her arms and dragged her off the path, and dumped her in the knee-high bushes. Without a backward glance he remounted, and the two riders rode back to their vantage point among the trees.

. . .

As DAWN BROKE IN a clearing in another part of the forest, Simon Carter, wood-carver and bow-maker, was preparing to leave home for a day's hunting, and to collect willow saplings. On his broad back he carried a leather quiver with a selection of brightly feathered arrows, and in his hand he gripped a large bow. He was reputed, at the age of forty, to be the best archer in the area, and could hit a rabbit at sixty paces, and knock a bird out of the sky.

"I'll try an' catch 'ee something for the pot on my way to the willow groves," he said. "I'll not be late."

"Good," his wife smiled at his serious face. She was a short stocky woman, with dark hair flecked with grey. "I shall be quite safe, Simon. Stop ye worrying."

"Aye, well just 'ee stay near the house, Pol'. There be strange things 'appening in these woods, and I ain't being worried for nothing. Ol' Marcus was certain he saw horse soldiers in the storm yesterday."

"So ye keep saying. Ol' Marcus is as blind as a mole, 'e wouldn't know a soldier from a poor traveller. Now get to ye work, an' leave me to mine!" She laughed. "I've been safe here these last twenty years, I reckon I'll be fine for a few more." She waved a plump brown arm and disappeared into the house.

Simon turned and tramped slowly into the forest, his feet splashing in the soggy earth. He made his way along his usual path, leading to a large grove of willows. The area was swampy, and was situated at the foot of the high ground. He was not learned, but he understood a great deal about trees and the wild life of the forest. He was known as an honest man, a good husband and a generous friend.

Normally, he was single-minded and moved methodically from one task to the next, but today he was distracted. There had been a report of a huge fire to the north and more than one report of strange soldiers in black. As he pondered on these things he became aware that something was missing. He stopped and checked his equipment.

"Well, bless me!" he exclaimed, "I've left me darn knife at home." Shaking his head, and muttering to himself, he began to retrace his steps. He had travelled about a mile from his cottage, and the sun was just beginning to rise in a cloudless sky.

He was only a short distance from his home, when he heard his wife cry out. It was a loud cry of pain and anger, and was quickly followed by a long agonising scream that echoed in the trees and was suddenly cut short.

Simon lurched down the path, his feet slipping and stumbling as he ran. Fear gripped him in an icy embrace, and the familiar path seemed unending.

"Pol! Pol!" he yelled as he came bursting into the clearing.

It all happened so fast.

There was a group of horsemen and foot soldiers dressed in black. Some had swords in their hands, others were milling about on their horses. He could see his wife lying face downwards, unmoving, in the doorway of their cottage. There was blood on the back of her dress. The soldiers had heard his approach and were already advancing towards him. Two horsemen charged down on him, their horses' hooves drummed on the damp earth. Simon raised his bow and with a quick movement of his hand unleashed an arrow that caught the first rider in the throat. The soldier rose in his saddle and collapsed over the back of the horse, his black helmet rolling into a clump of reeds.

Simon reached for another arrow, and was fitting it into his bow as the second soldier galloped up. Even as the sword arched down, Simon still attempted to draw his bow. The blade sliced into him a split moment before he could fire the arrow. Simon Carter died instantly.

• • •

JOHN WAS SOME WAY off when he heard a woman scream. It was a short cry of terror. He stopped and listened intently, trying to locate the direction of the sound. A second voice was calling a name, and John heard men yelling. He began to run through the forest in the direction of the commotion and was aware, as he did so, of the hated accents of the foreign soldiers.

A thick clump of holly barred his way and prevented him from running headlong into the clearing. Through the branches, John could see a small group of soldiers running towards a solitary archer, who had apparently killed one horse soldier, and was about to be attacked by a second. The archer was intent on drawing his next arrow when he was cut down. From the deep shadow of the forest John watched, his chest heaving, as Simon Carter was hacked to death. John felt the anger well up inside him as the soldiers cheered and kicked the dead body. But there was nothing he could do to help the unfortunate victim, and John was about to withdraw into the forest, when he noticed the woman lying in the doorway of the cottage.

At first he assumed she was dead, but as he watched he saw her hand move and her eyes blink open. She was obviously in great pain, but as her consciousness returned she began to drag herself towards a large log pile that was on John's side of the cottage.

The soldiers were about seventy paces away at the other end of the clearing, and were engaged in a spontaneous archery competition. They showed no concern over the death of their comrade, and appeared to accept dying as a natural part of their role as soldiers.

John moved quickly through the bushes, skirting the clearing, and arrived in the trees twenty paces behind the log pile towards which the injured woman was dragging herself. At the other end of the clearing the soldiers were still absorbed in their contest, using the dead man's bow in competition with their own.

Polly moved in a frantic, crab-like fashion, her knees and one elbow provided the movement, while her injured shoulder was hunched in the air. She reached the logs and squirmed into the shadows, out of sight of the soldiers, and fainted. John raced across the twenty yards that separated him from the woman and knelt down and lifted her head. She was breathing heavily, and as he tried to lift her into a sitting position, he felt the warm blood on his hand. She was quite limp, and he felt certain he could not lift her into the safety of the trees.

He checked the soldiers. They were still occupied. He tried to review his position: the woman was losing a lot of blood, and would bleed to death if the wound was not tended; yet, his position was dangerous in the extreme, and there was no way he could carry the woman any distance, if at all.

John closed his eyes and concentrated his mind on the problem. What to do? What would Old Mary have done? She would have used herbs to stop the bleeding. That was it! John realized he knew what to do. He recalled all those evenings when Old Mary had taught him the seemingly endless list of names and charms. It had been in preparation for this very situation. He gazed around and saw a leafy plant that grew in the shade of the logs, and felt instinctively that it would help.

He laid the unconscious woman face down on the wet grass, and opened the neck of her gown. There was a gash, the length of his hand, on her broad shoulder where the sword had sliced down, but the thickness of her course gown had broken the force of the blow. Although the wound was deep, it was not likely to be fatal, providing he could staunch the flow of blood. John pressed the thick green leaves against the wound and muttered the words he had been taught. There was a tingling in his hand, and the runes on his palm throbbed. He could feel a powerful current passing from his hand into the woman's shoulder, and he knew he could heal her. For the first time in his life he was using a gift he had been given, with the confidence and complete conviction of his power. This was what Old Mary had been promising: *When the time is right.*

His fingers worked quickly. He used Polly's shawl to bind the herbs to the wound and laid her gently on her back. Holding her head between both hands, he called her back to consciousness with a soft, yet persistent voice. Her eyes opened and she stared uncomprehendingly into John's face.

"You will feel no pain," he instructed. "You can walk. I will help you. You can walk if I am holding you. Do you understand?" He spoke with authority and with a quiet insistence.

She nodded slowly, and without a sound staggered awkwardly to her feet with John's arm supporting her uninjured side. The log pile was high enough for both of them to stand, yet still be hidden from the soldiers. Glancing back every few paces, John guided Polly towards the trees, keeping the log pile between themselves and the sight lines of the soldiers.

It was difficult to move through the bushes and trees without stumbling, but Polly moved on slowly without complaint, as though in a trance. John kept his hand firmly under her good arm, while holding his sword in the other. He kept glancing back, and was disturbed to see that they were leaving a clear path in the wet grass and muddy soil. When the soldiers discovered the woman was gone they would have no trouble in following her escape route. John's only advantage was that they would not be expecting him to be with her.

After a few hundred paces they came, unexpectedly, to a wide, frequently used path. There were deep wheel ruts and the impressions of numerous horses' hooves. Polly was still moving like a sleepwalker; her eyes were open but seemed fixed on some distant object a long way in front of her. John kept his hand under her arm and guided her over the path and into the shade of a dogwood thicket.

"You must sit down here, carefully," he said. "Lean your good shoulder against this stump." John manoeuvred her until she was as comfortable as he could devise, then he placed his fingers gently on her eyelids. "You will sleep now," he said, using the gentle persuasive voice he had adopted since using Old Mary's teaching. Without a murmur Polly relaxed into a deep sleep.

John walked back down the path to the place where they had emerged from the forest, and began to drag his feet across the ruts in the opposite direction to where Polly lay sleeping. It was possible that it might confuse the soldiers if they decided to give chase. He managed to cover only a few yards when he heard a sound further down the path. Was it the soldiers? John chewed his lower lip, as he stood in an agony of indecision. Finally, he stepped behind a tree moments before a lumbering hay cart moved slowly into view. From the shadows John observed it closely. It was pulled by two large, grey cobs, and was driven by an old man with an ample stomach and a bushy white beard. He wore a woven straw hat and his head drooped on his chest. He appeared to be asleep.

John stepped out in front of the horses, and they halted obediently, glad of the rest. The driver awoke instantly, and fixed a suspicious gaze on the young man who had disturbed him. His deep blue eyes widened as he saw the sword on John's shoulder.

"What d'ye want?" the old man growled.

"I need your help."

"Ye goin' to rob me?" he asked, looking hard at the sword.

"No, of course not. There's a woman over there," he said pointing down the track. "A local woman who's been hurt."

"Who's that then?"

"I don't know her name," John answered. He ran back to where Polly lay sleeping against the tree. Her injured shoulder was clearly visible, and flies buzzed around the dried bloodstains on her clothing.

"That be Polly Carter!" the old man exclaimed. He climbed down awkwardly from the cart. "What be the matter with 'er?"

John quickly explained the recent events, and described the death of Polly's husband. The old man was visibly upset, and took hold of the side of the cart to steady himself.

"Dead then?" he muttered.

"Yes. Did you know him?"

"Know him!" the old man clenched his fists. There were tears in his eyes. He fought to hold back the sobs. After a moment he whispered, "'E was me younger brother." He turned away, choking on his tears.

John was moved by the old man's sorrow, but the situation was too dangerous for further discussion. He placed his fingers on Polly's eyes and spoke gently but firmly, "Wake up, Polly. Wake up now. You will feel no pain. You must stand up."

The old man turned to watch as Polly slowly rose to her feet with John supporting her uninjured side.

"How d'ye do that?" he gasped, his emotion giving way to amazement.

"I'll tell you later. We must hide her in the wagon, and move away from here quickly. It's not safe."

The old man wiped his eyes with the back of his hand and nodded briefly. With remarkable speed for one who had appeared to be so aged, he jumped onto the wagon and began to remove some of the hay from the front of the load. It took only a few moments to create a deep hollow in the pile of hay. When he was satisfied with the depth of the hole, he helped Polly onto the wagon while John directed her movements with gentle, firm instructions. Polly behaved like a sleepwalker; she moved slowly and precisely and without any apparent interest in the proceedings. She eased herself into the hiding place and on instructions from John, closed her eyes and, once again, sank into an untroubled sleep.

"I've seen some odd things in me time, but nothin' to beat this," the old man said as he placed some hay over Polly's head. "Ye better hide that sword an' all," he added as he handed an old sack to John. They took their places at the front of the wagon, and before he gave the command to the horses, the old man turned and gave John a meaningful look. "I'm Will Carter," he said, as though that explained everything about him. "Who're you?"

"John."

"That all?"

"Yes. I was given another name, but I don't use it."

They rode on in silence with the cart bumping and creaking along the uneven track. The sun was high in the sky and the air was heavy with insects. John kept glancing back and Will did the same on his side, but there was no sign of pursuit.

"Perhaps they think that Polly crawled away and died in the forest. Maybe that's why they haven't come after us," John said.

"Maybe," Will grunted. He seemed overwhelmed with his loss. "Maybe they don't care."

After some miles, they came to a small village. "This be Reedsleigh," he muttered. The village consisted of a cluster of hovels and tumbledown thatched cottages, which enclosed an irregular green, in the midst of which children played and some cows were grazing. Smoke drifted lazily out of holes in the thatch and from crooked chimneys, and chickens scratched about below in the muddy ruts. In the open doorways grimy women prepared food or mended clothes. At one end a group of men were passing the time in idle conversation. There was a peaceful, unhurried air about the place.

Will directed the horse towards the knot of men. They stopped talking and watched, curiously, as the cart approached. John was aware that he was the focus of interest.

"They killed Simon!" Will yelled. The men were still some paces away, but the effect on the group was obvious. Their curious expressions changed to shock and anger. "Polly's 'ere in the wagon, she be hurt bad."

Will instructed the men as they carefully lifted the sleeping Polly out of the wagon and moved her into a large thatched cottage, which John understood was Will's home. Polly was laid on a rough bed of straw and a group of women hurried in with cloths, bowls and ointments. The older men assembled in the main living area, while outside the rest of the village gathered in a large murmuring crowd.

"This 'ere is John. 'E be an 'ealer," Will stated in his terse manner. He placed a strong hand on John's shoulder.

All eyes turned, once again, to John, who blushed with embarrassment. He carried the sword wrapped in the sack, and he was conscious of his youthfulness. They were all expecting him to do something wonderful, he could see it in their faces, and he realized that Will was an important man in this community. Will's hand on his shoulder was as potent as a crown on his head.

He bowed slightly and led the way into the sleeping area, where Polly lay sleeping peacefully on her side, with the damaged shoulder clearly revealed. He placed his fingers over her eyes and gently awakened her. As Polly's eyes opened there was a gasp of relief from the onlookers. John carefully removed the bindings, and undid the top of her robe revealing the thick, green leaves he had used as padding. Once again, he was conscious of the strange tingling in his right hand and of a sense of power. Slowly he removed the herbs to reveal the deep wound for all to see. There was a loud intake of air as they saw the extent of the wound, and this was followed by exclamations of wonder. The wound had healed over and the bleeding had completely stopped. Apart from the dried blood around the area, there was no redness and no sign of infection.

"I said 'e was an 'ealer," Will said, smiling around the room in a knowledgeable way. "We'll leave the rest t' the women."

The men moved back into the main area, while the women attended to Polly.

"You will feel no pain until tomorrow," John said, and gently closed her eyes. Even as he spoke the words, he wondered how he knew it to be true. He pondered this as he followed the men out of the room. Old Mary had said the power would flow when the time was right, and those who had power were like the mouths of fountains. "The power flows out and sometimes it

seems to have a will of its own. But beware you don't block it with pride."
It was a timely reminder. John promptly removed the haughty expression
that he was conscious of having adopted as he passed the line of admiring
faces. He moved to a position near the door, where he could observe the
deliberations of the elders of the village, without seeming to intrude.

Will sat in a large chair near the fireplace while the others stood or squatted
on their haunches. He described what he knew of Polly's injuries and of the
reported death of his younger brother Simon. At times his voice trembled
and he gazed around the room with wet eyes, overcome with emotion. A
number of men spoke of the late Simon Carter in glowing terms, and it was
evident Will's brother had been respected by those in the village.

Finally, there was silence, and after a suitable pause one of the older
men uttered a question that was on everyone's mind: "What we goin' t' do
then?"

A tall gangly man was the first to reply. "I reckons we find 'em foreign
soldiers, and sort 'em out." He shrugged his shoulders as he spoke and kept
raising his eyebrows in a nervous manner.

"That's all very easy t' say," a bald-headed man replied, "but we be dealing
with soldiers. That ain't easy."

"I'm not afraid of no soldiers!" a younger, good-looking man exclaimed.

"Nor me neither!" shouted a red-faced youth from the doorway.

"I'm not afraid neither, Hal!" the bald-headed man replied, looking fiercely
at the first young man. "That weren't my meanin'. The fact is there ain't
many young men in the village. Some of us," he gestured towards a group
by the fireplace, "was soldiers with the Crusade. We know what it means t'
fight soldiers. It ain't as easy as just talking about it."

"What you saying, Wilf?" the red-faced youth growled.

"Enough of this, Young Robin," Will interrupted. "We got no time for
this family feudin'. We got more important things t' do. I aim t' find these
foreigners and get me revenge. They's not going to kill me brother an' get
away with it!"

This speech was well received by most of the group, and there were
murmurs of, "We're with ye, Will."

"However," Will continued, "Hal has a good point, we don't 'ave to be
afraid of these soldiers, just careful." He ignored the red-faced Robin.

Robin glowered at Will and at the bald-headed man, but said nothing.

"'Ow can ye be sure it was soldiers did it?" All heads turned to face the speaker, a small foxy-looking man with a pointed nose. "After all," he continued, "we don't know if Simon really be dead. We only 'ave his word for it," he pointed at John. "Suppose 'e injured Polly an' made up the whole story!" He looked triumphantly about the room. Some of the others nodded in agreement.

John was speechless with indignation.

"What would 'e do that for, Dan Birch?" Will asked in a cold voice.

"'Ow should I know? Why don't ye ask 'im?" Dan said, stabbing a finger, once again, in John's direction.

"D'ye think I be stupid or somethin'?" Will replied. His voice was menacing. "I reckon I knows when someone is speakin' the truth, 'specially when 'e told me 'ow Simon was when he died, an' what the soldiers was like an' all." He paused, "also he could 'ave killed me with 'is sword if 'e had wanted to."

"What sword's this then?" Robin asked. He was still smarting from Wilf's rebuke and wanted to hit out at somebody.

"Show 'em ye sword," Will gestured towards the sack.

Reluctantly, John withdrew the sword from the sack and held it up in front of him, moving as he did so into the centre of the room. The bright light from the doorway and the flickering flames of the fire seemed to blend in an aura around the blade, giving it a strange radiance of its own. A loud gasp went up from the villagers, and they all took a step backwards.

Will was the only one who appeared to be unmoved by the experience. He sat in his chair and rubbed his nose as John lowered the sword. "Sit 'ere," he said, motioning to a stool in the recess of the fireplace. "I think the time has come for ye to tell ye story." He signalled for the door to be closed and for the assembled villagers to make themselves comfortable. There was a tense, expectant atmosphere, as each man understood this was no ordinary youth, and they were in the presence of a sword unlike anything they had ever seen. It was more than just a sword: it was beautiful and yet frightening, attractive but deadly. All their petty jealousies and feuds were forgotten, as they stared mesmerised by its strange hues.

"Now ye know why I believe 'im," Will said quietly. "Tell ye tale, John, we be ready to 'ear ye now."

John was not sure where to begin. It seemed important for these men to have some idea of the enemy they were intending to face, and he was desperate to enrol their help to search for Gwen, or if she had been recaptured, to gain her release. He decided to avoid any mention of the sign on his palm, as none had noticed it, and to concentrate instead on the strange happenings in the flower meadow, the night chase through the forest, and the fire.

"So that were thee what done that," the gangly man interrupted. "We 'eard of the fire this mornin'. They say it were a mighty big un." He coughed, shrugged his shoulders and looked embarrassed.

John described the black uniformed soldiers and the magic powers of their leader, but did not mention the strange encounter with Owl. Gwen, Tom the blacksmith, and the rescue of Polly Carter were the main parts of his story. When he finished, there was a long silence.

"Who be these soldiers then?" asked Wilf, the bald-headed man.

"I don't know," John answered. "They're not from this country. But I know their coming has something to do with the sword."

"'An the blacksmith, 'e had one as well?" Dan enquired. He stared at the sword, fascinated by its beauty.

"Yes, the leader of the soldiers has it now, and this belonged to his dead brother." He rested the sword across his knees.

There was a change in the atmosphere. The good humour and eagerness had been replaced by tenseness, as though all the room was waiting for something to happen.

"It must be worth a lot of money, with all the gold an' all," Dan Birch said. He had a voice like treacle. "More money than the whole village put together." His foxy eyes twinkled. "Perhaps we ought t' look after it for ye, it being so valuable." He winked significantly at the other two men standing with him. They had similar pointed noses. "Why don't ye let me an' my bothers take care of it for ye?" He smiled as he advanced towards John but his eyes were cold.

John sprang to his feet and raised the sword, holding the pommel with both hands. Dan suddenly found the sharp blade pointing at his stomach. He stopped, uncertain what to do. To continue forward was impossible, and to move the blade invited injury.

"Hands off, Dan," Will snarled. "The sword stays with John." He looked at the others. "Are we going t' rob him after he saved Polly's life?"

There was a loud chorus of "No!"

"Ye makin' a fool of yeself, Dan Birch," said Hal, gravely. His good looks combined with a powerful build made him an impressive figure.

Dan smiled apologetically, and held out his palms towards John. "I wasn't wantin' t' rob ye, boy. Only tryin' to 'elp." He moved back to the wall next to his brothers, laughing as though it was all a joke, but his eyes were cruel and his gaze remained fixed on the sword.

"I think this could be linked with the Crusade," Will said thoughtfully. "I think 'em soldiers be infidels. If so, they've come an awful long way." He paused and looked at John. "Could be they wants more than the sword. Could be them swords be just part of it. Whatever it be, it must be important, for they be takin' a mighty big risk. Anyways," he raised his voice, "they killed me brother Simon, an' I mean t' get me revenge. They may 'ave the girl an' all." He stood up and pulled his britches over his stomach. "Are ye all going t' lend a hand or are ye goin' to stay at home with the women?"

There was a roar of agreement led by Hal, and even the bald-headed man offered his support.

Will placed his hand on John's shoulder and led him outside. The sunlight was dazzling and the crowd looked dark in contrast. Will's cart was close to the door and he climbed up on the front and spoke to the assembled villagers.

He explained his plans clearly, but in few words. The younger boys were to fan out towards the high ground and look for any signs of the soldiers. They were to go on ahead, remain hidden and avoid any danger. The women were to arrange food for two days and be ready to defend the village if the soldiers came while the men were away. The men numbering about thirty were to collect such weapons as they had, and be prepared to travel within the hour. The plan was to march towards the high ground and hope the boys would have some news of the soldiers.

"The young 'uns be good woodsmen," Will explained as he climbed down. "If anyone can find 'em soldiers, they can."

John smiled, but his eyes were noticing many things as Will directed him back towards the house. The young boys were keen to be away, but harassed mothers were insisting on provisions, while fathers gave instructions on how to behave. The old men were giving advice to any who would listen, and the girls were being enlisted to help with the food. But even in this hubbub, John was aware that his sword was still the focus of many pairs of eyes. Some eyed it with awe, but others had expressions of undisguised greed.

Inside the house all was quiet. Polly slept peacefully, and the other women had returned to their own homes to prepare for the expedition.

Will produced a cold meal of cheese, dark bread and pickles, and this was washed down with weak beer. The two ate quickly and silently, each lost in his own thoughts.

"What will you do when you find the soldiers?" John asked.

"We'll see when we gets there," Will replied. "We needs to catch 'em by surprise if we is to 'ave a chance. Some of me neighbours be good with a bow, an' some fought with th' Crusade, but most of 'em 'ave more courage in their mouths than sense in their 'eads. There be only a few swords in the village, and hardly any spears. Wilf 'as a bit of armour, but most 'ave nothin'. They like a good scrap, but only if they be winnin'." He smiled sadly, "We be very poor really, but we'll do our best."

John stared at the dregs of his beer. "I don't think the soldiers want to fight. They seem to be looking for someone. Maybe it's Gwen. They want to get the sword back, I can feel sure of that, and..." he paused. "I think they may be looking for me."

Will looked steadily across the table at John. "Why d' ye think that?"

"Because of this." John showed Will the design on his palm. "I have the same marks as the sword." He thought of the old woman and added, "It is the mark of power."

Will said nothing, but thoughtfully swirled his beer around his mug.

"Is that how ye healed Polly?"

"Yes, I think so." John smiled self-consciously. "A few days ago I knew nothing, now I feel I know so much, and I don't know how I know it."

There was a knock at the door. "Ye ready, Will?" It was the gangly man known as Red.

"Give us a moment an' we be right with ye," Will replied. He turned to John. "If we finds 'em murderers, I knows what I got t' do. But if I goes down early in the fightin', you must take over see. That sword of yours'll act as a banner. They be good men in their own ways, but one setback an' they'll run 'ome like rabbits. Ye understand?" He gripped John's hand.

"I understand. But will they follow me?"

"Not you, John... the sword. They'll follow the sword." He paused and looked towards the door. "But when it be all over, watch ye back. Especially when them Birches is around."

Will disappeared into a dark corner and returned with a thick leather jerkin, leather gauntlets and a large old sword. It was chipped and scratched and the blade was dull.

"Not as good as yours," he said and smiled.

John smiled back, and watched as Will applied a wet stone to the edge of the blade. There was a warm bond between them, and he felt proud to be accepted by this strong old man who knew much, but said little. It was not difficult to see why he was the acknowledged leader of the villagers.

"I suppose rightly I should tell old Sir Edward what we is about," Will murmured. He worked the stone in deep thought. "However, 'e be old and not in good 'ealth, so he probably won't know until it is all over."

"Does he own this village?"

"Aye," Will nodded. "We don't see much of 'im. I attends to most of the problems, we just see 'is steward when it comes to tax days. I arranges all the work days on 'is lands."

When Will had sharpened the edge of his sword, he laid it on the table.

"Can I try ye sword for a moment?" he asked, and stretched out his hand.

Unwillingly, like a child giving up a new toy, John passed his sword to Will, hilt first. Will took the sword gently, with a kind of reverence, and held it with one hand on the golden hilt and the other supporting the flat of the blade. He examined the runes in silence and then glanced at John's palm. John realized he was standing with his right hand extended as if to catch the sword. Feeling self-conscious, he lowered his arm.

Will balanced the great sword in his strong right hand. But as he went to place his left hand on the pommel, in a two-handed grip, the sword sprang out of his hand as though on a spring and twisted in the air, the hilt facing John, the blade lancing down towards Will's chest.

It was over in a trice. Relief replaced the look of horror on Will's face, as John grabbed the hilt and stopped the forward movement of the sword, only a hand's width from Will's body. As John's right palm closed on the handle, the sword reverted back to a heavy and lifeless piece of metal, and it was hard to believe that a moment before it had possessed such energy.

In the instant of clutching the sword and preventing Will's death, John experienced a frightening sensation. He glimpsed a long, dark tunnel, down which he seemed to be flying at amazing speed towards a figure framed in a circle of orange light. The figure was huge with red hair and a face of terrifying ugliness. A vast hand reached out to grab the sword. John felt himself grip it with all his strength, and he was yelling something with great passion. There was a deafening noise and fiery flashes and a foul stench of corruption. In a moment, the horrible image was gone and John found himself alone in the silent, sunlit room.

John shook his head and rubbed his eyes with his left hand. It was some moments before he could focus. Outside, a thrush sang and excited voices called to each other. It seemed impossible to comprehend the horror he had just averted.

Will was collapsed across the table, and slowly slipped to the floor; his face an ashen grey, his eyes staring. Then, with great deliberation, like a man sleepwalking, he stood up and shuffled towards the big chair and folded into it as though his flesh was unsupported by bones. He blew out his breath in a long, tuneless whistle.

"I thought I be dead then," Will whispered.

John rubbed his forehead. Now that he had recovered himself, his mind was racing. "This sword belonged to one of the two foreigners I told you about. He died in the way you almost did." John paused. "I caused his death. I don't know how, but it was something to do with this sign on my palm, and my other name."

"Giles Plantard," Will said.

"How did you know?"

"Ye was yelling it as ye grabbed the sword." Will breathed in deeply.

"What does it all mean?"

"Seems to me ye sign and ye name be what controls the evil power in that sword."

"I had a vision of his awful face."

"The man ye killed?"

"Perhaps. But I think it was the other one, his brother. I felt his hatred and his anger; it was as though he had almost won and I stopped him."

"Why try to kill me?" Will pondered.

"Perhaps because you were holding it." John took a deep breath. "I think you are right, maybe I am the only one who can control this sword while that man lives." He looked into Will's troubled eyes. "He wants it back. I felt it in the vision."

"But he didn't succeed, did 'e?" Will stood up and rubbed his arms as though he was cold.

"Not this time," John said, "but I think he knows where it is now. You could all be in great danger."

"What will be, will be," Will said. He placed an arm on John's shoulder.

"I owe ye my life. I'll not forget." He patted John gently on the back of his head, and took up the battered sword from the table. "We got work to do," he said. He took a deep breath and, opening the door, walked out into the sunshine.

John remained alone staring at the fire. It crackled and hissed as the flames devoured the damp logs. The shimmering red heat had a hypnotic effect, and John found himself listening to a voice that gradually became indistinct. It was a sentence repeated over and over again: *You will have power some day.*

"What sort of power?" he spoke aloud to the empty room.

But there was no answer, just the sound of the burning wood. He placed the sword on his shoulder and left the house.

CHAPTER 9

T HE DAY WAS HOT and the villagers kept in the deep shade of the trees as they followed the winding tracks leading towards the higher ground. It was two hours before Will gave the order to stop. They reached a wide clearing, enclosed by tall elms, where two paths crossed at the foot of the hills. The younger men, who arrived first, were already sprawled around the bushes and propped up against the trunks; their first rush of excitement had spent itself.

"Any news?" Will asked to nobody in particular.

"Nothin'," one of the youths replied. "The young 'uns ain't returned yet."

"Who's keeping watch?" There was an awkward silence, broken only by the approach of some of the older men. A number of the youths stood up and looked at one another, waiting for someone else to answer.

"That's a good start. You all push on ahead like untrained hounds an' then you don't mount a watch. Ye could all be dead by now." Will spat forcefully into a clump of weeds. "From now on ye do as I tell ye or ye can all go 'ome. Understand?"

Nods and a few grunts followed this statement. Will waited until all the stragglers arrived, then climbed up onto a rocky ledge.

"Ye all agree to take orders from me?" Will spoke in a low voice, but one that carried over the assembled villagers.

There was more nodding of heads and muttered agreements.

"'Cos if not, now be the time to say." He paused. "Right then, this be the plan at the moment. We wait here until we get some news. When we knows where they be, then we can decide how to get even with 'em an' how to get the girl away."

"Let's just finish 'em off an' be done with," a voice interrupted. "I say we kill 'em all. I'm not afraid of 'em." The speaker, the red-faced youth who had spoken before in Will's house, looked around for support. A chorus of approval came from a small knot of other youths.

"Glad ye got so much spirit, Robin," Will answered with a tight smile. "But ye've never killed a man before. It's easier to talk about it than do it." The older men murmured their agreement. "So ye remember, ye do as I tell ye, or ye could get us all killed." He frowned. "If ye can't promise to follow me, ye better get 'ome now."

Robin pulled a face and bobbed his head about, and shifted back among his friends. He had made his statement, and the recognition was good enough for him. The fact he had lost the argument was not important.

Will posted two youths in each direction along the paths and then gathered a group of the older men together. John watched silently as Will took a stick drew a map in the dust.

"Unless I be mistaken, I think they be likely to camp in this area 'ere," he pointed to an area on the other side of the high ground. "There's a large flat area, with running water and a small lake. It be a natural defensive position, and one that can't be seen except from the top of this high ground 'ere." He pointed to the various parts of his map. "Anyone tryin' to get to it from the bottom would be sure t' be seen an' they wouldn't have a chance against 'em soldiers."

"What'll we do then?" Hal asked.

"Well, we'll wait to see if any signs of 'em be found by the lads. If 'em soldiers be camped in this place," Will pointed forcefully with the stick, "then we have no choice but to go up this side of the cliff and over the top, and get 'em from behind. They won't be expectin' us that way."

"That be if we can get up there an' all!" a voice interrupted.

There was a chorus of agreement and John quickly understood that the majority was unhappy with the plan.

"It just so 'appens I know a way up the cliff," Will said. "It 'aint easy, but I learned it off me father, an' he got it from 'is father." He stopped to let the significance of his statement sink in. "When ye look at that cliff, it looks like it ain't possible to climb it. But if I can do it, ye can all do it."

There was a general mutter of assent, but it was obvious that many of them thought it was impossible.

"Well then, we'd better wait quiet until some of the lads return. Then, we'll know if we 'ave to climb it or not." Will sat down against a tree and signalled for John to do the same.

"Why did you learn to climb this cliff?" John asked.

"'Cos there was a falcon's nest up there. We used to take a chick every year and train it. We never told nobody because they would all 'ave been wanting to take a chick." He smiled. "Every year we had a falcon we trained. It were good sport and then we would sell it to a local lord. It's been a good secret in our family."

"Now everyone will know," John said.

"Maybe. It would take a few times to get the hang of it, and it could be that if we 'ave to go up there to fight the soldiers, many of these fellows won't be going anywhere, 'cos they'll be dead."

There was a brief hubbub at the west side of the glade. Will staggered to his feet as a crimson-faced youth ran towards him.

"Ye got any news, James?" Will demanded.

"We found their camp," the youth gasped. He was hot and dripping with sweat. "The others are watching to see where they be going."

"Going?" Will exploded. "What d' ye mean going?"

"They be movin' out. We saw their guards, an' we had to stay hidden, 'cos they be very watchful." He sank down on the ground.

"Suddenly, they moved off an' we followed. They 'ad a camp over the other side of the mountain, on a high piece of flat ground. They could see everything, which is why we 'ad to stay put."

Will nodded. "I thought they'd have chosen that place."

"When they all started off, there was guards spread out at the back." James paused. "The rest of the boys is waiting at the camp site." He yawned loudly. "I didn't stop once," he added.

"Ye did well, James," Will said.

The youth looked pleased. "It were nothin' really."

"Is any one followin' them? Will asked.

"No. We thought it best to keep together an' not wander too far. Ye said we was only to find 'em."

"Ye did well," Will said. He looked at John. "Ye goin' to ask the question or shall I?"

John felt himself blushing. "Did you notice if they had any prisoners?" he asked.

"I didn't see none," James said. "But there was a lot going on and we couldn't get too close."

"Were there any women with the soldiers?" John asked.

"I don't think so," James answered. "Anyone got a drink with 'em?"

"You go and get a drink, James," Will said. "Ye did well."

As James moved away towards the other youths, Will signalled for the older men to join him.

"The soldiers be going away," Will said.

"Good riddance an' all," a voice muttered.

"So what we going to do now?" another asked.

"Well, nobody kills my brother an' gets away with it," Will said in a low meaningful voice. "I aim to follow 'em and do 'em some mischief. You going to help me?"

There was an unexpected silence. A few of the men looked awkwardly at their feet and kicked holes in the soil. Some looked uneasily at each other, all waited for someone else to speak.

The bald man called Wilf spoke first. "Well, it be like this, Will. If we had found them soldiers today and could 'ave a chance to fight with 'em, it would 'ave be fine. But if they be travellin' on, well we might be following them for days before we catch 'em, and we ain't got the food or provisions for a long campaign."

"I thought ye was my friends!" Will said. "They killed my brother! If they had killed your family I would 'ave supported you." He glared at them.

"It be different now, Will. We thought them soldiers would be staying in this area and likely attack our village. But if they be going," he paused. "Well, we got to remember they be soldiers, an' we could just be risking our lives for nothin'."

There was a general nodding of heads, and although the younger men were more inclined to continue, the older ones appeared united in their opposition. Will looked as though all the fight had gone out of him, and John was reminded he was looking at a man who was four times his age.

John had been half asleep during the previous hours. The events of the morning coupled with the long march and the heat made him feel lethargic, and he was content to follow Will and be guided by his directions and knowledge of the area. It was a welcome relief to leave the decision-making to someone else. However, in these few moments it had changed. Will had apparently lost his leadership, and nobody appeared to care that an innocent girl could still be held captive by the very soldiers who, only moments before, the villagers had been resolved to fight.

For the second time in a day, he began to feel a strange tingling feeling in his right hand holding the pommel of the sword. As his mind cleared, he felt an anger boiling up inside him like a sudden eruption of a volcano.

John held the sword above his head and advanced into the middle of the group, pushing into a number of the men and shoving them to the side. His eyes blazed and he looked stronger and taller, and much older. Many of the villagers were startled, unable to believe the change. A hush descended on the group as they stared at the raised sword. A beam of sunlight shafted through the high branches and the blade shone bright and deadly above their heads. John stood on a small mound making him taller than those around him. It was as though the sword acted as a magnet, pulling those on the ground to their feet and compelling others who would have moved away to return.

"Is this what your life has come to mean?" John demanded. "No courage, no honour, and no friendship? Can you sneak home like cowards and face the questions of your families and friends?" Some of the men shrugged their shoulders and looked at each other, but said nothing.

"You will not be able to sleep easy in your beds knowing you refused to help Will avenge his brother's death." John's voice was deeper and had a ring of authority. "We must follow these murderers and punish them. Each of you must do your bit. No one must be allowed to be a coward. You must support each other!" He paused, aware that all eyes were fixed on the dazzling blade he held above his head. "Will you join me?"

There was a chorus of agreement. Many of the men began slapping each other on the back and puffing out their cheeks; the talk was animated and optimistic. Once again the change had been mercurial. John was reminded of a bright day when the sun dips momentarily behind a cloud and everything looks dark and threatening until the light breaks through once more.

"Ye did well, John," Will said quietly.

•   •   •

THE GROUND WAS A long way down, and the steep summit of the cliff stretched up into a sky of cloudless blue. The air was thick with buzzing insects and whirling swallows; while high above, a solitary kestrel hovered, its keen eyes observing the gradual progress of the climbers as they snaked their way up the rock face.

Will climbed with a slow precision, and John concentrated on following each movement. It was the first time in his memory that he had climbed a rock face, and he found it both exciting and strangely relaxing. At the start there was a feeling of unreality, as the cliff appeared to be insurmountable. But Will led the group to a small rocky outcrop and pointed out a series of ledges and depressions, and the climb began.

As they ascended, more handholds appeared and the climb, while physically demanding, was not beyond the ability of any of them. "The big thing is not t' look down," Will said as he slowly heaved a leg up to the next ledge. "Just keep ye eyes looking up, and ye'll soon be at the top." He paused to catch his breath. "This'll make a young man of me yet."

The rock was rough and warm to the touch. Small dry plants and grasses grew in every niche and cranny on the steep surface. Overhead larks screamed in the still air and the sun shone down mercilessly. However, in spite of the heat, John felt strong and optimistic. The sword was strapped across his back and, as he climbed, he sensed its energy seeping into his body.

Each villager followed the steps of the man in front, and from a distance the line of bodies looked like a strange snake wriggling its way up the almost vertical side of the hill. When it was the turn of the last man to begin the climb, he placed his hands on the rock and, uttering a deep sigh, he lowered his head and closed his eyes. He was still in this position when Will and John reached the safety of the cliff top.

"The man you called Young Robin is still at the bottom," John said, as he peered over the edge at the struggling line of men.

"Ah, he would be an' all," Will gasped as he hauled the next man onto the hilltop. "Got no head for heights, that one."

"He's good at boasting, but not much use when it comes to really doing something," the first man agreed. He took over the role of helping the climbers over the edge.

Will lay on his stomach and stared down at the lone figure at the foot of the cliff. "He could be useful all the same," he said.

"Hi! Young Robin!" Will called. "I got an important task for ye!"

The young man looked up, squinting into the bright sky. "What?"

"I wants ye to go back to the village an' tell 'em what's happened!"

Robin dropped his head and kicked the earth with his feet. He seemed to be disgusted with his role as messenger.

Will took a deep breath. "Ye'll be in charge until we gets back!"

There was an instant reaction from below. Robin straightened up and adopted an aggressive stance.

"Are ye up to it? 'Cos we're counting on ye!"

"Don't ye worry about nothing!" Robin yelled. "I'll look after everything until ye all gets back. Ye can all count on me." He began to walk backwards waving to the men on the hilltop. "I'll be in charge!" he shouted, and at that moment tripped over a rock.

A great roar of laughter arose from the men on the top, and those who were still climbing smiled, in spite of their exertions. Robin jumped to his feet and waved as though nothing had happened. He ran towards the trees and disappeared from view.

"I just hope the village be still in one piece when we returns," one man jested. Only a short while before, he had arrived breathless with the message, and now he stood on the cliff's edge gazing down contemptuously at the trees below. He seemed to be in excellent physical shape.

"I don't think we have to worry, James," Will replied. "Hal's pretty wife won't allow Robin to get up to much!" Hal gave a broad grin.

"I think he got the worst end of the job," another youth commented. "All those women, an' only he to look after 'em!"

"Oh ah? Ye've a lot to learn, young fellow," Will winked at the older men. They all laughed.

While the last of the group were completing the climb, John tried to get his bearings. In front was the steep drop of the cliff and below, winding its way through the forested slopes, was the path that led back to Will's village. The sun had passed its zenith and was slightly to his left. In front was where the sun would set and north was to his right. He turned to face south, and his eyes followed the line of the escarpment, as it curved round to the south east.

"If we move on quickly we could reach the place where they've been camping," Will said. "An' if we can get there before late afternoon, we might still be able t' follow their tracks. Who knows? We may be able to find where they be camping tonight. What d' ye think, John?"

John nodded slowly. He felt pleased with the climb and with his new-found authority. He was in charge, and it felt right. He walked to the place where they had all scrambled over the edge, and turned to face them. A full step back and he would fall to his death; the danger excited him. The men were gathered in an uneven circle: some were lying on their backs; a few were standing; most were sitting on rocks. John positioned himself so that he had the sun on his back and the men had to shield their eyes to look at him. He held up the sword and light danced along both sides of its blade. It was hypnotic.

"You have all done well. Something to tell your children about."

There were some smiles and a few murmured comments.

"You can be heroes if you wish. Today is your chance to prove your manhood. Will knows the way to the soldiers' camp. We know they will have left, but I feel sure we can follow them." John felt it was true, he could follow them; he could do anything with the sword in his hand. He did not feel like a young man talking to older and more experienced men. He was their leader. He had the sword and he felt the power.

"I will lead you to the soldiers. We will march most of the night if we have to, and I will find their new camp. We will attack them while they sleep and with this sword I will win."

"We shall all win," Will added. He spoke quietly but firmly. "I wants me own revenge for the death of me brother."

John bit his lip and gave a weak smile. "You and I together," he waved his free hand, "will beat these soldiers, whoever they are. You are all brave men."

John hesitated. He felt he had lost his way. Until Will's quiet correction, John had been confident in his own ability to decide everything. Now, after that emphatic *We*, John was forced to review what he had said. Old Mary had given him a warning about this, but he could not remember what it was.

"There should be good pickings, when this be all over," Dan Birch called out. "Just think of them horses and I bet there be gold with 'em as well. We'll all be rich."

"'An' they has weapons as well. They'll fetch a tidy penny."

Everyone began to talk excitedly, and John stood alone on the rim of the cliff trying to remember something that a part of his mind refused to accept. He lowered the sword and gazed sadly at the ground.

Near his feet was a round flat stone that shone in the sunlight. John allowed his eyes to trace out the contours of the stone. It was like a face. The eyes formed first, green mocking eyes, and then the wide sensual mouth, with a flicking tongue. A large hooked nose developed, there was a lurid scar on the cheek and red hair framed a broad forehead. The mouth opened wider, and amid a forest of yellow broken teeth it formed a soundless scream of fury and hatred. John took an involuntary step back.

"Look out!" The cry brought him to his senses. He had one foot on the rock and the other was stepping back into the void. A strong pull yanked him forward, and John was catapulted over the round stone and onto a rough patch of shale in front of the nearest of the villagers. As he fell, he had a fleeting glimpse of the stone's face changing from exaltation to frustrated rage.

He staggered to his feet fighting waves of fear and nausea. He dropped the sword, and it lay a few feet away, glinting in the bright light.

"That was a close one. Ye nearly fell over the cliff." It was Will's voice. "If I hadn't got ye, that would have bin it. Ye want to take more care!"

"Thank you. I... I don't feel well." He ran awkwardly towards a patch of scrub and was very sick. The villagers had stopped talking and laughing and were regarding him with a mixture of genuine concern tinged with disdain. This was not how a leader behaved.

"Perhaps I should look after this until ye feel a bit better," Dan Birch said, as he reached out towards the sword.

"Don't touch it!" Will shouted. "Leave it be!" He rushed forward and placed his foot on the sword.

Dan's hand still reached for the hilt. He could not control the desire to hold it. His fingers touched the metal as another metal point forced his hand away. He looked up to see Will's sword pressing down on him.

"I said leave it be," Will growled. "Ye don't know how dangerous this is. It's not just a sword. I know what I be talkin' about."

"What are you then? His nursemaid or something?" Dan turned towards his brothers and the younger men. "He's gone soft in the head," he indicated Will with a contemptuous thumb. "I just 'ope your precious John can use that sword when the time comes, that's all I hope." He turned his back on Will and stalked off to stand by himself, looking at nothing in particular.

"Ye feeling better?" Will asked when John returned.

"Yes," John said. He picked up the sword and then went back to look at the round stone. It was just an ordinary stone. He kicked it with his foot.

"Ye ready to move on?" Will asked.

John nodded. He wanted to tell Will about the face and to try to explain what had happened. "You saved my life."

"'Makes us equal," Will replied. "Best hold tight to ye sword."

Without any comment the group moved off with John and Will in the front and the rest of the men, in small groups, followed behind.

"When we get to the soldiers' old camp, ye better take over again," Will said. "Ye'll need to get some fire in their bellies if we is to get 'em to follow the soldiers." He paused, "You were making a good speech up there and then something happened."

"I know," John said, "I did something wrong. It's not easy. I… I feel something is trying to destroy me, and yet I know that something else, something powerful, is looking after me. I don't seem to have much control over anything. I'm like a ball being thrown between two sides. I feel powerless." He squinted up at the sun as if searching for an answer; the horizon was obscured in a heat haze.

The journey across the hilltop and down to the high flat area Will had described, took less time than expected. It was only mid-afternoon when they arrived. The sun was still high in the sky and although hot and thirsty, the villagers were in good spirits. To many of them, this was the biggest adventure they had ever experienced.

They followed a winding track down to the open grassy plateau where the soldiers had recently camped. Just before they reached the level ground, John noticed a fox lying dead under a small bush. The animal's body was very swollen and its fly-covered eyes bulged out of its small skull. The mouth was gaping, revealing sharp, white teeth and jaws locked in a ferocious smile. It seemed an unusual way to die.

John dismissed further thought on the subject when Will called back to the others. "They been here an' all. Look at this!"

There was plenty of evidence of the recent occupation: smouldering campfires, horse droppings and the general mess that is caused by a large group of people.

"They was in a hurry to leave," Will said. "Perhaps they 'ad a hunch we was after 'em."

"They know we are," John said. The face in the fire and then in the stone had convinced him that the leader of the soldiers knew exactly where to find him. "I don't think they are concerned about us, it is something else that is causing them to hurry."

"Do ye think we can catch up with them?" Will's eyes were red with fatigue and his broad shoulders drooped.

"We have to. They have the blacksmith's daughter. I have to rescue her, and you," he touched the old man on the arm, "have a score to settle with them." John smiled encouragingly. He was feeling strong again. His mind was clear and the sword was, once again, feeling powerful in his grasp.

"There's water over here!" John called to the straggling men. He led the way to a deep pool that was fed by a small trickle of spring water that flowed down the rock face. He bent down to take a drink when something prevented him from dipping in his hand.

"Keep away!" he yelled to two of the villagers who had also bent down to drink. They looked up, surprise and irritation on their faces. "The water is poisoned! Keep away!"

He turned to the rest of the men who were shambling up to the pool. "The water has been poisoned by the soldiers. You must get water from the cliff." The men looked baffled and some stared at the pool, while others walked quickly to the side of the cliff to quench their thirst.

"How did ye know?" Will asked.

"Did you see the dead fox back there? I felt something was wrong, and as I bent down to drink I saw dead frogs at the side of the pool." He pointed to two small bloated bodies that lay nearby.

"Those murderin' heathens!" Will exploded. "They could 'ave killed us all." He stared at the frogs. "What a way to die."

They both walked over to the cliff and cupped their hands under a ledge to catch the water. When they had drunk they moved back towards the pool.

"Will, call the men over here. We need to discuss what we should do." It still felt strange giving an order to a man who was so much older and more experienced.

"Discuss?" Will echoed. "Ye don't want to discuss it too much. Most of them will be glad to do as ye tell them. Those that have a mind of their own will offer advice anyway. So ye tell 'em what ye think and let's see what happens."

He knew Will was right. Up on the edge of the hill John had felt convinced of his own abilities. But his near escape from death and the nagging warning of Old Mary, which was still hovering on the rim of his consciousness, had reduced his confidence. Now, however, he must provide the leadership if they were to have a chance of rescuing Gwen. He found himself smiling whenever he thought of her, and was determined to see her again.

As Will collected the men together, John held the sword with both hands and pointed it at the deep blue sky. Very slowly he began to turn in a continuing circle. He closed his eyes and concentrated on the soldiers and their leader. As he revolved, John imagined them as they had been when he had started the fire. He remembered the faces of the two soldiers who had nearly killed him when he was with Owl. He thought of Gwen and the touch of her hand as he had guided her through the bushes

The vision came quickly in a sudden flash of brightness. There was a river and a large flat boat. He could see the soldiers, they were hurrying down a wooded path. There was a house on fire. It was night and there was a lot of water. He could see Gwen… then the darkness was everywhere.

"Ye ill again?" It was Will's voice.

John opened his eyes. He was lying on his back on the grass with the sword clasped in both hands. The men were gathered around looking down at him. It was as though he was in a well and the faces were peering in.

John bounded to his feet. He was breathing quickly and his eyes were very bright. It was a sign. This was what he had needed to give him the confidence that had been lacking all afternoon.

"I know where the soldiers are!" he announced. The men looked at each other and some pulled faces. "I have just had a vision."

"I think ye've had too much sun," Dan muttered. Only his brothers laughed.

"Is there a river crossing near here with a large flat boat?" John asked. His gaze searched the faces.

"Ah, there is indeed," said a tall man with a thin brown beard. "That be Potter's Crossing. I went there last year." He turned towards the other men. "My cousin in Broadleaf was gettin' married, so I went over the river at Potter's Crossing. Cost I a half penny it did."

"Is it far?" John asked.

"We should get there 'fore supper time, if we gets a move on."

"Can ye guide us from here, Ben?" Will asked

"I reckon so," Ben replied.

"What if the soldiers 'aven't gone that way?" Wilf asked.

"We shall follow their tracks," John said, "and Ben will tell us if they are heading in that direction. I am certain they are."

"Did ye see this in ye vision?" Dan jeered.

"If it weren't for him ye would have drunk that water, Dan Birch, and at this moment ye would be a swollen corpse," Will said fiercely. "If he says he had a vision of Potter's Crossin', I believe him."

"We're going to Potter's Crossing," John said. He raised the sword above his head. "If any of you would rather go home to the women and join Robin, you can do so. But from now on we must be prepared to fight and there is no place here for cowards or those who want to cause trouble. Lead on, Ben!"

His determination and strength of purpose had returned and the effect on the other men was quickly apparent. As John moved off down the slope towards the forest, the rest followed, leaving Dan and his two brothers standing near the pool. After shrugging their shoulders the brothers joined the tail end of the group.

"Hi! Wait for me! What's the hurry?" Dan called after them.

The men walked briskly in small groups towards the cool shade of the trees. The trail left by the soldiers was easy to follow.

"I don't think Dan thinks much of 'im," Ben said, as he walked next to Will. He nodded his head towards John who was striding out ahead.

"I just 'opes Dan don't do nothin' stupid, that's all. Them Birches have always been a pain in the arse," Will replied. He smiled at Ben. "However, I be looking forward to catchin' up with them soldiers. They'll know the mistake they made when they killed me brother."

CHAPTER 10

WHEN GWEN AWOKE SHE was cold and she ached all over. She shivered violently and tried to stand up. Her left leg gave way under her and she fell to the ground and gave a cry of pain. Peter sat up with a start; he had been dozing fitfully since first light.

"'All right?"

"Yes. It's my leg, it's numb." She began to rub the circulation back into the limb. "I feel cold and damp. We must get moving and find some place to dry our clothes and get some warm food."

"I be cold as well, an' my leg hurts all the time." Peter got to his feet and began to beat his arms across his thin body. "Still I've 'ad worse nights."

"You have?" Gwen's voice was full of disbelief.

"There 'ave been many nights when I 'ad to sleep outside after my farder beat me." He rubbed his twisted leg.

"Beat you?" Gwen could not imagine such behaviour from a father. Tom Roper had never raised his voice to her, let alone hit her. "That must have been awful," she murmured.

"Oh it weren't that bad," Peter said, enjoying her attention. "I got used to it." He tried to think of something brave to tell her. "I used to get rats walk all over me."

Gwen shuddered. "What about your mother?"

"She was afraid of 'im. 'E would beat her something rotten." He yawned. "I 'ope 'e's dead."

"You mustn't say such things," Gwen said. She rose unsteadily to her feet. "You must not wish anybody dead."

"Why not then?" Peter protested. "Ye would wish 'im dead if 'e was ye farder."

"I wouldn't!" Gwen spoke sharply. "There must be some good in him."

Peter laughed scornfully. "Huh! What do ye know about anything! You've

129

'ad it soft! All ye life ye've 'ad it soft." He hobbled about in front of her, like an ugly gnome, his grimy face creased in an angry grimace. "Ye've 'ad it soft!" he bellowed, jabbing a dirt-encrusted finger at her. "Ever since ye were given to 'em!"

"What do you mean given?" She had been in the act of walking away from Peter's unpleasant display, but now she faced him defiantly.

Peter looked sheepish. "It's what me mother said. That's all."

"What did you mean?" She spoke with icy calmness, and her dark eyes bore into his. She took a sudden step towards him, and Peter, realizing she was taller than he was, backed away, tripped over a clump of ferns, and fell sideways in a tangle of limbs. "It's not my fault," he whined. "Me mother said it."

"Said what?" She was standing over him. He felt utterly demoralised.

"Alright," he gasped. "Me mother said we was not to speak of it, 'cos Tom Roper's wife, ye mother," he added quickly, "she weren't able to have no children. Then sudden-like she 'ave a baby, just like that, 'cept it were not a baby she 'ad but a child more like."

"A child? What do you mean?"

"Thee! It were thee that suddenly came. But ye weren't hers, ye was given to 'er, an' ye farder," he swallowed, "he ain't ye farder neither. Ye was given to 'em."

"I don't understand you," Gwen said and moved away from him. But, even as she spoke, she recalled a number of things that had seemed strange at the time, but which she dismissed as merely curious or unimportant. She had always felt a distance between her mother and herself. As a young girl she sensed she was different to the other children: always leading the games or remaining happily aloof when it suited her.

Sometimes, she had seen the older women staring at her and then turning away, and the old priest treated her with a particular deference that he did not show to the other young people in the village. Brother Matthew taught her to read Latin and to write with a quill, and corrected her village speech, insisting that she pronounced words as he did. Her father never objected to the special attention the old priest lavished on her, and she assumed Brother Matthew was lonely and that the other young people of the village were not interested in learning. But now? Her thoughts were in a whirl.

"It was a secret, see," Peter continued. He stood up slowly. "I were told not to say nothin'. All our village knew about it, but it sort of got forgotten. I only remembered it just then," he added weakly.

"What else do you know?" her voice sounded strangely distant.

"Well, one day, a while back now, I heard some talk about how ye was brought by a lot of horsemen in the night."

"Who were these horsemen?" Gwen insisted.

"I wasn't told," Peter looked sullen.

Gwen looked at his truculent face and knew she would get nothing more from him if she remained angry. With a great effort she smiled, her wide soft lips framing her white teeth, "I didn't mean to frighten you."

"Frighten me? It'd take more than a girl to frighten me." He straightened his shoulders and tried to look taller, but his face relaxed.

"It's just," she paused, "you gave me a shock." She wiped her eyes.

"There were something else," Peter said reluctantly. He dug his foot into the ground. "They say in the village that them horsemen were knights, and that ye was important to 'em. They said ye was special."

"Special?"

"They said ye was different to the rest of us."

"How am I different?" Gwen spread her hands. "Do you think I'm different?"

"Well, I don't know." Peter looked embarrassed. "Ye're better lookin' than them other girls in the village."

Gwen looked away and took a deep breath. "Do you remember anything else that was said. Anything at all?"

Peter searched his memory. This had been his longest conversation with a girl of his own age. He felt light-headed, and his ears were burning. He wanted to please her, to be her friend. "This be yours?" He produced a silver bracelet from under his shirt. "I found it in 'er cottage on the table with the meat and bread." He looked strangely shifty.

"It's mine!" Gwen laughed delightedly. "I never thought I'd see it again." She wondered why he had kept it hidden for so long, but was grateful to get it back. "Thank you." She slipped it back on her arm. "Do you know anything else?" She smiled encouragingly.

"There was some talk about ye being from some foreign place."

"Did anyone say where?"

"I don't think so." He scratched his ears with both hands. "Oh, now I remember, they said ye came from where ye farder, well, Tom Roper, went to fight. With them Crusaders."

Gwen was confused. Nothing seemed real any more, and yet everything Peter said had a ring of truth to it. Her skin was darker than the other girls, even in winter. Her hair was blacker, and her eyes were dark brown. Most of the other girls were shorter and stockier, with brown or red hair and blue or green eyes. She was different, there was some truth in that. She had perfect teeth, almost unknown in the village, and unlike the other young people, she did not have lots of relatives. Most families were related, but she had no uncles or aunts and no grandparents, in fact other than the Ropers, she had no family. Tom had explained that he and Elizabeth were the only surviving children in their families and that their parents were dead.

"If Tom Roper is not my father, then who is?" Gwen whispered.

"Well, ye can 'ave mine any day," Peter said. He shrugged. "I thinks we should be on our way."

"Do you know where we are?" Gwen asked. Her voice sounded distracted.

"No," Peter said, as they began to walk down the brightening path. "But if we follow this, we'll be sure to get to somewhere. Then we can get somethin' to eat. I be real hungry."

· · ·

The village of Nether Burstock was nestled in a hollow between two low hills. In the centre of the village was the usual green, which served as the market place and a grazing area for sheep and cattle. The houses lining the road were mainly small, wooden structures with thatched roofs and few windows. The only two buildings with any sense of permanence were the stone church, situated on one of the two hills, and an inn named The Wild Boar.

"I hopes to meet my husband there," Martha said, pointing to the inn. "That be the place where the merchants stay. There's an annual fair what lasts two days. The first is today."

Tom turned to watch the activity on the village green. Many stalls were already set up and others were being hastily erected. Dozens of people were bustling around, and the early morning air was full of calls and yells as instructions were issued and misunderstood. Behind the stalls was an area where the animals were to be sold, and a series of makeshift pens had been constructed in which sheep, cows and pigs complained loudly. Horses were tethered to long poles and chickens peered anxiously from woven straw cages. Everywhere there was movement and colour, and Tom felt an odd sense of security. So many people. Yet, it was only yesterday, and but a few miles away, when he had felt so alone.

"I'll stop over here." Martha manoeuvred the horse towards a huddle of similar wagons parked close to the inn. As she did so, a short, thick-set man with a bald head appeared from behind one of the wagons and began to wave vigorously in their direction.

"Who's that?" Tom asked.

"That be my Uncle Abel," Martha said. A big smile spread across her face. "I haven't seen 'im for a while. I'm glad he's here."

"Well now, Martha!" Abel said. He possessed a loud, deep voice and merry eyes. "How's my favourite girl?" He lifted her out of the wagon and embraced her warmly.

"Put me down! Put me down! Everyone will be watching."

Tom could tell she was pleased by the attention. He jumped from the wagon and stood behind Martha. Abel's eyes grew wide as the huge stranger appeared behind his niece.

"This here is Tom Roper. He be the smithy in Woodford. Tom, this be my Uncle Abel."

"Any friend of Martha's is a friend of mine," Abel replied. He clasped Tom's hand in a firm handshake. Then Abel's smile faded and he looked uncertainly at Martha. "Does Sam know?" he asked, nodding at Tom.

"Ye should be ashamed of yourself," Martha laughed. "Tom fixed my wheel for me. He's a good man who be searching for his lost daughter."

Abel looked so relieved that Tom had to smile. "If you'd introduce me to Martha's husband and then to as many of your friends as you can," Tom said. "I needs to find out news about some foreign soldiers that 'ave taken my daughter Gwenny."

"Soldiers in black uniforms?"

Tom nodded. "A big group of 'em."

"We've all heard of 'em," Abel said. His bushy black eyebrows knitted in a frown. "They say a lot of people have been killed by 'em. Nobody knows who they be, but some reckons they comes from the 'Oly Land."

"Why do they reckon that?" Tom asked.

"'Cos some claim they seen soldiers like 'em when they was with the

Crusade. Beats me why they should come all this way. It's not as though they have enough men to capture anything."

"I think they've come to capture people or maybe just get back certain things that was stolen from 'em," Tom answered. He rubbed his thick beard thoughtfully.

"Aye, well, there be a lot of people who'd like to hear your story, and some who may be able to help you find them soldiers. Ye say they got your daughter?"

Tom nodded. "I think so. It may be she escaped, but I don't want to take no chances."

"Right then. Ye come with me, and I'll get ye something to eat." Abel indicated the inn. "Martha, if you stay with the wagon, I'll tell Sam ye be here." He smiled at her, "Sam's done well with his weavin', he's sold almost all of it."

• • •

BY MIDDAY, TOM FELT like a new man. He had eaten a good meal, drunk a tankard of ale, and spoken to a number of men who claimed to know something of the progress of the soldiers. Martha's Uncle Abel was particularly keen to help and he spent the morning spreading the word. It became clear to Tom that many of the people were related or long-time friends, and for this reason he was quickly accepted. They were strong, cheerful men who possessed a variety of skills, but the man who impressed Tom the most was Martha's clever husband Sam.

"Normally I would never have left my wife by herself," Sam said, as he and Tom walked together near the village stream. "I certainly would not have done so if I had known about those soldiers." Sam was an unusual man, for although he was average height and slim build, what made him different was that he could read and write and speak Latin, and he used none of the local mannerisms in his speech. Tom discovered, from Abel, that Sam had been a novice monk, but had somehow managed to leave the order.

"What will you do now?" Sam asked as they crossed some stepping stones over the shallow stream.

"I mean t' buy a horse and some supplies and set out after 'em," Tom said. "I 've got me strength back now, and if you and Abel can set me in the right direction, I hopes to track 'em down."

"By yourself?" Sam was so startled that he stepped into the water.

"There be no reason for anyone else to get involved," Tom said gravely.

Sam sat down on the bank and took off his wet boot. "I have heard that old Sir Percival has gathered some of his soldiers and peasants and has marched towards the coast in the hope of catching the foreigners."

"Is 'e the local lord in these parts?" Tom asked.

"One of them. His lands stretch to the south and west of here. I think he sees this as a small raiding party from abroad, and his main concern is protecting his villages. If he finds that the soldiers have moved out of his area, he'll not waste time and money chasing after them." Sam pulled on his boot, and stood up as Abel approached from the inn. "What news, my friend?"

"The latest report from a forester, is them soldiers be making for Potter's Crossing." Abel's face was flushed with beer.

"Where's Potter's Crossing?" Tom asked.

"It's a ferry across the river Avon, south and east of here," Sam replied.

"'Ow long would it take to get there?" Tom was adjusting his belt as he spoke.

"By horse, you could reach it by nightfall," Sam paused, "if you knew the way." He stressed the *if*. "But, without a guide you could take days. There is thick forest to the south of here, and even the cleared ground is easy to get lost in. Near the ferry there are marshes, and if you lose the path you could be in trouble."

"An' that don't take no account of robbers, an' there be some of them around 'ere," Abel added.

Tom's mouth went down at the corners. "Well, I'll just have to try. That be all I can do. I can't risk them taking Gwenny." He began to walk towards the fair. "Perhaps ye could show me an honest horse trader, and I'll be on my way."

"Just a moment, Tom," Sam said. "I owe you a favour, and Abel here would like a bit of excitement. We'll come with you."

"I couldn't let ye do that," Tom said. He stopped walking and looked down on his two friends, who barely reached his shoulder. "You're both family men, and this is not your fight. I've bin a soldier, I can look after myself. I can't ask ye to come with me." He pushed out his lips and looked severe.

Sam clasped Tom's hand. "You haven't asked us. We've made up our own minds. We may not be trained soldiers, but we can show you the way." He smiled. "Able has something to tell you."

"There be a few others who want to come with us," Abel said proudly. "A friend of mine is willing to lend you a horse, and the rest of us can get hold of one an' all."

Tom stared hard at them both, then his large face relaxed. "Well, I…" he stammered. "I thank ye both." His expression became fierce again. "But I have money, and I'll pay for the horse," he paused, "an' anybody else's horse as well… an' we'll need weapons and supplies."

By mid-afternoon Tom, Sam and Abel and four other men were trotting out of Nether Burstock heading south. Each man had a sword and one carried a bow. The sun was still high and the day was hot and dusty. As they moved off, Martha stood beside her wagon holding Joan's hand and waving.

"Will father be long?" the little girl asked.

"No, my love," Martha replied brightly, "he'll be back in no time."

As they watched the men disappear in a cloud of dust, Martha sucked on her lower lip and tried to keep the tears from her eyes.

· · ·

Tom and his six companions rode hard for two hours before Abel called a halt near a small river. It was late afternoon and still hot. Each man was covered in grime and those who had been riding near the back were unrecognisable: their sweaty faces were caked in grey dust, and only their eyes seemed to have any colour. Each rider had wound some material around his head to protect his mouth and nose, but the fury of the gallop had loosened the makeshift masks, and the dust had found its way into their mouths, noses and eyes.

"We'll stop here for a while and freshen up," Abel gasped.

Without comment the men fell from their saddles and led their frothing horses down to the water.

"Don't let 'em drink too much at first," Abel ordered.

The horses were carefully watered and tethered to bushes. After removing their clothes, the men waded slowly out from the bank and sank into the shallow river, letting the slow current wash over them. The cool water was reviving, and gradually they began to think again.

"I work with horses all the time, but I never gets time to ride one," Tom said. "I reckon I'm going to be mighty sore tomorrow." He stepped awkwardly out of the river, trailing streams of water as he staggered towards his clothes.

"That were some ride," one of the men commented. "I ain't ridden like that for many a moon."

"Never at all, more likely," another answered playfully.

"You certainly set a hard pace, Abel," Sam said. "I'm just thankful I've been on a horse in these past weeks."

Abel pulled on his smock and wiped his face with the back of his sleeve. "Well, we've made good time," he said. "If we press on, we should make the crossing before dark."

The men gathered round as Abel began to draw in the dust with a stick. He drew a cross and a few feet away he traced out a long line with a small cross half way down.

"This is us here," Abel said, pointing to the first cross. "This is the river, and here's Potter's Crossin'." He began to make marks close to the river line. "This here's the marsh, and this is the main road to the Crossin'. He drew another line from the first cross towards a place below the marsh. "We can get to the Crossin' by a small path that takes us through the marsh. If we takes this way then nobody will be expectin' us." He nodded meaningfully to the others and touched his nose with his forefinger.

"I said he was worth his weight in gold," Sam said, and patted Abel on the back. "Tom, if those soldiers plan to cross the river tonight, we may yet be able to stop them. Lead on, Abel. We'll follow you!"

CHAPTER 11

THE ROUGH PATH WOUND on interminably. Tall trees on either side provided soothing shade from the sun, but the insects were numerous and their loud humming was almost threatening.

"There be more bugs here than in Woodford, that's for sure," Peter, said as he slapped his hand against his cheek.

"I wish I was back there," Gwen said. "This path doesn't seem to lead anywhere."

"I'm glad I'm not back at Woodford. There be nothin' for me there. Besides," he paused, "this ain't so bad really."

"I'm not sure what's good about it either," Gwen said. She was hungry, tired, and her joints were stiff from lying on the hard ground.

"Well, we'll be sure to meet someone soon, or reach a house maybe." He spoke cheerfully and, in spite of his limp, he seemed to have no trouble maintaining a steady pace.

Peter was not in the habit of examining his feelings, but he was aware of a new-found sense of purpose. He was free of the burden of his family and he had spent many hours with a pretty girl, for the first time in his life. Other than his sisters, he had never had the opportunity to talk to girls, and had viewed them with a mixture of suspicion and disdain. He had always been conscious of his limp, and the domination of his father had prevented Peter from having much spare time to indulge in idle conversation. Now everything was different, and he felt more confident and self-assured. He wanted, more than anything, to impress Gwen and to be able to continue their journey together, wherever the route might take them.

The path had gradually sloped up to higher ground, and as they trudged over the brow of a small hill they could see, below them, a stream flowing into a small pond. The flowing water had kept the surface relatively clear, apart from some rushes at one side.

"I could do with a drink," Peter said.

"Oh, yes," Gwen murmured, "and a chance to wash."

"Wash?" Peter echoed. It did not seem like a normal thing to do.

When they reached the stream, Peter lay on his stomach and stuck his head in the cool water, and drank noisily. Gwen knelt down and sipped the water from her cupped hands.

"You stay here," she said to Peter. "I'm going to the other side of the pond by the rushes. Don't look until I tell you."

Peter sat on the side of the pond with his feet in the water, watched the iridescent dragonflies and pretended not to look. He saw Gwen disappear behind the rushes, and after a few moments there was a splash.

"You can look now!" Gwen called from the middle of the pond. Her long black hair was plastered to the sides of her head, apart from the short piece on top, which stuck up. Her oval face and slender neck were deeply sun tanned and contrasted with the light brown of her shoulders. "Come on in – it's wonderful."

"I don't think so," Peter said, splashing his feet. He was feeling uncomfortable and yet strangely excited.

"Come on! It's so cool."

"I can't swim."

"It's only deep in the middle, you can wade in from the stream end."

"No, I don't want to. Thanks all the same." As she swam towards him he stood up and stared down at her. The water was clear with a greenish hue, and her long lean body was clearly outlined.

"Well, at least wash yourself…" she paused when she saw him staring at her, and with a quick movement turned around and swam leisurely away to the other side of the pond.

Peter stood watching her, conscious of burning cheeks and a pounding heart. Bravado and fear struggled within him. When she disappeared into the rushes he sat down moodily and tried to drown the water midges with his feet.

He was still sitting there when she reappeared. Her blue gown was hitched up above her knees, and her hair was piled up in a loose knot on top of her head. In her cupped hands she carried wild raspberries.

"Would you like some?"

"Uh, no. Well, yes, thanks." He felt himself blushing again.

139

She did not appear to notice, and they sat looking at the pond and eating the fruit. "It was lovely in the water, you missed something special."

Peter was sure he had, but was unable to answer. "We'd better get going," he said gruffly. As he stood up, he looked down at Gwen's cropped hair and had a vision of her in the water. He blew out his cheeks and made a puffing sound. Then he walked awkwardly towards the path.

Gwen stood up and followed him, a small smile played around her mouth and she shook her wet hair from side to side.

Soon, they came to a larger track and while they were debating which way to go, a man greeted them. He was sitting on an old cart pulled by two tired horses. It was a wide vehicle with a broad seat in the front and a pile of bulky sacks in the back.

"I can give ye a lift to the mill at Linford," he said. He was a thick set man with a bushy black beard with streaks of grey, and piercing blue eyes. He had a battered flat hat on his head and wore a brown apron. "I'm Nicholas the Miller," he said as he extended a large rough hand, and helped them onto the wagon. "Corn for the mill," he indicated the sacks.

"I'm Peter, and this is," he paused, "me friend Gwen."

The miller smiled, and after looking appreciatively at Gwen, he gave Peter a wink. Peter blushed.

Over the next mile Nicholas questioned them about their travels. Gwen did much of the talking, and described her abduction by the soldiers, her escape and her meeting with Peter. She did not refer to any of the stranger events, but kept her story to the basic facts. "So, I am trying to get some news of the soldiers to find out if they still have my father." She had some difficulty saying the word *father*, and tears came to her eyes.

The miller listened attentively to her story, frequently glancing towards her as she described her situation, and when he saw tears brim in her eyes, he was convinced of the truth of what she said. Peter sat on the other side of Gwen and added a few brief comments. He also avoided any reference to supernatural happenings, mainly because he had a limited imagination, and had failed to understand the unusual connections between some of the events that had occurred.

"That be quite a story," Nicholas said meditatively. "It so happens I've heard a fair bit about them soldiers in the past two days. I understand they've killed a few people an' all. When we get to the mill, it be likely my son Martin will 'ave something to tell us. There be nothin' like a mill for getting all the news."

The journey to Linford Mill was slow and hot, and Gwen soon dozed off, while Nicholas chatted to Peter about the mill and the problems of getting enough corn to grind. Peter was unused to being treated as an equal by a man of his father's age, and nodded and grunted at the appropriate places. But most of his attention was given to Gwen whose head had rested on his shoulder. He felt a warm glow of pleasure at this close contact.

Gwen did not wake until the horses stopped outside the mill house. Peter jumped down and helped her off the wagon. It was not something he would have thought of before, but the action gave him a sense of importance, especially when Gwen smiled her appreciation.

The mill was built of stone and stood next to a fast-flowing stream that turned a large wooden wheel. "This be the best mill in the area," Nicholas boasted, as he indicated the building with a sweep of his arm. "An' this is my son Martin. There be just the two of us.

A tall, thickset young man appeared, as if from nowhere, and began unharnessing the horses. He had dark features and broad muscular arms, and his thick neck gave a clear indication of strength. His fierce, blue eyes were fixed on Gwen, and he studiously ignored Peter.

"Who's this then?" He seemed to be speaking to his father, although his eyes never left Gwen.

"These be Gwen and Peter, they've 'ad a bad time with them soldiers we've been hearing about," the miller said, as he climbed out of the wagon. Martin said nothing but continued to stare at Gwen.

"So ye be Martin," Peter said, trying to get himself noticed. "Ye father told us about ye."

"Oh yes?" Martin said. He dragged his eyes away from Gwen and finally looked towards Peter. There was a slight curl of his lip as he noticed Peter's limp. "Did the soldiers do that?"

"No, I've always 'ad it." Peter spoke defiantly, but his tongue flicked over his lips.

Martin's eyes travelled slowly over Peter's thin body, then with a mocking smile he turned away. "Better get ye something to eat, it looks as though ye could do with it."

During the meal the conversation centred on the reports of the soldiers, and their flight towards the coast. Martin seemed reluctant to say much and kept his eyes fixed on Gwen, who appeared not to notice.

"So ye reckon they'll 'ave to cross the river then?" Nicholas said.

"Stands to reason if they be in a hurry to get to the coast," Martin replied.

Nicholas nodded. "I reckon they'll 'ave a boat handy some place. Possible they could travel down the river in small boats and meet a bigger one near the sea."

"Depends if they know this area. Then again, they must have 'ad some idea of where they was going," Martin said.

"I don't understand what they came for. It don't seem sensible t' me." The miller drank deeply from a pewter flagon of ale.

"Some of 'em that lives south of 'ere reckons them soldiers came to get something special. Or perhaps they came to take some prisoners," Martin said.

"One of them definitely wanted to capture me," Gwen said. She stared reflectively into space. "The other man, who looked like his twin brother, seemed to think I was important in some way. It was as though he was searching for me, but was unsure who I was."

"Now they seem to be trying to get back to where they came from," Peter added.

"An' good riddance an' all," the miller said, wiping his mouth with the back of his hand. "So what are ye going to do then?" he said looking at Peter.

"Well, I don't..." Peter began.

"We are going to follow them and make sure they haven't captured my father," Gwen interrupted.

"Supposin' ye do manage to catch up with them, which I doubt, what will ye do then?" Martin looked contemptuously at Peter. "Fight 'em?"

"Perhaps," Peter said. He stared down at his plate.

"Perhaps I better come along with ye," Martin said. He raised an enquiring eyebrow at his father.

"No, thanks, we can manage by ourselves," Peter said. His face was red and his bottom lip stuck out.

"Ye can't wander round the country and try an' fight soldiers with a good-looking girl like her with ye," Martin said.

His eyes travelled over her face. Gwen met his gaze with a frank, cold stare.

"What happened to ye hair?" Martin asked.

"The soldiers did it when they captured me. They threatened to cut off my head if my father did not surrender to them."

Martin turned to Peter. "What were ye doin' when all this was happenin'?"

Peter remembered very well what he had done at the time. His cowardly betrayal was like something out of a bad dream.

"He wasn't there," Gwen said quietly. "Peter rescued me from the house of an old woman who had drugged me."

Peter gave Gwen a grateful smile.

"That must have been very brave," Martin smirked. "Rescued ye from an old woman!" He gave a snort and stood up from the table. "Ye don't know this area. I knows it well, and I knows all the short cuts to the river. Besides ye'll need me if ye meets the soldiers."

He went to a corner of the room and picked up a short sword and scabbard, which he fixed to his belt.

Nicholas had been watching the sparring between the two young men, and was well aware that Gwen was the reason. For some weeks Nicholas had noticed that his son had become increasingly argumentative and bad tempered. There was no doubt his son needed to meet more young people of his own age, especially girls. It was about time he settled down. His son had worked in the mill since he was old enough to be useful and it was time for him to get away for a while. Also, Nicholas was aware that he probably could not physically stop his son from going. It was Martin who did the heavy lifting these days.

"I think Martin could be useful to ye both if he came along," Nicholas said. He turned to his son. "Ye could take the boat down the Willow to Olton's Weir and then carry it across the meadows to the River Avon." He turned to Peter. "The Willow's a small stream that flows near the Avon. That way ye would be following the flow of the stream and ye should be well down river before nightfall."

"Now," he said, turning back to Martin. "I'm not coming with ye, so I want ye to promise me ye won't do nothin' stupid. If ye comes close to them soldiers, I wants ye to remain hidden an' see if her father be with 'em. If so, then ye must get help. If not, then ye can all come back here again and we can talk it over."

Martin sucked in his lips and gave his father a brief nod.

"Ye remember now, nothin' stupid," Nicholas said. But he knew his son would do whatever he wished to do and nothing others said would alter anything. He wondered vaguely if he could call on some of his neighbours for help, but it would take time and he realized that the two young people, especially the girl, were keen to get going. "I'll give ye some food for two days or so, an' ye can have a couple of my old cloaks. It'll get cold at night."

As Nicholas bustled around, Martin led the way to the stream at the back of the mill. They walked past the slow-moving wheel and paused to watch the white water of the Willow roaring through the millrace. Further down the bank, where the water was less turbulent, there was a flat-bottomed boat lying in thick grass. Alongside, and almost hidden from view, was a long, thick pole. The boat was designed for two people, although there was a seat in the middle.

"It's a good boat for these waters," Martin said defiantly. "Ye ever been in one before?"

Gwen and Peter shook their heads. Gwen was excited by the prospect of the rapid travel, and relieved that there appeared to be very little walking to do. She was conscious of her weariness, but determined to continue. It was as though she was compelled to find the soldiers. This feeling of inevitability had been growing all day, and she found it almost reassuring.

Peter felt no such reassurance. He was clearly aware of his inadequacies, and he saw Martin as a superior competitor for Gwen's attentions. Earlier in the day he had thought only of the present, savouring each moment with Gwen. Now he could think only of the future, and he was frightened. He had never been in a boat in his life, he could not swim, and he knew he would have no chance if Martin decided to fight him. He stood gazing listlessly down at the ground as Martin dragged the boat to the water.

"Ye stayin' or ye comin'?" Martin said. He helped Gwen into the middle seat, and indicated that Peter should sit in the front. There was only one way to sit and that was with his back to the bow, facing down the small craft. Peter gingerly climbed into the rocking boat, lost his balance, and fell awkwardly onto the seat

"Look out!" Gwen cried, clutching Peter's leg.

"It won't do him any harm if 'e fell in," Martin cackled. "It's not deep. It don't go much above ye knees. That's why the boat has to 'ave a flat bottom."

"Hold on there!" The miller called as he ran down from the mill. He had some food tied up in a piece of cloth and a bundle of tattered cloaks. "I bought ye cloak as well, Martin."

Martin grunted and took the food from his father. Gwen used the cloaks as cushions. "We'll be off then," Martin said abruptly.

"Take care and don't try nothin' stupid," the miller said. He waved in a half-hearted way as Martin, standing in the back of the boat, poled the small craft through the water with great strength and skill. Soon the miller was out of sight and Peter glanced about anxiously as the boat sped along with the current.

The stream flowed through meadows where the scythed hay lay drying in the hot sun; along tree-lined banks, where herons and kingfishers perched, and through thick rushes where frogs croaked and otters played. Gwen was delighted with the journey, and her enthusiasm encouraged Martin to display his knowledge of the area.

Peter sat uneasily in the bow and watched in silence as Gwen and Martin exchanged stories, and pointed out the wild creatures that they passed. He had never been very interested in watching birds and animals, and he knew almost nothing about plants and flowers.

He adopted a bored expression and tried to avoid thinking about the next phase of the journey, when they would arrive at the river. He knew enough about rivers to know that they were often deep and fast flowing, and the thought of travelling down a river in the frail craft on which he sat was terrifying.

"Peter!" It was Gwen's voice.

"Yes?" Peter gave such a jump that he rocked the boat.

"I said, we be almost at Olton's Weir," Martin spoke as though to someone who was hard of hearing. "We'll 'ave to pull into the bank and carry the boat across the meadows. I'll stop now before the current gets too strong. If we goes over the weir, ye'll have to do some pretty quick swimming I can tell ye!" He gave his odd cackling laugh.

Peter glanced round and noticed how fast the water was running and heard the roar of the weir in the distance.

"How far is the weir?" Peter asked. He could not keep the panic out of his voice.

"Just round the bend," Martin said. He heaved on the pole and forced the boat towards the left bank. "This be the side that the current is strongest," he gasped, "but we 'ave to get across them meadows. Don't get so pop-eyed,

I won't let ye drown." He gave another loud laugh intermixed with grunts, as he forced the boat towards the bank, at a place where some giant willows overhung the water, and their leafy tendrils reached down to brush the cool surface.

The sarcasm in Martin's voice was lost on Peter, who was too concerned about the approaching weir. His mouth was dry and he was breathing rapidly. He reached out to grab an approaching branch, which hung down like a friendly arm.

"Don't do that, ye'll upset us!" Martin yelled. "Leave this to me!" He was aiming the boat so that it would pass to the shore side of the overhanging branches where he could bring it up on a small gravel bank. He had done this many times before, and was unable to appreciate how vulnerable Peter felt in the front, with the roar of the weir loud in his ears.

The branch was in reach and Peter grabbed it. The effect was to twist the boat round and cause Martin to lose his balance. He let out a roar and began to swear loudly, while he struggled to regain control. Gwen reached forward to restrain Peter, just as he stood up to try to pull himself, and them, towards the bank. The boat swung round violently, causing Gwen to fall backwards into Martin, who almost lost the pole. Without any guidance, the small craft careered away into the main current with Peter still holding onto the branch. There was a loud splash and a terrified scream as Peter catapulted into the rushing water, and was left hanging on to the trailing branch with only his head and shoulders above the surge. Martin, meanwhile, was fighting to get the boat out of the grip of the swirling current and into the safety of the bank. All Gwen could do was to shout encouragement to Peter and pray that Martin's great strength would prevent them from being carried over the weir.

Martin's huge muscles bulged as he pushed the pole against the current and slowly forced the flat boat towards the quieter waters. Suddenly, it was all over. The tenacious hold of the Willow was loosened and the boat scrapped up on the gravel.

"What about Peter?" Gwen wailed, as she clambered out.

"Serve 'im right. He's a cursed fool, that one," Martin gasped. He took some deep breaths and stepped out of the boat, quickly fastening a rope from the stern to a small tree. He glanced towards Peter who was still holding on to the branch and wailing for help in an hysterical voice.

"What shall we do?" Gwen said.

"He'll 'ave to wait until I gets me breath back," Martin said. He placed his hands on his hips and bent forward, taking great gulps of air. "He won't come to no 'arm for a moment or two."

"Hold on!" Gwen called. "We're coming."

It seemed to Gwen that Martin took an unnecessarily long time to recover. At last, he stood up and took the long pole and waded purposefully into the shallows, until at last he could rest the end of the pole against Peter.

"Take the pole!" he ordered. "I'll pull ye in."

"No!" Peter screamed. "I'll be washed away!"

"Hold on to the blasted pole, or I'll let ye drown!" Martin roared.

For a few seconds Peter wailed and cried for help. Finally, he grabbed frantically at the pole, and was yanked towards the shallows, where he collapsed on his stomach. He lay there, with his head just above the water line, shuddering and weeping hysterically.

Martin looked at him and spat on the ground. "Get up and stop blubbering like an infant." He turned to Gwen. "Come on, we'll go up to the meadow and dry our clothes and 'ave something to eat."

Gwen hesitated, looking anxiously at Peter.

"Come on," Martin insisted. "It'll give him time to recover." He picked up the cloaks and the parcel of food and climbed up the steep bank onto the meadow. He reached down and extended his hand to Gwen. With a final worried glance back at the bedraggled Peter, she allowed herself to be hauled up to the meadow.

After some time Peter climbed up to the sunlit meadow. He was shivering with cold, and felt utterly wretched. A few yards away Gwen and Martin were lying in the grass, each covered in a cloak, while their clothes dried in the hot sun. Larks screamed overhead in a cloudless sky, and the air was alive with the throbbing of insects.

He stood for a moment, blinking in the bright light, unsure what to do. The two bodies were an arm's length apart, yet he felt that, in some strange way, he was intruding. Gwen sat up and turned towards him.

"Come on, Peter, get those wet clothes off and have something to eat," she said, holding her cloak together with one hand and beckoning to him with the other.

"No, I'm alright," he said, trying to control his shivering.

"Peter!" her voice was firm. "Get those clothes off, and put this on." She stood up, holding her cloak around her, and handed him an old brown garment. He glanced around anxiously.

"I won't look," she said in a mischievous way.

"It's not that, it's just…" he was unable to explain. He rarely took off his clothes, and never in broad daylight in the middle of a field, and in the presence of a girl. The fact that Martin was watching him with a sardonic smile on his face was the final stage in Peter's humiliation.

"Go on," Gwen coaxed. "You can't go around in wet clothes, you'll become ill." She gathered her cloak about her and sat down next to Martin. "Hurry up," she called over her shoulder, "before Martin eats all the food."

The way she mentioned Martin, and the familiarity that was implied, was not lost on Peter. He turned miserably away and took off his grubby jacket and torn blouse. Then he wrapped the cloak around himself, before he removed his frayed breeches. Finally, when he had squeezed out the water, he draped the clothes over the tall grasses, where they hung like the motley rejects from a scarecrow.

"Ye better eat some food. We can't stay here forever," Martin said impatiently.

Peter sat down next to Gwen, who passed him some bread and a hunk of cheese. He chewed thoughtfully, as Martin described the next stage of the journey.

"It's not far. Over there, just past them trees." Martin pointed to a clump of willows in the distance. The land in front of them was gently undulating and much of it had been cleared to provide lush grazing meadows and hay fields. Nearby a herd of black cows was sitting out the heat of the day; a haze was developing, and the distant hills were just a smudge on the horizon.

"I've carried the boat on my back before now. Done it a few times by myself," Martin boasted. "It should be no bother with three of us." He looked towards Peter. "Not unless ye decides to run off with it!" He gave a bellowing laugh.

"I'm sorry," Peter said. He rolled a piece of cheese between his fingers. "I'm 'fraid of water. I can't swim. I've never been on a boat before."

"Well, ye'd better not lose ye nerve when we get on the river, 'cos that could be right dangerous. In parts it's too deep for me to pole, and the current can be real lively."

Gwen gave Peter a concerned look. "I can swim, so can Martin; you'll be alright."

Peter did not look convinced.

After a short while, Martin decided it was time to get dressed. Their damp clothes were cold on their hot skins, and it was agony fitting back into the garments. Martin pretended to be driven mad by the sensations, and played the fool. He yelled, jumped up, fell over and did head stands. Gwen laughed until she cried, but Peter pretended not to notice.

Eventually, they hauled the boat up into the meadow. It was much lighter than Peter had imagined, and it was easy to carry. Martin walked with the front part on his head, supporting it with one hand, and carrying the pole in the other. Peter and Gwen carried the rear end on their shoulders. When they came to hedges, they looked for a way through and passed the boat over the top. The ground was uneven and the heat was blistering, and soon they were forced to rest at more frequent intervals.

"How much further?" Gwen gasped.

"Almost there," Martin muttered. "It were cooler the last time I done this."

Peter was limping in a more noticeable way, but he made no complaint. His mind was focused on the river.

· · ·

When they reached the great Avon, the sun was already low in the sky. The river was broad and deep, and in the gathering dusk, the water looked like thick treacle. The sky was still blue, but the west was a glory of greens and pinks surrounding the setting copper sun. Shadows were forming among the trees, and the landscape was devoid of human habitation.

"We'll 'ave to see 'ow we makes out," Martin said. "If things go well, we may be able t' travel at night. But if it gets too dangerous, then we'll 'ave to continue the journey in the mornin'."

They spent a short while preparing for the journey before Martin launched the boat. Gwen volunteered to sit in the front and Peter clambered unsteadily into the middle seat. His terror was such that he did not trust himself to speak. Gwen smiled encouragingly at him as Martin pushed the light craft into the middle of the current.

The start of the boat ride was uneventful. The light slowly faded and the water took on a luminous glow. A bright half moon rose in a clear sky and a single bright star appeared beside it. Gwen marvelled at how peaceful it was. There was the steady splash of the pole as Martin reached back and lifted it up to push it down again in a rhythmic movement. A furtive quack of a duck or the splash of a jumping fish were the only other sounds.

Nobody had spoken for a while and Gwen pretended not to notice that both of the young men were gazing at her; one with a superior, confident smile, the other with a forlorn, pleading look. She was not prepared to think too deeply about them. She was grateful to one and sorry for the other. There was nothing more to it. She tried to focus her mind on what might happen if they caught up with the soldiers, but was unable to form a plan. There were too many unknowns. What would happen if they reached the mouth of this majestic river and there was still no sign of the soldiers. What then? She ran her tongue over her lips and tried to picture her father.

She stared into the silver water and began to imagine his face. Slowly, very slowly, an outline began to form on the rippling surface. But it was not the comforting features of her father that took shape, but a frightening, ugly face. She gasped. It was the evil creature who had chopped off her hair to force her father to surrender. The huge mouth opened wider and wider, repeating the same soundless word. Dark pupils stared malignantly out of red-rimmed sockets; the eyes were hypnotic. There was an urgency about the face, it seemed to be willing her to come closer. To come closer.

"Gwen!" It was Peter who grabbed her.

She fell back into the boat like a bent sapling that had been released. Her face was contorted with fear and she let out a long, deep moan that seemed to come from the deepest recesses of her mind. She sat hunched up, her face in her hands.

Martin stared at her in alarm, and stopped poling. His self-assured smile gave way to puzzlement, tinged with fear.

Peter knelt forward carefully and clasped both of her arms. "Are ye alright? Almost fell in the water ye did. 'Ad a very strange look on your face an' all."

She did not speak for a few moments, but breathed in and out deeply, her head between her knees. When she looked up, the moon illuminated her face and made her look pale and unearthly.

"It was him," she moaned. "The awful creature with the red beard."

"What d' ye mean?" Peter gasped. He looked quickly to both sides of the boat.

"I saw his face in the water. It was so frightening!" Gwen crossed her arms across her body and rocked slowly back and forth. She was breathing quickly and noisily.

"What's she on about?" Martin said. His voice was high and wavery.

"I think we should pull over to the bank," Peter said, turning to face Martin. "She's not feelin' well."

"Round the next bend is Potter's Crossing. That'd be a good place to stop." He began to pole the small boat towards the bank on the right hand side.

· · ·

THE HORSES WERE TIRED, and Abel was forced to slow the pace. The men were soaked in sweat, and it had not taken long for the dust to cake their faces again. The hard ride had taken its toll, and although none would admit it, each of them was close to exhaustion. Abel signalled for them to stop. "We'll have a final rest 'ere before we travel through the marsh. Be a good time to eat as well. Them horses are almost done."

As they dismounted, Tom noticed that Abel stood holding on to the side of his saddle. He was breathing hard, and had difficulty standing upright.

The men shuffled over to some brackish pools and used the brown liquid to wash off some of the dust that was encrusted round their eyes and mouths. "We'll find some water for the horses as we enter the marsh," Abel said.

They sat around in a tight group and said little. Each man was drawing on some inner strength to enable him to face whatever was ahead. They chewed slowly on strips of dried meat and pieces of flat bread, and drank sparingly from their water containers. In spite of their extreme weariness there was a sense of companionship in the group.

"Well, that was harder than I thought it would be," Sam said. "It's a long time since I rode in a hurry. However, it was certainly necessary." He gestured towards the fading light.

"Can ye find ye way through this marsh at night?" Tom asked.

"'Course 'e can. Got eyes like a cat," one of the men quipped. This brought a roar of laughter.

"I reckon I can find me way alright," Abel said. He smiled broadly, but his weariness was evident.

"Tell us what we will find when we get to the other side of the marsh," Sam suggested. "Then we can prepare ourselves."

The rest of the group nodded and murmured their agreement.

"I doubt if we'll get through the marsh until after sunset. It should be a clear night, and there be a bright half moon. At the Crossing there's a small cottage an' a bit of cleared ground. The ferryman lives there by 'imself. Everyone calls 'im Squint. Tough ol' man. 'E got this big old flat boat. There's a rope from one side to t' other, and 'e pulls 'imself across, and anyone else who don't want to swim."

Abel paused, while everyone tried to imagine the scene. "Now it's possible them soldiers 'ave got there before us. In which case I don't fancy 'is chances. However, if `e be still alive, then we can take the boat to the other side an' stop them crossin'." He looked at Sam. "What do ye think?"

"I agree with you, Abel. We need to approach very carefully," Sam said. "Perhaps we should leave the horses near the marsh and creep up on foot?"

Abel pondered this. "I think once we are through the marsh, me an' one other should go ahead to find out what's happened. The rest of you should keep on your horses, 'cos if there be trouble, the horses will give us an advantage."

"I'll come with ye an' all," Tom said. "It be only right that I do," he looked fiercely at the others.

"I was countin' on ye," Abel said, and patted Tom on the shoulder. Abel turned to the others, "Who else knows this place?"

The man with the bow raised his hand. "I been 'ere once before, when I were younger. I still remember what it looks like."

"Good for you, Walt," Abel said. "Ye'll be in charge when me and Tom goes ahead."

Walt pursed his lips and looked pleased.

Abel staggered to his feet. "Well then, we better be movin' before we loses all the light."

Sam moved up close to Abel and turned his back on the others "You alright, Abel?" he asked.

"Never been fitter," Abel said. There were beads of perspiration on his brow and his face was grey. He ran his hand over his bald head.

"'Tis not my business, but my Martha said you were ill this year, just after the snow went."

"It were nothin'. Don't ye worry about me." He smiled broadly and clapped Sam on the back. "Now," he said loudly, "we'll travel in single file. I'll lead, with Tom after me, and Walt next. Ye bring up the rear, Sam." He pulled himself into his saddle, and sat there for a moment, puffing out his cheeks. "Don't speak unless ye have to, and try to stop anything clinking together.

Remember this may turn out to be nothin', or it may turn out to be a killin'. Whatever 'appens, I wants ye all to get back safely." He smiled at each man, nodding his head as he did so.

They moved off at a brisk canter, but as the ground became softer, Abel slowed down to a walking pace. The path was still visible in the twilight, and the men had no difficulty in seeing their surroundings. Trees had gradually diminished in number, to be replaced by bushes and tall reeds. At times the riders passed through shallow brown pools ringed with thick tufts of dark green bog grass. Gradually, the light faded and the path disappeared. Abel continued on without a pause, and his quiet leadership inspired confidence in the others.

The journey became less pleasant as they ventured deeper into the bog. The mosquitoes were everywhere. Large and merciless, they attacked every piece of unprotected skin, and their high-pitched whine was a constant irritation. The horses suffered greatly with insects invading their eyes and buzzing in their ears. Without warning, a horse would stop and refuse to move forward, shaking its head up and down and whinnying loudly. Frogs croaked in massed unison, and silent owls swept low over the desolate landscape.

The water was deeper in places, and the mud clung to the horses' hooves, producing loud sucking noises. For brief moments the column of riders would move onto small areas of higher ground, only to return to the vile clinging mud of the swamp, with its foul stagnant smell.

Everything was bathed in an unreal silvery light, which increased the feeling that this was some awful nightmare. It was a fearful situation from which none of them could withdraw. There could be no turning back in this wilderness of mud and water, only the prospect of more mud and increasing suffering from the attacks of the unrelenting mosquitoes. Many of the men began to doze fitfully in their saddles, to be woken suddenly when their horse stopped or staggered. Even Tom, whose strength and determination was greater than any of the others, found himself nodding off to sleep.

One moment the horses were plodding sluggishly through the marsh, and the next they were striding nimbly up a grass verge to higher ground. The sudden change of pace stirred those who were dozing, and they awoke to find their horses were standing on a flat piece of raised ground. Ahead of them were the dark shadows of trees, while behind lay the evil bog, glinting horribly in the moonlight. The horses pawed the ground, anxious to be away from the torment of the mosquitoes, and to free themselves of the clinging mud.

Abel raised a finger to his lips, and faced each man. Then he indicated that they should follow him down a small path that led into the trees. Shortly after their entry into the forest, they came to a clearing. Abel climbed carefully out of his saddle and indicated the others should do the same. There was a menacing silence in the glade, and two of the men drew their swords, as they stared watchfully around. Abel stood in the moonlight and beckoned for them to come closer.

"Ye all did me proud," he whispered, and clasped each man's hand. "The river's over there," he pointed to the side of the glade. "Stay here while Tom and me goes to see if them soldiers be about. Keep an eye on our 'orses, and don't let 'em make a sound. The landin' is just over there." He pointed in front. "Walt," Abel hissed, "do ye remember where we are?"

"I never came this way," Walt murmured.

"'Course not," Abel agreed. "Ye remember where the cottage is?" Walt nodded. "We is behind the cottage and to the right. There be just a few trees between us and the open ground. The cottage is quite close. The front of it is about fifty paces from the river. Keep ye ears peeled, and if ye 'ave to be involved, then keep quiet about it, don't warn 'em that ye be comin'." Walt nodded again.

"I'm ready," Tom whispered. He had a heavy sword in his hand.

"Keep that bow handy, Walt," Abel said. "But don't go shooting us when we come back."

He walked quickly towards the trees with the large shape of Tom close behind. Then they melted into the shadows.

Sam and Walt and the other three men sat silent and unmoving on their tired horses. Apart from the usual night sounds, there was nothing to indicate that there were other people in the area, or that there was any danger.

CHAPTER 12

MARTIN MANOEUVRED THE BOAT against the wooden platform that served as a loading and landing dock for the ferry. The platform was more than three feet above the level of the water, and after he had tied the boat to a solid wooden strut, Martin carefully pulled himself on to the dock, his huge muscles bulging with the effort. He looked about quickly. Something was wrong.

The moonlight bathed everything in a deceiving white glow, making it possible to think that it was as bright as day, but only the general shapes were illuminated, the details were obscured.

"Give me ye hand," Martin whispered. He reached down and pulled Gwen up onto the dock, before he helped Peter. "There's something odd going on," he said quietly. "It don't feel right."

"Where's the ferry boat?" Peter hissed.

"That's mighty odd," Martin said. He pointed to a dark shape on the other side of the river. "Why would old Squint leave the boat over there, when his cottage is on this side?"

Gwen had been staring in all directions, like a wild creature testing the scents on the air. "The soldiers have been here," she muttered. "They could still be here."

Peter let out a strangled gasp. "What're we goin' to do?"

"The cottage is over there, just in front of them trees." Martin pointed along a path that curved to the left. "We better check that nothin's happened to 'im."

The worn path led from the landing up a steep stony slope and then across a wide flat area that was covered in high grasses and reeds. When they were on the landing, they were unable to see the cottage, but equally nobody in the cottage could see them.

They climbed carefully up the slope and peered over towards the cottage.

It was set back about fifty paces away from the river, and about two hundred paces to the left of the landing. They could see a faint light flickering in one of the windows.

"Perhaps Old Squint is there after all," Martin said.

"Why would he leave his boat on the other side?" Gwen asked.

"Search me," Martin said. "It don't make sense." He turned to Gwen. "Ye saw something when we was in the boat, didn't ye?"

"I saw a face in the water. It was the man who cut off my hair." She shuddered.

Martin thought about this for a moment. Then he drew his sword. "Ye got a knife with ye?" he asked, turning to Peter.

Peter nodded and produced the old rusty blade that he always kept hidden in his clothes. Martin inspected it and sniffed.

"This is what we'll do," he whispered. "Me an' Peter will go up to the cottage and see if we can find old Squint. Ye stay here an' keep hidden in this grass. Keep an eye on the boat an' all."

"Suppose the soldiers be there?" Peter could hardly keep his voice under control. He looked towards Gwen for help.

"We can't stay here all night," Martin countered, "and if them soldiers is there, then at least we'll know, and we can make a plan to see if they got Gwen's father. Unless we goes up to check, we don't know where we be."

There was an awful logic in Martin's argument, and Peter felt trapped. One part of him wanted to hide until it was light, but he could not allow himself to appear a total coward in front of Gwen. He nodded nervously and chewed on his lower lip.

Gwen reached out and put her hands on the arms of both of them. She gave them a squeeze. "Take care. Don't do anything silly. If it looks dangerous, then don't go near it."

Martin grunted and indicated for Peter to follow him. He kept to the side of the path, and advanced in a crouched position. Peter was convinced that Martin was enjoying himself.

Unwillingly, Peter imitated Martin and slowly they approached the cottage, stopping every few paces to check their surroundings. Martin put his face close to Peter's. "We'll creep up on this nearest side. We'll check the back, then we'll try and look in the window," he whispered.

Ducks flew up from the river, their wings making a loud drumming as they wheeled overhead. Martin listened intently as the noise of the birds faded, but there were no other sounds except an owl calling from across the river. "Come on," he urged.

They crept, bent double, up to the side of the cottage. Peter's heart was beating loudly and there was sweat on his brow. His leg was aching because of the crouched position they had been adopting, and he wished he were somewhere else.

They pressed their backs against the wall of the cottage. Martin edged his head round the corner to see what was at the back. "There's nothin' there," he whispered. "Just a back door, and some wood."

The moon illuminated the side and back walls while the front and the other side were in deep shadow. Peter's eyes searched the dark wood at the back of the cottage, and he was unaware that his mouth was wide open as if preparing for a scream. They edged back along the side of the cottage; once again Martin led the way. He peered round the corner and paused, letting his eyes get used to the darkness. There was a door with two small windows. The nearest window was the one with the flickering yellow light.

"Stay here and keep watch," Martin murmured. He edged round the corner and very carefully peeped into the room. Then he crept back to Peter who was glancing about in an agony of indecision: he kept thinking he could see shapes moving in the trees.

"What's the matter?" Martin hissed. Peter jumped and almost cried out.

"Over there, in front of the trees, I thought I saw something move."

Martin stared into the darkness. The moon was illuminating them both, but the trees were dark and mysterious. "I don't see nothin'," Martin growled. He relaxed his stance. "Old Squint is asleep in his chair. It's a candle in the window that's givin' that light. I think it be alright if we goes in. 'E knows me."

They walked round to the front of the cottage. Peter kept looking back, unwilling to believe it was his imagination. The door was ajar, and Martin knocked loudly, and entered.

A guttering candle gave just enough light for them to make out the main details of the cottage. There was just the single room with a curtained section to cover the bed. The main area was modestly furnished with a solid oak table, some stools and a large, crudely woven willow chair in which the old man was propped; his head rested on his chest. The fire was out in the grate and the remains of a meal were scattered on the table. Dry reeds littered the floor and crunched under foot.

"Now then, Old Squint," Martin said. He spoke in a loud, friendly manner. He walked over and placed his sword on the table, then he placed his hand on the old man's shoulder and gave him a gentle shake. The body collapsed to the side.

"Quick, bring me that light!" Martin said.

Peter carried the candle over to the chair and they could see that the front of the old man was covered in dried blood. There was a terrible gash in the chest, and the body was stiff and cold. He had been dead for some time.

Peter was speechless with fear. He had never seen a corpse up close. He wanted to pretend it was not true, that this was just a bad dream.

"He was a nice ol' man." Martin spoke softly. "He was a friend of mine. Now someone's gone an' killed 'im." He sniffed and wiped his eyes. "Do ye think it was them soldiers?"

Peter nodded. He could not draw his eyes from the awful sight. Martin blew out his lips and swallowed loudly. "Well then, it looks like they've moved on." His face hardened. "Them murderin' devils, what did they want to kill an old man for?" He took another deep breath. "We'd better get back to the boat and tell—"

The door burst open and three soldiers rushed in. At that moment two more appeared from behind the curtain. They had swords and short spears and they moved like panthers. The two youths backed behind the chair, but they could put up no resistance as Martin's sword was on the table. Peter quickly raised his arms above his head and watched in terror as the soldiers surrounded them. Martin folded his arms and stared defiantly back at the menacing weapons. The soldiers came within an arm's length and waited. Nobody moved.

Lights appeared in the doorway and two soldiers with flaming torches marched in and stood to each side, as a huge man entered.

Peter recognized him as the one he had encountered in the forest when Gwen's hair had been sliced off. In the flickering light in the small room the warrior was even more terrifying. His eyes flashed red in the torchlight as he stared contemptuously at the two young men. His red hair almost touched the ceiling.

"We have met before," he said grabbing Peter's thin neck with a huge hand. He had a heavy accent, but there was no mistaking the threat in his words.

"Please, sir, I ain't done nothin' wrong," Peter pleaded. The pressure on his throat was almost unbearable.

He pushed Peter against the wall with a dismissive gesture. Peter crumpled like a feather pillow, and lay shaking on the floor.

"Who are you?" the leader said. He tried to grab Martin by the throat, but even his great hand could not encircle Martin's thick neck. Instead, he attempted to grip Martin's shoulders, but was able only to use his hands to push the youth against the wall.

"I see you are strong. Who are you?"

"I be Martin."

"Martin?" The giant appeared to savour the name. "Where is the girl?" The question came out abruptly, like an arrow in an ambush.

Martin stared back, unmoved, at the evil face. His cheeks sucked in and he pursed his lips. "What girl?"

. . .

JOHN AND THE VILLAGERS followed the little-used forest trails towards Potter's Crossing. They had walked at a brisk pace for most of the journey, but when the early evening was upon them, the exertions of the day began to take their toll. John had noticed Will was limping, but by the grim, determined expression on his face, it was obvious the old man did not intend to give up.

When they reached a point where two paths crossed, John called a halt. "How far do you think it is, Ben?"

Ben furrowed his brow. "Well, I've only come this way once before. Last year it was, and I was with me two cousins. I reckoned we'd 'ave been there by now."

"It seems pretty clear that them soldiers came this way," Wilf said. He pointed to the tracks in front of them. There were numerous hoof prints, and something heavy had been dragged along.

"Almost too clear if ye think about it," Will said. "Almost like they was leaving us an obvious trail to follow."

This statement produced a hubbub of discussion. Some of the men got down on their knees to examine the tracks, which had followed a turning to the right. Others checked the remaining two paths. John stood in the centre of the intersection and watched with increasing foreboding.

Once again he felt it was his fault. He had assumed that Ben knew the way to Potter's Crossing and that it was simply a matter of seeing if the soldiers were going in the same direction. John had put his confidence in Ben and had failed to anticipate that the soldiers could be travelling a different route. His mind was racing. He wondered if this was a deliberate false trail, one that would lead them into a trap, or whether the soldiers were merely trying to escape by the fastest route. He needed to think.

His vision of the river and the large flat boat seemed to indicate Potter's Crossing. A cottage was on fire, and Ben had confirmed that there was such a cottage. Gwen was there, and it was happening at night. He tried to remember if there was anything else in the vision, but he could think of nothing. He needed another sign, something to help him pinpoint the exact order of events. John felt the weight of responsibility. It was necessary that he use the sword to give him the answers he needed.

He stood up, and with both hands lifted the sword above his head. Some of the men stopped what they were doing and watched. John was aware of them, but felt strangely superior. He slowly turned in a small circle and stared up at the glittering blade. He willed something to happen, but nothing did. He closed his eyes and continued to turn slowly. "Going to give us another vision, are ye?" He heard Dan Birch's mocking voice. There was a sound of scrapping feet, a thud, and a sudden exclamation. Dan's voice again.

John kept his eyes closed and concentrated on his previous vision, and tried desperately to get the sword to help him. But there was no tingling in his hands, there was no surge of energy. It was just like any other sword. John stumbled and opened his eyes. The villagers were staring silently at him, waiting for him to tell them what he had seen. Will was in front of him, and his eyes were smouldering. Behind him, lying on the ground, was Dan Birch.

"What did ye see?" Will asked. There was an anxious quality in his voice.

John looked slowly around the group of faces. All eyes were fixed on him. Some men had their mouths open, as though they were waiting for him to fill them with his wisdom. He could see Hal running towards him.

"Well?" Will urged.

"I saw the soldiers," John lied. "I... I..." The sea of faces moved closer: this was what they wanted to hear, this would help them defeat the invaders and get some plunder to take home. This was why they were going to follow him. John knew he must give them something to hold on to. He was young, he was a stranger, and he wanted these men to help him save Gwen. Up until now they had followed because of the sword. If the sword had lost its power, then it was up to him to lead them.

"The soldiers are not far ahead. We must go down... this way!" He pointed along the path that the soldiers appeared to have gone down. It seemed the obvious choice.

"Ye sure about that?" Will said.

"Yes," John said. He did not look Will in the eye. The rest of the men seemed to be content with his decision.

"We'll get some rest and something to eat. We will catch up with them at Potter's Crossing," John said, and added great emphasis to the word *will*. He had to prove his leadership, and if the sword had lost its power, then he would act as though it was still powerful. As long as the villagers believed in it, they would follow him.

A voice in his mind kept repeating Old Mary's warning: *Beware of vanity*. But he wasn't being vain, this was what he had to do, he could manage without the sword if he had to. Who cared why the men followed him, just so long as he could rescue Gwen... nothing else mattered.

As the villagers moved away in small groups to share their food and ease their tired feet, Hal arrived breathless and sweating.

"I found more signs of the soldiers," he said. He had been down the path that led straight ahead of them. "I found some fresh horse droppings. They was quite a way down the path, but there weren't no signs of any hooves. Then I came to a muddy bit and there were boot marks and..." he looked triumphantly around. "I found some deep rounded prints. I reckon they've put sackin' round the hooves of their 'orses to cover up their tracks." He looked proudly at the grim face of Will. "I reckons this is a false trail," he said, pointing down the path that John had chosen. Hal smiled at John and a couple of villagers who had gathered around him. "It were a good job I went as far as I did, or I would've missed that an' all." He strutted importantly over to a small group of friends, and the two men followed. They looked confused.

Will took a swig from his leather water container. "Ye sure ye chose the right path?"

"I'm sure," John said. There could be no backing down. He had made the decision based on his supposed ability to see into the future; to contradict his earlier decision would be to invite doubt among the villagers. He chewed on some cold meat and bread, and took a swig of Will's water. The sun was setting and he was anxious to get on. He called Ben over.

"Is this likely to be the quickest way to Potter's Crossing?" He pointed down the chosen path.

Ben nodded. "It could be," he agreed. "I'm not certain, of course, 'cos I've only been 'ere once before. It don't matter though, 'cos you know where we got to go." He spoke without any hint of mockery. It was clear that, apart from Dan Birch, the rest of the men had a complete and simple trust in John's abilities.

John avoided Will's questioning look and gathered the men together.

"We are close to Potter's Crossing," John spoke in a strong voice. He realized that he was enjoying himself, and that by making a decision, even if it was a lie, he had taken on the role of a leader. It felt good.

"We may catch up with the soldiers in a short while. If we do, there could be fighting. We need to punish them for killing Will's bother, and for murdering many other people. Remember, they tried to kill all of you by poisoning the pool." There were murmurs of agreement. "We need to rescue any prisoners, and there may be the chance of taking some of their gold. You could all be rich!" Another lie, but a necessary one. John knew many would have deserted before now, if it had not been that the expedition provided the opportunity for looting.

The men gave muted cheers and some raised their weapons. They were keen to get on, and the weariness of the long walk seemed to have left them.

"It will be dark soon, and we will need to travel carefully. We must not make any noise, and we will have to travel by the light of the moon." John knew these men were used to hunting at night; this would be no problem to them. "If any of you find any sign that the soldiers are close, then stop and warn the others. We'll walk in pairs. Will and Wilf will bring up the rear, and Ben and I will lead. The rest of you should keep close together. Carry your weapons and be ready for anything." John was not sure where his confidence had come from, but his heart was beating fast and he felt he could achieve greatness. He held the sword above his head; it was strangely heavy in his hand. "Follow me, and we will achieve great things tonight." There were muffled shouts of agreement; the atmosphere was charged with excitement.

"Which path are we takin'?" a voice called out.

"This one," John pointed along the well-worn track.

"Hal reckons them soldiers went down the path in front," Dan Birch said. "'E says they had put sackin' on their horses' hooves."

"It was a clever trick to get us to take the wrong path," John said. "We must get on, or they will be across the river before we can get to them."

It would have been so easy to agree to take the path that Hal had suggested, but John felt unable to change his mind. He could not, and would not lose face again. He was their leader; he had to make decisions. That afternoon he had lost control on the cliff top; he could not let that happen again.

There were some muttered comments, but the men formed up and John and Ben led the way at a fast walk. The sunlight was almost gone; the tops of trees were silhouetted in the evening sky, and the shadows were deepening on each side of the path. The men were wary and searched the trees and the way ahead for any sign of movement.

The path meandered through the forest, and they could see the clear tracks of the soldiers whenever the moonlight broke through the trees. They walked another mile, and still there was no sign that they were getting near the river.

Suddenly, there was a gasp from Ben. "There aren't no tracks. They've vanished!"

In a moonlit patch on the path they could see that the surface was completely smooth. There was no sign of hoof prints or of the heavy structure that had been dragged along the earlier sections.

"It's magic," someone whispered.

"Magic be damned!" Will said forcefully. "We've bin tricked."

He began to retrace his steps. After about thirty paces he stopped and began to examine the left side of the path. Others joined him.

John walked slowly back, checking the trees and bushes for any glint of metal or sign of movement. He felt uneasy and his earlier self-assurance was fading.

"Look what I've found," Will snarled. He held up broken branches which had been used to cover a break in the forest. Others helped him to remove the camouflage. In the dappled light they could see two large logs that had been dragged between the trees. The logs had been chopped with axes and there were notches where ropes had been attached. Behind the logs, there was a fresh path that had been made by a number of horses.

"They've made fools of us." Will spat out the words. "They wanted us to come this way. Then they've doubled back. We've come a long way round an' all."

"I knew I was right," Hal said.

"I thought ye said ye knew which way to come?" Dan Birch wheedled. "Didn't ye 'ave a vision or something?" He gave a derisive laugh.

John said nothing, but stood in the shadows with his sword resting on the ground.

"Did ye make a mistake?" Will asked.

"I saw the soldiers marching down a wooded path," John said. This time it was the truth; that was what he had seen in his earlier vision. "I thought it was this one. I was wrong." He spoke quietly, but with authority.

There was a pause, then Will spoke again. "Did ye say they was marching?"

"Yes," John answered. It had not occurred to him until then that he had seen no horses. What did it mean?

"No horses then?"

"None. I saw a cottage on fire. I saw a large flat boat, and I saw the girl, the one they had prisoner." He avoided mentioning her name. "Why would there be no horses?" He directed the question to the group.

"Ye tell us. Y're the one who claims to get visions," Dan Birch said. He turned to the others. "He's just a boy with a valuable sword. What I say is—" He stopped as Will's sword prodded his throat.

"Shut ye mouth, or I'll take ye head off, so help me I will." Will's eyes were big and white in the moonlight. His breathing sounded like a bull snorting. "If ye can't speak in a helpful manner, then ye hold ye tongue."

Dan's two brothers reached for their weapons, and advanced on Will from behind. John saw them clearly in the moonlight and stepped out of the shadows, raising the sword with both hands and resting it on his shoulders. The two men stopped and were uncertain what to do. There was no movement from the other men.

"Dan Birch," John said, "you might not like me, but you and your brothers will do as I say, or go home." He spoke slowly, and gripped the sword tightly with both hands. He wanted the sword to react, but it remained just an inert and heavy piece of metal. For some reason it had lost that strange energy that had made it so wonderful and so terrifying.

John stood alone, and realized that this was a crisis. Even without the sword he must rally the men. He knew that if he had been older there would have been no questioning of his authority. But the sword had given him a taste for leadership. He liked it, and nobody, especially Dan Birch, was going to take it from him.

"You all know I cured Polly." John spoke slowly, placing emphasis on the important words. Some heads nodded in the moonlight. "You know I saved you from drinking the poisoned water." It was not a question but the stating of an accepted fact. "You have seen the power of this sword." He let the words sink in. "I will lead you to the soldiers, and with your help I will defeat them. You will all be heroes, and you will be able to return to the village as rich men." Even as he spoke the words, he knew it was a lie. But it did not matter; a leader had to do this.

He turned to Dan Birch and moved the sword from one shoulder to the other. In the moonlight Dan was convinced that John was going to attack him. He flinched, raised his right arm to ward off the blow, and gave a small cry like a child makes when it gets hurt.

"I won't harm you Dan Birch, but you must support me from now on, or leave now."

"'E didn't mean nothin'." One of Dan's brothers moved up and placed a protective hand on Dan's shoulder. Will lowered his sword and moved behind John. "It's just 'is way. We'll keep an eye on 'im," he murmured. There were hoots of derision from some of the other villagers.

The other brother had also approached, and as John stared into their shadowy faces, he sensed that they would not forgive him, or Will, for what had occurred.

John faced the other men. "We have the choice of either going back the way we came, and going down Hal's path, or cutting through the forest and following the trail the soldiers took when they doubled back." There was a silence and John realized that Will was right: they did not want to make decisions, they wanted someone to lead them.

"The quickest way is probably through the trees," John said. "The river must be quite close. We know the soldiers are near, so be ready for anything." He waited for any comment, then led the way into the trees, while Will rounded up the stragglers. The three Birches positioned themselves in the centre of the column, and Hal travelled next to John.

• • •

THE HUGE MAN RELEASED his grip and appeared to step back. Then, with a lightning movement he slapped Martin across the face. He gasped, but remained unmoved. The leader took a step forward, his face close to Martin's, enveloping him in a wave of foul breath. Martin lunged forward and brought his fist up into the man's stomach. Immediately two spears were pressed into his throat and Martin was rammed back against the wall. The huge man staggered slightly, and then continued as if nothing had happened.

"You will tell me about the girl, or you will die, painfully. So will your friend." He delivered a mighty kick at Peter, who howled like a puppy.

"I think you will tell me," he said, his voice was like silk. In one movement he reached down and dragged Peter to a standing position.

Peter's eyes were wide with fear and he trembled like a leaf in the wind.

"Where is the girl? I know that you can tell me. I could find her myself, but it will be quicker if you tell me." He raised a huge fist in front of Peter's face.

"Don't 'it me, sir, I ain't done nothin'," he sobbed.

"Where is the girl?" the giant yelled. "Tell me!"

Peter screamed with pain as the fist hit him in the cheek. His head banged against the wall, and he would have slumped to the floor if the other huge hand had not prevented him from falling. His screams reached an hysterical pitch as the massive fist prepared for another blow.

"I'll tell ye!" he blubbered. "I'll tell ye! Don't 'it me again, sir."

"Well?" the stranger roared.

"She's 'iding in the grass down by the ferry!" Peter cried, his voice cracking with emotion.

"Coward!" Martin spat out the word like a blow. The spears dug deeper into his throat.

"Keep them alive until I have the girl," the leader said. He walked towards the door and all but two of the soldiers followed. One kept his spear against Martin's neck, forcing his head against the wall, while the second held a sword in one hand and a burning torch in the other. Peter lay on the floor whimpering like a small child, and hating himself for his weakness.

• • •

TOM AND ABEL MOVED silently through the remaining trees, and after a short while they found themselves, as Abel had predicted, behind the cottage and to the right of it, with the river in front.

There seemed to be some activity around the building, and the two men sank down to watch. By the moonlight, they could see a number of shadowy shapes move into the forest directly behind the cottage; the nearest was only a stone's throw away. After a few moments they disappeared among the trees.

"Those were the soldiers," Tom hissed. "It looks like we've caught up with 'em before they crosses the river."

"Maybe, maybe not," Abel cautioned. "They didn't look like they was in a hurry to cross. They be up to something, an' we better see what it is, before we makes any plans."

"We've been lucky to see 'em 'an all," Tom muttered. "If we had arrived about now, we would not 'ave known there was any of 'em in the trees there. Now, we knows that we can't cross straight to the cottage."

"If we gets back in the trees here, and makes our way down to the water's edge, we could move through the rushes and get in front of the cottage. From there we could 'ave a view of anything 'appening on the river," Abel suggested.

Tom nodded, and they both crawled carefully back into the deep shadow of the trees, and they made their way slowly towards the river. The water was cool and inviting as they gently lowered themselves in. Around them bull rushes grew in thick patches, and above them the riverbank sloped up towards the high grasses that covered the cleared area. They waded steadily through shallow water, until the rushes thinned as the water became deeper.

Abel indicated that they would have to crawl up the bank, and take their chances in the long grass. The river had a silver glow, and they could just make out the dark shape of the ferryboat on the other side of the river.

"I didn't see no horses," Abel muttered. "I reckon they've taken them over the river. But if that's the case, why haven't they left this place, and continued to wherever they be goin'?"

"I think they be setting a trap for someone," Tom whispered. "Or they be meeting someone 'ere. One of the two."

They crawled up the bank and crouched in the tall grass. The outline of the cottage could be easily identified, and a small yellow light was burning in one window. There was no sign of any soldiers.

"Look!" Abel whispered. "What's going on now?"

Two figures had suddenly appeared from the direction of the landing and were creeping up to the cottage from the other side; one was much larger than the other, and carried something in his hand. They vanished round the side of the building and then, after a brief interval, the larger one moved back into view and looked briefly into the lighted window. He then disappeared round the cottage and immediately both figures reappeared, and passed in front of the lighted window and went through the door.

"What do ye make of that?" Abel muttered.

"Well, I don't think they be soldiers," Tom said.

"Hush," Abel said. He pointed to a number of black figures that had risen up out of the grass near the ferry landing. Others came out from the trees behind the cottage. One of the shapes was enormous.

"I know who that be," Tom hissed.

The figures grouped near the door and then rushed in. Two torches were lit and by the red light, the huge man could be clearly seen before he entered the cottage.

"'E must a giant," Abel gasped.

"He was the one that slashed me daughter's hair," Tom said grimly.

Someone screamed in the cottage, and they could see the torches moving about behind the windows.

"What shall we do?" Abel asked.

"I reckon we must see what 'appens. I needs to find out if they got me daughter."

The door burst open and a group of the soldiers came out, followed by the giant. More torches were lit and the soldiers ran towards the landing, dipping about like fireflies. Others were called out of the woods, and they began to search the tall grass. The leader could be seen standing on the landing, directing the operation.

"I reckon we could get to the cottage and see who they got in there. There be at least one soldier inside, 'cos I can see him movin' with 'is torch," Tom said.

"We'll be seen as soon as we get near the lighted window," Abel said. "An' when we goes through the door, they won't be able to miss us." He paused. "Wait on now, there be a back door, I remember. It leads into Squint's sleepin' area. That way they won't see us. Not unless they got others waiting in the trees."

"Let's try it," Tom said. He was a man of action, and he worried that even while they discussed their plan Gwen could be in danger.

They edged their way back down the bank, once more battling through the reeds, and crept quickly among the trees until they were level with the side of the cottage. Both men lay on the ground surveying the scene and trying to control their heaving chests. They were wet, muddy, and covered in scratches.

"I be getting a bit old for this," Abel panted. They watched as lights moved back and forth near the ferry landing. "D'ye think we should slip back and tell the others?"

Tom shook his head, "If we leave this place we won't have any idea what is going on when we return. We better get in that cottage right soon, and find out who those others were. I reckon there could be at least two soldiers in there, so we best take care."

"We 'ave to 'ope there ain't no others in them trees behind the cottage," Abel said.

As they raced across the open ground, they could hear men yelling from the direction of the landing. They reached the side of the cottage and paused to catch their breath. Abel checked the back, and they both crept up to the small rear door. Inside, they could hear two voices talking in a foreign tongue, and the sound of someone sobbing.

Abel raised the door latch very carefully, while Tom checked the forest behind. Slowly, Abel prised open the door and peered into the room. To the right was Squint's narrow bed; on the left was a large wooden box, and coming across at an angle was a heavy curtain pulled partly to one side. Abel crept up to the gap in the curtain, and saw a thickset youth who was standing against the back wall with a spear to his throat. The young man had his eyes closed and the soldier was only half in view; the owner of the other voice was completely hidden behind the curtain. Abel could not tell if there were any other soldiers in the room. After a moment's hesitation, he beckoned for Tom to join him. They gripped their swords, nodded to one another and charged through the curtain at opposite ends.

Tom burst through his side of the curtain and found a heavy table between himself and the soldier with the torch. The element of surprise was lost, and the soldier had time to raise his sword before Tom could get to him. Abel fared no better, for he had to get over Peter's prostrate body before he could strike the man with the spear. The soldier turned quickly and jabbed at Abel as he was attempting to jump over Peter. It was at that moment that Peter sat up, like a released bowstring, knocking Abel off-balance. The spear sank deep into his thigh.

Tom edged round the table, and the soldier thrust the flaming torch at him, and tried to jab with his sword at the same time. Tom parried the sword stroke, and with a powerful upward movement knocked the torch from the soldier's hand. Within seconds the dry reeds on the floor had caught fire, but nobody took any notice.

As the soldier drew back his spear for a second thrust at Abel, Martin jumped on the man's back and enveloped him in a powerful bear hug. The soldier was unable to move as Martin's huge arms crushed the man's ribs and prevented him from breathing. The soldier's eyes bulged, as he fought to retain consciousness.

Abel dropped his sword and fell on top of Peter; covering him in blood. Peter was so terrified that he was incapable of helping, and he lay on the floor screaming like a banshee. Abel fought to remain alert, for he knew he had to staunch the wound, or he would die. He hit Peter with the back of his hand. "Help me! Damn ye! Help me!" he roared. The fire was spreading rapidly.

Tom quickly recognized his opponent as an experienced fighter, and it was only by utilizing his great strength that the blacksmith was able to beat off the soldier's furious attacks. As Tom parried another powerful stroke, the fire reached the place where the soldier was standing. The man cried out in pain and, momentarily, lost his concentration. Tom seized the opportunity and ran straight at his enemy using the sword as a spear. The soldier stepped back into the fire, dropped his guard, and was unable to avoid Tom's sword cut, which passed through the leather body armour, and delivered a mortal wound.

Tom took a step back, and ran round the table. He dragged Abel away from the encroaching flames and pulled him out of the back door. The room was full of smoke and Peter was coughing and screaming at the same time. He crawled painfully towards the back door through which Tom was dragging Abel. Peter glanced back and, amid the leaping flames and smoke, saw that Martin was still struggling with the soldier. It seemed impossible that he could escape in time.

Outside the air was cool on the skin and it was easier to breath. Tom dragged Abel behind the stack of logs about ten paces from the blazing building. Behind this shelter he lay Abel on the ground and attempted to stop the loss of blood. Abel groaned loudly. It was a bad wound, but Tom had seen similar injuries during his time with the Crusade. He worked feverishly, cutting away Abel's clothing and using the material to block the flow. He tore off a piece of his own shirt to act as a bandage. It was all he could do for the moment, and he hoped that Abel was strong enough to last the ordeal until help arrived.

The cottage was a raging furnace. Long red tongues of fire poked out of the doors and windows, enveloping and consuming the dry thatch. The heat was almost overpowering. As Tom stood up, the roof collapsed in an explosion of flames and sparks that burst into the night sky like a small volcano. He staggered back shielding his eyes from the hot embers that rained down. Everywhere was chaos. Behind him a bloody battle was being fought, and he could hear cries of rage and pain and the dull clank of swords clashing together. Horses and men were thrashing about in the bushes, and there was the constant thwack of bowstrings and the screaming of the injured. Over by the landing the torches had been extinguished and dark shapes were running towards the trees. He wondered what had happened to the youths in the cottage, and was tormented by indecision: should he stay with Abel, or try to help defeat the soldiers?

At that moment a group of horsemen galloped out of the woods from the side of the flaming building. He thought he recognized Sam and Walt by the light of the inferno. They were speeding across the clearing and would pass in front of what remained of the burning cottage. Tom feared they might ride past without seeing him, and he ran round towards the landing side of the fire, shielding his face from the intense heat as he did so. So fierce was the conflagration that Tom was forced to veer away and, with his arms over his face, he ran straight in front of the galloping horses.

It was too late for the riders to change course. In the noise and searing heat of the burning cottage they saw a large figure suddenly appear, his head was covered and there was a sword in his hand. In the instant they were upon him and he fell under their thundering hooves.

· · ·

"I KNEW I WAS right about them soldiers," Hal said. He seemed to be looking for approval.

"Yes, you were right," John said quietly, picking his way over a fallen tree.

"I need your eyes to help me follow this trail. You've proved yourself to be an excellent guide."

"I'm good at huntin' at night an' all," Hal said. He seemed pleased.

They waited while the rest of the villagers closed up, and then they marched in single file through the trees. For much of the time it was easy to follow the route the horses had taken. Although nobody spoke, John worried that the file of men seemed to make a lot of noise as they crashed through the tangled undergrowth.

Hal was leading with John directly behind him. They kept up a fast pace and John was sweating in the warm night air. Hal stopped when they reached a piece of moonlit open ground, and examined a sandy area. "Look 'ere," he said in a loud whisper. "There seems to be three horses. The main group must 'ave gone down that path I followed."

John nodded. He was puzzling over the point that Will had made: there had been no horses in the vision. What did that mean? He guessed he must be close to the river, and soon this riddle would be solved. It was good to be near the end of the journey.

They followed the trail of the horsemen over uneven ground. Thick blackberry bushes and clumps of thistles had forced constant detours in the open spaces where trees had died or blown down. On each side there was thick forest and the possibility of danger. As they came to the top of a steep rise, Hal stopped and listened carefully. The others closed up and waited to discover what was happening. There was silence. Suddenly, off in the distance, faint noises could be heard: voices were yelling in a strange language.

"'Sounds like them soldiers," Hal whispered.

"I think we're near the river. Those sounds may be coming from Potter's Crossing," John said. As he spoke, a pale reddish glow appeared above the black silhouettes of the trees. It flickered and increased in intensity.

"Something's on fire!" Hal called back.

"It might be that ferry man's cottage," Ben said.

John turned to the shadowy shapes behind him. "That was part of my vision! Keep together. Don't make a noise until we know what's happening. Follow me!"

There was a sudden rush forward. John was trying to keep up with Hal, who was running like a rabbit. On both sides men, determined not to be left behind, were pounding through the trees. Many of the villagers were cursing loudly as they careered down the slope through tangled bushes, while others were laughing with the excitement of the moment. There was no order, and no way of stopping the headlong rush.

They were getting closer to the fire, and as they charged down the last part of the slope, the flames could be clearly seen, like beckoning fingers, over the tops of the trees. Hal was four paces in front, barging his way through bushes and low branches, and John could hear the grunts and gasps of others close behind. His legs pounded the earth, his lungs were bursting, and he felt cold fear suddenly replace the wild exhilaration of the impetuous rush. But it was too late for caution.

As they reached the fringe of the trees, John saw Hal stop in mid stride. He gave a high-pitched scream, rose up on his toes, spun round and collapsed. In the flickering glow of the fire John glimpsed the arrow in Hal's chest. There were black shapes among the trees. Arrows. Screaming. John was unable to stop, tripped over the falling body, and careened into a tree. He had a split-second recollection of how sad everything was, before the darkness enveloped him.

CHAPTER 13

G WEN WATCHED ANXIOUSLY AS the two youths crept along the path towards the ferryman's cottage. She had felt uneasy from the moment their boat was tied up at the pier, but was unable to point to anything in particular. The two young men were helping her, and it would have complicated the situation if she had insisted they all stayed together.

The moon was very bright in a cloudless sky, and she could see the outline of the flat ferryboat on the other side of the river. She crawled into the tall grass, where the land sloped up to the right. From this vantage point she could just make out the cottage with its faint yellow light. In front was the track that led to the cottage and to her right was the broad road that led down to the ferry landing on her left. Behind her was a dark band of gracefully curving willows growing close to the water and merging with larger elms and birches further up the slope. She edged back into the deep shadows of the trees, where she felt less vulnerable, and hid herself behind the hanging fronds of a willow. Her dark colouring enabled her to blend with the tree, yet still have a wide view of the clearing.

She wondered if Martin and Peter had reached the cottage, and strained her eyes to see any sign of movement, but could see nothing. As she stared into the darkness, there was an unexpected flare of light from two torches burning outside the cottage. She wondered what it meant. By the fitful light of the torches she could see dark shapes moving about. The soldiers were there!

If they caught Peter, she had no doubt they would soon find out everything that they wished to know. The awful face in the water, the leader of the soldiers, he would be among them, and Gwen felt certain he wanted her. In the flower meadow near Woodford, the first assailant, who must have been a brother, had certainly meant to capture her. This second man had not been so certain in the forest. But now he knew, and was determined to find her. She had no idea why this hideous creature was plotting to harm her, but she was convinced he was. She shivered slightly in the warm air.

The torches disappeared, and there was a bright light from inside the cottage. Moments later the torches reappeared and quickly increased in number. They were coming towards her!

It was as though she had planned for this event. Without any conscious decision, she climbed out through the back of the willow and crawled rapidly down to the riverbank, about fifty paces up from where they had moored the boat. Quickly removing her blue gown and folding it into a tight bundle, she placed it on her head and fastened it with the belt around her chin. Then, very slowly, without making a splash, she slipped like an eel into the water and swam up stream and towards the other bank, her head held high. With strong strokes, Gwen soon reached the safety of an overhanging willow on the opposite side. She peered out from beneath the protective covering and tried to understand what was happening on the other bank. Men with torches were shouting to each other and searching the place where she had been only minutes before. She guessed Peter must have been captured.

Then a rosy glow appeared in the sky, followed by a sudden eruption of bright sparks and dense smoke. She knew it must be the cottage. The torches on the opposite bank vanished, and in the still night air she could hear the unnerving sounds of a battle. Gwen wondered who could be attacking the soldiers.

There was a splash and a grinding of rope on wooden pulleys and she saw the ferryboat move like a phantom across the silvery water. When it reached the other side, a number of men on horses galloped up the bank and disappeared from view. The cries and yells increased, then slowly subsided. The glow in the sky faded and silence returned.

Gwen was beginning to feel cold, and knew she would soon have to leave the protection of the river. The problem was on which side would she be safer? The question was almost immediately resolved, as shadowy horsemen appeared on the steep slope leading down to the ferry on the opposite bank. The men dismounted and led the horses onto the boat. She could not see how many men were involved, but she could hear their strange voices and some bursts of brutal laughter. She guessed the soldiers had won the battle.

The ferry made three crossings while Gwen stayed concealed in the cold water. When there was no more movement on the ferry landing, she swam silently towards the opposite bank, holding her head high above the water.

She climbed out and hid in the comforting shadows of the trees, listening for any sound, and trying to control her shivering. After a few minutes she took off the bundle from her head and began to rub herself vigorously with handfuls of grass. Then she donned her blue robe and moved cat-like into the forest in the direction of the clearing.

Gwen reached the cleared area of the ferry at the place where the road joined the clearing. She guessed she was at the furthest point from the cottage, which had been reduced to a smouldering heap. There seemed to be no movement anywhere, but she was too cautious to venture out into the open. She followed the tree line for a few paces, until she was parallel with the road and away from the clearing on her left. The road was bright and bare in the moonlight, and she felt very vulnerable as she glided across. Nothing happened. Gwen took a deep breath and decided to press on through the trees in the direction of the cottage.

She worried about Martin and Peter and wondered if they were alive and free, or whether the soldiers had captured them. The possibility that they were dead was not something she wished to think about. There had been many others involved in the battle, and perhaps she could find some of them to learn what had happened.

The ground began to slope up to her right, and rather than be too close to the clearing, she began to climb. The trees formed a thick canopy above, allowing only patches of light to filter through. On her left and some paces away, she imagined the clearing: moonlit and dangerous. As she edged forward in the darkness, her bare foot felt something hard. Gwen bent down, and her hand touched the cold outline of a sword. She had never held one before, but picking it up gave her a feeling of security and its presence proved she had reached the area of the battle. She advanced with extra caution, her strong arms holding the sword in front of her.

It was when she reached a point just above the smouldering cottage that she heard a sound. It was a deep, resonant groan of a man in pain. She tiptoed towards the sound. The trees were thinner and some larger patches of light filtered through. As she edged slowly round a stunted sycamore, she came face to face with a large, old man propped up against a fallen trunk. His eyes were closed, but in the dim light she could see his chest heaving.

Gwen knelt down next to the old man, laid down the sword and touched his shoulder. "Are you alright?" she whispered.

He was immediately awake. He stared wide-eyed at her, his lips moving, but making no sound, like a fish in water. A deep gurgling cough shook him and his eyes closed again. Gwen saw he had a water bottle hanging from his belt. She lifted the bottle to his lips and he tried to drink, but most of it trickled down his chin. He coughed again and lay back, gasping for breath.

After a few moments he summoned up his remaining strength and tried to speak. "I'm dying... stabbed in the back... Dan Birch did it." He coughed and lay with his mouth open for a few moments.

"It's alright. Don't try to speak. Save your strength," Gwen said.

He shook his head slowly. "'Don't 'ave much longer... we came to find a girl... you?" he murmured. "The boy, John, 'ad a sword... we came to 'elp 'im find... Gwenny." He coughed, and she used a scarf round his neck to wipe away the blood that had appeared on his lips.

"I'm Gwenny," she said. Only her father had ever called her by that name.

"Good," he gasped. "Good... John's 'round 'ere somewhere... saw 'im fall... tried to 'elp... stabbed..." He was racked with a bout of coughing, but he fought to tell her something important. His hand grasped hers and he tried unsuccessfully to sit up. His eyes stared at some point behind Gwen's shoulder. "Dan stole... sword." His voice gave up and he coughed weakly.

Slowly, his eyes closed, and his breathing became more laboured. She knew he was dying and held his hand. After a few minutes he stopped breathing, and she wept.

She did not know how long she knelt beside the body. He had seemed a fine old man, and someone he knew had stabbed him in the back. He had also mentioned John, the youth with the sword. She remembered him: his dark hair, his handsome face, and the strange motif on the palm of his hand that produced in her such a strange and exciting sensation. Gwen said a prayer over the dead man, and rose unsteadily to her feet. Tiredness and a great sadness threatened to overwhelm her.

An owl screeched somewhere in the trees. Gwen tried to clamber through some thick undergrowth, and found it was too difficult in the dark. She stepped back and decided to find a suitable space to rest until dawn, when she could see where she was going. The owl called again, a long insistent hoot. This time she took notice. Gwen moved tentatively towards the sound.

Another call echoed in the silent forest. She wondered if it meant anything. There was more space between the trees, and moonlight filtered down, creating strange patterns on the forest floor. The owl hooted again, and she could see its dark shape flying above her. It alighted on a branch and, after giving another loud cry, flew down to the left of her in a long glide. She turned and followed the owl. It had alighted in an oak about thirty paces away. There were fewer bushes and fallen branches, and she made quicker progress, using the sword to clear a path.

When she came across another corpse, it unnerved her. In the grey light she had thought it was a log. The body was of a young man. He was lying on his back with an arrow in his chest. There was a surprised expression on his face.

Gwen bent down and closed his eyes. His skin felt cold and he had been dead for some time.. He did not look like a fighting man, and had the clothes of a poor peasant.

The owl called again. It was perched on a branch that hung above some thick undergrowth. Gwen picked her way slowly towards the bushes, and could see dimly that something had carved a passage through the vegetation. Dawn was starting to break and the increased light revealed a pair of boots sticking out from under the leaves. She parted the undergrowth and found the body of another young man.

He was lying face down, and as she crawled in beside him she could see he was still breathing. Gwen was unable to turn him over in the bushes, and was forced to drag him out by his feet. He groaned, but did not stir. It was difficult to move him, and she was panting with the exertion. Once he was out of the bushes, she turned him over and recognized the youth who had rescued her twice before.

"John," she whispered, "Oh John!"

He had a lurid gash on his forehead, stretching down to just above his right eye. The blood had congealed, but the area was puffy. The eye was black and swollen and his upper lip was cut.

She needed to get some water to clean his wounds, but the river seemed a long way off and she worried about finding him again. Looking around she realized the owl had disappeared.

· · ·

THE LIGHT GREW STRONGER, and Gwen was able to see others had also fallen in the battle. About five paces away a thin man with a bald head, lay huddled grotesquely under a small alder. He had died with two arrows in him, and in his hand he still clutched a small, rusty sword. As she stared sadly at him she noticed he was carrying a leather water bottle, similar to the one the old man had carried. She bent down and unhitched it.

Gwen tasted the water and found it cool and refreshing. She splashed some on her face, and got to work. The dead man had a sharp knife in his belt, and she used this to cut off a piece of his shirt. Returning to John, she used the material and the water to wash away the dried blood and clean the grime from his face. Next, she removed the dead man's jacket and used it as a pillow for John's head. She felt no guilt in taking from a dead person; her concern was with the living. Finally, she tore a long strip of the material and used it as a bandage to keep the wound clean.

Later, she explored the area and found two more bodies: one was a tall man with a thin brown beard, the other was a youth who had been shot in the back by an arrow as he had been running away. She found that they all carried water bottles and small cloth bags with dried meat and cheese inside, and she collected these together and ate a small meal, taking care to leave some for John when he recovered.

It was still cool in the forest, although the sun was well up, and Gwen began to feel chilled as soon as she stopped moving about. She had covered John with his own cloak, and there was little more that she could do for him until either he recovered, or help arrived. She spent some time dragging the dead bodies closer together, so that they could have a decent burial when their friends arrived to look for them. After her exertions, she gently washed John's face again, hoping to waken him. He groaned softly but remained unconscious. Gwen continued to trace the contours of his face with her fingers: the high cheekbones, the strong jaw and particularly the full, soft lips. Using more of the water she gently dabbed away the congealed blood on his upper lip, then holding her breath she leaned over and kissed him, her mouth barely touching his. For a long time she sat gazing at him, memorising every feature. When she closed her eyes she could still see his face.

At about mid morning she decided to take some more definite action. She placed the water bottles and the food bags close to John's body, in case he awoke while she was gone. Standing up, she looked around and checked the forest for landmarks, and grasping the sword in her right hand, she stepped carefully down the gently sloping ground in the direction of the ferry landing. It took only a short time until she emerged from the trees, almost directly behind the gutted cottage. There were small wisps of smoke coming from the debris, but the main fire was out. Nothing moved in the clearing. All around was the aftermath of a fierce battle: there were bodies near the cottage, two dead horses lay in the tall grass close to the path, and a number of weapons were scattered around. The ferry landing was deserted and the boat was on the other side of the river.

Gwen did not wish to look at more corpses, but from the safety of the trees, she forced herself to check each body to see if any resembled her father. None did, so she retraced her steps and arrived back to find John sitting up holding his head in his hands.

· · ·

DAN BIRCH FELT ELATED as he led the defeated villagers on the long trek home. He had never wanted to help John, or get revenge on the soldiers for the killing of Will's brother. His family disliked the Carters, and Dan had a particular hatred for Will. From an early age, Dan had been in trouble with other villagers, and it was always the Carters who enforced the law. Now Will was dead, and Dan possessed the sword he had coveted from the moment he saw it.

"Both them Carters be dead now, and we won't 'ave nobody telling us what to do," Dan said to his two brothers. The two men only grunted their agreement. They did not share Dan's good humour, as both were suffering from minor wounds and, unlike Dan, had gained none of the spoils of war.

It was dawn, and the east was ablaze with pinks and blues. The birds were singing and the cloudless sky promised another hot day. Many of the villagers were limping and had minor injuries caused by their headlong flight away from the soldiers' arrows. Some had tried to fight, but their swordsmanship was no match for the professional fighting men, and the villagers were easily routed. Even though it was now light enough to see each other clearly, no one took the responsibility for checking who was missing.

As they shuffled along in a disorderly group, many cursed Dan Birch, for they had seen him stab Will in the back, as the old man tried to help John. They had seen Dan grab the golden sword and in the chaos of the battle escape into the forest. Will had tried to follow Dan, but after a few yards had collapsed in the place where Gwen found him.

Now Dan Birch led the group, and carried the sword on his shoulder, just as John had done, and the villagers knew their lives would never be the same.

They made slow progress during the hours of darkness, and in daylight were still uncertain as to the exact route back to their village. The path they were following looked well used and most were confident they would soon meet someone who could help them.

They came to a small cleared area leading to a shallow stream, much reduced by the recent lack of rain, with a rutted ford and a deep pool on one side.

"We'll stop here for a while," Dan announced. He was in no hurry.

He led the way to the water and, holding the sword on his shoulder with his left hand, he used his right to splash water on his face. As he bent down to cup the water into his mouth he paused to look at his reflection. There was something different about it. His eyes seemed to be staring back at him with a grim ferocity. Dan felt his heart beat faster as the face in the water changed rapidly to a demonic vision. Huge red eyes and a vast screaming mouth filled the pool. Dan let out a choking cry and backed away from the water. He waved his arms, pointing furiously at the stream and jabbering incomprehensibly.

The others looked at him strangely, but were either too tired or too sick to worry about his odd behaviour. Dan felt the sword slipping off his shoulder and tried to hold it with both hands. It twisted in his grip, and he staggered about struggling to retain a hold on the weapon. He presented a bizarre sight as he wrestled with the sword, gasping and grunting with the exertion, and making horrible faces. Dan made short frantic runs, interspersed with slight pauses when he seemed to be trying to dig his feet into the dusty earth.

"What in hell is 'e doing?" one man said.

"'Tis almost like he were being pulled by that sword," another commented.

By now everyone had stopped to watch Dan's convulsive progress down the path they had just come along. Suddenly, a strange thing happened, and they would only remember how the sword seemed to fly into the air, hover a moment and plunge down towards the thin, agitated figure. Dan gave a last desperate scream as the sharp blade pierced his chest, then he fell backwards onto the grass. At that moment, a huge black horse galloped out of the trees and raced towards Dan's body. The rider was enormous, and had a full red beard. As he reached the body, he leaned over and the sword appeared to jump into his hand. The rider let out a great roar of pleasure, and pulled brutally on the reins, causing the animal to rear up in the air. Then the rider turned the horse, and brandishing the sword, he cantered back into the trees.

The two Birch brothers were the first to react. They ran towards the body of their brother, while the rest of the villagers stood rooted to the spot, their mouths sagging and their eyes staring out of their heads.

"I think Dan be dead," someone whispered.

"'An' good riddance 'an all," another man said. "At least we won't 'ave 'im to worry about."

"That rider took the sword," another murmured.

"An' good riddance to that an' all," the second man said. There was general agreement to this statement, and they began to move slowly along the path, leaving the Birch brothers to carry Dan's body as best they could.

· · ·

GWEN GAVE A CRY of delight and ran towards John. He did not appear to hear her and did not react until she placed a hand on his arm.

"What happened?" he muttered. His voice was low and he appeared to be in pain.

"You have a deep gash on your head and your face is badly bruised," Gwen said. He was in no fit state for more detail. She lifted a water container to his lips. He tried to hold it himself, but his co-ordination was poor. He took a few sips then eased himself back onto the makeshift pillow. "I must sleep a bit," he mumbled, and promptly did so.

While he slept, Gwen sat close to him, and slowly chewed on some of the cold meat. Her dark eyes smiled as she watched him sleep. He was quite tall, with long wavy black hair and, his skin was, like hers, deeply tanned. She guessed he was about her age. He had a strong neck, a well formed nose, and she remembered his dark, sparkling eyes when he had rescued her from the soldiers. His hands were large with long, pointed fingers. He was handsome even with a bruised eye. She would enjoy nursing him back to health and getting to know him. For the first time for three days she felt happy.

There were so many unanswered questions. So much had happened in the past few days leaving Gwen with little opportunity to reflect on things. She wondered why John had travelled to Potter's Crossing, and who the peasants were who had tried to fight the soldiers. She thought of Martin and Peter, and worried if they had been captured or killed. Things had happened so quickly, allowing little time to consider them, and she felt guilty about her lack of concern for her two missing friends. Her head nodded and she dozed in a sitting position, with her head on her knees.

It was late afternoon when Gwen awoke; she was curled up and lying on her side. There was a cloak over her, and a fire was crackling a few feet away. She sat up to find John returning with an armful of twigs.

"You're better?" she enquired; it seemed impossible that he should have made such a recovery. She rose stiffly to her feet and stretched slowly in all directions.

John watched her through his one good eye. "Yes, I feel fine. My head hurts, but I'm lucky it was nothing worse." He indicated the bodies that were lying under the trees. "I can't find my sword," he said.

"Someone called Dan Birch stole it."

"How do you know?"

"I found an old man over there," Gwen indicated towards the denser area of trees. "He had been stabbed in the back, and before he died he told me Dan stabbed him and stole the sword."

"Oh," John's voice dropped. He stood looking at the ground. "Poor old Will. He was a good friend to me. Are you sure he's dead?"

Gwen nodded. "I sat with him for a long time after he died." The memory made her cry. It started as a small sniff and developed into a body-shaking spasm. All the anxiety, sadness and terror of the past few days contributed to her overwhelming passion, and she gave herself to it without restraint, shaking violently on her feet with her arms to her sides and her head bent forwards.

John stood staring at her. He felt awkward in the presence of such grief. Slowly, hesitantly, he approached her, and gently placed his arms around her. She buried her face in his broad shoulder and wept until she was exhausted. For a long time they stood, silent in each other's embrace, until a pheasant fluttered noisily onto a nearby tree.

They parted quickly, and both seemed embarrassed. Gwen wiped her eyes and ran her hands through her hair. She felt the short hair and turned away. "I must look awful," she protested.

"No," John said. "No, you look…" he paused, "wonderful." He said it with such feeling that she laughed.

"The closed eye suits you too," she joked.

They both giggled. The relief was so great that they wept with laughter, and ended up holding their sides unable to laugh any more. They sank to the ground and propped themselves against a tree. The restraint between them evaporated, and they sat quietly, regaining their composure.

"Dan Birch must be a very unpleasant man," Gwen said at last.

"I doubt if he will be alive now." John's fingers gingerly traced the extent of his wound. "I seemed to be the only one who could hold the sword without danger."

Gwen frowned and looked thoughtfully at John. "I think you and I should tell each other our stories. There is so much I don't understand. So much has happened to me in the past few days, that my life before seems unbelievably dull." She smiled. "You start, and then, if it's not too late, I'll continue."

Both of them sensed it was a precious time to be explored. They could have set out to find help, but instead they sat and listened to each other's stories. The sun set, and they plied the fire and sat around it and chewed on the dried food that was left, while the almost unbelievable accounts of their adventures were exchanged, and the questions asked. Finally, it was pitch dark. The moonlight filtered through the trees and the fire flickered and produced bright sparks that floated into the leafy canopy.

When Gwen completed her story, they both sat silently for a while, just staring at the fire. There were so many unanswered questions, but all of their strange experiences seemed to have a single starting point: the connection between Gwen and John and the riddle of their heritage.

"I want to know who I am," Gwen said, breaking the thoughtful silence. "Tom has been good to me, but it appears he is not my true father."

"I have no clear memory of any parents," John said. He described his vague recollections of a sea crossing and a man who may have been his father. "He was a tall man, I don't remember him saying much; I think he was ill. I must have been very young. There were many men in armour. I think someone said he died." He stared into the fire, trying to dredge the depths of his earliest memories. It must have been winter time, he remembered the snow. "I seem to have vague memories of staying with different families, but Old Mary is the only one I really remember."

"Peter said I was given to the Ropers by a party of knights. He said I'm different to the other village girls. Do you think I'm different?" She turned to face him. It was important to her to know how he felt.

"I think you are quite different to other girls I met in the village," John said. "Your skin is darker, your hair is blacker and you…" he paused, "well, you're very beautiful."

Gwen felt the blood rush to her face, and was glad of the darkness. She gave a scornful laugh, "Beautiful with cropped hair!"

There was no look of humour in John's face. "Your hair will grow, that's nothing. I am talking about the real you. There is something wonderful in you, something that sets you apart from other girls of your age." He did not know how he knew this to be true, for his experience of girls was very limited.

He was so intent in articulating his thoughts, that Gwen felt she had to change the subject, no matter how pleasant the content. "Perhaps you should get some sleep," she suggested. "That head of yours is going to take some time to heal, and tomorrow we should be trying to get some help. These bodies will need burying."

John nodded absent-mindedly, and gave a long yawn. "Umm, I feel very tired," he said. The nervous energy that had enabled him to talk and listen for so many hours, suddenly ebbed away. He curled up with the undamaged part of his head resting on the makeshift pillow, and was immediately asleep. Gwen piled wood on the fire and covered John's unconscious body with his cloak. She looked about for a place to sleep, and tried, unsuccessfully to get comfortable. After a while, she got to her feet and stood for a moment looking at the outline of John's body in the glowing firelight, and a mischievous smile crossed her face. She tiptoed over and carefully lay down beside him and pulled the cloak over herself. As she snuggled into his back, she smiled contentedly and fell into a deep and carefree sleep.

They awoke at the first light. Gwen slipped quietly into the forest while John sat with his face in his hands. His wound felt raw and his head throbbed; he tentatively inspected his eye, peering first with one eye then the other.

"How did you sleep?" Gwen asked. She rubbed some water on her face and tried to comb out her hair with her fingers.

"I slept well," he yawned. "How about you?"

"The best sleep I've had for days." She turned away so he could not see she was laughing. He appeared to be unaware she had spent the night cuddled into his back.

After a cursory check of their sleeping area, they made their way down to the ferry crossing. The early morning sun warmed them, and the bright light cheered their spirits. They crossed the tall grass to the path and walked quickly towards the ferry landing, trying to avoid seeing the dead animals and the unknown corpses. There was an unpleasant smell in the air.

"It doesn't look as though anyone came this way yesterday," Gwen said.

"Everyone will be staying at home in case they meet the soldiers." John looked carefully around, but there was no sign of their enemy.

When they reached the crossing, they could see that the ferryboat was moored securely against the other landing. "They must have taken Martin's boat as well," Gwen said. "But I don't see it on the other bank."

They washed themselves in the cool river and Gwen tended to John's wound; it seemed to be healing well and his eye was less swollen. However, it had become a lurid blue and black, and the eye itself was a mass of red.

"It looks very sore."

"I'll live," John joked. He was feeling stronger, and he no longer experienced the dull ache in his head. He smiled encouragingly at her.

"Well, now we have to decide what we are going to do?" Gwen said.

"We can go back," John pointed up the road that lead to the landing, "and try to find a place to eat. Or we can swim this river and try to discover where the soldiers have gone. They may still have your father." He paused. "I favour crossing the river."

Gwen did not reply; she stared up the road, and there was a far-away look on her face.

"Gwen?"

She jumped slightly, and looked at John with a lack of recognition. She slowly shook her head and rubbed her hand over her brow. "I'm sorry, I had a very odd sensation." She took a deep breath. "I saw a party of knights galloping along a road. I think they're coming this way."

"You saw them?"

"Yes, as soon as you pointed down the road, I had a vision of many men on horses, and the leader wore chain mail with a white tunic with a large red cross on it."

Two weeks ago, John would have scoffed at this, but so much had happened that he was prepared to believe in visions, especially if Gwen claimed to have had one.

"If your vision is of something about to occur, then we should wait and see," John said.

"I have not had it happen to me very often. But it was so vivid, John. I know they are on their way."

They sat together on the warm planks of the landing, and gazed expectantly up the road. After a few minutes they could hear the steady drumming of a large number of hooves. They stood up and exchanged glances, staring at a point where the top of the road disappeared.

First, there was a dust cloud, followed by the tops of the lances and the heads of the knights and then the first horseman appeared over the rim of the hill. Gwen let out a loud gasp: the leader wore chain mail under a white tunic and on the front of it was emblazoned a large red cross.

The horsemen slowed to a trot and finally to a walk, as they approached the two young people. The leader was looking around at the burnt-out cottage and the fly-ridden corpses littering the open ground. He stared intently at John, and noted the blood-stained bandage and the battered face. He towered over them. His large white horse was frothing at the mouth. Two of the riders moved up on either side of the leader, while the rest, numbering at least forty men, remained back at a respectful distance. There was a sense of order and professionalism in the way they sat quietly on their horses.

"Were you part of this?" the knight demanded. His voice was strong and forceful and he spoke with authority. He had a full grey beard and blue piercing eyes.

"Yes, my Lord. I was leading a group of villagers from Reedleigh. We were trying to catch up with the soldiers, but they ambushed us in the woods over there."

"You were leading them?" The voice was sharp. "Why would these peasants follow you?"

"Because I had a sword. I took it from one of the leaders of the foreign soldiers."

The knight stared down at John and his expression was one of incredulity. His face was glistening with sweat and he was tired and impatient to be moving on, but there was something about the way the youth spoke and held himself, in spite of his injuries, which interested the knight. "What is your name?" he barked.

"John."

"You have another name?" the knight sounded irritated.

John swallowed and licked his lips. He felt overawed by this man. "I am told that my real name is," he took a deep breath, "Giles Plantard."

This statement had an immediate effect on the knight. He leaned forward in his saddle as if to get a closer view of John, and the sneer on his face vanished. "Tell me about the sword," he hissed.

"It had a strange design on the pommel," John said. He was trying to use the minimum of words. "The same as this." He held up the palm of his hand, and revealed the strange runes.

This action had an even more dramatic effect on the knight and on the two knights that were with him. All three dismounted and shuffled towards him; their limbs were stiff after the frantic gallop.

The leader grasped his hand and stared intently at the design on John's palm. He breathed in deeply and looked meaningfully at the other two knights.

"You lived in the hamlet of Reedleigh?" his voice was expressionless.

"No, my Lord. The soldiers had murdered one of the villagers of Reedleigh, and I helped the dead man's wife who was injured. The villagers decided to help me find the soldiers, especially as I carried the sword." John felt he was expressing the situation clearly and concisely, yet the knight was clearly expecting something else. "I've been living recently in the village of Woodford."

There was a sharp intake of air by all three knights. The name of the village seemed well known to them.

"And you," the knight turned his attention to Gwen. She was standing slightly behind John and had remained silently watching as the questions had been answered. "What is your name?"

"My name is Gwen, my Lord. I have lived for many years in the house of Tom Roper, the blacksmith at Woodford. I have come to understand he is not my real father." Gwen looked down at the ground as she spoke of Tom, as her eyes had filled with tears. In doing so, she missed the looks of amazement on the faces of the three knights.

The leader stared intently at both Gwen and John. He seemed to be comparing their faces. He reached forward and raised Gwen's left arm; his eyes were fixed on her silver bracelet. He lowered her arm and nodded his head thoughtfully. Finally, he turned away and consulted with the other two knights in an urgent whisper. One of them ordered two of the horsemen over to the river. The riders quickly discarded their battle dress and, with obvious enjoyment, swam to the other bank where they untied the ferry and pulled on the rope to bring the craft across.

The other knight climbed back on his horse and directed the majority of the men to serve as a burial party, and the remainder to collect up the weapons and keep guard. The leader climbed back on his horse, and commandeered the two horses from those who were operating the ferry.

"Can you ride?" he asked kindly. His attitude was almost deferential.

Gwen said she could, and John only nodded; it was not something he remembered doing. Yet, he felt confident that he could.

They both climbed on to the sweating horses, which stood waiting patiently, tossing their heads to rid themselves of the flies swarming around them.

"There are more bodies in the trees behind what was the cottage. Those are the villagers of Reedleigh," John said. "I don't know who these others are." He indicated the corpses in the grass.

The leader nodded and gave some more orders. He trotted back to where John and Gwen sat waiting on their mounts. "We will return to my castle. There you will be well looked after. We shall be there by midday." He spoke in short sharp sentences, leaving no room for misunderstandings. "I am Sir Richard de Godfroi."

The ferryboat completed its crossing, and the two soldiers dried off in the sun. Sir Richard spent a few moments checking on some details with the first knight, and then, accompanied by four soldiers, he walked his horse down to the boat. He dismounted and led the horse carefully down a short ramp and onto the ferry; the others did the same.

The ferry was more like a flat raft than a boat, but it did have a makeshift rail along both sides for people to hold on to and, when the river was in full flood, to give the horses extra security.

When they reached the other bank, two of the soldiers were set on guard. The other two acted as an escort to the knight, and brought up the rear, with Gwen and John in the middle of the small group.

"Reports indicate that the enemy has headed for the coast, but we won't take any chances. Keep alert." The knight set off at a canter, and John found that, although his horse behaved perfectly, it was an uncomfortable ride. Gwen was having far less trouble and he tried to copy her actions, but he was painfully aware of the two soldiers who travelled behind and who could see his lack of horsemanship.

CHAPTER 14

T HE COLUMN OF HORSEMEN kept up a steady pace and nobody spoke. The area was well treed and showed more signs of habitation than they had previously encountered. There were barns and animals in the fields, but strangely, only a few men were working. They passed through one seemingly deserted village, where only the dogs greeted them. The two soldiers forced open the door to the pub, and discovered the majority of the inhabitants hiding beneath the tables. When the soldiers enquired about *the enemy*, as the knight referred to them, the villagers claimed to know nothing. The knight sat upright in his saddle staring straight ahead like a stone statue, giving a terse grunt when one of the soldiers gave his report. John and Gwen felt intimidated by Sir Richard and kept silent. "Ride on!" was all Sir Richard would say.

Finally, when John was beginning to wonder how much longer he could endure the discomfort of his saddle, they reached their destination. It was a shallow valley through which a small stream flowed, and on both sides was a ragged cluster of poor cottages with thatched roofs. A wooden bridge crossed the stream, and the path led to a stone fortification on a nearby hill. The castle was not large, but was of sturdy construction. It was built halfway up the slope to give increased height to the walls, which had four turrets and a large wooden gate. Inside was a courtyard, which surrounded a rocky mound, on which was built a large stone rotunda with a massive iron gate.

The outer walls enclosed a number of rambling wooden buildings. These housed the soldiers and the horses, together with pens for animals and barns for food storage. At one side was a large well and close by were several workshops where blacksmiths were hammering out swords and spears, and other men were making wooden barrels and leather goods. Chickens and dogs were everywhere and children played in the mud, while their mothers prepared food. On the walls, well-armed soldiers paced about and monitored the steady flow of people through the main gate. After the isolation of the past two days, it felt strange for Gwen and John to be surrounded by so many people.

They dismounted in the crowded courtyard, and John almost fell out of the saddle. His legs ached and his head had begun to throb. He was relieved when some ragged stable lads ran forward to take the reins and lead the horses away.

"Give them a good rub down mind!" Sir Richard ordered. Then he walked towards a large, proud man who was dressed as though he had some authority in the castle, and whom John came to understand was the steward. The two men walked slowly towards the well in heated discussion. Then the steward clapped his hands and a number of servants came running to receive their orders. After he had dismissed them with a cursory wave of his hand, he continued to talk to Sir Richard.

Gwen and John were fascinated by all the activity going on around them, and John remarked on this to a woman who was carrying water in wooden buckets. " 'Tis not normally like this," the woman said. "Sir Richard called in all the men to help fight them invaders." She hurried away as Sir Richard returned. The self-important steward had disappeared inside the rotunda.

"Come with me. My steward will arrange for you to have new clothes, and some refreshment awaits us." He did not pause for any response, but strode towards the rotunda. The heavy gates were open and a guard stood to attention as the knight approached. Sir Richard led the way up a narrow flight of stone steps into a large circular room. The walls were covered in faded heraldic banners and an unusual array of weapons. Long curtains in deep blues and reds had been used to soften the effect of the stone, and some had been hung to divide off parts of the room. On the far wall, a winding staircase disappeared into the space above.

To the left of the entrance was a massive empty fireplace surrounded by two large chairs and some benches. On a small table was a flagon of wine and some goblets, and on a long refectory table in the centre of the room was an assortment of cold meats, cheeses, pickles and round loaves of bread. There was an ornately carved chair at the farther end and plain benches on both sides. A smaller, but equally ornate chair was at the nearer end.

The knight poured red wine into three pewter goblets and indicated that they should each take one. He raised his goblet and Gwen and John did the same. "To the Holy Grail," he said solemnly. He fixed them both with a thoughtful stare. Gwen smiled awkwardly and murmured the toast, while

John stared back, his mind racing. Old Mary had said he was the Keeper of the Grail. What was the connection?

"You aren't drinking," Sir Richard said sharply.

John flinched. He raised the goblet to his lips and drank deeply. The wine was good and he felt better than he had done for a while. "What does it mean to be the Keeper of the Grail?" he asked.

The old knight's eyes widened and then immediately became hooded. He took a deep draft of his wine, then slowly advanced until he was an arm's length away. John found himself having to raise his head as the knight frowned down at him. Sir Richard was still wearing his chain mail and high leather boots, and seemed immense in height and stature. "Who told you about the Keepers of the Grail?" he used the plural form and John absorbed this fact.

"I lived with an old woman called Old Mary; she told me that my name was really Giles Plantard and that I was the Keeper of the Grail," John replied.

There was a long pause as the knight considered this information.

"How long were you with this woman?" he asked.

"Almost a year," John said. "I have only vague memories of anything that happened before I arrived at her cottage." John paused. He wanted to say more but was unable to form the words, and ended up shrugging his shoulders.

The knight nodded curtly. He turned to Gwen. "You are the one I have been looking for," he smiled, and there was something gentle and adoring in the way he gazed at her. "But you," he faced John, and his expression hardened, "I had not expected to find."

The knight finished his wine with a great swallow and turned to get the flagon. Gwen gave John a questioning look. He widened his eyes and gave small shrug of his shoulders. The knight returned with the flagon. "We have a lot to discuss, and if you are the people you appear to be," he frowned, "you will have much to learn about your responsibilities."

He refilled his goblet and turned to Gwen. She declined, as she was unused to wine. Sir Richard rang a small bell and a young serving woman appeared at the main door. "Take Mistress Gwen to her chamber, and wait on her," he commanded. The woman smiled and curtsied, and indicated that Gwen should follow her up the winding staircase. "We shall eat when you are ready." He watched Gwen leave the room before filling John's goblet.

"There is much that you must tell me, but first you must change your clothes and have that wound attended to. Then we will eat." The steward descended the stairs and gave a short bow. "Everything is prepared my Lord."

"Good." Sir Richard turned to John. "From now on you will be treated like a gentleman. One of my servants will wait on you. If you have any other needs my steward will attend you." The steward bowed stiffly in John's direction. It was the first time, as far as he could remember, that anyone had ever bowed to him. It was a strange experience, yet one he enjoyed. "Thank you, my Lord," John said. He felt a warm glow of pride.

"If you will come with me, sir," the steward said. He led the way towards the stairs.

John placed his goblet on the small table and followed the man out of the room, remembering, just in time, to bow towards the knight.

The second floor of the rotunda was used for accommodating guests. Grey stone walls partitioned off the individual areas, each of which had a heavy brown curtain across the entrance. John's room was large in comparison to the sleeping area he had enjoyed in Old Mary's cottage. The furniture consisted of a simple sleeping pallet, a wooden box for storing clothes and a stool. A narrow open window allowed in some light, and through it John was able to look down onto the courtyard and have a view of the main gate. Across the ceiling huge oak beams supported the upper floor. John wondered, briefly, why such strong supports were needed, as they were double the width of those on the ceiling of the main room. However, it was only a fleeting concern.

On the wall was a plain oak cross, and on a small plaque were the Latin words *Deo non fortuna*. He bit his lip with excitement, he knew what it meant: *God not fortune*. In all the time he had stayed with Old Mary, he had never had the chance to see any writing, yet he knew how to read! This was a discovery that sent his mind into a whirl. What did it indicate about his earlier life?

"These are your quarters, my Lord," the steward said. "I hope the clothes are suitable." He regarded John steadily under thick bushy eyebrows, and his deferential attitude seemed like a mask hiding his true feelings.

John calmed his racing thoughts. "Does Sir Richard have a wife?"

"No, my Lord, Sir Richard's wife, Lady Margaret, died while he was away on the Crusade. Will that be all, my Lord?" He gave a slight bow and withdrew, carefully drawing the curtain after him.

John washed thoroughly and then called the servant to dress his wound. The man attended to his hair and took away his old clothes which had become little better than rags. He donned some brown leggings and a white linen under tunic with rucked sleeves. The servant helped him into a blue over tunic, which reached down to his knees and had decorations around the neck and the hem. Around his waist he wore a thick leather belt and there was a choice of sizes in the soft brown leather boots that were laid out for his inspection. Finally, the servant placed a rich burgundy cloak on his shoulders and attached it with a gold pin.

"What do I look like?" John asked the servant.

"Ye looks like a Norman courtier, m'Lord," the man replied.

John tried not to look too pleased, but in truth he could not believe his good fortune. He remembered Old Mary's prophecy: *You will have power some day*, and he wanted to believe the time had come. He sat on the box and reviewed the past hours. The knight had recognized the sign on his palm, yet Sir Richard said he was looking for Gwen. And the knights knew the name of her village. John furrowed his brow; there were a lot of things he still did not understand. He dismissed the servant and stared out of the narrow window.

In the courtyard there was increased activity as the rest of the soldiers arrived back. Many looked hot and exhausted, and the wives and younger women were bringing buckets of water for them to drink and pour over themselves. The two Norman knights had dismounted and were giving instructions to the stable lads; both men looked tired, but still held themselves aloof from the activity around them. John admired their discipline and their complete confidence in their own authority.

A few moments later they clattered past his curtain towards their own sleeping quarters, calling for their servants in loud, angry voices. While John listened to the running servants attending to the knights' demands, he practised walking around the bed, swirling his fine cloak. He wondered what Gwen would say when she saw him dressed like a lord, and felt excited at the prospect. On his way down to the great hall he saw the small area where a servant slept next to the stairs, and noticed the steps continued up to another floor. By the light of a guttering torch fixed to the wall, he could see round the dark well of the stairs to where a solid oak door barred further discovery. John wondered what was so important that it needed such a strong door to protect it, and decided to ask the knight when the opportunity arose. Perhaps it had something to do with the huge oak beams. He pondered this as he descended the stairs into the main hall.

John gave an involuntary gasp when he saw Gwen. She was dressed in a flowing white gown with a long, semi-circular cloak of deep purple. Her black hair had been braided with ribbons into long plaits, and covering the top of her head, and the cropped hair, was a small white veil which flowed over her shoulders and down her back, and was held in place by a simple gold fillet round her forehead. She looked wondrously beautiful.

She did not notice him for a moment as she was speaking earnestly to Sir Richard who had changed out of his military gear and was in Norman attire similar to John's. They both turned to face John, and he felt a chill pass through him as though this was a scene that was already changing and would never be repeated. He needed desperately to make it last. He wanted to be part of this way of life.

At the meal, Sir Richard sat at the head of the table with Gwen on one side and John on the other. The two knights who ate with them were introduced as Nicholas de Montford and Simon de Rochley; both men appeared to be in their mid thirties. Before they sat down, Sir Richard said the grace in Latin and then the servants brought in an array of food. There was a haunch of wild boar decorated with herbs, a well-grilled joint of beef, a roasted swan, and a large carp. The servants also brought in an assortment of pies, jellies and round loaves of dark bread. John had never seen so much food on one table, and was careful to notice how the knights behaved.

Each person had a large pewter platter and ate with a knife and with their fingers. The knights carved their own meat, taking slices from whatever took their fancy. A servant attended to Gwen, cutting the meats and placing them on her platter. There was red wine on the table as well as weak beer, and the pompous steward constantly refilled their goblets.

Sir Richard had a hearty appetite and ate large quantities of meat. The two knights ate less, but drank considerably more wine. John noticed the servants seemed very wary of Nicholas de Montford, especially one young women who could scarcely control the shaking in her hand when she served him.

The conversation during the meal was about horses, travel and hawking. There was no mention of the day's events, and no attempt was made to question Gwen or John as to their identity or on their recent encounters with the enemy. As the topics of discussion were outside their experiences, Gwen and John said little. John noticed how the two knights vied for Gwen's attention, and talked loudly of their own accomplishments. Gwen seemed to enjoy being the focus of the conversation and smiled frequently, while John became more and more aware of his own lack of knowledge. Before the meal he had felt important and dashing in his new clothes, and he had been delighted to have servants to wait on him. But these knights took all this for granted. Money and servants were of no importance; they had always enjoyed these things. He wondered what these men still desired, and what were their ambitions?

When the meal was finished, the servants cleared the table and brought more wine, oat cakes and cheese. After this they bowed their way out of the room.

"Now we can talk about the main issue of the day," Sir Richard said. He turned to Gwen. "When we met today, our forces had just returned from your village of Woodford, but we were too late it seems." He gave her a hard searching look. "We have known of your existence in that village with Roper the blacksmith, since old Sir Maurice of Ridefort persuaded him to give you a safe home. How long have you known he was not your father?"

"Only during the last few days, my Lord," Gwen said. She looked down at the table. "He has been good to me, and I will always think of him as my father."

"Did he ever tell you anything about yourself?" Simon de Rochley said. He was a slim, muscular man with thin cruel lips and a scar near his left eye.

"No, I thought I was his daughter."

"And who do you think you are now?" Nicholas de Montford asked. He was the larger of the two knights, and had heavy features and a ruddy complexion. What was most noticeable were his thick lips, and the way the lower lip sagged down in one corner, giving him the appearance of always talking out of the side of his mouth.

"I have come to believe that I am important in some way," Gwen said, choosing her words with care. "The soldiers in black were keen to capture me."

"Tell us what happened," Sir Richard said.

Gwen recounted her story from the time the foreign warrior had tried to capture her in the flower meadow. She described all of the strange events and detailed John's role in twice rescuing her. She spoke of Peter and Martin and of her hope of freeing her father.

The servants brought in fresh candles for the table and placed flaming torches in the wall brackets. The servants refilled the goblets and bowed out of the room, as Sir Richard continued the questions. "What happened to your friends, Martin and Peter?"

"I don't know, my Lord," Gwen said. "I hope they escaped. Perhaps they went with John's villagers? I did not see their bodies around the cottage the morning after the battle. I have good reason to hope that they survived, have

I not?" She directed her question at everyone at the table. John noticed how the two lesser knights nodded encouragingly, while Sir Richard pursed his lips and concentrated on his wine.

There was a pause and Gwen looked quickly round the table; her face was flushed. "Well, who am I, my Lords? And why the secrecy?"

"My dear," Sir Richard said quietly. "You are a beautiful and intelligent young woman, but you are also a member of a very important bloodline. Your family have, for hundreds of years, been protected and venerated by people such as ourselves, who are privy to your secret. When you were very young, a series of terrible events occurred and the enemy discovered the identity of many members of your family. These were grim days for our brotherhood, but in the year of Our Lord 1095 we launched the Crusade and attempted to regain the lost Kingdom of Jerusalem for the Christian church. This we achieved four years later." He took a sip of wine.

"At the same time we managed to rescue some small fragments of what had been a great dynasty. You were one of those who was rescued. But the enemy was powerful and had spies everywhere. In the year 1101 we returned to England only to find that the enemy was waiting for us. It was impossible to guard you all the time, as our order was weak and reduced in numbers after five years in the field of war. I was with Sir Maurice when the Order decided to hide you, and Tom Roper was his choice." He smiled sadly.

"Each time we thought of bringing you back to the comfort and status to which you should have been accustomed, we would discover fresh evidence of treachery and betrayal. I think it was because we kept such a regular watch on you, that we eventually revealed your hiding place." Sir Richard paused and nodded to Nicholas de Montford who seemed eager to speak.

"We did not know the enemy had landed in such large numbers until after the big fire. We had to get the men in from the fields and give them some brief training and then we marched to Woodford to give you our protection." He leered at Gwen.

"We even crossed at Potter's Crossing," Simon de Rochley added bitterly. "We must have missed them by a few hours. Perhaps they did not wish to engage us." His voice was slightly slurred with the wine.

"I think that Potter's Crossing was where they had intended us to meet up with them," John said. He had not spoken for a while, and the whole picture of the events was now clear in his mind. "They hoped to re-capture Gwen, kill me and regain the sword.

Simon de Rochley turned his attention to John. He regarded him for a few moments with an ironic smile on his lean face. "I think perhaps it is time for you to tell us about this sword you claim to have had, and how you come to have that design on your palm." He spoke in a patronising way, hardly opening his thin lips.

John felt the blood rush to his face. He knew he was being insulted, but was unsure what to do about it.

"Before you start, we'll have a short break," Sir Richard said firmly. "There are a lot of arrangements to be made for tomorrow, and we may receive fresh reports of the enemy's position." He stood up and stretched. "Nicholas, I want you to check the horses. Simon, you'd better see what state the men are in. Make sure they don't get drunk; we may have to march at first light." He bowed to Gwen, turned on his heal and disappeared through the main door, followed closely by the two knights.

"What does it all mean?" Gwen said. She yawned and rubbed her eyes. "I'm feeling so tired. It's been a long day."

"I think you will be well looked after, whatever happens," John said. "But I don't think they believe me."

"This bloodline, what is that about?" she rested her forehead on her hands. She felt exhausted.

"I think it is the key to everything that has happened," John said. He looked cautiously towards the door, and lowered his voice. "What do you think of these people?"

Gwen raised her head from her hands and looked at him quizzically, "I don't know. I think I trust Sir Richard, but I am not sure about the other two. How do you feel about them?"

"I don't think I like them. It is just a feeling, but there is something unpleasant about Nicholas; the servants are terrified of him. Simon unnerves me; he is so cold and calculating. Sir Richard seems pleasant enough, and generous," John indicated his clothes, "but I think he is a fanatic. Have you noticed the way he looks at you? It is as though you are a princess or," he waved his hands as if searching for a suitable word, "a – a goddess."

"Don't be silly," Gwen said, pouting her lips. "I may be part of some great family, but that's all. I think he's just being kind." She sat up and glanced towards the door. "I agree with you about the one called Nicholas; he doesn't take his eyes off me." She gave a little shudder. "I think you need to watch Simon. I don't think he likes you." She was going to say more when the main door opened and Sir Richard entered. Gwen and John stood up, after exchanging warning glances.

Sir Richard walked towards them with a preoccupied expression on his face, then seeing Gwen he smiled. "My dear, you are looking tired."

Gwen curtsied and gave a brave smile in return. "My Lord, it has been a long day. Many long days!" she added with a laugh. "With your permission I shall go to my room."

"Of course, my dear." Sir Richard rang the bell, and a servant girl appeared from the floor above. "Attend to the mistress," he ordered. As Gwen went to leave, he reached for her right hand and raised it to his lips.

"What you have told us tonight is almost unbelievable. It is a miracle. But you are safe now, my dear, and I vow you will never be exposed to such dangers again. From this hour on you will be guarded continually and, when it is safe to do so, you will be taken to France where the main part of our order is situated. You have much to learn about the great role you will play."

Gwen went to respond, but changed her mind, and merely curtsied before leaving the room with the servant girl.

He turned to John. "We have much to thank you for. Without you the enemy would have gained its greatest prize," he smiled at Gwen as she left the room. "You must also be tired, especially with that wound. Your story can wait until another time."

John felt that he had been dismissed, as though he was of no great importance. Yet, he also felt relieved. His strange and magical experiences seemed even more improbable in the formal luxury of this military setting. At that moment the two knights returned.

"Where is Mistress Gwen?" Nicholas asked as he picked up his goblet.

"Gone to bed," Sir Richard said.

"Already?" Nicholas sounded disappointed. "None of those lazy messengers has returned," he complained. He swore an oath and muttered about what he would do if they failed to return before morning.

"The men are tired, but they will do as they're ordered," Simon said. "They're hoping we won't have to travel at night." He gave an ironic laugh and drank deeply. He staggered slightly.

"We are all hoping we won't have to travel at night," Nicholas said. He sank into a big chair by the fireplace. "Still, not a bad day all things considered." He spoke out of the side of his mouth.

"God has answered our prayers," Sir Richard intoned.

John was still standing near the refectory table, but it was as though he did not exist. "With your permission, my Lord, I shall go to bed." John tried to be as formal as possible to avoid any further sneers from Simon.

Sir Richard turned to him and nodded. Relieved, John turned to go.

"Just one moment." It was the voice of Simon de Rochley. His words were slurred. "You were going to tell us about that sword." He swayed towards John and placed a strong, rough hand on his shoulder. "That magic sword." He emphasised the word magic, his voice heavy with sarcasm.

"I captured it from the warrior who attacked Gwen. The blacksmith had a similar sword."

"Captured?" Simon mimicked. "You mean he fell off his horse and you picked up his sword!"

"That's not true," John replied hotly.

"Do you know anything about this sword the blacksmith is supposed to have had?" Nicholas directed his question at Sir Richard.

"Yes, he had a particular sword all right," Sir Richard stared unseeing at the open fireplace. "We captured it in Jerusalem. It was a sacred object to the enemy. Sir Maurice brought it back with him and decided to give it to the blacksmith as a token of the girl's importance." He turned to face John. "What happened to that sword?"

"The blacksmith was taken prisoner by the soldiers when he tried to rescue Gwen."

"He must be a coward, or he would have died fighting," Simon mocked.

John shook off Simon's hand. "He fought bravely, but the leader threatened to kill Gwen if Tom did not surrender. That is why Gwen has her hair cropped on the top; the leader pretended to cut off her head." This statement had a sobering effect on the knights; they had all noticed Gwen's hair.

"You said you had a sword that you took from the first leader. What happened to it?" Sir Richard spoke softly. The other two men stared at John contemptuously.

"It was taken from me when I was leading the villagers against the soldiers at Potter's Crossing." He realised he had not impressed the knights. "It was dark, and we could see the cottage on fire, and as we approached the edge of the forest the soldiers ambushed us. The man in front of me was hit by an arrow, and I believe I tripped and knocked myself unconscious on a tree."

"How could you have been leading and yet be behind this man whom you tripped over?" Simon jeered. "I think you're a liar."

"Just trying to impress the girl with your stories," Nicholas added.

"I'm no liar," John protested. He felt hurt and humiliated by their accusations. "Gwen found an old man who was dying of his wounds; he told her that Dan Birch, one of the villagers, stole the sword from me when I was unconscious."

Simon spat on the floor, and refilled his goblet, then ignoring John he sat in the other large chair near the fireplace. There was a long silence, and John wondered how he could extract himself with some modicum of dignity.

"When we first met at the ferry, you said the villagers followed you because of the sword," Sir Richard said. "What did you mean?"

John was relieved at the break in the sullen silence. "I was the only one who could hold the sword," he said. "When others tried, it seemed to become alive and tried to stab them." He was aware of the knights looking at him as though he was half-witted. "The warrior, who almost captured Gwen, would have killed me with the sword." He spoke quickly, stumbling over his words, "but I... I held up this hand with the imprint of the same design that was on the sword, and I yelled my other name... the name Old Mary gave me... Giles Plantard!" He was breathing heavily. "The sword jumped into the air and it... it went straight through his chest... it killed him." John licked his dry lips and tried to control the strong emotions that gripped him. "The sword was evil... but I, I was able to control it."

The three knights stared at him. John stared back defiantly. It was Sir Richard who finally spoke. "How did you lose the sword if you were the only one who could control it?"

John swallowed and looked at the floor. This was the question he had feared, the one he had not wanted to face. "The sword lost its power when I," he screwed up his eyes, "when I no longer deserved to control it." He opened his eyes and looked up at the ceiling. He knew he was speaking the truth. "I wanted to impress the villagers, and I pretended that I had a vision of where we would meet the soldiers. It was untrue. The sword became like any other sword... just a heavy piece of metal. It was because of me, because of my pride... Old Mary warned me to avoid misusing my power... many of those men are dead because of me. "It was the first time he had acknowledged his responsibility.

It was a powerful and emotional speech and the fact that it was unbelievable did not matter. Even Simon was temporarily silenced by John's sincerity. Sir

Richard placed a tentative hand on John's shoulder." Where do you think the sword is now?

"I think the leader of the soldiers will have it. He was desperate to get it back. I seemed to have the power to oppose him, but Dan Birch was just a stupid, greedy man. I am certain he will be dead by now." John took a deep breath. He was thankful to have been able to confess his weakness. It was a great relief, and he felt light-headed.

"You tell a good story," Nicholas de Montford mocked, "no matter how unbelievable."

"The boy with the sword!" Simon roared. He finished his wine in a single gulp and threw the pewter goblet in the fireplace. "You can show me how to use a sword!" he yelled. His words were barely understandable. He tried to rise out of the chair but collapsed back in to it, and lay sprawled in a heap.

"You have done well," Sir Richard said gently. "Now you should get some sleep." He rang his bell and the steward appeared. "See the young gentleman to his room," he ordered.

The steward bowed and led the way. John bowed to Sir Richard and ignored the other two. As he followed the steward up the winding staircase, he felt strangely at peace.

He must have slept for a while, for he was woken by a loud crash, as though a heavy body had fallen. He could hear muffled cursing and the deliberate, heavy steps of people trying to climb the stairs. John had not undressed, but was sleeping on top of the bed with his cloak over himself. He sat up and crept over to the heavy curtain. He pushed it cautiously to one side until he could see the area of the staircase, and was just in time to observe some shadowy forms climbing the stairs to the upper floor. As the figures reached the top, their shadows were cast back down the staircase. Then the door closed at the top and everything was dark again.

He climbed back on his bed, and wondered what the knights were doing. He estimated that it was after midnight, and he thought it was strange that they should be engaged in military planning at such a late hour, especially as Simon de Rochley was so drunk. John dozed off again. He had a dream about a sword. It was always just beyond his reach. There was a rough sea and the sword was moving towards a large sailing ship. John was running across a beach and his feet were sinking into the sand. It was like running in a marsh. The waves were crashing on the shore, huge mountains of white water, and he knew he had to stop the sword from getting to the ship. He ran into the foaming brine, but the sword was always just out of reach. A big white, curling wave was towering over him, and there was a voice screaming and the sword was....

He was wide-awake and drenched in sweat. Outside an owl screamed. John wiped his face and tried to calm his racing breath. The owl cried out again, an urgent, insistent call. After a few moments he heard another sound: men were coming down the steps.

John tiptoed to the curtain and peered out. He could see Sir Richard holding a torch, while the other two knights climbed carefully down the stone steps. There was a whispered exchange, then Sir Richard continued down the second staircase, and the two knights carefully made their way along the corridor, past John's curtain and into their own sleeping quarters.

The owl called again, and John remembered his own experience with the strange man in the forest. It was Owl! There was no doubt in John's mind that he was being called, and he knew what it was he had to do.

He pushed the curtain silently to the side and crept out onto the stone corridor. Moving swiftly in his stocking feet, he came to the foot of the stairs where the young servant was curled up on a mound of straw like a domesticated animal. He could hear her heavy breathing. At the top of the stairs the weak flame of a torch flickered to one side of the great door he had seen earlier.

John stood at the bottom of the staircase and listened carefully. Apart from the steady breathing of the servant, there was no another sound. The owl had stopped calling.

There were sixteen stone steps to the top of the staircase, and when John reached the final one, he looked back down the dark grey tunnel and held his breath. At any moment he expected a voice to cry out or a dark shape to come rushing up the stairs after him.

The door was massive, and by the weak light of the torch he could see the strong hinges. There was an iron hand grip that one pulled to open the door, and the key had been left in the lock.

John gripped the handle and pulled, and the door slid silently open. Whoever had been in charge of the key had been too drunk to even turn the lock.

He eased his way through the door and closed it gently behind him. There was light in the room. John was intent on entering quickly and closing the door behind him, and failed to take any notice of the chamber other than to satisfy himself that nobody else was there.

When he turned round, he was confronted with a sight such as he had never experienced. The small wooden church at Woodford was his only clear memory of a religious building, and although he had some dim recollection of a stone chapel, he could not remember where. In front of him was a temple laid out with great complexity and precision. He was spellbound.

The room was large and circular, with a vaulted ceiling. In the centre of the floor was a sunken area with three steps down to a mosaic circle, in the centre of which a yellow flame was burning. Around the circular wall at equal spaces were thirteen stone seats, and there were seven narrow windows letting in glimpses of the night sky. Around the wall, three braziers glowed a deep red, and in the centre point of the ceiling was a complex design of interlaced patterns in the shape of a cross. There were other designs on the floor representing swords and shields and strange runes. It was like nothing he had ever heard of, and he shivered involuntarily. Now, he understood the need for the huge beams supporting this room.

There was something unpleasant about the place. Perhaps it was the odd sickly smell that clung in the cold air, or maybe it was that everything was composed of hard stone. There was no softness in the room, and John wondered what weird ceremonies were performed there. Someone had gone to enormous lengths to construct something that was both perfectly symmetrical and, he assumed, had some precise significance. John was not sure what he was looking at, but he was certain it was important. His eyes moved slowly round the room as he tried to memorise exactly what he was seeing. Did this have anything to do with the bloodline that Gwen was supposed to be a part of? Was he linked to the same family? He shivered. There was something unclean and frightening about this temple, if that was what it was, and he wanted no part of it.

The owl called again, and he was jolted back to reality. He sensed it would be dangerous to be discovered in this room. If it was as secret as he supposed, the knights might kill him for daring to intrude into their sanctum.

John walked quickly to the door and opened it a fraction; he was breathing quickly and a pulse vibrated in his throat. He checked there was nobody outside, and eased his way through the great door. He pulled it back into place, ensured the key was in the same position as he had found it, and climbed swiftly down the stairs with agile, cat-like strides. The servant was still asleep, snoring gently, and there was no movement in the corridor. He paused for a few seconds to listen for any sound, and at that moment the owl shrieked once more. John was certain it was a warning. He hurried to his room and slipped silently through his curtain and immediately curled up on his bed, wrapping his cloak around him.

A minute later he heard someone pass his curtain on their way to the stairs. There was a long pause, a muted exclamation, and he heard the servant girl cry out. After some muttered conversation, John heard the shuffling steps returning. They stopped. Then he heard his curtain being pulled softly aside. He lay still, trying to breath in a steady manner, straining his ears for any sound of movement. After what seemed a long time, he heard the swish of the curtain being replaced and the feet moved off down the short corridor.

His dreams were a confusion of stone temples, swords and shadowy figures. Once again, he was on a beach with his feet sinking deeply into the sand. There was a loud, raging sea and a large sailing ship was heading out into the storm and he could not stop it, because of a noise and… people were shouting and someone was shaking his shoulder.

"Wake up, young sir. Wake up!" The steward 's bloated face was leaning over him.

John sat up and tried to get his thoughts together. It was early morning and a grey light was filtering through the narrow window.

"What is it?" John mumbled.

"Sir Richard wants you down stairs immediately," the steward said. He hastened out of the room and left the curtain slightly open. John climbed off the narrow bed and stretched himself. He heard feet in the corridor and glimpsed two servants running past. There were some angry yells and the servants darted back carrying a collection of belts, swords and helmets. The two knights followed, grumbling loudly. John waited until they had reached the staircase before he ventured out, and was in time to see Nicholas lash out with his foot at the second servant, who had not moved fast enough. There was a resounding crash as the equipment and the servant fell down the stairs. Nicholas gave a raucous, triumphant laugh.

As John walked towards the stairs he could hear the knights bellowing and the softer voices of the servants trying to placate the angry men. The maidservant, who had slept at the foot of the stairs, bobbed a curtsey as she passed John on the way to Gwen's room with a bowl of water. One side of her face was red and puffy.

By the time John reached the foot of the stairs, he was in a grim mood. No man, he reasoned, had the right to treat his fellow beings in this way. He was particularly annoyed that one of the knights should have hit the servant girl, merely for not staying awake. The main hall was awash with activity: servants were bringing in food, helping the three knights to don their chain mail, and sorting out the leather belts and boots. There were soldiers rushing in with information and receiving orders from Sir Richard, who appeared to be dealing both with the soldiers and with his steward. The two knights seemed more concerned with their own attire. There was a lot of shouting and cursing, and John felt that this did not bode well for the day. He walked up to Sir Richard, and kept his back to the two knights.

"Ah, there you are. Sleep well?" Sir Richard did not wait for a reply. "It would appear the enemy has outwitted us. I have been sending out scouts to cover all the roads, but it appears the enemy went down the river on that ferry boat last night." He rubbed his grey beard. "'Not surprising we didn't get any reports of their movements." He paused to give a quick order to the steward. "It seems they must have crossed the river and hidden themselves just up stream. It would explain why they hadn't destroyed the ferry. I was puzzled by that."

"Would they all have been able to fit onto that small ferryboat, my Lord?" John asked.

"The reports indicate that they left their horses behind. Apart from one black horse, there were no others on the boat. The boat could reach the mouth of the river by this evening. If we get a good start, we may still be able to intercept them, before they escape. "Better get something to eat, we may be able to use you." John did not respond immediately, and the knight drew his own conclusions. "That is, if you feel well enough to ride." He hurried towards the door where a group of soldiers was waiting.

John scowled. Yesterday he would have been pleased and proud to be included in the expedition, but after the events of the previous night, his views had changed. He glanced towards the other two knights: Nicholas was sitting on a bench while an inexperienced and nervous servant was pulling on his boots. "You useless idiot!" the knight bellowed. Behind him Simon was standing, glowering, while a servant hastened to attach his sword belt.

Avoiding their attention, John grabbed a pewter mug, filled it with milk and took a long drink. He cut himself a hunk of bread and moved back towards the staircase. At that moment Gwen appeared. She was dressed for riding and carried a whip.

"You're not going with them?" John exclaimed.

"Of course I am. The soldiers may have my father." She said the last word defiantly.

"I don't trust them," John said. He quickly told her about the strange temple at the top of the building. "These are not ordinary knights, and they treat their servants cruelly." He glanced round to ensure they were not being observed. "We don't have to go with them."

"I don't trust them either," Gwen said, "especially Nicholas de Montford. But I have no choice. I must find out if those foreign soldiers have my father." She looked appealingly at John. "We have come so far, we can't give up now."

John did not answer. Before Gwen appeared, he had made up his mind to escape with Gwen as soon as the opportunity arose.

"Look, you don't have to go. I know they will protect me," Gwen said. She took his hand and raised it to her lips. "But I don't want to lose you."

John melted. He gripped her hand with both of his. "You stay in the castle, I'll travel with them. It's silly for you to go. You can't fight."

"I have to be there when they find the soldiers," Gwen said. She looked him in the eyes. "I think you know I have to."

John swallowed hard. He was about to renew his plea, when a strident voice called Gwen's name. John let go of her soft hand and turned to face the room.

Nicholas de Montford strode towards them. He was in full chain mail, under a white tunic emblazoned with a red cross. He bowed low to Gwen and raised her hand to his thick lips. "Welcome, Mistress Gwen, I see you intend to join us." His smile revealed a mouthful of yellow, uneven teeth.

Gwen gave a tight smile and a half curtsey. "Thank you, my Lord."

"Allow me to escort you to the table," he offered his arm in an exaggerated flourish and, by doing so, turned his back on John, whom he had not acknowledged.

"John is also coming on our expedition," Gwen said pointedly.

A look of irritation crossed the knight's face, to be replaced almost instantly with a false smile. He turned to John. "Perhaps you will wish to lead us today," he spoke mockingly, "or perhaps not, now you have lost your…" he paused, "magic sword." He gave a loud guffaw and strode towards the table dragging Gwen along with him.

John stayed where he was and fumed inwardly. He watched Nicholas assist Gwen with her chair. He sat on one side of her and Simon took the other seat.

John approached Sir Richard who was giving instructions about the provisions. "My Lord." The knight turned and regarded him with a fierce stare.

"I feel quite recovered. My wound has healed well, and I wish to join you on your expedition," John said.

"And so you shall," Sir Richard said. He smiled broadly. "You must not take to heart anything that Nicholas and Simon say. They find it hard to believe things they have not experienced. When we return from this sortie, you will be able to tell your story. If you are the person I think you could be, then they will soon be bending their knee to you!" He laughed again.

"My lord, I shall need a sword," John said.

"Yes, of course, and a dagger as well." The knight looked at John's strong build. "Can you manage a shield?"

"Thank you, my Lord," John bowed and cast a furtive glance at Gwen who was being feted by the two knights.

"Choose your weapons," Sir Richard said. He made an expansive gesture towards a pile of weapons, and went to speak with the two knights. John selected a short sword, with a leather scabbard; a battered shield, that was not too heavy, and a bright, sharp dagger. When he turned round, Simon de Rochley had left with Sir Richard to organise the soldiers, and Nicholas was encouraging Gwen to go with him to check the horses.

"You'd better come with us, John," Gwen called to him across the room. "Nicholas will need to find you a horse." She pretended to gaiety.

"I'll find you a horse. There's no need for you to come," Nicholas said, darkly.

"I'd better come with you, my Lord," John smiled innocently at the sullen knight. "Sir Richard is almost ready to leave. Besides, I want to select a quiet horse."

"A quiet horse!" Nicholas echoed. "From what I heard about your riding yesterday, I think I should find you a donkey." He gave Gwen his arm and propelled her through the door and into the courtyard. John followed close behind, gripping his sword in one hand and clenching the other in a tight fist.

After a short while they were ready to leave. The weather was changing, and the clear blue sky was gone, replaced by dark clouds and a brisk wind. Already there was a dampness in the air.

"'Looks like we be going to have a wet ride an' all," one of the soldiers moaned as John walked by. He looked about the courtyard. There were about forty men in total, and most carried weapons and supplies. They sat on their horses, impatient to be off. Some joked with wives and other family members, while others sat quietly, absorbed in their own thoughts. At one side was a large, rickety supply wagon that was to follow behind with the spare horses.

Before they moved off, Sir Richard called a brief meeting with the two knights and included Gwen and John in the group. He seemed anxious and vaguely depressed.

"I have bad news. The latest reports are that they have passed the village of Ashley and could reach the mouth of the river by early evening. They are moving faster than I would have thought possible. Moreover, although they will have to pass close to the castle at Christchurch, the estuary is wide and it is possible that they could escape without being noticed. I have sent messengers to the garrison at the castle, and they may be able to intercept the boat. It depends if there is a galley in the harbour, or at least some fishing boats."

"My Lord, I doubt if the ferryboat will cope with rough water. If the soldiers are hoping to meet a larger ship, they may have to arrange for the transfer up river. It should allow more chance for them to be noticed," John said.

Simon de Rochley made an impatient snort. "We should not waste time discussing theories. We need to get down to the estuary as soon as possible and hope that the scouts do their job this time."

Sir Richard nodded. "Mount up and ride hard!" he yelled. He urged his horse into a canter and the rest of the group followed. John positioned himself behind Gwen's horse and tried not to think of the stiffness in his thighs.

Overhead the clouds darkened and the first drops of rain began to fall. The wind increased and became a strong south-westerly, and as the day unfolded the weather conditions deteriorated. The road that had been dry dirt and loose stone the day before, became a quagmire. Those at the back of the column suffered from the muck thrown up by the hooves of the lead horses, and the deep ruts caused their horses to stagger. Occasionally, the branches of great trees hung low over the way, forcing the riders to duck or pull up suddenly. Some men galloped into the branches, causing them to whiplash back, injuring the riders behind. By the time they paused to take a rest at midday, they had lost four of the original party.

"Those oafs can follow with the supply wagon," Simon de Rochley said. He made no effort to disguise his contempt for anyone who could not ride well.

"You must remember, Simon, that many of these men rarely get the chance to ride a horse," Sir Richard said.

Simon grunted and made no further comment. He was indifferent to the fate of the common men. Their suffering was their own fault and not his concern. He refused to get to know them or become friendly with them; they were merely beasts of burden, and whether they lived or died was immaterial, as long as he was able to accomplish his aims. This expedition was what he had been trained for, and he was anxious to reach the mouth of the river before the enemy could escape. He considered himself to be in peek physical condition, and he was desperate to avail himself of any chance that might gain him some reputation in the field of war. "We must press on," Simon urged. "The weather is slowing us down."

John noticed that Simon's horse was in more of a lather than the other horses, and there were bloody marks in its haunches where Simon's spurs had been cruelly applied.

"You ride well, Mistress Gwen," Nicholas de Montford said. He had removed his helmet and made a fawning smile. Gwen sat upright on her horse and appeared to be enjoying the experience. She gave Nicholas a nod and turned her mount to speak to John. The knight scowled and replaced his helmet. It was a rounded piece of armour with a flat top and two slits for the eyes and one for the mouth; it made him look both sinister and impersonal.

"I feel we are coming to the end of the affair, and I have no idea how it will end." Gwen moved her horse close to John's.

"I wish you hadn't come," John said. "I don't have a good feeling about this."

Gwen smiled encouragingly. "I had to come. I could not have stayed in that awful place by myself, wondering what was happening." She looked into his dark eyes. "Also, I wanted to be with you."

John tried not to be affected by this comment; he was still smarting from the insults he had received from the knights. "I am surprised that Sir Richard allowed you to come," he said moodily. "Especially as he thinks you are someone important."

"He was not in favour at first, but I pointed out to him that I would be safer with all of you than by myself, especially as we did not know if the enemy had left any of their group behind." Her smile was infectious, and she used it enticingly. "If we catch up with the soldiers, I have promised Sir Richard I will keep back from the action." She looked demurely down at her saddle. "Also Nicholas has said he will protect me." She watched John's reaction under hooded lids.

John frowned and stuck out his lips. "If anyone is going to protect you it will be me," he muttered.

Gwen laughed and reached for his hand. "I had hoped you would say so." She removed the thick silver bracelet she wore on her left wrist. "I want you to wear this for me today. If all goes well, you can return it to me later." She forced it over his hand and onto his wrist. "Take care, for my sake."

John flushed with pleasure. Words failed him, and all he could do was nod briefly before wheeling his horse and joining Sir Richard. Nicholas de Montford had witnessed the exchange, and swore quietly under his helmet. How he hated this young upstart.

CHAPTER 15

THE RAIN PUMMELLED DOWN, drenching the riders. Their capes no longer hung loosely over their shoulders, but clung, sodden to their backs, like thick skins. The path was waterlogged and difficult to follow, and the wind howled in their ears and buffeted them with powerful gusts. The pace slowed, until at last they were only able to proceed at walking speed.

Their route took them close to the village of Avon, but there was no news of the foreign soldiers, and the villagers were distrustful of such a large body of horsemen.

"This road takes us directly to Christchurch, but we are no longer in sight of the river," Sir Richard said. They had stopped near a grove of large oak trees, and the men were getting what shelter they could. "I think we would be wasting time if we kept striking out for the river to check if they are in sight." The other two knights nodded their agreement. Sir Richard wiped the rain from his lined face. "If we press on we may reach the castle before nightfall; at the very least we can get some shelter from this accursed weather. At the best, we may get word of their position before they reach the mouth of the river."

Gwen was no longer enjoying the journey, but her mind was composed, and she was determined to accept the discomforts. While the knights were cursing the weather and the tardiness of the other riders, she stood quietly by the side of her horse, patting its neck, and saying nothing. There was a chance to eat, but few had any appetite.

John had pressed on to the village of Sopley, with two of Sir Richard's more experienced men, to seek information. The village was close and John returned before the main group left the shelter of the trees. He was feeling more confident of his riding ability, and was beginning to enjoy the experience, in spite of his unease about the outcome of the expedition.

"The enemy are some way ahead of us, my Lord," he reported to Sir

213

BARRY MATHIAS

Richard. "The boat passed down the river at about midday; it was seen by some fishermen. They said the men on board were like black devils, and the villagers were too scared to continue fishing." He smiled. "Which was lucky for us, or we would not have had the report."

"Well, we are still in the race," Sir Richard said. "We seem to have lost two more men. Lame horses so the others tell me."

"Lame horses!" Simon scoffed, as they rode away. "Lame hearts more likely!"

At times the rain eased and they would dare to hope it would stop, but always their expectations were dashed when the deluge renewed itself with increased ferocity. Cold and exhaustion were beginning to take their toll, and it was only the prospect of dry quarters in the castle at Christchurch that prevented others from dropping out. From bits of conversation he overheard, John understood that most of the men were quite happy not to catch up with the foreign soldiers.

It was still light when they came upon two ragged men pulling a small cart which was filled with fish. The fisherman smiled awkwardly at the knights, fearful of what they might do.

"How far is it to Christchurch?" Sir Richard bellowed. His voice was carried away by the wind.

"Ye'll be there by dark if ye trots a bit, m'Lord," one of the men answered.

"Where is your boat?" Simon shouted.

The men looked anxiously at each other. "We be poor men, sir. The boat is owned by all our family."

"I didn't ask for the history of your family!" Simon roared. "Tell me where your boat is!"

The men looked quite beaten. "M'Lord, the boat is over there," the older man indicated with his hand towards a small path joining the road. "'Tis only a very small craft," he added.

"You have just been fishing?" Nicholas demanded.

The men looked hopelessly at one another. "Yes, m'Lord," they answered together.

"You are not going to be punished," Sir Richard interjected. The fishermen looked relieved. "We need your help." Both men nodded furiously. "Have you seen a large flat boat with a party of soldiers and a black horse?"

214

"Oh yes, m'Lord, we sees 'em a short while back. We was just pulling in our nets when we sees 'em."

"Where did you see them! Get on with it!" Simon bellowed.

"Just opposite where we keeps our boat. There be a small creek up yonder," he indicated up the path. "We was rowin' for shore 'cos our net be full and we 'ad to land to pull it in 'cos we 'ad caught so much fish. It were a monstrous catch," he indicated all the fish in the cart.

"Yes?" Sir Richard said encouragingly, trying to prevent Simon from assaulting the man.

"Just as we was starting to pull in the net, we sees this boat ye talked of, and it were in trouble." The older man was feeling more confident. "The currents is strong there and the tide be coming in and meeting the river goin' out, and what with this wind an' all, it was fierce out there and dangerous if ye don't know the waters."

"Go on," Sir Richard urged. "What happened to it?"

"Well, m'Lord, the current took they to the other side, and we sees 'em is near the rocks. Then a strange thing 'appened." The older man stopped and looked at the younger man as if for confirmation.

"Get on with it before I have you thrashed!" Simon de Rochley shouted. His voice was barely carrying into the pounding wind.

The younger man spoke. "It were like this. We could just see 'em in spite of the rain and the surf, and they was close to the rocks, when suddenly the sea went quiet. Just in that part near the rocks. One moment there was lots o' white water and next there it were, calm as a pool."

"Then what happened?" Sir Richard asked. He moved closer.

"We could see this big fellow with a red beard, it were quite far off, but we could see 'im clearly. 'E was wavin' this big sword an' all." The young man faltered, and the older man nodded encouragement. "Then they gets past the rocks, against the current mind, an' they be safe in the cove across from us. I never seen nothin' like it." He shook his wet head from side to side like a seal. "'Specially as the sea gets rough again as soon as they be in the safety of the cove. That be real queer."

The men were quite serious, and had obviously seen something outside their normal experience. They looked uncertain what to do.

"So the soldiers in black are safely on the other shore! Why could you not have said so in the first place!" Simon demanded.

Sir Richard ignored this outburst, and spoke encouragingly. "You have done well. Now tell me, what did they do after they were safe on shore?"

"Well, m'Lord, we was like to lose our catch what with the wind and the net being so full," the elder man said. "So, we sets about getting the net on shore, and when we looks again, there was nothin' there."

"Nothing there!" Nicholas echoed. "What do you mean?"

"It's true, sir," the younger man added. "The boat and all them people and the 'orse had all gone. As though they be swallowed up. As though they never be. They was…."

"Gone! Yes! So you said," Nicholas snapped. "How much of this are we to believe?" He turned to Richard. "It is very convenient that if we go to check their story, there is nothing there!"

"We did not tell them about the leader or his red beard, my Lord," John said, ignoring a snarl from Nicholas. "I believe these two men. The one we seek has strange powers."

"These are stories for the stupid and ignorant!" Simon de Rochley yelled; he looked meaningfully at John. "I suggest we go and look for ourselves."

Sir Richard dismissed the frightened fishermen, and both men dragged the cart away at great speed, stumbling over the uneven ground. As they passed the end of the column, two soldiers leaned over and each took a fish. The fisherman pretended not to notice, and were soon lost in the gathering gloom.

The knights led the way along the winding path to the creek where the fishermen kept their boat. It was a bleak place with stunted vegetation, broken rocks, and a large expanse of mud and sand. The creek was a shallow depression between two brown muddy banks, and was partly filled with water to about knee depth. A sturdy rowing boat was moored at the far end of the channel, attached by a rope to a seaweed-encrusted rock. Beyond the boat a narrow stream, enlarged by the heavy rain, rushed to meet the incoming tide.

The horsemen rode to the end of the creek, where they could see the whole of the seascape. To their right the river flowed into the estuary, broadening as it did so, until by the time it reached the sandy promontory on which they stopped, it was at least half a mile from shore to shore. Opposite, on the other side, was a shoal of rocks on which the incoming sea crashed furiously, sending plumes of white spray high into the air. On the river side of these rocks was a sheltered cove. There was no sign of a boat or any human habitation. Nothing moved except the waves and the scudding clouds.

"Look over there!" Sir Richard yelled. All heads turned to where he pointed. The opposite shore rose up to become high rocky cliffs, which stretched out towards the sea then curled around to almost enclose the wide estuary, like a narrow, crooked finger. On their side the shoreline was relatively straight, ending in a rocky outcrop on which the castle's towers could just be glimpsed. This craggy rock and the end of the high cliff formed a wide entrance to the estuary, and the curving cliffs provided a sheltered bay and a safe anchorage. "That's Hengistbury Head!" Sir Richard called out to those nearest to him. The information was passed along the column.

John leapt up in his saddle. "There it is!" he cried. "That's the ship!" They all peered across the storm-battered bay and there in the shelter of Hengistbury Head a large ship was riding out the storm.

"What ship is that?" Sir Richard asked, peering into the battering rain.

"It's the one I saw in a dream. It is the one the enemy are going to escape in!" John shouted back.

"Are you mad?" Simon de Rochley yelled. "Do you expect us to believe any more of your childish stories? I'm not one of your superstitious peasants!" He rode his horse between John and Sir Richard, forcing John's horse off the edge of the promontory and down onto the shingle beach. "Richard, we must get to the castle and see if they have had any reports. We have spent too much time listening to clowns and idiots." He turned his horse and followed by Nicholas de Montford he cantered back towards the road.

Sir Richard peered into the failing light for a few more moments, then signalled to his men to follow the two knights. He and Gwen waited while John rode his horse up from the beach. "Ride close to me and tell me about this dream," he bellowed, trying to get his voice to carry over the thundering of the waves and the roar of the wind.

It was dark when they reached the castle, and the heavy wooden gate was closed. A sentry challenged them, and they were forced to wait in the storm until torches were lit and the guard was able to identify who they were.

"Is Sir Michel de Tournier here?" Sir Richard demanded. The sergeant of the guard confirmed he was. "Tell him Sir Richard de Godfroi is here, with other noble company. I need shelter and food for my men."

The sergeant disappeared, the door was opened and the riders dismounted and walked their horses through into the stone flagged courtyard. Everyone was drenched and tired, and shivering from the cold wind and lack of warm food. Gwen kept silent throughout the last part of the journey, and concentrated on keeping alert and aware of her surroundings. The rain and wind was intense, forcing her to summon up her personal reserves of strength in order to remain in the saddle. As she climbed off her horse she realised her legs were quite numb, and she held on to the saddle to keep her balance.

John saw her stagger and moved up behind her. "How are you?"

"I'm well," she murmured. Then added, "Oh, I'm so glad to be here!" She gave a forced laugh. "I'll take your arm if I may."

John helped her towards the main building, where the knights were being greeted by a group of other knights. Sir Richard was speaking confidentially to a tall dark-haired man who listened carefully, and gave Gwen a long, hard stare.

"This is Sir Michel de Tournier," Sir Richard said. "And this is Mistress Gwen," he smiled, "although that will not be her name for much longer."

Sir Michel bowed and took her hand and raised it to his lips. "Mistress Gwen, I am honoured to meet you. My castle is at your disposal."

Sir Richard indicated John. "This is John, who may yet prove to be of great use to our cause." John and the knight made formal bows to each other. "He claims his other name is Giles Plantard," Sir Richard said quietly. A shocked expression came over Sir Michel's face, and was replaced, instantly, by a courteous smile. "Indeed? You are also most welcome," he said.

He took them into a great hall, where a huge fire burned and where servants were rapidly preparing a banqueting table with an array of food, including five types of fish, huge crabs, and plates of shellfish. Sir Richard's soldiers meanwhile were taken to the guardroom to be warmed and fed on more basic fare.

Sir Michel's wife, an austere, grey-haired woman, led Gwen away to change her clothes, and the knights and John huddled around the fire while servants brought goblets of hot mulled wine. Nicholas and Simon made a point of ignoring John, but refrained from other insults out of respect for Sir Michel.

"We are here to do battle with a group of foreign invaders," Sir Richard said. "They have killed a number of people, and may have some captives. We believe they have headed for this direction."

"We have had strange reports of them for a few days now," Sir Michel said. "Do we know who they are?"

"They are the enemies of The Order and set on destroying the Holy Grail," Sir Richard spoke gravely and there was a reluctance in his voice, as though even mentioning these things was difficult for him.

Sir Michel frowned and looked sidelong at the assembled knights. "We will talk more of this later." He relaxed his face. "However, we have received no news of these invaders in this area."

"Tell me about the ship in the bay," Sir Richard said.

"Ah, you noticed it, did you? That is a very strange vessel," Sir Michel agreed. He turned to a short, stocky knight, "This is Louis Saint Clare. Tell them, Louis, about the ship."

Louis moved closer to Sir Richard. "The ship first appeared on a high tide about fourteen days ago," he said. "It must have entered the bay during the night, for the first thing we knew of it was when it was leaving on the morning tide. We were unable to get any details about its purpose or its cargo."

"Tell them about the fishermen," Sir Michel urged.

"Fisherman!" Simon de Rochley gave a derisory laugh.

Sir Richard raised his hand to silence any further comments. "Do go on. Tell us about the fishermen."

"That morning, some men were gathering shell fish on the opposite shore at first light, and they claimed they saw a large party of foot soldiers and cavalry dressed in black and making their way inland along the path towards the village of Wick," Louis said.

"Naturally, we investigated this report, but nobody at Wick had seen anything unusual, so we did not consider the information important, until some days later when we received other reports of soldiers in black who were terrorizing the countryside." He paused. "It was at this point we connected the soldiers with the ship out there."

"When did the ship return?" Nicholas asked. He was keen to be noticed.

"They must have returned during last night, for we did not see them until the low tide this morning," Louis answered. "By that time, this storm was blowing and it was too dangerous to cross the bay in such foul weather. Perhaps we will be able to inspect it tomorrow."

"Perhaps it will be gone by then," Sir Richard said. "What do you think, John?"

"I think so," John said. He straightened his shoulders under the steady gaze of the knights. "I think they intend to leave on the next full tide. This is why they have moved so quickly in their journey back from Woodford."

"What makes you think they will try to leave on the next tide?" Sir Michel asked. He looked puzzled.

"He dreamed it twice," Sir Richard said, ignoring a snort from Simon de Rochley. "I believe him. Just as I believe the report we were given by two of your local fisherman: they saw the enemy land on the opposite shore." He looked firmly at Nicholas and Simon. "There are some very strange things happening at the moment, and we must explore them and not dismiss them."

"When is the next full tide, my Lord?" John asked Sir Michel, who looked quickly towards Louis.

"The tide is just over half way in at the moment," the stocky man replied. He screwed up his face in deep concentration.

"Is there any way we could get over to the ship?" Sir Richard asked, his voice pleaded for agreement.

"Not in this weather, and anyway they would see or hear us long before we reached them, and it would be no easy matter to try to attack a ship of that size." Sir Michel was adamant.

"I don't believe they are on board yet," John ventured to speak. Sir Richard nodded encouragingly. "I think they will wait until the last moment, in the hope that the storm will die down." He pushed out his lips and took a deep breath. "In my dream," he paused, waiting for a roar of laughter. There was none. "In my dream, I saw the ship in the place where it is now. There were high cliffs on my right, and a long sandy beach. My feet were sinking into the sand."

"That is how it is on that beach," Louis said, "when the tide comes in it is almost like quicksand." Nicholas gave Simon a questioning look. Simon shrugged his shoulders.

"What else did you see?" Sir Michel asked quietly.

"I was chasing one of the swords." He looked round at the questioning faces. "There are two identical swords, and they have strange powers in the hands of certain people."

"I will tell you about them later," Sir Richard said to the others. "Continue!" He gestured towards John.

"The soldiers were pulling away in a boat, and I was unable to reach them in time. I knew there was another reason I had to stop them, apart from the sword, but my dream was not clear." He was speaking quickly and breathing heavily. "The storm was raging and huge waves were crashing on the beach. I tried to wade out, but it was impossible." He stopped speaking and his eyes were focused into the far distance. Everyone remained quiet, looking at his distraught face.

"I think it is time you all got out of those wet clothes," Sir Michel said, breaking the tension. "The servant will show you where to go." He indicated a young man who bowed and led the way.

When Sir Richard and the others had left the room, Sir Michel stood with his back to the fire and gathered his own knights around him. They spoke rapidly, exchanging views and considering options. They were still discussing their plans when Gwen returned, accompanied by Sir Richard, John and the two knights.

"We have a plan, of sorts," Sir Michel said. "I suggest we eat while we discuss it." He turned to Gwen, who was wearing one of his wife's dresses. "Mistress Gwen, you are a delight to the eyes. I salute you." He gave a deep bow.

Gwen blushed and returned a curtsey. "I am not used to such gallantry, my Lord."

"You will soon take your rightful position," Sir Richard spoke fervently, "and the years of drudgery will fade away. From now on you are under our protection." His watery blue eyes flashed and he picked up his goblet. "A toast: to beauty, to youth and the preservation of the Holy Grail!"

The knights raised their goblets and drank deeply. John watched Gwen, as she looked quickly from one to another. He could not tell if the attention of all these men pleased her, for she seemed to be acting a part, and disguising her real feelings.

During the meal Louis explained some of the problems. "We have a small harbour below the castle, but it is outside the estuary. It would be almost impossible to sail into the estuary from the harbour because of the direction of the wind, and the added problem of the high seas." By way of explanation he added, "The wind is coming from the west, which means we would be sailing directly into it. This would be possible in normal weather, but very difficult at this moment."

"Does that mean the ship in the bay will be locked in as well?" Sir Richard asked.

"For them, the wind could not be better," Louis Saint Clare said. "They will be able to cross the bay with the wind behind them, then beat at an angle through the mouth of the estuary and safely into the ocean."

"Is there no way that we could get to the other side tonight?" Sir Richard persisted. He frowned at Louis.

"There is a way, but it will not be easy," Louis said, he looked towards Sir Michel.

"We have a galley ship in the harbour. It was captured from pirates, and has been moored there, unused, for many months." Sir Michel helped himself to more food. "We have the men to operate the galley, but they have no experience of handling the oars, and in this foul weather there is a risk that, with sufficient fighting men as well on board, the ship could capsize.

"The most dangerous part would be coming through the mouth of the estuary," Louis said. "The galley will be low in the water, and there are monstrous waves hammering on Hengistbury Head. With an incoming tide that is on the flood, we could be overwhelmed very quickly."

"If only sailors were on board, would that be easier?" John asked.

Louis looked at him as though he was half-witted. "We would have very little problem if the galley was lighter and higher in the water. But what would be the use of that? These men are not trained soldiers."

Simon de Rochley grunted loudly in a derisive way.

"If the galley could get into the estuary and keep to this side, we could join the vessel by rowing out to it," John continued. "There is a small creek at the point where the estuary begins to narrow, and there is a sturdy rowing boat there, we saw it earlier."

"I know the place," Louis said. He furrowed his brow and rubbed his large fleshy nose. "It is a possible idea. There is a small sheltered bay opposite, where we could disembark."

"It is the best idea so far," Sir Michel said.

"Then we should try it!" Sir Richard said loudly. "I have not come all this way to see those heathens sail off before our eyes." He looked fiercely around the table.

"We will have to move quickly, if we are to catch them before they reach their ship. The tide is rising fast," Louis Saint Clare said.

"Are we all in favour of this?" Sir Michel asked.

The knights thumped the table to show their approval. John noticed that Nicholas de Montford was the only one who was not thumping the table;

his attention was concentrated on Gwen who was staring in horror at a large pewter plate. She seemed to be mesmerised and her lips were moving, but she made no sound.

"Are you ill, Mistress Gwen?" Sir Michel's wife asked in an alarmed voice.

John stood up and moved behind Gwen. He looked down onto the plate but could see nothing. Gwen shuddered, and continued to stare wide-eyed as though at some hideous apparition. The knights had stopped speaking and watched in awkward silence. "Is she having a fit?" Sir Michel hissed.

John placed both hands on her shoulders and concentrated his mind on supporting Gwen. He closed his eyes and was able to recall the strange signs and symbols that Old Mary had insisted he learn. It was the first time since losing the sword that he had experienced these echoes. The symbols formed a pattern in his mind, and he felt he was forcing this mosaic out into the dark night to a place where the enemy lurked. He envisioned himself crossing the black raging waters and focusing on a piece of flat ground where the soldiers stood in a dark circle, within which the giant with the red beard stood with his hands raised before him and his eyes closed. In front, were the two swords of power. Their blades were crossed and glowed in the dark.

In his mind's eye John plunged down towards the swords, thrusting the pattern of symbols before him like a shield. As he hurtled downwards, the leader's eyes snapped open like a trap, and anger and disbelief flashed across the evil face. John experienced a split second of intense exhilaration while the world seemed to disintegrate.

Gwen was screaming and her voice gave him the point on which to concentrate as he fought to escape the blackness. In a moment, it was all over. John opened his eyes and the room was spinning, and he was sprawled over Gwen's chair. She had slipped to one side, but both her hands gripped his right arm and her head collapsed against it. The knights stared in total bewilderment.

John disentangled himself and rubbed his face. Gwen staggered to her feet and took his arm, holding on tightly to it as though to a lifeline. She began to weep piteously, her body shuddering with each sob. John placed his arm around her, and led her to a seat near the fire.

"What happened to you? Are you recovered?" Sir Michel said to Gwen.

"What did she see?" Sir Richard asked, placing his hand on John's shoulder. The other knights gathered round.

"It was him," Gwen whispered hoarsely. "He was controlling my mind until you broke the spell." She gripped John's hand.

"I don't understand," Sir Michel said.

"My Lord, the leader of the enemy has strange and awful powers," John said. "He is capable of reproducing his face on bright surfaces such as water, fire or pewter, and even stone. It has happened to me a number of times, and Gwen has had one such experience before this."

"Do you mean this man can control your minds from a distance?" Sir Richard asked; he raised an aristocratic eyebrow in disbelief.

"My lords, this man is evil; he has powers that are terrifying," Gwen said, struggling to control her emotions. "He wants to destroy both of us." She looked at John.

The knights were unsure what to do. They wanted to believe Gwen, and had witnessed her sudden emotional upset. But for most, the concept of magic was beyond their understanding.

"If this man is so powerful, why are you still alive?" Sir Michel asked quietly. His shrewd eyes scanned their faces.

"I have a sign on my hand that has saved me in the past week from certain death," John said. "I think he wants to kill me, but he also wants to capture Gwen. I don't know why." He showed his palm to the other knights, who made no comment.

"Have you recovered?" Sir Richard said to Gwen.

"Thank you, my Lord," Gwen said. She attempted a smile, but her eyes were red with crying and her face was flushed.

"If we are going to use the galley, I must organise the men," Louis said, changing the atmosphere.

"Good! Do so," Sir Michel commanded. "The rest of us must saddle up our horses and be ready at the creek when the galley arrives. We shall have to board the ship as quickly as possible. If we are to catch them, we are going to need a deal of luck, and all the strength and courage we can muster. May God help us!" He raised his goblet, and the knights drank deeply.

As the others prepared themselves, Nicholas de Montford approached Sir Richard. "I don't think it would be wise to leave the girl by herself," he said.

"What do you suggest?" Sir Richard asked, his face flushed with the wine.

"I think I should stay here with her to ensure that she comes to no harm. For all we know there may be some of the enemy on this side of the river. She is very valuable to our cause; one of us should protect her, and it had better be me."

"What about John?" Sir Richard said thoughtfully. "Should he stay?"

"I think not," Nicholas answered. "You will need all the help you can get, and we are still unsure about him. If he is able to prove himself in a battle, The Order will accept him more easily."

Sir Richard nodded. He turned to John who was watching the knights don their armour. "You will come with us. Your help could be valuable. You have your weapons, go and make sure you have a good horse." John was pleased to be included and left the room with a swagger; he felt he was slowly being accepted. It was not until he was in the courtyard that he remembered he had not told Gwen what he was doing.

Sir Richard turned to Gwen, "You will be well cared for while we are away." He kissed her hand and bowed.

"Thank you, my Lord," Gwen curtseyed. "You also must take great care."

Sir Richard went to speak to his steward, and Gwen sat down in a chair to await developments. The other knights had rushed off to supervise their horses, except for Nicholas, who remained drinking near the fire. He reminded Gwen of a self-satisfied pig, as he guzzled more wine.

"I am leaving Nicholas de Montford to guard and protect you while we are away," Sir Richard said, as he raced past her chair. He waved an arm as he hurried out of the room, his mind already focused on other problems.

Gwen wanted to protest, and stood up, but it was too late. She turned slowly to face the smirking Nicholas. "I would have thought you would have wanted to take part in this great battle, my Lord." She smiled coldly, her lip quivering with loathing. She sat down and looked about the room for some distraction.

"My duty to you comes first," Simon said smoothly. He bowed. "It will give us the opportunity to…" he belched unexpectedly, his foul breath enveloping her like a cloud, "get to know each other." He sat down opposite her; his eyes were red rimmed and bloodshot. Sir Michel's wife had gone to organise the servants, and Gwen felt obliged to remain until she returned.

"What about John?" she asked.

"He could be very useful to Sir Richard, and it will be a chance for him to prove," he smirked, "his manhood." He slurred the last word, raising his eyebrows and twisting his mouth in mockery.

"I want to see him before he goes," Gwen said, rising to her feet.

"You must not upset yourself, you are still suffering from the effects of your," he struggled with the words, "unfortunate experience." He spoke out of the side of his thick lips. "John will be up to see you before he leaves." He gently forced her back into the chair, and was pleased to hear the horses departing the castle.

. . .

JOHN RAN TO THE stables, and quickly chose a horse. An excited groom attended to the saddle and harness, chattering on about how he would like to have taken part in the attack on the enemy. As John walked the horse to the courtyard, the other knights were already mounted and yelling orders to their grooms. He looked for a servant who could hold the horse while he went to check on Gwen, but as he paused, Simon de Rochley strode up to him and took the reins from his hands.

"Find yourself another horse!"

"My Lord, that is my horse," John protested.

"I said, find another horse!" Simon growled, his voice was full of menace. He swung himself quickly into the saddle and, without another glance at John, trotted over to the main gate.

John was outraged. As he stood fuming, Sir Richard rode up on a powerful, white stallion. "Where's your horse? Come on, we haven't any time to lose!" He signalled to a groom. "Get him a horse at once!"

Humiliated, John hurried after the groom, and was the last one out of the stables. As soon as Sir Richard saw him, he nodded to Sir Michel, who gave the order to move out of the castle. John twisted in his saddle, hoping to catch a last glimpse of Gwen, but she did not appear, and he cursed himself for his negligence.

In spite of the darkness the knights and their men rode at a swift pace, and John discovered what it was like to be at the back of a group of horsemen in such conditions. It was still raining, but the earlier intensity had abated to be replaced by a thin, steady downpour that was whipped into their faces by strong gusts of wind.

The road had been reduced to a quagmire, and the mud was thrown up into the air by the horses in front, making it impossible to see anything. In order to survive, John held on tightly, closed his eyes, and relied on his ears to tell him what was happening.

The tortuous ride seemed unending, and his mind wandered back to Gwen. He was angry with Simon for preventing him from going back to her, but blamed himself for being so full of his own importance and forgetting to bid her farewell. When he thought of Gwen a warm feeling enveloped him, and he was able to ignore the rigours of the ride. Her beauty was undeniable, but so was her sweetness of nature as well as her strength of character. When this episode was over they would find a way to leave the knights and travel back to Woodford. He screwed up his eyes as a large dollop of mud splattered in his face.

The thought of the village reminded him of the blacksmith who might still be a prisoner, and if the knights could rescue Tom, he would be a welcome companion on their journey home. John was sick of the whole business. Although Sir Richard had treated him kindly, he knew the other knights might never accept him. His brief moments of feeling important had been a sham. Why should he be important? Apart from the device on his palm he was no different to any one else. He began to doubt the incredible things he had experienced. Nobody believed him. After tonight, he wanted to forget about the enemy, the sword, and the knights. After tonight....

He was jerked to wakefulness when his horse veered suddenly to one side, and he was able to apply the reins just in time to avoid a collision. The leaders had pulled up abruptly, and were trotting more carefully down the path to the creek. Overhead a half moon gave intermittent light as thick clouds raced across the sky.

High tide was fast approaching, and the creek was full. They could just make out the fishermen's broad boat, which was floating low in the water at the end of its rope. Even in the creek there was a heavy swell, as waves spent their fury at the entrance, racing along the inlet, raising the thick fronds of seaweed, and then retreating with a hollow sucking sound.

Some of Sir Michel's soldiers pulled the boat to the side. "It's half full of water, m'Lord!" one of the men shouted.

"Pull it ashore and empty it out!" Sir Michel commanded. This was not easy to accomplish, as the boat was heavy, but the men set about the task while the knights dismounted and led their horses down to the shore.

They were appalled when they saw the violence of the sea. Angry white breakers surged towards them; huge waves piled one on top of another as they roared up the beach. The noise was fearful: the wind howled, the rain smacked against their faces and the waves thundered with unremitting fury. For brief moments the moon illuminated the raging world in front of them, but it was impossible to see across the estuary.

"I hope Louis can manage the galley. I had not realized the conditions were so bad!" Sir Richard yelled. He stood close to Sir Michel.

"He has lived here all his life, he knows these waters. This would not be the worst storm he has encountered," the knight replied. "Our main worry will be getting this fishing boat alongside the galley. It could be a difficult operation." The men emptied the boat, refloated it, and moored it in the creek, just beyond the range of the surf.

Sir Michel gathered some of his men together and they formed a tight circle while they discussed the situation. After a while he returned to where Sir Richard and Simon de Rochley stood staring glumly at the tormented waters. "Those men have had experience in ships and boats. They say they will be able to ferry us from the beach to the galley."

"I've fought many times on land," Sir Richard said, trying to make his voice heard above the din of the storm, "and I have no fear of dying in battle. But I have no experience of this," he indicated the white surf. "I shall be mighty glad when my feet touch the land on the other side."

"Don't worry, old friend, my men will get you over there!" Sir Michel shouted. "Our big hope is that the enemy soldiers have delayed embarking. This storm is really in our favour!"

Sir Richard shook his head in disbelief. Next to him, Simon de Rochley and some other knights scanned the wild seascape for any sign of the galley. John was standing back from the main group mesmerised by the drama of the scene. The tempestuous sea brought back memories of an earlier time when he had been in a large ship racked by violent storms. It was more of a feeling than a clear memory, like a dream half-remembered. There was a tall, sick man, who may have been his father? John felt a deep sadness, for he could not remember what his father looked like.

His mind turned to Gwen. Tom was important to her, even if he was not her real father. If he was still a prisoner then he must be released. John was determined to prevent Tom from being taken into slavery, and even more determined to prove himself worthy of Gwen's attention. Attention? No, that was not the word. Admiration? Perhaps. There was another word, but he did not feel able to use it. His mind avoided the deep emotional impulses that his body tried to impose. He must consider one thing at a time. He forced his thoughts back to the problem of locating the galley.

"My Lord," he leaned towards Sir Michel, "should we light some torches to help the galley find us?"

"We don't want to alert the enemy," Sir Richard interrupted.

"I think it is worth the risk!" Sir Michel yelled back. "We don't want the galley passing us in the dark."

It was hard to get the torches to burn in such conditions, but eventually a pair were ignited, and Sir Michel ordered two of his men to get back on their horses, and hold the torches aloft. The rest of the men lined the higher ground watching for any sign of the galley.

Sir Michel went to converse with an older man with white hair, then he went down to the creek and gave some orders. Two men clambered into the boat and prepared the oars. Sir Richard walked over to watch. "Old Will says the galley will have to stay out about a hundred paces, just the other side of the surf!" Sir Michel bellowed. "I'll have the men ready to row out the moment the galley appears. The boat will take another five people."

Sir Richard nodded. His eyes were stinging from the rain, his joints ached, and he felt an unaccustomed weariness. He shook himself angrily, and marched briskly after Sir Michel, tripping awkwardly on some driftwood as he did so.

They walked back to face the waves. At that moment the galley was sighted, a dull shape rising and falling in the big swell beyond the surf. The men began to yell and wave, although it was impossible for their voices to carry beyond a few feet.

"Richard!" Sir Michel yelled. "You and Simon, and you," he pointed to John, "can go first with two of my knights. I'll stay to organise the boarding, then I'll come on the last run."

Everyone had to wade out into the muddy creek and clamber on board. The sizeable swell in the narrow channel added to the difficulty. John sat shivering in the bow looking down the boat, with Sir Richard and Simon facing him. The two rowers sat in the middle facing the stern, with Sir Michel's two knights facing them. There was no rudder, and the rowers were totally responsible for the safe direction of the boat.

"Good luck! I hope those in the galley have seen our lights, or you may have to come back!" Sir Michel shouted. "God be with you!"

The rowers moved cautiously down the heaving channel until they were near the point where the waves were crashing. At a signal from a man on the beach they rowed out on a great wave as it was falling back, and were immediately engulfed by a second wave. The boat reared up, and for a moment appeared in danger of being thrown back on the beach. But the rowers, who were strong men, heaved on the oars and the small craft disappeared over the back of the breaker, into a trough and up again onto the next wave.

The five passengers gripped the seats or the gunwales, and held on for their lives. The boat was tossed and buffeted as each mighty wave threatened to overwhelm it. Rogue waves would suddenly smash in from a different angle, soaking the men and almost swamping the craft. After what seemed an age, they were in a heavy swell with fewer breaking waves. The worst of the white breakers were behind them.

"Use your helmets to bail!" Sir Richard yelled, and the knights set about reducing the level of water.

"The galley! It's over there!" John shouted, and pointed to their right, where the ship was wallowing in the heavy swell, as Louis and his men tried desperately to locate the position of the smaller craft.

The two rowers manoeuvred the boat with great skill, until they were on the down wind side of the rolling galley. The rowers at the back of the ship tucked in their heavy oars to allow the fishing boat to pull along side. The deck of the galley was more than four feet above the height of John's head, and he looked forward to soon being on a sturdier vessel.

Boarding nets were thrown over the side of the galley and Simon agreed to go first. He flung himself across the gap between the two craft, and although his hands caught the rope, his feet failed to find a purchase, and he was completely submerged as a huge wave swept past. He clambered quickly up the net, and laboured to get over the side of the galley, as his sword became entangled with the ropes. Sir Richard was also submerged in the heavy swell, but fought his way up the netting, cursing loudly. John saw there was a good time and a bad time to jump. He waited until a wave lifted up the boat, and jumped at the highest point. When he grasped the net he was above the level of the next wave, and was able to get over the side without a complete soaking.

The other two knights learned from John, and climbed aboard without mishap. The rowing boat immediately turned for the lights on the beach, and the galley attempted to maintain its position as best it could. The men straining on the heavy oars in the small boat looked frail and vulnerable in the threatening sea.

The next three journeys were successful, and although each round trip was accomplished with great speed, Louis was worried about the tide. "It is now at the flood," he said to Sir Richard, who was shaking from his immersion in the cold water. "We will need to hurry."

Sir Richard nodded, and yelled to the departing rowers, "One more time!"

Those on the galley waited anxiously for the last boatload that would be carrying Sir Michel. The sea was a maelstrom, and the galley was caught by waves from different angles. John noticed that there were more breaking waves, but he kept his thoughts to himself. Many of the men were bailing, and those on the oars had great problems keeping in position.

"Here they come!" a voice called.

John stared into the blinding spray as the small boat lurched over the brow of a dark wave and dropped down with great force into a trough, only to be buffeted by the next wave. One of the rowers lost his grip on the oar, and the small boat went broadside into a white-topped breaker and was swamped. It all happened so quickly. The soldiers on the pitching galley watched helplessly as the seven men were catapulted into the water like rag dolls. Arms flayed the water as the men tried to swim towards the safety of the ship, their bodies bobbing like corks in the wild sea. Sir Michel and another knight were in full chain mail, and within moments they had disappeared from view, overwhelmed by the seething waters. The other three soldiers tried to untie their harnesses and swords, but their efforts tired them, and in the terrible conditions they were soon sucked under. The two rowers survived by holding on to their oars and keeping close to each other. When ropes were thrown from the galley they were able to tie them around themselves and were dragged, exhausted, onto the deck.

Sir Richard gazed wildly into the darkness, hoping against the truth of his own eyes that Sir Michel might still be alive. "He was a good man," he lamented. "A good friend, and an important member of our Order."

"Do we continue or turn back?" Louis asked.

"We must go on!" Sir Richard roared. "The enemy must be defeated! If we go back now, Sir Michel's death will have been for nothing."

Louis gave the order and the galley turned up river, making an angle towards the opposite shore in order to avoid being caught broadside by the waves. The rowers grunted with the effort as they manhandled the heavy oars.

"Everyone on the oars!" Louis shouted. "Join me on the tiller!" he called to Sir Richard.

Each man took a part as they manoeuvred the heavy craft towards the safety, and the danger, of the approaching shore. All around them the wind howled and the waves crashed over the sides, as the storm reached its peak. It seemed to be the darkest moment of a dreadful night.

CHAPTER 16

IN THE CASTLE, THE violence of the weather forced the few remaining guards to take shelter. Soon most of them were asleep, after consuming the wine that Nicholas de Montford had sent to the guardroom. The soldiers remarked on this unusual act of generosity, but gladly consumed it without worrying about the reason. The servants retreated to their straw pallets and were soon in the exhausted sleep of those who eat poor food and are overworked.

Below, on the seaward side, huge waves slammed into the rocks and exploded over the stone breakwater of the harbour. Their thunderous roars echoed around the castle, competing with the cacophony of the lashing rain and the howling wind.

In the main hall the fire crackled and glowed as the drafts played upon the smouldering logs. Sir Nicholas poured himself another goblet of wine and stared lasciviously at Gwen, who avoided his gaze. She was tempted to join Sir Michel's wife when she retired to bed shortly after the knights had left, but Nicholas had protested that he would be left alone, and that they would soon get a report of how things were developing. Gwen also had a strong feeling that she was safer in this room where she could keep a watch on Sir Nicholas, rather than in her bed, where he could approach her without warning.

"You're a beautiful woman, but you don't say very much," Nicholas complained in a slurred voice. He had been drinking steadily all evening, and had some trouble pronouncing his words.

Gwen sat opposite him staring stonily into the fire. She was furious that Nicholas had deliberately prevented her from saying goodbye to John, and she maintained a frosty silence throughout the evening. Her thoughts centred on Tom, whom she continued to think of as her father, and she wondered whether he was still alive. She worried about John. It seemed strange that the knights would have wanted him to go with them on what was obviously such a risky venture, especially as he was not a trained fighter and had nothing to contribute as regards local knowledge. If he was *special*, as the knights insisted she was, then why had they risked his life in this way? Finally, she considered her present situation. Why had Nicholas agreed to stay with her rather than do what he was trained for, which was to fight the enemy. He was a large, ungainly man with small red eyes reminding her of a wild pig. His wide mouth curved down in one corner, and with the effects of the wine, his thick lips had flopped apart revealing his ugly teeth.

"I could make you very happy, you know," he tried to rise from his chair. "You are nothing at the moment," he emphasised the word nothing, "but with my help we could have it all." He gave a drunken giggle. "We could have the power to run Christendom and old Richard would have to do as he's told." He stood up and swayed from side to side.

"My Lord, you have had too much wine," Gwen said. She tried to sound bored, but her knuckles were white as she gripped the arms of her chair.

"I never have too much wine," Nicholas boasted. "Now it's time you gave me a kiss!" He lurched towards her, and tried to place his arms on both sides of her chair. Gwen realized his intention and darted out under his outstretched arms, and retreated towards the fire.

Nicholas was unable to stop his forward motion, his hands grabbed the sides of the chair, but his great weight continued to propel him onward. The empty chair tipped backwards and Nicholas careered over the top and collapsed, head first, on the stone floor. He gave a low moan and lay still.

Gwen was unable to believe the horror had faded away so easily. Only a moment before, she was his potential victim, and now Nicholas was merely an unconscious mound of flabby flesh. His powerful shoulders rose and fell with each laboured breath. She was relieved he was not dead, but she feared his great strength. He might make a rapid recovery. It was not safe in the castle.

She ran up the stairs to her sleeping area, and fetched a thick, dark coloured cloak. A servant girl was snoring gently at the top of the stairs, and Gwen glided silently past without waking her. In the main hall Nicholas still lay face down on the floor, but his position had changed, and as she tiptoed past, he groaned and tried to raise his head. She raced towards the outer door.

In the courtyard, she woke the drowsy guard and ordered him to take her to the stables and find her a horse. He knew better than to ask questions, but he could not resist observing, "It's a wild night, m' Lady."

"I know it," Gwen said abruptly.

The guard shook his head, grabbed a smoking torch and led the way to the stables. The stone courtyard was awash with mud and debris, and the angry wind buffeted Gwen, and tugged at her loose clothing, which would suddenly billow up causing her to lose her balance. She clung on to the arm of the guard who hurried her into the shelter of the stable. By the time she was out of the clutches of the wind she was already soaked to the skin.

A young boy was asleep on a pile of hay, a wistful look on his grubby face. The guard shook him roughly until he awoke, and ordered him to saddle up a horse. The boy stumbled off, bare-footed, into the shadows and soon emerged leading a large mare. He struggled with the heavy saddle, and Gwen ordered the guard to help. The man did as he was ordered but made it obvious that he disliked doing so.

"You're not dressed for this type of saddle, m'Lady," the guard said. There was a mocking note in his voice.

"It does not matter," Gwen said. "Hurry!"

When the horse was ready Gwen stood on a pile of hay and the boy brought the horse to her so she could climb into the saddle. She did not want to ask the guard to help and carefully tucked the folds of her dress under her legs, ignoring his blatant stare. Next, she arranged the cloak tightly about her body to conserve her body heat; her teeth were chattering with the cold. The raging storm was not inviting, and she had no idea where she was going to ride to on such a night, but the alternative was even more frightening.

"Open the main gate for me!" she ordered.

The guard made a face, but did as he was told. As she left the stables, she turned to the boy. He smiled nervously up at her. She reached inside her cloak and took a coin from the purse given to her by Sir Richard. "Take this," she said. She tossed a silver coin to him.

"Oh, thank ye, m'Lady!" The boy said. He stared at the coin in amazement.

"Keep it safe. It will help you someday." She turned and urged the horse out into the rain-swept courtyard. The guard had opened one of the main gates, and stood hopefully to one side. She urged her horse into a trot and passed though the gate without a sideways glance. The guard scowled and slammed the gate. In the stables the small boy tested the coin with his teeth.

· · ·

AFTER HER BOLD EXIT from the castle, Gwen slowed the horse to a walking pace. The dark road was hard to follow, and she could see her way only when the moon broke through the clouds. The drenching rain began to ease, but the wind showed no sign of abating. She passed a few frail cottages clustered near the castle, and followed the road along which Sir Richard's party had previously come. Gwen was already feeling a lightness of heart, and although she had no definite plan, her escape from the castle raised her spirits.

Her only thought was to retrace her earlier journey and find the creek where they had met the fishermen. John's plan was to ferry the soldiers out to the galley from the creek, and she hoped to be able to meet up with some of Sir Michel's men. Perhaps, John would still be on the beach, as she was certain Sir Richard, and particularly Simon de Rochley, would not have wanted an inexperienced young man with them. She was still puzzled as to why he had been asked to join the expedition. With these and other thoughts she occupied her time, as she made her way carefully down the deserted road, a lone and vulnerable figure in a violent world.

The creek was easier to find than she had hoped, but the wind seemed even stronger, and she was forced to dismount from the horse and lead it towards the sea. The beach was deserted and, apart from the red embers of a dying torch, there was no evidence that anyone had been there. Gwen was dismayed, and stood helplessly staring into the darkness, feeling a great sense of loneliness. Where was John? Had he ventured out into this wild sea? What if he had been forced to go? If they were drowned, what would she do? Lost in her thoughts, she walked down to the beach, leading her reluctant horse behind her.

The roar of the sea and the ferocity of the surf caused the horse to panic. It whinnied loudly, and reared up in fright, threatening to strike Gwen with its powerful hooves. She struggled desperately with the terrified animal and was compelled to lead it back down the side of the creek towards the road. She groped her way in the darkness until the clouds parted for a moment, and she was able to tether the animal to a weather-beaten bush.

The horse whinnied loudly again, its eyes huge and white in the blackness, and in spite of the howling wind, she thought she heard an answering neigh. "Of course," she spoke aloud, "their horses must be somewhere around here awaiting their return." She could not understand how she had failed to think about this. Leaving the horse securely tethered, she followed a small track to her right, and in less than a hundred paces came upon a shallow depression in which a small red torch flickered wildly in the gale. Many horses were tethered closely together, and sheltering on the other side of them was a group of figures.

Gwen advanced from the side, and was almost next to them when the nearest man jumped up with a cry.

"It's all right. I'm a friend!" she yelled. She did not know what else to say.

She was immediately surrounded. Rough hands grabbed her arms and her hood was pulled back. One of the men held the weak flame of the torch close to her face. "It's a girl. Her that were with Sir Richard!" a voice shouted.

From the darkness a broad, familiar shape appeared in the lighted circle. "Gwen?"

"Martin!" She could not believe her eyes. "I thought you had been killed or captured by the soldiers."

They embraced each other warmly. "I thought you was dead as well after Peter gave you away to that red-haired giant!" He was shouting to be heard above the battering of the wind.

A man in chain mail, who appeared to be the leader, placed his large arms around their shoulders and shouted in their ears. "We 'ave to stay with the horses, but there's no reason why you two can't get some shelter! Old Ned here will take ye to 'is place."

After a short ride, Gwen and Martin reached Ned's cottage. It was a small, one-roomed structure made of stone and wattle and with a thatch roof. It was dry and warm, and a fire glowed in an open hearth. Ned lit a tallow candle, which gave off a sickly smell and a weak yellow light. "Ye be welcome to stay 'ere and keep warm," he said. "If we hears anything we shall send word. I've tied the 'orses round the back, out of the wind." He banked up the fire, then opened the door and disappeared into the storm.

"Martin, it is so good to see you again!" Gwen said as she huddled round the fire. By the light of the flickering candle she saw that Martin had hardly any hair in the front of his head and that his eyebrows had almost disappeared. His face was blotched and scarred.

"Oh, your poor face! What happened?"

"It's nothing much. It'll heal. There was a fire in the cottage, see, an' my 'air caught the flames as I got out. It were nothin'." He smiled bravely. Later, he told her how the soldiers had captured Peter and himself, and how Peter had betrayed her to the leader with the red hair. Then he told her how a large man had burst in with another older and smaller man, and how they had fought with the soldiers. "'E was a good man with a sword was the big fellow, the other got speared by one of the soldiers, but I settled 'im," Martin said with grim satisfaction.

"Tell me about the big man," Gwen said urgently. "What did he look like?"

"Big 'e was, with very strong arms and shoulders, bigger than I," he spoke with pride. "'E had a big black beard and, oh yes, I remember, the smaller man called 'im Tom."

"Tom? Was his name really Tom?" Her voice shook with emotion.

Martin slowly nodded his head, as understanding crossed his face and his eyes grew serious. "Were he your father?" he spoke slowly.

"Yes!" Gwen's face was animated and her eyes sparkled in the firelight. "He's alive and free, and all along I thought he was still a prisoner with the soldiers. This is the best news I could have received. What happened next?

Martin looked into the firelight and nervously touched his face. "It were a bit confused like. I was not too sure what 'appened." He sat down heavily on a small three-legged stool and watched the fiery sparks float up the chimney.

"But you must have seen him. Did he get out of the cottage safely?"

"Yes... yes, 'e did," Martin spoke with obvious reluctance. "'E dragged the wounded man out of the back door, and I were forced to get out of the front." He relapsed into silence and nervously massaged his burnt eyebrows.

"What is it, Martin? What happened next? I must know!" She grabbed his left arm and willed him to look at her. The yellow light of the candle and the glow of the fire made Martin's face look strange and frightening. "Please tell me, Martin. If it is anything bad, then I must know it. What happened to my father?"

"Well, I was burned real bad at the time, and I just ran for the river. I ducked my head in the water an' then I went to go back to see what were 'appening like." He paused and licked his lips. "There were a lot of them soldiers running back from the ferry towards the fire, and then a group of horsemen galloped from out of the woods and this man, your father, he comes running out in front of them and 'e..." Martin turned away from Gwen. "'E was knocked down by the horses. They galloped over 'im."

"Was he dead?"

"I dunno. I think so." He cleared his throat. "The horsemen stopped and then it got confused. There was a lot of fighting and some of them soldiers were on horses as well. I didn't see much more 'cos one of them soldiers came at me, an' I didn't 'ave no weapon, so I jumped in the river and swam down stream. 'E didn't follow me."

Gwen sat in silence. It was difficult to grasp. To have such good news destroyed so quickly was overwhelming. She sat numbed and unable to speak. The fire crackled in the hearth, and outside the wind pounded against the door, and the candle trembled in the draft.

She turned quickly towards him. "He was not there when I went down the next morning. I would have seen him. I was looking for you and Peter. I would have seen him if he had been near the cottage. He could still be alive." Gwen's voice had a pleading quality. She needed reassurance.

"Yes, 'e could be, I suppose," Martin did not sound convincing. He remembered how hot the fire had been, and he had seen Tom fall near the flaming building. It was possible the fire had consumed the body. "Where's John?" he asked, trying to change the subject.

"I don't know," her voice was flat and lifeless, and tears trickled down her cheeks. "He went with the knights to try and cross the bay. The soldiers are on the other side." She sniffed and rubbed her eyes.

"I learned something about that from them fellows I was with. They said it were madness to go out in a small boat in this weather, but that Sir Richard 'ad no choice if 'e were to catch them soldiers."

Gwen nodded absent-mindedly. She felt depressed, but her positive nature struggled to find some good in the situation. "They would be safe once they reached the galley, and John does have a charmed life." She bit her lip and tried not to give in to the misery threatening to engulf her.

Martin was looking into the fire. "They told me that the last time the boat went to the galley it sunk."

Gwen sat up with a start. "Did they rescue those on board?"

"I don't know. They couldn't see what 'appened. But the boat didn't come back."

"Do you know who was in the boat?"

Martin paused. "Yes, I remember they said that Sir Michel was in the boat with some of 'is men."

"So John must be safe on the galley?" The intensity of her voice indicated her concern, and Martin felt oddly resentful.

"How did you get here, Martin?" Gwen realized she had not asked an obvious question. She wiped her eyes.

"Well, after I swims down river, I be tired and I finds a dry place and I sleeps for a long time." He spoke in a way that seemed to make everything so simple. "When I wakes up, it were the middle of the day, an' I be hungry. But first I checks to see what 'ad happened at the ferry. The cottage was still smoulderin' and there were a lot of bodies around." He rubbed the tufts of hair on his forehead. "There be lots of flies and it were hot, so I followed the path down river. I thought I would soon reach a village. I stayed the night with an old man who 'ad a shack near the water. The next day, that be yesterday, we 'ad reports that a lot of them soldiers had gone down river on the ferryboat. So, I sets out after them, to try and warn people an' see if they 'ad you captive like."

He tried to be casual about it, but Gwen could sense he was quite emotional. She was touched by his simple friendship towards her.

Martin placed another log on the fire. "What do we do now?"

Gwen shook her head. It was early morning and the events of the night had begun to take their toll. "We could stay here and wait for Old Ned to bring us any news, or we could go back to the castle."

"Why did ye leave the castle in the middle of this storm?"

"There is a knight there named Nicholas de Montford. He was supposed to be protecting me, but instead he got drunk and tried to assault me," Gwen said. "He's a foul creature." She shuddered with the memory.

Martin was outraged. "A knight behaved like that!" He had no real experience of knights, but held the general belief that they were of a higher order than the rest of the people and somehow behaved differently.

"He is just an unpleasant man," she answered. "But, if you are with me he won't dare try anything. With luck he will be asleep. He was very drunk when I left."

"Well, it'll be better than staying here," Martin said. As if to confirm his view, the feeble candle blew out.

"I wonder what is happening across the bay," she said. She gazed into the

THE POWER IN THE DARK

fire and had a strange feeling of light-headedness. It was as though she was being lifted up. A picture started to form in the red ashes and for a moment she feared she was about to see the awful face she had seen twice before. But instead, she began to be drawn into the darkness behind the embers, into the storm and above the beach. She was high up and falling like a bird towards the other shore. She could hear the waves crashing on the rocks and there was blackness all around. Suddenly, the moon illuminated the scene, and she could see a group of men in silver armour crouching behind rocks while other men, in black, fired arrows at them from higher ground. There were bodies on the sand. Then, she saw John. He was running down the beach towards the river, leaving the other men. He had outrun the arrows and was disappearing along a path up the hill side. He did not look back.

"Gwen! Gwen!" She felt Martin's hand on her shoulder and she began to come back. It was like coming out of a pond that has thick weeds and scum on the surface. It was difficult to get free.

"Are ye all right?"

"Yes," she murmured. She rubbed her face with both hands. "I had a vision of what is happening over there." She pointed vaguely towards the door. "I have never experienced anything like this before. John said it happened to him. Now I know what he means."

Martin was overawed. "What did ye see?" His eyes stared out of his blackened face.

"Sir Richard's men are trapped in a small cove and the soldiers are firing arrows at them. I saw John... he was running away."

Martin made a face. He had never met John, but had already decided that he did not like him. "Perhaps he don't like the people he was with," he suggested ambiguously.

"We must get back to the castle and see if we can get help to them," Gwen said. She was aware of how unlikely this was, but she could not allow her gift of seeing to be wasted.

Outside it was still dark, but the moon was bright, and although the rain had eased, the wind was as strong as before. They found the horses tethered to a post at the back of the cottage, and travelled back to the castle as quickly as the conditions would permit. Martin pounded on the gate but it was some time before a sleepy guard appeared. Gwen was relieved it was not the same one who had saddled her horse. The guard recognised Gwen but was suspicious of Martin.

"He is a friend of Sir Richard's. Open up!" she ordered.

The gate opened, and leaving their horses in the courtyard, they raced up to the main hall. There was no sign of Nicholas de Montford, but Louis Saint Clare and some other men were sitting in a dejected group drinking wine. He jumped to his feet as soon as he saw Gwen. "Mistress, you should not have been out in such a night."

"I had no choice," Gwen answered. She felt in command of the situation. "Has Nicholas been put to bed?" The manner in which she spoke conveyed a clear message to the knight.

Louis nodded slowly and said "Ha!" in a knowing way. His face changed. "We have bad news. Sir Michel is dead. He was drowned as he tried to reach the galley."

"I heard the news at the beach. I'm sorry." She paused. "Does his wife know?

The knight shook his head. "She is asleep. The news will be just as bad in the morning."

Gwen nodded her sympathy. Then she introduced Martin and accepted a chair that was offered. She turned to Louis and spoke with quiet authority. "My Lord, you will find it difficult to accept what I am about to tell you, but I want you to listen carefully." Louis regarded her with interest.

"When you delivered Sir Richard and the others to the far side of the bay, you took them into a deep water cove where they were able to wade ashore. The cove has a number of large boulders on the beach, and one of them has a large round hole in it. There is a low, steep cliff that completely encloses the cove, apart from a narrow beach that stretches back up towards the river, and from this beach there is a small path that leads up a hill. On the seaward side there is a rocky outcrop." She had been speaking quickly, but her eyes had not left those of Louis Saint Clare.

He gazed back at her and nodded. "That is correct. But I believe you are a stranger in these parts?"

"Yes, my Lord, I have never seen that place before tonight."

There was a murmur from the other men, but Louis continued to regard her with uncritical interest. "Do go on," he said.

"Sir Richard and his men are trapped in the cove. The foreign soldiers have archers and have killed at least two men. If Sir Richard does not get help, he and his small army will almost certainly die, and the enemy will escape."

"How do you know this?" Louis asked. His voice indicated curiosity rather than disbelief.

"I know it by the same way I could describe the cove to you, my Lord. I had a vision."

This statement produced an excited hubbub among the men, but Louis only smiled. "I believe you, Mistress Gwen. It does not surprise me that at such a time you should show your power. It is what I would expect with your position in The Order." He dropped to one knee in front of Gwen, and held up his sword, point down. "To you I pledge my life."

Gwen had felt confident as she entered the main hall, but she expected to have considerable problems convincing Louis, and the rest of the men, of her sincerity. Louis's complete belief in her, and his reference to her place in The Order, came as a shock. She felt her cheeks redden and passed her tongue over her dry lips.

"My Lord, please rise," she said, and placed her hand on his shoulder.

Martin stared as though in a dream. None of this made sense. He had come to support Gwen and, if necessary, stand up to a knight who did not deserve to be a knight. Things were simple and straightforward in his mind, and he was unnerved by events outside his experience. He watched as Louis stood up and sheathed his sword. He kept his head bowed. The rest of the men had risen to their feet.

"Mistress, what should we do now?" Louis's question was so direct as to be childlike.

"Is it possible to use the galley to get back into the bay?" Gwen said thoughtfully.

"It is possible," Louis spoke slowly. "The sea is not as great as it was earlier, and with enough people to man the oars we could get through to the bay. However, we could not take many men in armour, as the ship would be too low in the water." He gave a mirthless laugh. "Not that we have many men left!" He looked around at the others. "It will be dangerous, and we are all weary, but our friends are in even greater danger. Do we try it?"

There was unanimous agreement, and Louis gave some brief orders concerning the preparation of the galley and the mustering of extra men. As the hall emptied, he turned to Martin. "You look like a useful man, have you been on the sea before?"

"I've spent most of my life on rivers, m' Lord. I reckon I can manage."

"Good." He smiled at Gwen. "I am afraid you will have very little company,

Mistress Gwen, but perhaps you would be able to break the sad news to Sir Michel's wife?"

"No, my Lord, I am coming with you," Gwen said.

Louis's face lost its cool composure. "That is not possible. This will be very dangerous and no place for a woman. Besides," he looked her straight in the eyes, "sailors consider it unlucky to have a woman aboard."

Gwen was shaken by this, but still determined to get her own way. So much was happening, and this was certainly the final part in a series of events that were changing her life. There was no going back, and she felt her vision was another indication that she should be there to ensure the defeat of the evil creature who sought to ensnare her. Her eyes flashed. "Do you consider it unlucky, my Lord?"

"No, but I am not a real sailor. I am merely a soldier who often travels by water."

Gwen smiled warmly at him. "You acknowledge me as important in The Order?" Louis nodded. "And you believe in my vision?"

"Of course, my Lady, which is all the more reason for you to remain safe within this castle."

"I shall not be safe while Nicholas de Montford remains here," she retorted. "I believe my vision was meant to help us against the evil powers of the enemy. If I was with you and had another vision, it might prove to be decisive. But, if I was back in the castle, there is no way I could communicate with you." She placed her hands on his shoulders, and realized she was as tall as he was. "I can disguise myself as a man, the others need not know, and Martin will protect me." She turned to Martin who nodded in agreement. "Much is at stake, you need all the help you can get."

Louis was uncertain how to act. His instincts told him it was wrong to have Gwen on board, but his simple belief in her power, combined with the fact that she was the most attractive woman he had seen in a long while, made him indecisive.

"I may be able to help you," Gwen insisted. "Louis, you must let me come." Her voice was warm and persuasive, and her use of his name was the deciding factor.

"You may come," he said quietly. He looked confused and blinked as though in a bright light.

"Thank you, Louis," Gwen said and kissed him lightly on the cheek.

Louis smiled broadly and blushed. Then he looked serious. "Come with me, both of you." He led the way to a small chamber where there was an assortment of tunics, boots and pieces of chain mail. In one corner there were leather belts and harnesses, and a number of swords, shields and short spears; some were dull and rusty.

"This is what I keep for peasants whom we need for guard duty." He smiled at their questioning faces. "I look after the military provisions for the castle, including these things and the ships."

He turned to Martin. "I suggest you get a shield and a sword and some boots, if you can find any to fit. Then we will leave you, Mistress Gwen, to change yourself into a man. But you must hurry! I shall meet you both in the main hall." He rushed off to take command of the preparations.

Martin waited outside as Gwen made some quick choices. In a short while she opened the door and beckoned him in. She was wearing a heavy, brown tunic, loose trousers, rough leather boots and a chain mail hood that covered her hair and much of her face.

"Help me with this," she said, pointing to a leather breast plate. Martin quickly buckled it on and handed her a thick belt. "I would not know you were a woman," he said. "Truly, I would not."

"I shall take it as a compliment," Gwen said as she fastened her cloak. She fitted a short sword into her belt, and led the way to the main hall, where Louis was anxiously pacing around.

He looked carefully at the two younger people. "Good," he said. "Very good." He walked quickly through a wide door and down a winding flight of steps. Gwen and Martin had to rush to keep up. At the bottom of the steps they could hear the thunder of the sea. Louis turned to Gwen. "Remember to keep close to me, and if anyone asks you a question, let Martin answer. Once we are afloat everyone will be too busy to notice, and the wind will be too strong for conversation."

As they stepped onto the stone causeway leading to the harbour, the wind slammed into them and was all-powerful. It came in great gusts that threatened to lift them off the ground, and they were forced to walk half-bent towards the galley, where the last members of the crew were clambering on board.

Gwen had imagined a larger vessel. The galley had eight oars on each side and two men to each long oar. The benches on which they sat were tiered, so that a third line of men could help with the oars in bad weather or in battle. There was a single mast and an area at the bow and stern for the fighting men to assemble. At the stern was a large tiller that needed two men to control it in high seas. It seemed very frail in such weather, but the seamen looked strong and determined.

Several men carried torches that illuminated small areas of the wharf and made odd shapes of the faces of the soldiers, which were partly hidden by their helmets. Everything seemed unreal, and Gwen had to concentrate her tired eyes on the swaying gangplank in order to avoid falling into the harbour. Martin's strong hand guided her across and she staggered awkwardly as her feet touched the rolling deck of the galley. Even in the relative safety of the small harbour, the water was rising and falling violently as massive waves surged past the stone breakwater.

Gwen and Martin followed Louis to the stern and tried to keep out of the way of the crew who were preparing to cast off from the jetty. No one took any notice of the two young soldiers who kept close to Louis; the rest of the soldiers were situated at the front of the vessel. The tide had turned, and the moon shone down brightly from a clear sky. Although the rain had stopped, the wind was as strong as ever. At intervals, great waves burst over the stone causeway drenching those in the galley, and when Gwen looked towards the sea she was terrified by the wide expanse of tormented water.

Louis glanced towards her and smiled grimly. "I did warn you, Mistress Gwen, it will not be easy." Then he took pity on her and added, "This is nothing to how it was last time we set out."

Martin spoke briefly to the helmsman, who confirmed that the most difficult part was getting out of the harbour and through the wide entrance to the bay. "Tide's turned, and it'll be a mighty hard pull into the bay, but once we're there this craft should be able to manage."

When all was ready, Louis gave the order to cast off, and the galley slowly manoeuvred into a position where the men could get maximum rowing power as it approached the entrance to the sea. As the oars dug deep into the water and the galley started to move ponderously forward, Gwen saw a large figure in chain mail swaying down the causeway waving frantically, his voice lost in the wind. As she watched a large wave swept over the quay, enveloping Nicholas de Montford and knocking him down onto the rough stone surface. She smiled, in spite of her fear.

Louis did not notice Nicholas, as his attention was fixed on the difficult task of judging the wave patterns to avoid capsize as they left the harbour. "Now!" he yelled and the rowers dug deeply into the water. The boat lunged forward, and they were almost out of the harbour when the next wave surged in. The galley rose up in the air, but its weight brought it crashing down and the oars dug in once again, sending a shudder through the boat. Gwen and Martin sat huddled together, gripping on desperately to any projection. While Martin stared anxiously ahead, Gwen closed her eyes and prayed for help.

CHAPTER 17

THINGS WERE NOT GOING well for Sir Richard. The whole expedition seemed cursed. The terrible storm and the sudden and shocking death of Sir Michel had been but a prelude to other disasters. Sir Richard, as the senior officer, was now in command, but apart from some hurried words with Louis Saint Clare, he had little idea of the terrain on which he was to land. In his mind was only a rough outline of a plan: he hoped to land in the cove and find the enemy before they escaped in their ship. No other planning was possible.

The landing was a military failure, and would have been a total disaster if it had not been for the bravery and organization of Simon de Rochley. Instead of beaching the galley and using all the men available, Sir Richard insisted that only the trained soldiers, both his and Sir Michel's, would do the fighting. He ordered Louis to take the galley back to the harbour and pick them up at daylight when Sir Richard imagined he would have defeated the enemy, and when the storm would, hopefully, have blown itself out. He also instructed Louis to be alert to any movement by the sailing ship, and if it tried to leave the bay, Louis was to try and intercept it.

The deep water in the cove enabled the galley to get close to the beach, but the power of the surf made it difficult to remain in one place, and the men were forced to jump from the tossing galley into rough water that was shoulder deep. Thunderous waves broke over their heads and a fierce undertow off-balanced them. In the darkness, with their heavy armour and weapons, and with the beach only dimly outlined, many of the men panicked. The pounding surf injured some of the soldiers, others lost their weapons and a few refused to jump until the galley got closer. The result was a disorganized rabble that floundered ashore to be met by a hail of arrows that shafted out of the blackness like avenging demons.

Sir Richard stayed in the water encouraging his men as best he could, and it was left to Simon de Rochley to lead a spirited attack on a group of bowmen who had taken up a position on some rocks in the middle of the small beach. In the darkness and confusion, he succeeded in driving them back to the low cliffs where the rest of the enemy were lodged. Two of his men were killed in the encounter, and at least one was serious injured, but he had at least secured a place behind which they were able to rally their forces and take breath.

When they took stock of their position, it was quickly realized they were effectively trapped as the enemy could hold them there indefinitely. Sir Richard summed it up: "There is only one path up to the top of the low cliffs, and although we could certainly reach the path in the darkness, we would be easily picked off as we climbed up. We might try to climb the rocks at the same time as some of us charged the path, but our losses would be great, and we are not sure of their numbers or their positions."

John had been one of the luckier ones in the landing, and had helped Simon de Rochley dislodge the bowmen. He did not fight with anyone, but his ferocious yells and the speed with which he approached the enemy's position helped to cause the retreat. He even heard a gruff acknowledgement from Simon.

John was excited and keen to show what he could do. Although lacking Simon's power with the sword John continued to have complete faith in the power of the runes on his palm. If he met the leader again, John felt sure he could cause the sword to act as it had done against the first warrior in the Flower Meadows. He felt it was essential to get out of this stalemate on the beach and challenge the leader of the enemy face-to-face. Also, he wanted to impress Simon de Rochley. John moved closer to where the knights were standing. "My Lord, can we not move along the beach towards the river and try to get out that way?" he suggested.

The howling wind and the crashing surf made discussion difficult, and after the chaos of the landing Sir Richard was still trying to get his thoughts together. "Well?" he snapped, turning to a local soldier, "Is it possible?"

"It's possible, me Lord, but first we'd have to get past that rocky overhang, and they certainly 'ave some men up there. But, if we gets past them, the beach is completely open. There be a lot of small rocks, especially in the sea, but nothin' much to hide behind. Also, there be only one path up to the cliff top, unless ye follow the beach for a long way until it becomes the river. It's possible we'd be in a worse position with them bowmen than we be now."

This was not the information Sir Richard had been hoping for.

"Any more suggestions!" he barked. No one spoke. There was a loud crack, as an arrow hit the rock at an angle, narrowly missing the huddled group.

"I reckon they can see us better than us can see 'em," one of the soldiers observed. No one said anything, but each noticed that the moon seemed to be bathing the cove in light, while leaving the edges of the low cliff in deep shadow. They were at a grave disadvantage, especially as only two of their soldiers had bows, the rest having been left on the opposite beach.

"We shall have to stick it out until dawn!" Simon bellowed. "In daylight, when we can see what we are doing, we can charge their positions."

Sir Richard gave a quick nod, as though he had come to the same conclusion. "The chances are they could be gone by then," he muttered. "I think it is only the storm that is keeping them here." He sounded dispirited, his shoulders had sagged, and he resembled a tired old bear baited to exhaustion.

John moved closer until he stood next to Sir Richard. Simon was sitting on a rock close by. "If you could cause a diversion, I might be able to get down the beach before they noticed me. I am the youngest, and probably the fastest runner. I could get help."

Sir Richard head snapped up, his face was illuminated in the moonlight, and he gave John a hard stare. He turned to Simon de Rochley. "What do you think?"

Simon shrugged his shoulders. "It might work. It would be better than just waiting here for the dawn." He stood up and positioned himself close to Sir Richard so that John was behind him. "It might also sort out the other problem. If he dies there is nothing to worry about, and if he lives and does something useful, it might help his case with The Order."

The older man nodded in agreement. He turned to John. "You can have a try. First I want you to talk to him," he said, pointing to a short, thickset man. "He knows the area and can tell you how to get to the nearest village. In the meantime I shall agree on a diversion with Simon."

There was a distance of about forty strides from the safety of the rock to the narrow fringe of beach that separated the dark cliff from the white pounding surf. John reckoned that the narrow part was only ten strides, and once past there he would be on the other beach and heading for the start of the path leading up the steep, low cliff.

"We just got t' hope all their soldiers be involved with keeping us penned up, an' perhaps the path has no guards," the thickset man said.

John removed his heavy leather breastplate, the chain mail hood, his gloves, and the thick sword belt. He decided to take only a dagger, as he did not intend to fight in the conventional way. On his left wrist was the silver bracelet Gwen had given him, he gave it a squeeze and tried to imagine her asleep in the castle. His heart was racing, but he had no fear, only excitement. The local man was explaining how to get to the nearest village named Wick, but John merely pretended to be interested, as he had made up his mind to double back around the enemy soldiers and try to confront the leader with the red hair.

"Is that clear to ye, m'Lord?" the man asked, pitching his voice above the howling of the wind.

"Yes, thank you," John answered distractedly. His mind was on the short sprint he would do in a few moments. The wind was against him, but it might mean the archers would not be too accurate, and once he reached the rocky outcrop separating the two beaches, the bowmen would not be able to shoot at him without revealing themselves to Sir Richard's bowmen. He would need to sprint as fast as he could to get beyond the range of the bows, and hope there were no soldiers guarding the path.

Simon approached. "Are you ready?" His face wore its usual sardonic smile.

"Yes," John said. "I'm ready." He tried to keep his voice neutral.

"We will make a mock assault up the beach and create a lot of noise. The aim will be to draw their fire. Once their arrows are discharged, you will dash for the shelter of that rocky outcrop. Our two archers will cover you. With the wind and the dark, you have a good chance. Once you have started to run, we will return back here." He looked into John's eyes. "I wish you luck," Simon said slowly, emphasising the word luck.

John turned to face the wind. Forty strides. He noticed Sir Richard was busying himself with organizing the men and ensuring they all carried shields. It was obvious he did not want to speak to John. Was it guilt, or was he simply delegating that duty to Simon? John dismissed the thought and loosened up his limbs. He discarded his cloak, and waited for Sir Richard to lead the charge.

At a signal, the men rushed around the rock and followed Sir Richard up the centre of the cove, banging their shields with their swords and yelling loudly. A flight of arrows was immediately discharged at them, and John took off after the first arrow thudded against the rocks.

He ran like a greyhound released from its leash. The sand and shingle was hard under his feet. He avoided a small rock and in moments he was close to the outcrop, but decided not to stop. His boots pounded the narrow fringe of sand between the two beaches. It was steeper there, and his right leg took most of the strain. Soon, he was past the outcrop and into the wide expanse of rocky beach. The wind was slowing him down, but the moon enabled him to see the larger rocks. An arrow streaked past him and he changed direction, running diagonally up the beach, until he could see the white line of the path against the darker vegetation growing on the cliff.

He had a strange feeling he was being watched, and for the first time he began to experience fear. If the enemy were waiting for him at the top of the path he would be unable to avoid getting killed. His legs continued to pump automatically. The path was closer now, and there was no sign of any bodies on the cliff. He reached the bottom of the path. It was steep. He threw his weight forward and, bent almost double, raced up the path. The feeling of being watched increased, and he was almost crying with anticipation as he burst over the brow of the cliff, his lungs heaving with the exertion. Nobody was there! To his left, on the seaward side, he thought he could see some distant movement. He veered quickly away to the right, his chest was aching and his legs felt like jelly.

After some time, when he was well away from the cove, he turned inland, running steadily across a flat area of stunted grasses and low bushes. When he had counted to three hundred, he changed direction again and began to run back towards the sea, and running parallel with the bay. He no longer felt he was being watched and, with the wind behind him, his confidence increased and he relaxed into his running. He had no idea what lay ahead, but was prepared for what he expected to be an inevitable, final confrontation. He remembered his dream of the storm, the sinking sand, and that awful feeling of loss. He ran faster.

. . .

THE GALLEY PLUNGED AND rolled like a wild thing as the oarsmen strained to propel it through the turbulent sea and into the estuary. The wind came in long tortuous blasts, seeming to stop any forward movement, as though time was suspended. Gwen closed her eyes as yet another wave burst over the side and slapped across her face. Martin yelled in her ear, "We're through the entrance! Louis reckons we could reach the shore in a short while."

Gwen opened her eyes and tried to put on a smile. She felt nauseous, and the violent movements of the ship threatened to make her vomit. Another wave slopped over her, and her teeth began to chatter. Why had she come? The clarity of purpose she had possessed in the castle was fading, and her reasons were no longer realistic. She would be of no help to anyone, least of all to herself. She thought of John: had he really been running away? Perhaps the two of them were no longer important, and perhaps their contributions to the present events were finished? Could it be that all their suffering and struggles had been for nothing? Her head throbbed, and she covered her face with her hands.

Louis stood near the helm and barked out his orders. He glanced at Gwen. She did not look like a soldier any more, just a frightened girl with seasickness. He grimaced; he should never have allowed her to come with them. Looking over the moonswept waters he could just discern the outline of the large ship riding out the storm in the left hand corner of the bay. Louis had considered trying to board the ship, but the storm made it almost impossible, and he had no idea how many fighting men were on board. It would be best if he could rescue Sir Richard first. They could worry about the foreign ship later.

The galley was slowly approaching the shore to the seaward side of the cove. The best place to land would have been in the cove itself, but if Gwen's vision was to be believed, and he did believe in her, then there would be no point in landing in the same trap as Sir Richard. The area he was heading for was the one place where he thought he could beach the galley without grounding it on rocks. It would be dangerous, but was the only option. This time they would row the galley into the beach and drag the anchors up above the tide line. It would put the ship at risk, but there was more chance of getting the men safely through the surf.

Martin stood up and watched as the galley lurched towards the shore. Amid the rolling surf, there were areas where the sea burst up in frothing fountains as it encountered sunken rocks. Far to the right was the cove where Sir Richard was supposed to be trapped. Martin hoped Gwen's vision was accurate, but he was not completely convinced. Visions were not part of his limited experience of life.

Louis guided the galley towards the shore. He passed a message to the rowers to prepare for hitting rocks. Some of the men at the bow were ready to jump ashore with the anchors, while others prepared to fight the enemy, if they should be waiting. Louis wondered if the galley had been noticed either by Sir Richard's men or by the enemy soldiers. It might be possible for Louis's men to get from the beach to the cliffs without being seen. In that case, they would have the advantage. But, if they had been noticed, the landing would be difficult and perhaps deadly. He shut out the awful thought and concentrated on the final approach. Oars crashed on rocks; the galley hurtled forward on a mighty wave, and there was a loud grating sound, like a landslide. The galley's bow hit the beach, and the ship swung broadside to the pounding surf.

The men in the front scrambled over the side and ran up the beach with the anchors, while others fanned out on both sides to cover the landing from surprise attack. Louis urged everyone to get out of the galley and onto the stony sand as the violent surf threatened to swamp the ship. The large heavy oars were raised and stowed, and the rowers grabbed their weapons, jumped into the shallow water and staggered up the beach.

Martin helped Gwen to her feet, but she was reluctant to make the jump from the galley into the churning waters below. She balanced on the side of the tilting stern and tried to control her heaving stomach. Just as she was preparing to jump, the ship shuddered from a powerful wave, and she was catapulted into the raging surf. The weight of her leather armour dragged her down and she had difficulty rising from her knees. The undertow of the falling tide dragged her back and she was immediately overwhelmed by the next wave. As she struggled in vain to get to her feet, Martin's strong arms lifted her up, and she was carried, coughing and spluttering to the safety of the shingle beach.

Louis could not believe his luck. In the first few minutes of the landing, he was able to use ropes to drag the stern of the galley round, so that the waves no longer threatened to swamp the ship, and with the falling tide the bow was already out of the water. All the time he was supervising this, he expected to hear the screams of his men as the enemy arrows cut them down. But nothing happened.

Now, he could turn his attention to the next stage of the operation. He had known this beach from early childhood, and realized there were three possible plans. He knew there was a narrow path up the steep cliffs, which would be quite difficult to climb with weapons and armour, but not beyond the abilities of any of his men. However, the first few soldiers would be very vulnerable to attack. Alternatively, they could wait a while until the tide receded, when it would be possible to wade around the rocky outcrop separating the beach from the cove, where Louis believed Sir Richard's men were trapped. From the cove, there was an easier path up to the top of the cliffs. The third option was to march down the beach until they were nearly opposite where the foreign ship was at anchor, and follow a narrow path that led up to the top of the high cliffs. As they stretched seawards, these cliffs gradually increased in height, until they formed the rocky promontory known as Hengistbury Head. It would be a hard trek along the beach, and would, once again, leave them exposed to attack.

Louis had a short discussion with some of his men, and presented the three options. His helmsman expressed the feeling of the group. "My Lord, we've risked our lives to cross this bay in the worst storm in living memory, and we did it to rescue Sir Richard and his men. Many of 'em be our friends as well. Therefore, there be no point in fighting our way round to the cove, just to join them in their trap. We could 'ave beached the boat there to start with. If we goes down the beach, we may succeed in cutting off the enemy from the ship, but we would also be sitting ducks if them wished to attack us. I think we should make use of the short time we has, before the dawn breaks, to climb this cliff. Them who be unable to, can guard the galley." It was a thoughtful speech and the others nodded in agreement.

"It will not be easy in this wind, but if we can reach the top without being detected, then we should be able to defeat them, or at the very least release Sir Richard from his trap." Louis patted the helmsman on the shoulder and nodded to the others. He scanned the moonlit cliffs, thankful there was no sign of any enemy soldiers. "This is almost too good to be true," he said thoughtfully.

Gwen was feeling sorry for herself. She was sitting on a smooth rock, holding her head. She was wet, bruised and had been very sick. She shivered in her wet clothes. "I've never been on the sea before, and certainly never in a storm like this one," she moaned. She looked at Martin, "I'm sorry to be a problem." She wrapped his cloak tightly about her chilled body, in a bid to stop the shaking spasm that gripped her.

"Oh, no. That's all right," Martin replied awkwardly. He was not used to anyone being ill, especially a woman. In the moonlight, he could see that Louis was preparing to climb the narrow path leading to the top of the cliffs. The men were bunched around the start of the path, each determined not to be the last up. Martin was anxious to take part, but did not know what to do about Gwen. Louis hurried back to them. "Have you had any more visions?" It seemed a strange request on the wind-torn beach.

Gwen shook her head. "They never come when you want them to," she said with a rueful smile. Her body trembled violently, as though experiencing a personal earthquake.

Louis made a face, his quick eyes noting Gwen's condition. "I want you to stay with her, Martin. It would not be safe for her to climb the cliff. I am leaving two men to guard the ship. If we are lucky, we shall be back by dawn," he spoke rapidly, but with authority. He made a short bow to Gwen, and was gone.

It was a difficult climb to the top of the cliff, and although it was not high, it would have been a death sentence for any man who slipped. Louis had positioned two bowmen in front, followed by two swordsmen and then more bowmen, with the rest of the foot soldiers at the rear. He hoped that the first men could reach the top before they were challenged, but by having the archers near the front he was allowing the small force to fight back even if they were caught on the cliffside.

The path was steep, and parts of it had crumbled away to just the width of a foot, which forced the men to shuffle along with their backs to the wall and their palms clutching the rough surface. As they inched their way upwards, the wind clawed at their clothing and sudden strong gusts threatened to dislodge them.

The first man reached the top and, with gasps of relief, dragged himself over the edge and on to a flat grassy bank. He quickly slipped his bow from his shoulder and selected an arrow in readiness. As more of the men reached the safety of the summit, they fanned out in a large semi-circle, each soldier counting himself lucky to have survived the climb.

Louis was amazed at their good fortune, and urged them on at a half-run towards the cove. The area was covered in small bushes providing excellent cover, and in the strange half-light of the moon, each man imagined every dark shape was the enemy. In moments, they reached the outcrop of rock stretching out to the bay, and providing the seaward side of the cove. They approached carefully, checking each bush as they passed, becoming more confident in their movements as they closed in around the top of the cliff.

"They've gone!" a man yelled to Louis.

"If they were ever here!" another called out.

"Of course they were!" Louis roared. He believed utterly in Gwen's vision, and was both angry at the wasted effort and relieved there had been no killing. He rushed to the top of the cliff and looked down into the cove. It was bathed in moonlight, and he could see at a glance that Sir Richard's men were not there.

· · ·

IT HAD TAKEN ONLY a short time for Louis and his men to climb the cliff path, and Martin had watched with mounting excitement as the shadowy shapes reached the top and disappeared. "Well, they've got the worst part done!" he shouted. There was a longing in his voice, which even the wind did not disguise.

"I'm sorry to have held you back!" Gwen called back guiltily. She wished she had not insisted on coming, yet a part of her knew why she had come, and it had nothing to do with Martin, Sir Richard, or Louis. She had made the dangerous journey to be reunited with John.

"That's all right," Martin said; he did not sound convincing. He sat down next to her behind a rock that sheltered them from the worst of the wind. Somewhere, down the bay in front of them, was the foreign ship, and to the left was where the dawn would break in a short while. Behind them was the solid outline of the galley, like a huge beached whale, where the two guards walked about trying to keep warm. They kept their anxious eyes fixed on the cliff, as if they expected, at any moment, hordes of foreign soldiers to surge down on them.

"I wonder what's 'appening?" Martin said.

"I wish I knew," Gwen replied bitterly. If only she could use her ability to *see* things when she wanted, and not have it happen in the random way it occurred. They sat silently, staring down the beach, and Gwen's thoughts turned, once again, to John. She wondered if her vision had been correct, or whether he might still be in the cove with Sir Richard. If he was running away, as she had seen him in her vision, where was he running to? She knew he did not like Simon de Rochley, and perhaps he was the reason for John's departure. Since her time with John at the ferry crossing, she frequently found herself wondering about him. There was no doubt she felt attracted to him, and she thought it safe to think he found her attractive. She subconsciously touched the cropped area of her head. Now, Martin was another matter. He was a friend, but she was not attracted to him. She closed her eyes.

"Who's there?" Martin exclaimed. He jumped to his feet as a group of armed men suddenly surrounded them. Gwen awoke with a start and screamed in terror. Martin drew his sword, his eyes were blazing, and he sheltered Gwen with his broad body. She continued to scream for help as the dark figures drew closer, their weapons gleaming in the moonlight.

A voice boomed out, "Mistress Gwen, what are you doing here?" It was the unmistakeable voice of Sir Richard.

• • •

As JOHN DREW CLOSER to the cliff, he could hear the thunder of the surf above the howl of the wind. In spite of the conditions, he kept up a rapid pace, running in long strides supported by the springy grass. He kept a close watch on the shadowy landscape, looking for any sign of movement, and was within fifty strides of the edge of the cliff when he veered to the right to avoid a clump of low bushes. Without warning, the earth collapsed under his feet, and he crashed to the ground, his foot in a rabbit's hole. The fall winded him and he lay on the grass gathering his tattered wits. The ankle did not feel too painful, and it seemed he had escaped with only mild bruising.

Eventually, he was able to breathe normally, and was about to sit up when he heard something on the wind: a voice or the sound of a horse. He froze. The only people likely to be on top of the cliff in this weather were the foreign soldiers.

Very slowly, he raised his head over the bush and his eyes searched the flat moonlit landscape. He could see nothing, and was about to leave the security of the bush, when a shadowy figure rose up near the edge of the cliff, quickly followed by another. They ran, bent double until they were away from the precipice. Then they stopped and arranged their weapons. Within moments, similar dark shapes, like black incubi, were silhouetted in the moonlight, all moving quickly to what seemed an assembly point.

John watched with apprehension, as he feared they knew where he was and were preparing to rush his hiding place. However, after a few muttered orders in their strange language, they marched swiftly along the edge of the cliff towards the sea. There were more than a dozen of them, and many carried bows. He looked behind, but could see no others, and concluded that this was the rearguard. He considered how lucky he had been. A few more strides and he would have literally collided with them.

As John watched them disappear into the darkness, he tried to review the situation. The enemy was escaping to the ship, while Sir Richard sheltered behind the rocks on the beach, believing the cliffs were lined with bowmen. He must alert Sir Richard. The enemy soldiers were out of sight, but the wind was blowing towards them, so he would have to be certain they were out of earshot before he began to yell. He ran to the edge and looked down into the cove. It seemed deserted, and he guessed that Sir Richard's men were hiding behind the rocks. The wind threatened to blow him over, and he was forced to lie prostrate on the edge. He cupped his hands and yelled as loudly as he could, only to hear his voice snatched away in the mighty gusts that swept the cove. He quickly realized it was useless.

Now he was in a panic. The enemy who had tried to kill him and capture Gwen, who had killed numerous innocent people, who had captured Tom, and who had stolen the sword, were escaping. These fiends were about to get away, and there seemed nothing he could do about it. He remembered his dream, and he knew that no matter what, he had to be on the beach when they were trying to escape. He started to run, and his feet were driven by his anger; he was determined to catch them before they reached the path down to their ship. He had no idea if such a path existed, but he knew they would have planned for this, so he had to stay close.

As John disappeared into the shadows in the direction of Hengistbury Head, the first of Louis' soldiers scrambled over the edge of the cliff on his way to relieve Sir Richard in the cove. Although the soldier and his companions did not know it, they had missed the enemy by less time than it took to unload the galley.

·　·　·

ON THE BEACH SIMON de Rochley organized the men into a defensive position while Sir Richard tried to update himself on the latest information.

"This is most unexpected," Sir Richard said. Seawater was still dripping from him. "When we waded round from the cove and I saw the outline of the galley on the beach, I thought it must have shipwrecked after dropping us off."

Martin explained how Louis had attempted the rescue mission after Gwen had described her vision of Sir Richard and his men being trapped in the cove.

"I saw John running down the beach and up a path to the top of the cliffs. Was that true?" Gwen asked, her voice betrayed her emotion.

Sir Richard was impressed. This was further evidence of Gwen's powers. "Yes, it was true, my dear. He volunteered to get help, and we arranged a diversion while he made a run for it. We don't know if he was successful." Gwen's face revealed a mixture of pleasure and apprehension.

The old knight turned to Martin. "Where is Louis now?"

Martin pointed to the steep path. "He climbed that cliff to attack the enemy soldiers who 'ad ye trapped. In this wind 'tis impossible to hear anything, so we don't know if they've been fightin' or not." He paused. "They got to the top without any trouble though."

Sir Richard was thoughtful. "While we were wading round here, not one arrow was fired at us. I think the enemy has retreated down towards Hengistbury Head. They hope to get aboard their ship now that the worst of the storm is past. Louis may have clashed with them, but the chances are that they avoided him as well. It was a clever move on their part." He waited while Simon joined them. In a few words Sir Richard explained what had happened.

Simon cast a critical eye at the steep white slash in the cliff. "It could be very dangerous for Louis and his men to get back down that path."

Sir Richard agreed. "We shall have to send someone up there with a message. If we hurry down the beach, and Louis and his group are able to move quickly along the top of the cliffs, we may yet be able to save the day!" His tired eyes blazed with fanatical zeal. He turned to Simon. "They have both of the Swords of Power with them; we must stop those getting to the ship. We have the opportunity this day to achieve a great victory for The Order. I want you to march the men along the beach, I shall catch up with you after I have made contact with Louis. Good luck!" He and Simon clasped arms. Sir Richard surveyed the cliffs as Simon ran back to the assembled men and urged them down the beach. His violent threats faded into the wind as the darkness enveloped them.

The moon was shining directly on Sir Richard's face, and he looked pale and tired, and there was something unnatural in his enthusiasm; it was like the last bright light of a meteor. He placed his arm on Martin's shoulder. "Martin, you must go up the path and give Louis a message. Can you do it?"

"'Course I can, m'Lord," Martin felt both honoured by the order and affronted by the question.

"Good. Tell Louis the enemy has deceived us. Tell him they are in retreat to their ship. I want him to advance along the cliffs towards Hengistbury Head as quickly as he is able. He is to try to attack them as they are making their way down to the beach." He was breathing heavily through clenched jaws. "Good luck!" He patted Martin on the back.

"Take care!" Gwen said. She felt strangely vulnerable as Martin prepared to leave. He was so strong and dependable, and now she would be left with only Sir Richard. She forced a smile. "I shall see you later." She gave him a quick kiss on the cheek. Martin smiled broadly in the moonlight, and without another word trotted over to the start of the path. In moments he was a mere shadow on the cliff face.

"Now we must catch up with the others," Sir Richard said. "Your soldier's attire is quite convincing, so if we join battle with them, you must keep out of the way. Remember, you are a very special person." He took a deep breath and guided her forwards. They began to walk quickly along the sloping beach.

After only a few dozen paces, Gwen was finding the going difficult. The small, soft shingle caused her boots to sink in with each step, and the effort of dragging out her foot before she could move forward was tiring. Sir Richard was also having difficulty, and the weight of his chain mail and weapons, combined with his wet clothes, caused him to sink in even further. They laboured on for a while until Gwen grew concerned about the old knight. He was panting and making strange groans, and it was clear he was close to exhaustion.

"Can we stop for a moment, my Lord?" Gwen asked. It was for his sake, as much as for her own. The wind carried her words down the beach.

"No time," he gasped. "We must hurry if we are to catch up with... with...." He made an odd gargling sound, dropped to his knees, clasped his throat, and fell sideways onto the beach. He rolled on his back and lay quite still with his eyes open, staring at nothing.

Gwen knelt down beside him, speechless with terror. She felt the pulse in his neck. There was none. Sir Richard de Godfroi was dead.

. . .

JOHN RAN CAREFULLY. HE did not wish to fall down another rabbit hole, nor did he intend to come unexpectedly upon the soldiers. He was beginning to think they had taken another route, when he saw a slight movement in the grey-blackness ahead. It was almost dawn, and his eyes longed for light. He stopped and listened, but could hear only the wind. But ahead there was more movement.

He felt his position was stupidly dangerous. Where would retreating soldiers look, but behind! To get close to them, he would have to approach from a different direction. He started to run inland, forcing himself to keep alert and to run faster. After counting to a hundred, he resumed his previous direction, but this time he had to try to hold the route in his mind. John could feel the imprint of the runes pulsing in the palm of his hand; it gave him renewed confidence, and he quickened his speed.

A rabbit burst from cover near his feet, and John almost tripped. He took this as a warning, and decided to stop. To his left was the bay, and somewhere, either in front or behind him were the soldiers. If he was to achieve anything, it was necessary to get back to the bay. He began to run in short bursts. The stunted bushes provided an illusion of cover and he was close to the cliff when he stopped behind a thorn bush to check his position, and glad of the break, he rested his hands on his knees. At that moment, silhouetted against the brightening sky, he saw the leading soldiers marching towards him. He ducked down and waited, fearing he had been seen, but the soldiers marched by. Their voices were loud and confident.

John was preparing to do another flanking run, when he saw them stop, about thirty paces from where he was hiding. As he watched they seemed to decrease in number. Like ripples they vanished from view until only one soldier was left. He gave a quick look around and disappeared.

After a short pause, John forced himself to leave the security of the bush. He crept up to the point where the soldiers had been, and saw a broad path leading down the side of the cliff to the beach. In the gloom he could see their dark shapes against the whiteness of the path. He stepped back, uncertain what to do. After leaving Sir Richard in the cove, John had been quite certain it would be pointless to try to get help from a sleeping village some distance away. His intentions were to meet up with the leader and challenge him for the ownership of the sword. Now, staring down at the departing soldiers, he realized how naïve and childish his plan had been.

The soldiers below did not include the leader, who almost certainly was safe on the beach, or might even be on board the ship. John carried no weapon other than a small dagger, and even with a sword, it would have been stupidity to take on a group of trained soldiers. He was racked with indecision. The imprint of the runes on his palm possessed no more life than the nail on his thumb. He felt weary and despondent and his muscles trembled with fatigue.

Something shot past in front of his face. The shock was so great that John jumped back from the precipice, as though on a whipcord, and just in time to avoid another black shape whistling past him. Arrows! In front he could see dark figures advancing rapidly along the cliff. He crouched down and ran for cover behind a clump of gorse as more arrows passed overhead.

John cursed his carelessness. The soldiers he had been following had not been the rearguard after all. He wondered how long it would be before he was surrounded. There was only one thing to do, and that was to run, and risk an arrow in the back. He could hear orders being yelled and men answering. He paused. He could understand them. They were local accents.

"It's me, John!" he yelled, his voice was barely able to penetrate the wind. "Don't shoot! It's me, John!" Another arrow clipped the bush. He yelled again. To be killed by his own side in the final stage of this incredible adventure seemed pointless and unfair. The men were creeping closer, and John yelled once more. He was not a hero, but neither was he a coward, and he was not prepared to run from Sir Richard and his men. Sir Richard! John had not thought about his name. He cupped his hands together and yelled at the line of dark shapes. "Sir Richard! It's me, John! Sir Richard!"

Someone called his name, then he heard a voice yell out, "John? If it is you, stand up!"

Slowly, fearing some soldiers might not have heard, John stood up with his hands in the air. Ghostly figures ran forward with swords in their hands. In the dim light he could see the small, stocky shape of Louis.

"Louis!" John said, "I thought you were the enemy!"

Louis clasped John's shoulders. "John! We thought you were one of their sentries. It is lucky for you that the wind is so strong, or my archers would have killed you." As he spoke, a large muscular figure joined them. He came close and gave John a long, searching stare. In the dim light John could tell that he was still a youth, although a powerful one.

"So you're John," he said slowly. "I'm Martin."

After the brief greetings and explanations, John led Louis to the edge of the cliff. Dawn was breaking and a thin line appeared on the eastern horizon. Down at the beach, however, darkness held sway, but they could just make out the figures of the enemy soldiers reaching the end of the path.

"Sir Richard's men are advancing down the beach. If we hurry, we should be able to stop the enemy getting on board the ship, and we may even be able to catch them in a trap, for a change!" Louis spoke cheerfully, but he held no illusions about the chances of success. He led the way, and John and Martin brought up the rear.

. . .

THEY WERE GETTING CLOSE to the foreign ship, and Simon de Rochley was hot and his legs ached. The forced march had been arduous, and Simon had used threats and physical force to persuade his men to stay together. The night's adventures and the difficult march in sinking shale had exhausted them, and it was doubtful if they would fight well. Simon called a halt, and the weary men rested on their swords and spears, and some collapsed on the ground.

"Get up, you scum! We could be attacked at any moment!" he yelled, but his words were ignored. He stared down the beach, trying to penetrate the gloom, but could see no sign of Sir Richard. Simon kept remembering John, the accused upstart, had claimed to have had a dream about this very beach with its sinking sand. He dismissed the thought as his eyes searched the empty beach. Sir Richard was nowhere to be seen.

"The old fool," he muttered fiercely. "Where in hell's name has he got to?"

At any moment he expected to make contact with the enemy, and his small force seemed too tired to care. He resolved to wait for a short while, to give Sir Richard time to catch up, but if he did not appear, then Simon was prepared to order the attack himself. He did not worry if the men hated him; they were mere peasants, little better than animals, and he was a nobleman and a member of The Order. They would do as they were told, or he would cut them down himself.

He walked over to the men who were lying on the ground. He had his sword in both hands. "Get up!" he roared. He kicked one man hard in the side of his hip. The soldier cried out in pain and staggered to his feet. The others did the same.

"We are close to the enemy. A few hundred paces and we should be there! Keep together, and pass along any order I give you."

He could see the resentment on their faces in the iron light of the pre-dawn, and he knew they did not share his desire to fight. Simon did not care, for peasants were not involved in the major movements of life; they were just beasts of burden as far as he was concerned. To achieve his own aims, he would trample and manipulate them as he saw best. He raised his sword above him. "This is an important moment in your lives. You will be able to tell your children how you fought against the heathen who dared to invade your country. You could be heroes!" There was a half-hearted cheer.

Simon arranged the swordsmen so that they formed a semi-circle, and the two archers were positioned among them. The wind was blowing from behind and, with the thunder of the surf, it was difficult to transmit orders, and impossible to do it quickly. The beach sloped steeply down from the high water line to the sucking surf, but above the high water line to the base of the cliffs, the surface was flatter, but dotted with large rocks and the roots of great trees. As the beach had become steeper, Simon had moved up towards the cliffs. However, the rocks and driftwood caused the men to bunch up and lose their defensive position. In the moments before the dawn they found it difficult to discern what each shape and shadow belonged to, and the heightened sense of expectation Simon had generated, quickly faded to be replaced with sullen resignation as they plodded on.

· · ·

WHEN THE ATTACK CAME, it was unexpected and ferocious. Although Simon knew there was a chance of an ambush, he had not given it serious thought. In his mind, the enemy soldiers were in retreat and wanting to get on board their ship. Consequently, he had imagined he would come upon them as they were vainly trying to escape. The reality was quite different.

A shower of arrows rained down, and a number of men were struck, their screams and yells carrying on the wind. The remaining men ran about seeking cover that did not exist on the open beach. Simon rallied his small force and they made a slow and disorganized charge in the direction from whence the attack had come. Another flight of arrows claimed more casualties before Simon saw the elusive bowmen darting back behind rocks in the shadows of the cliff.

He screamed a defiant yell and led the charge, attempting to inspire his terrified men. They had no choice but to follow, and were soon into hand-to-hand fighting. Simon fought like a man possessed. He battled his way to the seaward side of the high ledge of the beach and sought to out-flank the enemy position. He used both hands to wield his sword, and his powerful strokes smashed a path before him. In front a soldier opposed him with a short sword and round shield. Simon clenched his teeth and swung a savage blow against the upturned shield. The opposing soldier was knocked to the ground by the violence of the blow, and lay there expecting the next one to end his life.

Simon raised his sword for the final stroke, but was distracted by an unbelievable sight. Travelling at enormous speed towards him on his left side, was a huge figure who seemed to be flying across the ground. Simon spun round, his eyes wide with fear. In the diffused grey light a giant in full armour galloped past on the lower level of the beach, carrying a sword that glowed in the dark. Simon had never believed John's story about his so-called magic sword, but in the instant Simon knew he had been wrong. He stared amazed as the figure disappeared into the darkness, galloping in the direction of Sir Richard like a black spectre. Distracted by what he had seen, Simon turned to continue the fight, and saw, to his horror, he had left himself unprotected for too long. The enemy soldier was already thrusting up at him. Simon tried vainly to bring his own sword across to parry the stroke, but he was too late.

CHAPTER 18

I N THE MIDDLE OF the empty beach, Gwen waited for the dawn, and for the help that she was confident would come. Beside her lay the corpse of Sir Richard. She had arranged his body, placing his hands across his chest, and had laid flat stones over his eyes. She picked up his sword and held it carefully in both hands, testing its weight. With great care, she plunged it, blade first, into the sandy shale above his head, and sat down to watch the sun rise. It was all over, and there was nothing more to do. She would wait.

Her mind began to sort out the various implications of Sir Richard's death. He had been a senior knight of the strange Order he had constantly referred to. Did his death mean that Simon or Nicholas would now assume command? She shuddered. It was another reason for her, and John, to get away and return to the village. Gwen tried to imagine the village of Woodford without Tom, and her eyes filled with tears. The smithy could not be her home any more, and Elizabeth would find her only a burden. There was no point in returning. Her thoughts turned to John. She wondered if he had managed to get help from the nearby village. She was glad he would not be involved in the final battle, which she imagined was probably happening at that moment. With Louis's men above and Simon's men below, there was a good chance they would defeat the enemy. But where was the enemy's terrifying leader?

She sat up with a start as a shiver ran through her body and sweat broke out on her brow. She was suddenly aware that with the two Swords of Power, the leader of the enemy was unassailable and the outcome of the battle was not so certain any more. Gwen remembered John's description of how he was able to control the sword in the encounter with the other supposed brother, and wondered if John's power over the sword was gone forever.

However, she was glad he was some miles away seeking help. Perhaps he would find her in the morning, and they could decide what to do.

It now seemed likely the enemy would escape, and Gwen felt detached and unemotional. She did not want to be special or mistaken for someone else, she just wanted to get back to normal living. Even as she wished it, she knew things could never be the same again. The past days had seemed to go on for ever, so much had happened, and for what?

The wind was less violent than before, but still blew in strong gusts. Gwen removed the chain mail hood weighing down on her head, and shook her hair out in the wind. It was difficult to unfasten the leather breastplate, but after some fumbling, she managed to undo the wet leather buckles, and the heavy armour dropped on the sand. She wrapped her damp cloak about her and began to pace up and down. The first glimmers of light appeared on the horizon. With the new day, the enemy would leave and it would all be over.

White-topped waves crashed on the shingle, the roar changing briefly to a sucking, crunching sound before the next breaker rolled in. The storm was abating and the tide was going out. Everything was coming to an end. But just as the retreating waters seemed intent on dragging away the beach, so Gwen felt the enemy was still dangerous. She had a feeling of impending danger, but put it down to the anti-climax, and the fact that she was sitting with a dead body.

She did not react immediately when the towering horse galloped out of the gloom. It seemed impossible for a living creature to be so big. She tried to get to her feet, but in her panic she lost her balance and fell awkwardly on the shingle. Everything seemed to be noise and movement, dominated by the awful crashing of those terrible hooves. High in the air, she could see a sword that glowed in the iron-grey light of the dawn. Gwen twisted round and reached up for the pommel of Sir Richard's sword. There was a desperate fury in her actions. As her fingers touched the metal, the sword was struck with a blow that sent it skimming over the stones. She struggled to her feet, as a huge hand grabbed her left arm and effortlessly lifted her up and swung her, face down, over the front of the saddle. She screamed loudly, but the only response she got was a blow to the head from the pommel of his sword. She was mildly stunned, but in her pain and terror she heard him give a loud cry of exultation. "I have you now, and everything I came for is achieved!" He called out in a strange language, and the horse turned and began to gallop back along the beach.

. . .

As they descended the steep path, John kept turning to check if the soldiers were anywhere to be seen.

"'Looks as though they've gone back down the beach," Martin said. He did not have to shout, as the wind was not so fierce as it had been on the top of the cliff.

"They must know Sir Richard is coming along the beach, and are preparing to attack him," John said. "But it does not make sense. Why would they risk defeat, when all they have to do is get on that ship?"

They continued the descent in silence, watching the hurrying shapes of Louis and his men in front. The dawn light was seeping through the dark sky and everything was grey and indistinct. John felt a warm glow in the palm of his hand, and a thought came to him like an unexpected toothache. "The leader! Where is the leader of the enemy?"

"What do ye mean?" Martin said. He was concentrating on not slipping on the sandy path.

"There has been no sign of the leader, and now the soldiers have gone back down the beach. If he was on board the ship, they would have joined him. He must still be around here. But why?" John felt he was close to something important. "He has the swords of power and the only other thing he seems to want is to capture Gwen and kill me. I don't think he can kill me, and Gwen is safe in the castle."

"No, she's not," Martin interrupted. "She come with Louis and me in the galley."

"Where is she then?" John had stopped in his tracks.

"She be down on the beach with Sir Richard. He sent that knight called Simon to lead the men towards the ship. But Sir Richard, 'e gives me a message to take up the cliff to Louis, an' when I went off, 'e and Gwen was far behind. There were just the two of 'em." Martin stopped. The realisation of the danger to Gwen was slowly sinking in. "We'd better get down that beach pretty quick," he muttered. "Gwen could be in trouble." He began to descend at a rapid pace.

Louis had reached the bottom of the path where the noise of the battle could be heard in the wind. He divided his men into two groups: one to proceed along the higher level and the other to follow the waterline. "Martin, you come with me. John, go with the Sergeant on the lower level."

The two young men did as they were told. Each was anxious to get down the beach as quickly as possible and, although neither would have admitted it, they were glad to be away from each other.

The action was close at hand, and by the dawn light they could see that Simon's men were being badly mauled, and were fighting a hopeless retreat. Louis ordered his bowmen to fire a volley of arrows and then charged the rear of the enemy. Those of Louis' men on the lower level were able to fire up at the invaders while the swordsmen attacked from a third angle. Soon the battle was spread all over the beach as each side tried to out-manoeuvre the other. The remains of Simon's men rallied when they understood that rescue had arrived, and without Simon to bully them, each man fought bravely. Most of Louis' small army was made up of fishermen and local bowmen, and were no match for the professional soldiers. In spite of their disadvantage, the Wessex men fought hard and it seemed that they must win the day, by force of numbers.

Down on the lower level, John was fighting along side a burly Sergeant; a tough, experienced soldier who had served with Louis on a number of occasions. The Sergeant had given John his throwing spear. "Stay behind me an' stay close. Ye guard me back." John was anxious to get past the heaving mass of fighting men and run down the beach to find Gwen, but he knew he could not leave until it was certain that Louis had won the day.

The Sergeant was soon engaged in a fierce sword fight on the edge of the upper level of the beach, and John was dodging from one side to the other, trying to use his spear against the enemy soldier who was a big man and surprisingly quick on his feet. He understood what John was trying to do, and managed to force the Sergeant to retreat at the very moment when John was attempting to pass behind. The Sergeant swung his sword and stepped back, and the side of the sword hit John across the front of his helmet, knocking him down the slope. He fell backwards and landed heavily on the wet stones, winded and confused, while above him the Sergeant and the enemy soldier continued to exchange blows.

John sat up and rubbed his forehead; he could feel the swelling coming up. In the tumble, he had dropped his spear, and as he reached out for it he saw a sight that caused his eyes to widen. Galloping towards him was the huge, black horse and in the saddle was the man he most feared, wielding the golden sword. John stood up, uncertain what to do, but saw in the instant the body of Gwen slung across the neck of the horse. The huge rider was controlling both the horse and Gwen with his left hand and was waving the sword in his right. As the horse and rider careered down on him, John grabbed the spear and flung himself towards the sea, convinced that the horse would run him down.

Instead, the powerful beast veered towards the edge of the upper level of the beach, enabling the giant to use the great sword to deliver a mighty slash at the Sergeant, who was knocked senseless to the ground. The force of the blow almost threw the rider as well, and the horse skidded in the loose stones. With great skill the rider maintained his balance and prepared to continue his gallop down the beach.

John leapt forward and held up his palm. The runes felt cold and lifeless. "I am Giles Plantard!" he yelled. "Giles Plantard!"

The great horse reared up as the rider tried to turn the horse in order to get a better view of the young man who kept moving round on his blind side. "So! It is you! The final piece of the puzzle. I have waited a long time for this moment."

Again John held up his palm and shouted his name, but still nothing happened. The rider gave a scream of triumph. "It's finished for you! My brother died because of your meddling. Now I have my revenge." He spoke with a strong accent, but with a complete grasp of the language. He backed the horse towards John, who darted behind it. The rider cursed and tried again to get a clear thrust at his elusive enemy.

In John's mind, this seemed like a replay of the skirmish in the flower fields. But then he had felt inspired, now he felt vulnerable. He willed himself not to give in, and his anger replaced his terror. He had never used a spear, and was unwilling to throw it for fear of injuring Gwen. Instead, he tried to get close enough to be able to thrust it at the huge body.

As if sensing John's intention, the rider dug in his spurs and galloped off down the beach, leaving John running behind yelling wildly. Around him the battle was coming to a climax, and the enemy soldiers were trying to regroup, and to effect a retreat down the beach after their leader.

Without warning, the horse came to an abrupt stop. The rider turned the horse violently, causing it to rise up on two powerful legs and paw the air, like a dragon rampant. Then he was galloping back, hunched forward, leaning over Gwen with the sword held out in front like a lance. John noticed how wonderfully the sword glowed in the half-light, and he remembered the pride he had experienced when he carried it. People had respected him with the sword and he had known power. Men were prepared to follow him, but somehow he had lost it all. As the images flashed in his mind, he thought of Old Mary and her numerous warnings, and felt the outline of the runes glow in his palm. Was that the key? He was not doing this for himself, he was doing it for Gwen. His palm was throbbing like an open wound. He raised his hand, palm out in front of him, and faced the approaching horse and rider without fear and without pride. John took a deep breath and prepared to shout his other name.

The giant reacted with horror when he saw the upturned palm and the glow emanating from it, and turned the horse in full gallop. The huge creature slewed round on the beach and its legs almost collapsed under it. The rider dug in the cruel spurs once again, and the powerful beast regained its balance and broke into a gallop, back in the direction of the ship.

John knew he had the power; he held his palm directly pointed at the retreating stranger, and began to intone, "I am Giles—" A violent buffet pushed him to one side, as two soldiers tumbled down from the upper level of the beach. John tried to get up, but the flaying bodies battled around him and he was forced to crawl along the beach until he was far enough away to avoid their wild sword fight.

When he got to his feet, the horse was far down the beach, and this time John knew the leader would not be waiting for his men. In a few minutes Gwen could be on her way out to the ship. He threw down the spear and began to run, his legs sinking into the shingle and his heart beating fast. As he ran he wondered what had prevented him from saying his name immediately the runes had begun to tingle in his palm. If only he had completed his name before being involved in the fight. If only... His legs pounded into the loose stones and his lungs felt as though they would burst as he raced after the retreating figure.

He could see clearly now. The ship was nearer to the shore, and there were two rowing boats pulled up on the beach. John was getting closer. The horse had stopped near the pounding sea, and the giant was lifting Gwen from the saddle, as though she was just a bundle of clothes. There were a number of men standing near the boats, and some were loading things from the beach. There seemed to be an argument, men were fighting among themselves. One boat had been launched and a big wave almost overturned it; the men were rowing hard and the huge man was standing in the boat waving his arms and shouting orders. He was escaping! John was almost there. He rushed into the sea, but his palm was cold and he knew he had failed.

Then the dream came again, and he was in the dream and the dream was reality. Huge waves were still crashing on the beach as the tide withdrew, and his feet were sinking in the mixture of sand and estuary mud. On board the ship the crew were raising the sails, which flapped in the strong wind, and he was yelling as waves broke over him, and experiencing again the great feeling of loss.

At last, he understood the deep sadness of the dream. His loss was not the sword, it was Gwen. John stood there, beaten and helpless, as waves broke over him. The ship tightened its sails and the anchor was raised, and the vessel moved forward towards the wide mouth of the bay, gathering speed. The storm was abating and the ship easily coped with the breaking waves as it turned majestically towards the sea. Then it was gone.

He stumbled to the shore, not caring what happened to him. To his left, the other rowing boat was still pulled up on the sand and there were a number of bodies lying near it. John stood swaying backwards and forwards, his chest heaving, and gazed numbly down the beach. The battle was over, and in the distance he could see a small group of men in black uniforms standing together in a tired, dejected group while a short stocky man in a white tunic supervised the surrender.

The wind was still strong, and John felt cold and tired. He wanted to sit down, and wandered aimlessly towards the boat. On the sand, two men in black were lying dead with weapons still in their hands. A third was draped over the bow, apparently killed as he tried to launch the boat. A fourth body groaned slightly as John approached. The man was half hidden behind a pile of provisions, but there was something familiar about his sturdy frame. "Martin!" John cried. "Martin!"

John bent down and lifted the large head on its thick neck. Martin was unconscious, but breathing regularly. He had wounds to his arms and there was blood on his face and neck. John checked for any serious wound and could find none. He tried to lift the limp body, but was unable to. So he contented himself with raising Martin's head on a mound of sand, and arranging his limbs in a comfortable way.

As John stood up, Louis and a small group of men approached, waving enthusiastically as John turned to face them. He waited for them in silence, too emotional to speak.

"We beat them, and sent them packing!" Louis yelled. "What's been happening here?"

"It's Martin," John said. "He must have tried to stop them escaping." He bit his lip, and tears welled up, and he started to shake uncontrollably. "They took Gwen," he blubbered. "They took Gwen!"

Louis said nothing. He embraced John in his powerful arms and then released him. The men had moved round to attend to Martin, and Louis walked over to the large rowing boat, and stood there for a moment staring at it silently. John was slowly regaining his composure when Louis returned.

"There are some things that are beyond our comprehension, and some things that I believe are beyond our control." He took John's arm and led him to the boat.

John wiped his eyes and wondered what it was that Louis wanted him to see. In the bottom of the vessel, lying like a beautiful sea-creature, was Gwen. As John stared in total amazement, she slowly opened her eyes.

CHAPTER 19

I T WAS TWO WEEKS before they felt strong enough to leave the castle, and another five days to travel to Woodford. John and Gwen knew they would soon have to come face-to-face with the big changes in their lives. People had died; new friends had been made; they had matured, and the emotional bond between them was still so new they did not know where it would lead. Nothing would ever be the same.

They parted with Martin on the third day of their journey. It was an emotional farewell, as both knew the debt they owed to him. However, during the two weeks in the castle, he had come to recognize the bond between John and Gwen, and he knew he could not seriously hope to have any long-term relationship with her, no matter how much he might wish it.

Martin had told them about the last part of the great battle, describing the incidents about which only he knew. After John and Martin were assigned different areas on the beach by Louis. Martin had seen the giant gallop past on his black horse, and assumed he was intending to capture Gwen. Martin fought his way clear of the melee, and ran back towards the ship, keeping close to the cliffs. He hid behind some rocks and watched the two rowing boats land. There were three men in each boat, and he watched them recover the stores and baggage that had been dumped by their comrades. As they were finishing this task, the leader returned with Gwen. He was in a foul temper and hit some of the men, causing them to lose their attention to the other things that were happening around them. It was at this point that Martin attacked the second boat, and at the same instant the leader, seeing John advancing rapidly down the beach, scrambled into the first boat that was already afloat, and pulled hid horse on board.

There was confusion and panic, and Gwen was tossed into the second boat as the soldiers tried vainly to launch it and fight off Martin's ferocious attack at the same time. As the first boat ploughed through the breakers, the giant realized that Gwen's boat was unlikely to get off the beach, because Martin was wreaking havoc with the crew. The leader appeared to want to return, but the conditions prevented him.

John remembered seeing the leader standing up in the boat and waving his arms. It all made sense. Martin fought like three men in one, and because the soldiers were determined to launch their boat, he was able to fight them one at a time.

"It were nothin' really," he protested modestly, but his wounds told a different story. "If ye gets in any trouble again, ye knows where to find me." His eyes watered when Gwen kissed him farewell, and his handshake with John was abrupt. As he rode slowly away, he turned and ran his hand over his face. "My father won't recognise me an' all!" He waved one more time.

They returned to the castle of the dead Sir Michel de Tournier, and found that Nicholas de Montford had left to attend to *urgent personal business*, and was unaware of the deaths of Sir Richard de Godfroi and Simon de Rochley. It fell to Louis to inform Sir Michel's wife of the sad news, and he took charge of the running of the castle during the poor woman's grief. He was a perfect host to John, Gwen and Martin, and although he was genuinely sad to see them go, he gave them horses and food for the journey.

"Go in peace," Louis said, as they prepared to depart. "You, my lady Gwen, are a very special person to The Order of which I am but an unimportant member." He pursed his lips. "We have lost three of our best knights: Sir Richard, as you may have guessed, was the most senior, but Sir Michel was also high in honours, and Simon de Rochley was a most experienced fighter. They will be much missed, and for some time our Order, in this part of the world, will be greatly weakened. I have no idea what I should do with you both," he smiled at John, "but I have no intention of keeping you as prisoners. Perhaps The Order will want to offer its protection when we have healed our wounds, but for the moment you are free to go or stay as you wish."

Gwen kissed him softly on both cheeks, mounted her horse, and slowly followed John and Martin out of the castle.

As their horses trotted down the road from the castle, Gwen gave a final wave. "Sir Richard was a good knight, but obsessed with power. Louis was the only knight we met who was also a pleasant human being."

When they were in sight of Woodford, it was refreshing to be embraced by its tranquillity and silence, after the tension and excitement of the past weeks. The journey had been long, and although they had taken it slowly, it was now late afternoon and they were both hot and in need of refreshment.

"I know that Old Mary will not be there," John said reflectively. "I believe she came only to instruct me, and awaken my mind." He wiped his brow. "I shall miss her; she was the only family I have ever known."

Gwen sighed. "I know that the smithy will be there, but it will not be the same without Tom. Did you ever meet Elizabeth?"

John shook his head, "I remember few people other than Peter. I lived most of my time in the cottage, and it was a good way from the village."

They approached Woodford from the southern end. There were no people anywhere and, apart from the swallows swooping around the small buildings, the village appeared uninhabited. They passed one poor hovel, and the next habitation was the forge. Even though it was a hot day, there was a curl of smoke coming from the chimney of the cottage. "Elizabeth hates the summer, she sneezes all the time, and stays huddled around the fire," Gwen said, indicating the smoke.

The forge was empty and the furnace was cold, but everything was clean and neatly arranged. "Elizabeth seems to have made this into a shrine," Gwen said. Tears rolled down her face, as she gazed at the implements that Tom had used with such great strength when he had been alive.

They dismounted from their horses, and John wiped her eyes and kissed her gently on her lips. "We don't have to stop here," he said. "We have money and horses, we could travel on to a new life."

Gwen shook her head. "No, we're tired, and I owe it to Elizabeth to let her know that I am alive. She might not care very much, but I owe her that."

The horses were uncomfortable and in need of a drink, and they banged their hooves noisily on the stone floor of the smithy.

As Gwen turned to lead John into the cottage, a loud, familiar voice called out to them. "I'm not mending horses' shoes at the moment, better get on to Little Woodley!"

John and Gwen froze and their faces went pale. That voice? Out of the shadow of the house limped a large man with one arm in a sling and a leg in wooden splints. He had a bandage around his head, and his face was badly scarred, but there was no doubt that it was Tom Roper.

"Father!" Gwen screamed. She ran forward to embrace him, and had to restrain herself from jumping into his arms. Tom was overcome with emotion and there was much hugging and handshaking.

"We thought you were dead," Gwen sobbed.

"I nearly was an' all. But I shall be right as rain before the winter. Ye mark me words."

There was so much to talk about, and the conversation carried on into the night, long after Elizabeth had sneezed her way to bed.

"What happened to Peter?" John asked.

"Oh him!" Tom sniffed loudly. "Peter was not hurt much, and when Sam and his men rescued us, 'e pretended to be the great hero." Tom rubbed his injured leg. "When we got back 'ere, 'e tried to stand up to 'is father, but it didn't work, and 'e left the village. I don't know where 'e's gone now."

"Poor Peter," Gwen said. "He never really had a chance."

Later, as the last embers glowed in the gate, and when Tom was snoring behind the curtain, Gwen asked the question that had been on John's mind for much of the journey home: "Do you think it's over?"

John stared into the fire. "I think it's over for the moment," he said. He reached for her hand. "We must get on with our lives, and face things when they happen. Who knows what the future may hold."

"But what about The Order? They have been watching this village for years, ever since I was given to Tom. Do you think they will leave me alone if they believe I am so important to them?"

"I don't know," John said staring into the fire. "I still have the outline of the talisman on my palm, and it seems we are both somehow connected to The Order. However, The Order is in disarray, and the foreign giant has gone back to where he came from. He has the swords, and that could well satisfy him." He turned to Gwen. "I want you to have this back." He removed the silver bracelet from his wrist and gently replaced it on hers. "This bracelet has an importance that we have yet to discover, and we need to know more about this blood line and how the Holy Grail comes into it. I still don't understand what Keeper of the Holy Grail means." He smiled at her.

"What do we do then? Are we to search for these answers?" Gwen gripped his hands. "What about us?"

"We have our lives to lead. I may decide to help Tom with the smithy." He shrugged. "Who knows what we will do." He yawned loudly. "Tomorrow, I suggest we start again, and try to put the past weeks out of our minds."

They sat together, in companionable silence as the embers faded in the grate.

Outside, an owl hooted in the dark, and away in the distance among the tall trees of the ancient forest another owl answered.

A BRIEF NOTE FROM THE AUTHOR

Thank you for reading *The Power in the Dark*. The story continues in *Shadow of the Swords* and *The Keeper of the Grail*. There are many unanswered questions that echo throughout this remarkable tale of power, love and bravery. Until you have the next two books in your hands, may I suggest you reread *The Power in the Dark*? There is so much more to be absorbed if you read between the lines!

May the Power be with you.

Barry Mathias

LaVergne, TN USA
27 July 2010
190960LV00001B/18/P